CINDY DEES

CLOSE
PURSUIT

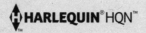

Recycling programs
for this product may
not exist in your area.

ISBN-13: 978-0-373-77848-5

CLOSE PURSUIT

Copyright © 2014 by Cynthia Dees

All rights reserved. Except for use in any review, the reproduction or utilization of this work in whole or in part in any form by any electronic, mechanical or other means, now known or hereafter invented, including xerography, photocopying and recording, or in any information storage or retrieval system, is forbidden without the written permission of the publisher, Harlequin HQN, 225 Duncan Mill Road, Don Mills, Ontario M3B 3K9, Canada.

This is a work of fiction. Names, characters, places and incidents are either the product of the author's imagination or are used fictitiously, and any resemblance to actual persons, living or dead, business establishments, events or locales is entirely coincidental.

This edition published by arrangement with Harlequin Books S.A.

For questions and comments about the quality of this book, please contact us at CustomerService@Harlequin.com.

® and TM are trademarks of Harlequin Enterprises Limited or its corporate affiliates. Trademarks indicated with ® are registered in the United States Patent and Trademark Office, the Canadian Trade Marks Office and in other countries.

Printed in U.S.A.

www.Harlequin.com

This book brings my writing journey to date full circle to where it began with a love story based on a real person's tragedy. It seems fitting, then, that I dedicate this book to those who have been with me since the beginning.

To my family, who've put up with
this crazy writer's life and kept me laughing.

To my literary agent, Pattie Steele-Perkins,
for keeping me sane and talking me down off bridges.

And to my BWFF—Best Writing Friend Forever—
Jade Lee, for sharing everything else.

I couldn't have done it without you guys.

CHAPTER ONE

KATIE MCCLOUD STUDIED the barren valley at her feet and shook her head. *Mars. It looks like freaking Mars.* Who'd have guessed anywhere on Earth looked like this? Of course, she'd had to go to the foothills of the Himalayas at the intersection of Nowhere and Uninhabitable to find it.

She ducked inside the makeshift shelter tucked between two giant boulders and looked around. It would be a tight squeeze for two people and their gear. But this trip wasn't about having all the comforts of home. She really was trying hard to think of it as a grand adventure, but her personal pep talk wasn't sinking in at the moment. Her brother had promised it would be like primitive camping. Maybe if she was primitive camping in *hell*.

"Come help me," her partner-in-crime, Alex Peters, called low from outside. She slipped out just as a cloud of dust rained down on the opening. Coughing, she batted the local gray grit out of her hair and glared at him on the hillside above her. "What are you doing?"

"Camouflaging our tent."

"You didn't have to camouflage *me*."

A rare smile crossed his face. "You do want us to remain hidden, right?"

"Well, yeah," she groused. "If they find us, we'll be killed."

Which was pretty crazy if she stopped to think about it. And which was why Katie was trying hard *not* to stop and think about it. Her brothers did this kind of stuff all the time, and everything always turned out fine. How tough could it be? She'd spent most of her adult life insisting to all of them that she could do the same sorts of wild things they did. And getting laughed at for saying it or, worse, patted on the head like some kind of cute puppy. This was her chance to prove she was the real deal once and for all.

Her confidence temporarily bolstered, she joined Alex on the steep slope above their little hideaway. She stumbled on rolling gravel, and his hand shot out to grab her elbow and steady her. As always, her pulse leaped at the contact. Surely he knew how totally hot he was. If he did, he didn't give any hint of it as he let go of her arm and turned his attention back to hiding their tent. She gathered up an armful of scrawny, dead weeds and scattered them across the canvas surface.

"Too much," he said critically. "The tonal value of the tent's green contrasts too much with the dead grass. It draws the eye to the tent." He slid gracefully down to the edge of the tent roof and removed most of the plant material.

"And when did you become an expert on the tonal values of tent canvas?" she asked tartly. Not that she doubted for a second that he was correct. In the few days she'd known him, he'd surprised her multiple times with the esoteric tidbits he knew. Her brother had warned her that Alex Peters was brilliant. As in off-the-charts-genius brilliant. But in her experience, intellect and common sense were two entirely separate things.

Alex stared at Katie warily. He did that a lot—look at her as if he thought she was about to leap on him and tear his shirt off or something. Not that it hadn't crossed her mind. He was pretty gorgeous in a dark, tortured kind of way. That combination of dark hair and light eyes was surprisingly sexy.

He answered her question laconically, "They made me take an art class my last year as an undergrad at Harvard."

"How old were you then? Twelve?"

"I didn't start college until I was thirteen," he replied absently, obviously already focused on something else entirely.

Her brother had told her Alex graduated from Harvard at sixteen with a degree in mathematics. Master's in statistics and probability from MIT at seventeen, and well into PhD work in cryptography there before the wheels had come off his life. Maddeningly, her brother hadn't said a word about what *that* meant. Just that the wheels had come off.

At thirteen, she'd been trying to convince her parents to let her wear makeup and her brothers to quit calling her Baby Butt. As she recalled, she'd developed an abiding hatred of math that year, too, compliments of pre-algebra. Thankfully, her degree in early elementary education only required basic mathematics.

The sun slid quickly behind the looming mountains, and day became night in minutes. The temperature dropped nearly as precipitously. The two of them retreated into the tent to huddle near the propane heater.

"You're sure they'll come?" she asked Alex over

a pouch of freeze-dried beef stew reconstituted with water warmed on the top of the heater.

"D.U. put the word out," he answered. "They'll come."

Doctors Unlimited was a low-profile international aid organization that sent medical personnel into the most remote and dangerous corners of the planet. Katie still didn't know a whole lot more than that about the group, even after she'd gotten the call from her brother that it needed her help. Mike was military intelligence, although he couldn't officially admit it. But everyone in the family knew he'd been a SEAL and probably still worked with the teams as an intel analyst.

She'd half suspected this trip was some sort of undercover SEAL op until she'd met Alex, who *no way, no how* was a SEAL. It wasn't just that he ran to the lean and elegant rather than stupidly buff. He was more...cosmopolitan...than she associated with most of the guys on the teams. He was James Bond, not Rambo.

And then, of course, there was the whole bit about his actually delivering babies out here. She didn't doubt SEALs could deliver babies—Lord knew, they could do just about everything else—but she couldn't see one successfully posing as an obstetrician for weeks or months on end. Although, how Alex had gone from mathematician to physician during the black hole of time her brother wouldn't speak of was a mystery to her.

"This area looks completely deserted," she announced.

He shrugged. "You saw the same maps I did. Karshan's a good-sized village, and it's less than a mile up the river from us."

"How will word spread that we're here? And to whom?"

"Women gossip faster than the internet," he murmured absently.

She'd already lost him again. His gaze was fixed on the heavy boxes of medical equipment they'd carried up there from the Land Rover, which was hidden under a brush pile down by the river at the bottom of the narrow, steep valley. Emphasis on steep. Her legs and back were going to kill her tomorrow.

She bloody well hoped they didn't have to move this camp anytime soon. Their first two camps had been in caves in much more accessible locations than this mountainous crevasse. Twice Alex had woken her up with an urgent warning that the rebels were coming, and it had been relatively easy to throw their gear in the Land Rover and bug out.

At this time of year, Zaghastan, high in a remote region of the Hindu Kush, was as barren and lifeless as the moon with vast stretches of gray granite mountains and wind-scoured valleys. She huddled deeper into her high-tech mountain climber's coat as a burst of frigid air rustled the canvas overhead. "Feels like snow," she commented.

"Humidity's under ten percent. Any snow will fall as virga."

"And what is virga?" she asked with the long-suffering patience she'd learned working with kindergarteners.

"Precipitation that falls from clouds but evaporates prior to reaching the ground. Although technically snow is a solid, so the correct term in this case would be sublimation and not evaporation, of course."

"Of course," she echoed drily. Being with this guy was like traveling with an encyclopedia. And he had about as many emotions as one. Either that, or Alex Peters was freakishly, inhumanly self-disciplined. Either way, she felt completely inadequate in his presence. As for her, she let everything she felt and thought hang right out there for everyone to see. It was so much easier that way. No secrets. No surprises. No head games.

Still, there was one thing she knew that he didn't—the local language. The natives of this region spoke an ancient tribal tongue not used anywhere else on earth—except in a small community of Zaghastani expatriates living in Pittsburgh. She'd learned it during her three-year stint there with Teachers Across America, educating their children.

It turned out she had a gift for languages. Absorbed them like a sponge. That, and the rules of hospitality in Zaghastani culture dictated that teachers be invited into parents' homes. She'd picked up the dialect like candy. It had helped her teach the kids English.

"Storm's blowing in," Alex observed.

She huddled closer to the tiny heat source, and her knee accidentally bumped his. He drew his leg away fractionally, and her fantasies about him were dashed yet again. Clearly, he didn't think she was in his league. Either that or he was gay.

"I thought you said we'd only get virga," she said a tad peevishly.

"That doesn't mean it won't get cold and windy. At this altitude, it's not uncommon for temperatures to drop well below zero."

She winced at the thought. Give her a nice, cozy fireplace, fuzzy socks and a cup of hot chocolate, and she was a happy camper. Less than one day on this mountainside and she was ready to pack it in and head home. Even a cave would be a step up from a canvas-covered crack in the rocks. At least they had the mountain at their back to block the wind a little.

"We should have some business before morning," he announced.

"Why's that?" she asked curiously. Was he psychic, too?

"Female mammals tend to give birth in the worst possible weather. It suppresses the movement of predators and enhances survivability of the gravid female and her offspring during the birth process."

Well, okay, then. This trip was going to be nothing if not educational, apparently. Alex commenced rummaging through his boxes of equipment. He looked frustrated, as though he'd misplaced something. "Can I help?" she asked.

"No."

That was Alex. Mr. Monosyllable.

Intense silence fell around them, disturbed only by the flapping of canvas.

"Seems like the only predators around here are the husbands of the local female population," she remarked to fill the void. She hated quiet. She hadn't grown up with five older brothers for nothing. Their house had been a zoo. But Alex seemed to prefer the transcendent silence.

He lifted one of the boxes effortlessly and shifted it into the corner. He might run to the lean side compared to her buff brothers, but he was stronger than he looked. He commented, "I doubt the husbands are the problem. It's an eighty-five percent probability, plus or minus about three percent, that conservative religious zealots have been the ones killing the midwives."

Slaughtering them, more like. Religious extremists were killing not only the midwives, but all women who advocated women's rights or who represented female power in their communities. It was obscene. And largely unreported in the media. The massacre had prompted Doctors Unlimited to fund this secret mission into Zaghastan to deliver babies, in fact. When her brother had asked her to go along and translate, she wasn't about to say no to helping women just trying to survive childbirth. She'd also just finished her gig with Teachers Across America and had yet to land a permanent teaching job or even decide where she wanted to live. And then there was the bad breakup with the latest rotten boyfriend to get away from. Her friends called her the asshole magnet for good reason.

"I'd suggest you get some sleep," Alex said briskly. "You look like you need it."

Her eyebrows shot up. "Hasn't anyone ever taught you women don't like to be told they look like crap?"

He looked vaguely startled—a first for him. "I beg your pardon?"

OMG. He really doesn't know that? "Women don't like to be told they look bad."

He frowned, his formidable mind obviously examining her statement from ninety-two different angles. "I suppose that's logical if a woman is insecure about her appearance for some reason."

"News flash, Einstein—*all* women are insecure about their appearance."

"I have no context within which to place that remark."

Oh, for the love of Mike. "Are you always such a geek?"

For just a second, something incongruous—and totally non-geeky—flashed in his eyes. Amusement. Male appreciation. Desire.

What. The. Heck? Where did the geek go?

She did a sharp double take, and his eyes were back to being as guarded and clueless as ever.

ALEX CONSIDERED KATIE—or at least the tip of her nose where it poked out of her sleeping bag. She could prove to be a serious problem. For a self-professed dingbat blonde, Katie had already showed herself to be deeply intuitive. Smarter than she let on. God knew, she was easy on the eye. The first thing he supposed most people would notice about her was the lush, golden hair falling in soft waves around her face. Or maybe her bright blue eyes. Or maybe even her slender, attractive figure.

Frankly, the thing he'd keyed in on first was her smile. It was warm and genuine and filled a room. He would like to think his mother had smiled like that. But, knowing his father, the man would never have gone for an open, loving woman. His old man would have gone for an ice bitch with a heart as hard and cold as a diamond.

Which would, of course, be more in keeping with his mother's early and complete disappearance from his life. He had no memory of the woman whatsoever. Had no idea what happened to her. Never seen a picture. Never even heard a name.

A loose rock rolled outside, and he jerked to full alert. He shed the sleeping bag he'd wrapped around his shoulders and slid into the shadow beside the tent flap. He shook a razor-sharp scalpel out of his sleeve and slid it into his palm.

A low voice whispered on the other side of the canvas and then devolved into the persistent cough most of the locals had. *Dammit.* He didn't understand a word of what the voice was saying. But it was female. He pulled the flap back, and two lumps of black cloth crouched in front of him. He gestured for them to come inside. The scalpel went inconspicuously back inside his sleeve as he moved to the back of the tent.

"Katie, wake up." He gave her shoulder a shake through the down sleeping bag. She felt small and fragile under his hand. A temptation he couldn't afford, dammit.

"Wha—" she mumbled as she rolled onto her back. Heavy sleeper. Must be nice to be so naive. It had been a long time since he'd thought the world was safe enough to sleep like that.

"I need a translator."

She sat up sharply. "Oh!" She looked over at the two women huddled by the door and said something in the native tongue. It was a guttural and clumsy-sounding language.

"You're on, Doc," Katie announced. "The one on the left is in labor. Older one is her grandmother. Says she's worried because her granddaughter is young and small."

"How young?" he bit out.

Another exchange of words. Then Katie answered grimly, "Fourteen. Her first baby."

One of the burka-wrapped shapes bent over just then and gave a low moan. Grandma propped up the girl as the contraction gripped her.

All the deliveries had been routine so far. Adult women, mostly on at least their fourth kid. But a first-timer barely into her teens? This could get interesting. His training in obstetrics was superficial; he was primarily a trauma surgeon. But all doctors were required to pull an obstetrics rotation in medical school. The men in prison with him who had constituted much of his on-the-job medical experience hadn't given birth to a hell of a lot of babies—which was to say, *any* babies.

He'd pulled a short stint in a maternity ward to deliver a few more kids before he'd been sent out here. But he'd never seen a case like this. Nothing like trial by fire to earn his stripes as an obstetrician.

"Get the girl onto a cot. I need her out of her clothes but covered enough to keep her warm. I'll crank up the heater while you ladies take care of all that," he instructed.

It was forbidden for males of any stripe, even doctors, to look at any part of a woman in this part of the world, especially where he'd have to look to deliver a baby. But with all the local midwives dead, he was the only show in town. The Doctors Unlimited folks in Washington, D.C., had explained that it would be a death sentence for him and his patients to be caught. But the D.U. staff had believed—correctly—that local women would risk it anyway.

Crazy thing, that. Women wanting to have a fighting chance at surviving childbirth. What *were* they thinking? He snorted sarcastically as he turned up the propane heater. Without proper care, one in three women in this part of the world died in childbirth or soon after from complications. Doctors Unlimited and other aid organizations had spent the past several decades training midwives, and the mortality rate had dropped to rates commensurate with the West. Until this past winter and the midwife massacre.

He commenced meticulously scrubbing his hands and forearms over a bucket of water so cold it made his fingernails turn blue. How in the hell was he supposed to work under these conditions?

A muttered argument ensued behind him, and Katie announced, "The girl doesn't want you to examine her or help unless things go badly."

"And how am I supposed to know things are going badly if I can't look at my patient?" he snapped.

She sighed. "They want you to tell me what to look for."

"That's absurd. You have no medical training whatsoever."

"That's what I told them. She's adamant, though. And embarrassed."

"But I'm a doctor—"

"And she's a young, terrified girl who cannot read or write and will be beaten to death by her husband if he catches her here."

"Then why did she come?" he demanded, low and angry.

Katie came over to stand directly in front of him. Her eyes were huge and beseeching as she looked up at him. "Because she's more scared of her baby dying than of dying herself."

He stared down at her, seared by the zeal in her eyes. He grumbled, "This sucks."

"Welcome to life as a female a thousand years ago."

He just shook his head. "The first thing to do is see if the baby's presenting headfirst. You'll have to use a speculum and a flashlight since it's so dark in here." The lone lantern was barely bright enough to read by, let alone perform surgery by.

Katie gulped and headed for the laboring girl, who was moaning again. He glanced at his watch. Contractions were under two minutes apart. "Do you know what a speculum is?" he asked.

"Every woman who's ever had an ob-gyn exam knows what one is," Katie replied frostily.

His lips twitched with humor, and he was glad her back was turned to him. "How far is she dilated?" he asked.

"There's about a silver-dollar-sized opening," Katie reported a moment later. "What does a head look like?"

"Like a wet, hairy balloon pressed against the cervix."

"Then we've got a problem. I'm seeing pink skin. And it's kind of pointy. Maybe bony. Like, umm, a baby bottom?"

"Breech presentation," he bit out. "You're going to have to talk our reluctant patient into letting me help."

But Mama was having no part of it. It was outrageous that he had to stand there and do nothing when he could be attempting to turn the baby before it entered the birth canal. Although given how small Mom was, that would be a dicey proposition at best. He really needed to consider a C-section sooner rather than later.

"Tell her I want to discuss a C-section."

Nope. Abruptly hysterical Mama was having none

of that. Grandma wasn't keen on the idea, either—something about not being able to hide the evidence of a doctor helping her granddaughter.

This was no way to practice medicine.

The tension in the tiny space mounted over the next hour as the girl's labor progressed and her moans turned into sharp cries of pain. "Don't let her push!" he ordered. "At all costs, she mustn't push."

The cries turned into screams muffled by a pillow the grandmother pressed over the girl's mouth. *God, this is barbaric.*

"I can set an epidural. Give her painkillers. At least let me put a heart monitor on the baby," he all but begged.

"I'm sorry, Alex. She's not budging."

"Katie," he ground out urgently. "Find a way. Make her understand that she and her baby are in grave danger. This is why she came to me. Let me do my job!"

His impotent fury mounted as the girl's screams turned into long, keening moans indicative of exhaustion and delirium. He didn't need anyone to tell him the patient was no longer progressing in her delivery. Katie finally turned to the grandmother and said something sharp.

"Okay, Alex. Grandma says to ignore her granddaughter and come help."

Thank God. As he expected, the girl was so far gone into the agony of a difficult birth that she barely noticed him working frantically to shift her baby into some sort of birthable position.

"I need her to push with the next contraction."

Katie stood by the girl's head, translating his instructions, although he doubted the mother was paying the slightest attention at this point. The girl's body heaved of its own volition, and he went to work. He pulled the baby's slippery ankles clear and hung on desperately until the next contraction. The girl screamed, one long continuous keen of agony as he all but tore the child from her body. It was that or risk the child suffocating in the birth canal.

"It's a boy." He suctioned the baby's nostrils and rubbed the child vigorously. Finally, the infant drew a shuddering breath and let out a wail. Not as lusty as Alex would have liked, but the kid was alive. He cut the cord and thrust the child at Grandma to wrap up and warm up. He had bigger problems at the moment.

This girl was too narrow-hipped and too damned young to be having babies, and the delivery had torn the crap out of her. She was bleeding heavily, and one supply he and Katie had not been able to haul in had been refrigerated whole blood.

He went to work fast, racing against time. The mother's screams quieted. Not that he wasn't causing her intense pain. She was merely bleeding out. Dying.

"Tell her to fight," he ordered.

Katie leaned down to speak in the girl's ear.

"Say it like you mean it," he growled.

Katie raised her voice and began demanding that the girl open her eyes. That she live for her son. And while Katie tiraded like a drill sergeant, he fought like hell, his hands flying to stem the worst bleeders. It took a full five minutes to avert disaster, and nearly a half hour to stabilize the girl. Once the meatball work was done, he settled down to the slower and more meticulous business of cleaning up the mess.

Of course, Grandma told him to make sure all the

stitches were internal and hidden. *There mustn't be any evidence of modern medicine, no sirree.*

After another hour, Grandma asked something and Katie translated. "She wants to know if they can go soon. They've got to get the girl back home before dawn."

"She can't move!" he exclaimed. "I just sewed her back together. I don't need her up, running around and tearing out all her stitches."

Katie threw his own words back at him. "We have to find a way to get her home."

Sonofabitch. "Where do they live?" he asked in resignation.

A short conversation. "Family compound on the edge of the Karshan village."

"I'll carry her as far as it's safe," he announced.

Katie's eyes flickered in surprise. "None of it is safe."

He rolled his eyes and scooped the girl up off the cot. Aware of how rough the terrain was going to be for their little trek, he elected to haul the mostly unconscious girl in a fireman's carry, slung across his back. Grandma led the way. Katie followed behind her, carrying the baby in a cloth sling in front of her. The child had yet to nurse and he had no idea if the difficult birth had injured the infant. But he was given no chance to examine the baby. The sky was lightening behind the mountain peaks across the valley.

The hike down to the river was hellish. It was frigid and dark, and the ground was slippery with frost. Plus, every stray noise could be a local religious hard core with a gun and no sense of humor about their presence in this valley. Grandma's cough worsened in the cold night air, although the sound might work to their advantage by announcing that their little party was locals.

At least the sound of rushing water muffled it as they reached the valley floor. Grandma led the way along a footpath beside the river for nearly a mile. But then she stopped and whispered something to Katie, who translated.

"Their compound is over the next rise. She'll take her granddaughter from here."

He eyed the short, heavyset woman. "How?"

Katie's answer was sober. "She'll find a way."

Reluctantly, he transferred the new mother to the old woman's back, draping the girl's arms over Grandma's shoulders while Katie looped the cloth sling holding the baby around her neck so it hung down her front. The old woman nodded her thanks and slowly trudged away from them under her load.

Madness. This is utter madness. He muttered, "It will be light any minute. We need to get under cover."

He gestured for Katie to lead the way back. Or more accurately, he took the rear guard position that put his body between her and the most likely direction gunfire would come from. The hike back to their hideyhole seemed to take forever. Maybe it was because his shoulder blades kept anticipating a bullet between them. Or maybe it was because he'd gotten no sleep last night. Or maybe it was because he was more than half convinced the two of them weren't going to make it out of this damned valley alive.

GLANCING FURTIVELY AROUND the mobile command post to make sure no one was close enough to overhear him,

Mike McCloud pinged Alex Peters's satellite phone and scribbled down the current GPS coordinates on a scrap of paper. As soon as he had it memorized, he would destroy it.

"Hey, Mikey," someone said behind him. He forced himself not to whirl around guiltily and greeted the uniformed soldier casually. He checked his watch. Too late to set out tonight. But tomorrow he'd track down Peters and his little sister and set up surveillance on the mysterious doctor.

Why in the hell a man with a past like Alex Peters would wander out here to deliver babies—as if it was actually some sort of humanitarian calling for the brilliant bastard—was anybody's guess. Maybe Katie, who'd been sent in to live with the bastard, would catch wind of what Peters was really up to at the end of the world.

But in the meantime, he'd be damned if he was letting his baby sister get hurt on his watch.

CHAPTER TWO

AFTER THE FIGHT to save the girl, something changed between her and Alex. But she had no idea what, exactly, it was. He watched her more than before. Studied her, even. He still didn't talk much, but his interest was tangible. Had he finally figured out she was a reasonably attractive person of the female persuasion, or was he merely observing her like bacteria growing in a petri dish?

The next few days settled into a pattern for Katie. Haul water up from the river. Haul supplies up from the Land Rover. Sleep. Eat. Attempt to wash herself, her hair, her clothes. And at night, help deliver babies. Women came from all over the valley to have them. Most times, they brought someone with them—a mother or sister or cousin.

Alex taught the companions all he could about the basics of childbirth and safe aftercare while Katie translated for him. She got good enough at the speech that she could do it without prompting from him.

She slept mornings and evenings, and he slept most of each day, which left her at loose ends to entertain herself much of the time. She had a fully charged tablet reader she'd loaded up with books before she'd come up there. The battery was supposed to last several weeks, but at the rate she was using it, the charge would run out in a week. She dreaded not knowing what she would do to keep herself from going stir-crazy then. Never in her life had she been anywhere this completely disconnected from…everything. No television, no internet, no phones, no electricity, no people. It was just her and Alex. The last two people on earth until some laboring woman crept to their door. No wonder Adam and Eve had been tempted. Sheer boredom would have driven them to having sex if the serpent hadn't tricked them. Goodness knew, her own mind was wandering in that direction more frequently than she'd like. It was hard not to think about sex with a man as hot as Alex living in such close proximity.

That flash of fire she'd seen in him when he'd fought off death and saved that girl and her baby riveted her. She was a little ashamed to admit to herself that she'd taken to teasing him. She went out of her way to brush close to him, to incidentally touch him now and then. But he remained frustratingly unresponsive in the face of her broad hints. The man was a machine of self-control. Frankly, it made her a little crazy. Just once, she'd love to see him let go and show her that passion again.

Sometimes, she watched Alex sleep. His face looked completely different then. Relaxed and open, his features were handsome. More striking than ever. His hair was coffee-colored, hovering between brown and black, and his skin retained a hint of a tan.

Must be nice. She had two skin colors: porcelain white and lobster red, the latter achievable by either unfortunate sun exposure or the ever-popular "see who can make Katie blush the worst" game. If she was really careful, summertime yielded enough freckles close enough together that, from a distance, she could pass for a little tan. But that was as good as it got.

Parked on the camp stool, she planted her elbows on her knees and her chin in her hands to study Alex Peters, M.D. She guessed he was around thirty. Although his eyes sometimes looked like he'd lived hard for that age. What was his story? Mike hadn't told her much. And she'd been so desperate to get out of the wreck of her love life and move on to a fresh new start that she'd let her brother talk her into coming halfway around the world—literally—with a total stranger.

Alex Peters remained a mystery to her. Why would a guy like him shift from math to medicine? Where was he from? What was his family like? Did he have any hobbies? What kind of women did he prefer? What kind of sex?

She started as his eyes opened without warning; his gaze drilled into her like a silver laser. "Is there a problem?" he rasped. His voice was husky with sleep and so sexy her toes curled in her clunky hiking boots.

"Nope," she answered cheerfully to hide her embarrassment at being caught staring at him. She hastily opened her tablet reader and turned it on.

"You were looking at me."

She looked up innocently. Not a chance she could lie her way out of it. He'd caught her red-handed. So instead, she took the direct route. "I wasn't aware that's a crime."

He took his arms out of his sleeping bag and linked his fingers behind his head. His naked arms. The upper reaches of his bare chest peeked out of the nylon shell. A sprinkling of dark hair was visible on it. And muscles. Lots and lots of mature-man muscles that, truth be told, she found intimidating. The guys she'd dated had been college types or recent grads who still acted and looked like students. She revised her opinion of Alex from lean to deceptively muscular. The guy must wear a tuxedo like a god.

"You're staring again," he announced.

"It's rude of you to point it out," she retorted. "Ladies are allowed to look."

"Are gentlemen allowed also?"

If she didn't know better, she'd say the doctor geek was flirting. Would wonders never cease? She fanned the tiny flame carefully by flirting back slightly. "Hello? It's *expected* that guys will check us out. Why else would we girls go to so much trouble to look so good?"

"I haven't gotten the impression that you're a big primper."

"That's because there's no power outlet for my blow-dryer, and the wind makes my eyes water too much to keep on eye makeup long enough to make it worthwhile."

"You brought a blow-dryer out here?" he blurted. He had the bad grace to burst into laughter.

She scowled at his amusement. "Hey, I brought power converters. In my world, primitive camping is a motel instead of a Marriott. Nobody told me there would be no electricity *at all* in this godforsaken place. I was under the impression there would be, oh, I don't know, walls and a roof for us."

"You don't need to primp. You're fine the way you are," he replied.

Hark, a compliment out of the good doctor! "Apology accepted," she replied magnanimously.

He blinked, startled, like he hadn't meant it that way. The man might be as hot as a god, and he might be smart as a whip, but he had a *lot* to learn about women. He reached for his sleeping bag's zipper, and she turned away hastily. Who knew how far down his nakedness extended? She'd already figured out that, as a doctor, he wasn't tremendously inhibited about the human body.

She asked over her shoulder, "So, does your Spidey sense say we're going to get a lot of business tonight?"

"No. We'll get the night off."

She turned in surprise— *Whoops.* He was just pulling jeans over spandex biker-short things. *Okay, then.* The deceptively muscular thing extended to his legs and ass, too. She silently dubbed him Gluteus Aleximus.

He glanced up, caught her staring and broke into a grin so hot her eyelashes singed. "Like what you see?"

"*Uhhh...shrmph...wuh...hwa...*sure," she managed to get out.

His grin widened.

Jerk. He'd embarrassed her on purpose. Oh, two could play that game. She hadn't grown up with a houseful of brothers for nothing. She could give as well as she got when it came to practical jokes.

While she pondered revenge, she busied herself heating up the little propane hot plate and scrambling the eggs someone had brought last night. She and Alex were frequently paid in bread, jugs of yak milk and these oversize eggs she hadn't had the courage to ask the source of. Geese, maybe? Or something weirder?

Chickens. In her world, every egg came from a chicken, and she was sticking with that mental image.

She'd tried to explain to the local women that Doctors Unlimited was paying the two of them, but that didn't stop their patients from showing their gratitude.

"So, Doc. Why do you think there won't be any babies tonight?"

He glanced up from the bucket, where he was washing his hands. "I listened to the radio while you were sleeping. A rebel force is moving into the area."

"Again?" she complained. "I swear, it's like they're following us!"

"Noticed that, did you?" he asked drily.

She did a double take. *Seriously?* They were being tracked somehow? The thought chilled her to her bones. "Why would somebody track us?" she blurted.

"That's a damned good question," he bit out.

She recoiled from the tight fury in his voice. Did he think the rebels were chasing him? Why? What was the big mystery around him, anyway? The six-hundred-pound gorilla in the corner of the tent was why her intel–Special Forces brother had asked her to come out here with Alex in the first place. Surely she was not the only person in the entire United States who spoke Zaghastani. And why did Mike drop that cryptic comment as he dropped her off at the airport to keep an eye on Peters and see if she noticed anything odd about him or why he was heading out to Zaghastan to deliver babies? Only odd thing so far was that the guy seemed totally immune to her general hotness and willingness to let him jump her bones.

Alex circled back to the original conversation. "If fighting breaks out between the rebels and the locals, any women in labor tonight will stay home."

"I dunno," she responded. "These women are already braving pretty dangerous obstacles to get to you. I doubt a little gunfire will slow them down."

"The rebels are well armed and violent. When they come, they'll crush everything in their path."

Yeah. Like the two of us. She shook her head, unconvinced, and declared, "I'll bet you five bucks we deliver a baby tonight."

The effect of her challenge on Alex was shocking. He went utterly still, and she thought she saw a shudder pass through him. From this angle, it looked as if he actually paled. The tension abruptly emanating from him was terrible in its intensity.

She was on the verge of asking him if he was okay when he turned abruptly. His gaze was hooded. Dark. And his entire being was suddenly sharply, dangerously alive. It was as if she'd woken a sleeping tiger. And now the beast was not only awake, but he was hungry…and on the hunt.

"Shall we make the wager a little more interesting?" he purred. The sexual energy in his voice raked across her skin like claws.

Whoa. She asked cautiously, "What did you have in mind?"

"What do you like best in all the world?" he asked.

"Ice cream," she answered promptly. It was the first thing that came to mind.

"Better than sex?" He sounded skeptical.

She shrugged. "I stand by my answer."

He replied huskily, "Then you haven't had good sex."

The promise of just that was thick in his throat. She didn't dare let her gaze stray south to see if he was as turned on as she was, all of a sudden.

"I think we have the terms of our bet then." Her gaze snapped to him as he prowled across the tiny space to less than arm's length from her. "If you win, we have a date to eat ice cream together. If I win…" His mouth curved up in a smile that was pure sin.

Her jaw dropped. "No way!"

His heavy lids might hide the fire blazing in his eyes, but they in no way diminished it. "A woman daring enough to travel halfway across the world, to brave a war zone and death threats, living alone in the wilds with a stranger…" He shrugged. "I thought you were…more."

More what? her brain shouted. *More than average? More than a nice little schoolteacher? More than a desperate wannabe in a family of adventurers and warriors? More than a fraud?*

Stung, her gaze narrowed and she glared at him. She thrust her hand out truculently. He stared down at it uncomprehendingly.

"Are we shaking on the bet or not?" she demanded.

His gaze lifted to hers, and if it had been hot before, it was an inferno now. Never breaking eye contact with her, he reached out slowly with his right hand and grasped hers. Heat built between their palms that scalded her all the way up her arm and down to her core. His fingers were strong. Capable. She'd watched that hand perform miracles. And right now, it claimed her fingers possessively, promising heretofore unimagined sensual delights.

His grip finally fell away and he broke the stare, turning away from her sharply. His rib cage lifted once short and hard. At least he wasn't entirely unaffected. As for her, she was panting like a dog in a sauna.

Holy crap, I just agreed to have sex with him. What on earth had she been thinking? She'd known since she was about seven years old not to let boys goad her into accepting dares. He'd just manipulated her like a master, damn him.

Of course, if she was lucky, she'd win the bet and get an ice-cream sundae out of the deal. That *was* the lucky outcome…right?

ALEX STRETCHED OUT on the cot in the corner. He'd turned down the lantern hanging over the bed, intentionally wreathing himself in dark shadows. It was easier to watch Katie that way. She was pretending to read—she hadn't advanced the screen on her e-reader for ten minutes.

She'd been as nervous as a cat in a roomful of rocking chairs and squirt guns ever since they'd made their bet. It was highly entertaining watching her alternate between wishing to win the bet and wishing to lose. Her face was a constantly changing mosaic of emotions ranging from chagrin to suspicion that he'd set her up—which he had, blatantly—to reluctant lust and back to chagrin.

If he were going to lie to himself, he'd say he'd made the bet with her to relieve the boredom and distract her from the building danger. To add a little spice to an otherwise tedious and miserable assignment. But the truth was he found her fascinating. She was such a girlie girl. But more compelling was how she reminded him of a shiny new penny that had never been nicked or tarnished. What must it be like to never have had anything bad happen in one's life? To be *good.* The concept was completely beyond his comprehension.

A shocking compulsion to end all that innocence rolled over him. Most men would call it simple lust. But he knew it to be more.

The girls at his various universities had all been many years older than him, deeply intellectual and far too cool to pay any attention to the skinny kid blowing out all the grade curves in their classes. At the opposite end of the spectrum had been the groupies in the casinos. Hookers, showgirls and hangers-on looking to trade their bodies, and even their souls, for access to his bank account. Not that he particularly held it against them. They were using what tools they had to climb out of life's cesspool, while he used them to climb into it.

There had been a few older women looking to take on the role of his missing mother—social workers, counselors, even a professor or two—who tried to mentor him along the way. Their hearts had been in the right place. Hell, they might even have had decent advice for him. But he hadn't been ready to hear it. Not back then. Not before his life imploded and he sent himself to hell.

Some would say he'd always been in hell and had just managed to find a stairway down to a deeper circle of it. They were also the ones who tended to declare him a lost cause. Doomed to wallow in his own black pit of despair, forever. He was inclined to agree with that crowd.

A faint rumble rolled down the valley, and Katie looked up sharply, startled.

"It's just thunder," he murmured drowsily, pretending to be half-asleep.

"No, it's not. That was a mortar explosion," she retorted tersely.

"And you know this how?" he asked with more alert interest.

"Three of my brothers are in the military, the other two are in law enforcement and my dad's an ex–Green Beret. We lived on army bases when I was a kid." Another explosion sounded, closer this time, and she announced with certainty, "And *that* was a rocket-propelled grenade."

Fuck. Supposedly harmless little Katie McCloud kept throwing him monkey wrenches. He needed her to be no factor in this mission. A know-nothing civilian translator who'd never been overseas and had no field experience. Naive. A bit of a dingbat. Manageable, dammit. But instead she was a dangerous wild card. What the hell was going on out here around them? Around him?

This job was supposed to be about redemption. About doing something decent with his life at long last. About escaping the clutches of his father, at least for a little while. Was it too much to ask to have *one* moment in his life to do what he wanted with it? If it wouldn't have been completely paranoid of him, he would half suspect his father was behind the rebels managing to stay on their heels like this.

Katie was so damned quick on the uptake. Hell, he already had her half-trained to be a decent surgical nurse. She was intuitive. Attractive. *And she could fricking tell mortars from RPGs.* He swore silently and with great fervor. Why hadn't anyone told him that about her?

"A patient will come to us tonight," she declared.

"Still holding out hope for that ice cream?" he asked lightly. Her gaze snapped unwillingly to his. *Mmm-hmm*. She was thinking hard about what would happen if he won the bet instead of her. Hell, so was he.

Ever since they'd come out here, he had exercised iron will not to let his mind stray to the possibilities between them—alone in the wilds, bored, attracted to each other. He didn't know what had come over him when he'd suggested the bet this afternoon. She'd broken through his self-discipline somehow, and he didn't have a clue how she'd done it. And *that* worried him.

He'd carefully locked away the darker side of his soul and kept it under tight wraps. But damned if he wasn't dying of curiosity to see how she would react to that other side of him. The dangerous one that corrupted everything and everyone it touched. He'd never dreamed she would actually accept the bet. The odds had been overwhelming that she would run screaming from such a risky wager. Unpredictable, she was. An outlier in his experience with women. It made her damn near irresistible.

She seemed so straightforward on the surface. An all-American girl. Her insistence on washing her hair every other day, even if the water was barely above freezing, spoke of care for her physical appearance. And the way she accessorized her mannish mountain jacket with frilly, fringed scarves and fuzzy earmuffs shouted of her need to demonstrate her femininity. Growing up in the houseful of brothers explained that, he supposed. Ten to one she polished her toenails.

He swore violently at himself. No more odds. No

more bets. He was done with all that. Down that path lay damnation and ruin.

She moved to stand in the doorway as darkness fell, gazing down the valley, her arms wrapped around her middle. He watched her become a silhouette against the twilight and then a mysterious shadow blending with the night. A need to consume her, body, mind and soul, burned in his gut like brimstone.

Was she regretting their bet? A gentleman would let her out of it since it seemed to disturb her so much. But then, gentlemen didn't often make it down to his end of hell. And a deal was a deal, even if it was with the devil.

He announced grimly, "I'm going to get some sleep. You should do the same. We won't get many nights off while we're out here."

She turned to glare at him. "Are you always so sure of yourself?"

"If you're asking if I'm always right, pretty much, yes."

"That's arrogant."

"Just stating the facts." He couldn't resist adding, "Odds are you won't get much sleep tomorrow night. Therefore, you should sleep tonight when you can."

Her mouth sagged open. Amused at her burgeoning outrage and disinterested in enduring a lecture from a ruffled female, he lay down on his cot, presenting his back to her.

"Someday, Alex Peters, something or someone is going to come along and knock you off that pedestal of yours. I sincerely hope I'm there to see it."

He snorted. That had been taken care of a very long time ago. But she had no reason to know it, and he had no reason to tell her. The past was over and done with. They'd told him to start a new life. To move forward. Too bad no one had told him how.

KATIE LISTENED TO the quiet sound of Alex's breathing. Every minute or so, it was punctuated by an explosion of one kind or another from outside. She identified ground fire and artillery and heard the change in pitch when attack helicopters rolled in on the distant battle. Even if it was still several miles away, gradually, gradually, it was moving closer to their position.

What if Alex was right? What if this area was overrun by the low-intensity brush war raging across this barren region? She'd heard war stories around her family's kitchen table for long enough to know that no war was low intensity if a guy was on the ground, caught in the middle of it. If only she could call whatever brother of hers was closest to this corner of the world and ask him to find out exactly what was going on. She hated not knowing what was headed their way. But no. She'd been determined to do this on her own. Heck, her cell phone wouldn't work even if she went hundreds of miles in any direction from here.

A new sound outside sent her to the door of the tent. It was a high-pitched scream, like a fighter jet, yet too quiet to be an airplane. Still, it sounded close. Perplexed, she scanned the sky. Her jaw dropped as she spotted a drone. It was big—the size of a small airplane. More interesting, it had a huge, bulbous protrusion on its belly. That was some sort of radar scanner.

She ducked under the tent instinctively. Alex had mentioned something about the tent canvas having metal fibers woven into it that prevented radar and infrared systems from seeing through it. Apparently, the special tents were standard gear for D.U. doctors. It helped them avoid being detected when they were treating patients in a hostile area.

The drone moved on, cruising at a leisurely pace. It pulled a big one-eighty turn at the head of the valley and commenced flying back down it. That looked like some sort of search pattern. What on earth was it looking for? More to the point, who was flying the darned thing? Who had that kind of military resources, and what were they doing in this remote corner of the world?

She was tempted to wake Alex, ask him to pull out the satellite radio and have him get an update from the neutral observers who were tracking the rebels and their movements. Alex hadn't turned the thing on since they'd fled their last cave. Of course, she was also tempted to get down on her knees and pray for a woman in labor to stumble through the door right about now, too.

Sex with Alex Peters? The notion had her tied in so many knots she could hardly see straight. Surely he wouldn't make her go through with it if he won the bet. Thing was, she'd been raised to keep promises and honor her word. And he struck her as the kind of man who would demand no less of her.

What in the heck had she been thinking to agree to such a crazy wager? She *hadn't* been thinking. Her impulsive nature had gotten her into a pickle *again*. Like it always did. Would she never learn?

Although how bad could sex with the good doctor be? He'd been genuinely shocked when she'd chosen ice cream over sex. Did he know something about it

that she didn't? He was a doctor. Did they talk about…
that stuff…in medical school? Teach students the anat-
omical secrets of fantastic sex? Lord knew he was attractive. Strike that. He was a hunk. *Smexy*—smart
and sexy.

She didn't usually go for the silent, brooding types.
But she had to admit, he wasn't so bad to be around.
Exuberant guys had a tendency to exhaust her with
their drama. Sure, she was the exuberant type herself,
but, at the end of the day, drama wasn't her thing. At
least Alex was predictable…most of the time…when
he wasn't making shockingly inappropriate bets with
his coworker. Predictably intellectual. Predictably
clueless about women. Predictably—and infuriat-
ingly—enigmatic.

Her brother had been specific in his instructions to
her. Earn Alex Peters's trust. Get into his good graces.
Find out if he was up to anything besides delivering
babies out here in the middle of nowhere. She'd asked
Mike what he suspected Alex of, but her brother had
fed her a bullshit line about not wanting to taint her
impressions of the doctor. What was the deal with
Alex? Who *was* he? And why had she been sent into
a war zone to watch him?

She paced the tiny tent until her legs ached. Finally,
Alex woke enough to mutter, "Lie down, Katie. You're
keeping me awake with all your fretting."

She did as he asked, but she tossed and turned for
much of the night. Yet again she checked her watch.
God. 4:00 a.m. Good news: the shelling was finally
winding down. Bad news: no women had crept to the
tent asking for the baby doctor.

She was so frantic not to lose the bet that she was

seriously considering heading for the nearest village to go door-to-door looking for women in labor. Okay, she wasn't serious about canvassing the neighborhood for business. But she *wanted* to do it.

As the first hint of dawn touched the peaks at the opposite rim of the valley, she reluctantly admitted defeat and burrowed deeper into her sleeping bag. What had she done? Why did she have a feeling deep in her gut that she had jumped off a cliff and just didn't know it yet?

KATIE WOKE WITH a jolt and was stunned to see sunlight inching in the tent flap. "What time is it?" she demanded, disoriented. She looked around and was alarmed to see that the tent was empty. Where was Alex?

"Almost two o'clock," he answered from outside.

She leaped out of the sleeping bag, shocked. Her feet hit the cold dirt, and she hopped uncomfortably from foot to foot until she could slip into her unlaced hiking boots. She gathered her hair up in a high ponytail. Today was hair-washing day, and she already dreaded dousing her head in ice water. But it was better than having greasy hair.

Alex ducked inside the tent and handed her a steaming mug of coffee. Their fingertips brushed as they made the handoff, and her pulse leaped wildly. She looked up at him involuntarily. One corner of his mouth turned up in sardonic amusement at her jumpiness. It was official. She'd made a deal with the devil. To have sex. *Ho. Lee. Crap.*

Freaked out, she stared down at her mug of coffee unseeingly. Slowly, slowly, her pulse returned to normal, leaving behind a low-level background hum of panic. She would figure out a way to dodge the bullet. After her coffee.

She inhaled the bitter aroma with great relish. It wasn't that she was the world's biggest fan of coffee, but it was the smell of home. Of the civilized world beyond this isolated valley. Of life's little indulgences.

"Thanks," she murmured. As usual, Alex didn't reply as he moved past her to the back of the tent. But today, she followed up with, "Why don't you ever say 'you're welcome' or something to that effect?"

"It's redundant. I've already done something polite or thoughtful and the recipient has acknowledged it. There's no need for further exchange."

"Are you always so…cold-blooded in your approach to human interactions?" she asked curiously.

He moved shockingly fast to stand right behind her. Her pulse leaped at his proximity. Was he going to collect on the bet right now? She started to feel light-headed, and her legs trembled so badly with an urge to bolt that they would barely support her weight.

"No, Katie." His voice was barely more than a whisper sliding across her skin. "I'm not cold-blooded about everything."

Her breath hitched, and she had to force herself to take her next breath.

A single finger touched the nape of her neck right where her hair met bare skin. It drew slowly down her spine to the top of her T-shirt. "For the record, I'm not going to fall on you and ravish you like some clumsy, horny American boy."

She turned sharply, mostly to escape that disturb-

ingly sensual caress, but also to stare at him in surprise. "You're American, aren't you?"

"I am a citizen, yes."

"But?"

"But I was born abroad. And my father did not raise
me particularly American."

"What about your mother?"

"No mother," he bit out.

She replied drily, "Last I heard, there's only been
one documented case of immaculate conception." She
added even more drily, "Assuming, of course, that you
accept the Bible as valid documentation. And even
then, it was the male parent in absentia."

His eyes were the roiling gray of a thundercloud as
he stared down at her. What on earth was he thinking
to send that turbulence through his eyes? She continued looking back at him expectantly.

After a moment, he muttered, "Let me guess. You're
not going to leave the subject of my missing mother
alone until I give you an explanation."

She smiled triumphantly. "Congratulations! You're
finally learning to read women, grasshopper." A scowl
crossed his face, but she waited him out. She had a lot
of experience outlasting stubborn males in her family.

Finally he shoved a hand through his hair, standing it up in short dark spikes all over his head. "My
mother left my father, or vice versa, when I was an
infant. I never knew her, and, no, I don't know the circumstances behind it." He added sharply, "And don't
tell me you're sorry. I never knew what it was like to
have a mother, so I have no frame of reference to measure whether or not it was a loss."

"Do you always intellectualize painful things?" she asked him.

Her question seemed to stop him in his tracks, and he studied her intensely. He looked as if he'd turned the full power of his formidable mind to analyzing her. His reply, when he finally spoke, shocked her. "Has anything truly terrible ever happened to you?"

She had to think about it for a minute. "Our dog died when I was in college. That was really sad. And my grandmother died a few years back."

"Let me guess. She was a hundred and ten years old, lived a rich and productive life, died in her sleep and everyone praised her full life and bemoaned her premature passing."

"She was ninety-five," Katie answered a little defensively.

He stepped close to her, and she was abruptly aware of how much taller he was. His head tilted down toward her as he murmured, "But you've never had everything you believed in ripped away from you? Never experienced regret so bad it burns a hole through your gut that won't heal? Never made a mistake that costs you everything?"

She shook her head, her stomach fluttering so much she felt sick.

"If you had any sense, you'd run away from me as fast as you could, little girl."

She bristled at being called a little girl, and her spine stiffened. "I can take anything you can dish out to me."

"We'll see about that," he replied so low she barely heard him.

If she didn't know better, she'd say his eyes burned

for a moment with a hot, unholy fire. But on second look, it was just a trick of the late afternoon sunlight reflecting off his light gray eyes. Still, the fire reached out to her, tempting her, enthralling her, arousing something restless and dangerous deep in her belly.

Eventually he swore under his breath in some foreign tongue she didn't recognize. But it was definitely cursing. He turned away and headed outside, grabbing the water bucket as he went. She listened to his angry footsteps retreating down the path to the river and, very slowly, let out the breath she'd been holding.

Alex was surly and uncommunicative when he returned from the river, his hair wet, and he retreated immediately into the tent to take a nap. She mimicked him and washed her hair. She brushed it out as she perched on the flat boulder outside and waited for the sun to set beyond the mountains. It was risky to sit outside like this in plain sight of anyone who happened by, but she got horrendously claustrophobic inside the tent, especially when Alex's brooding presence filled it so completely. She found it strange to sit in silence like this and just contemplate existence.

His earlier question disturbed her. So what if nothing tragic had ever happened in her life? That wasn't her fault. She and her family had been lucky. She got the feeling he hadn't been so lucky, though. A desire to know him, to know the source of the darkness she sensed in him, rattled in her gut…along with trepidation at what she might learn. People didn't get that dark without some serious crap in their pasts.

It was windy today, and the dust in the atmosphere made for a spectacular sunset that stretched high up into the heavens. As beautiful as it was, it also marked the inevitable passage of time. Would Alex insist on collecting his winnings when he woke up? He'd said yesterday that he doubted she would get much sleep tonight. Was he referring to the bet, or patients, or something else altogether?

How had he been so certain he would win, anyway? Suspicion took root in her mind that he'd heard something on the radios or gotten inside knowledge of some kind and thrown the bet. He seemed like the kind of man to whom winning would be more important than splitting ethical hairs over how he won.

"Time to douse the fire," Alex announced quietly from behind her.

She nodded and kicked dirt over the little campfire. Its light would be visible for miles after dark, and they dared not announce their presence like that. She figured the local men had to be getting suspicious by now. All the women sneaking out at night to have their babies, and all of them coming back alive? Something was up with that. The ones who gave half a crap about their wives and daughters might tacitly approve of a doctor to the extent that they didn't rat out her and Alex. But, eventually, someone radical would say something to the seriously hard-core religious types in the area.

Desperate to keep Alex's mind off sex as she ducked into the tent behind him, she asked, "How much longer do you think we'll be able to stay here before we have to move?"

"I give it two more days. Call it a twelve percent probability of our being discovered tonight. Double that tomorrow, and double it again the day after."

Crud. Mental math required. Twelve times two was

twenty-four, times two was forty-eight. "That's almost even odds in three days," she blurted.

"Like I said. Two days from now, we're out of here."

"Should we leave tonight?" she asked in alarm.

"We should certainly think about starting packing."

Awesome. Maybe he would be so tired after packing up tonight he wouldn't want to collect his winnings. Although, part of her—a tiny part—was curious about what sex with him would be like. He seemed really sure of himself when the subject came up. Would he be gentle or fierce? Vanilla or...not? He probably wouldn't fumble about clumsily; she would bet a hundred bucks he knew his way around the female body very well, indeed.

She dived into the task of packing with gusto. As long as she was moving, he couldn't have his wicked way with her. For his part, he busied himself with the boxes of medical gear, hauling them one by one down to the Land Rover. To date he'd never let her look inside any of them. When she'd asked about them, he'd only shrugged and said he'd crack them open if and when they needed the supplies inside. Whatever was in the boxes was heavy. Alex moved carefully down the hill in the darkness before the moon came up.

She'd just gotten back from carrying down a bag of miscellaneous camping gear they could do without for the next day when an explosion ruptured the night.

"Uh, Alex?" she said quietly. "That was pretty close."

She jumped when his voice came out of the gloom right behind her. "No more than a half mile."

And how, exactly, did a physician know how to judge distance on artillery fire? She opened her mouth to ask him, but another explosion, even closer, silenced her. Alex's arm went around her waist as he sprinted up the hill and all but threw her past him into the tent.

She tried to ask him what the heck that had been for, but his hand went over her mouth as he yanked her back against his hard body. Heat seeped through her clothing, and had she not been straining to hear what had flipped him out, she might have relished it. But as it was, she stood tense and silent in his arms.

There it was. The sound of people moving down by the river. Maybe a half-dozen by the sounds of their scuffling. A voice floated up the hill...a male voice... saying something in the local dialect about engaging the rebels in the lower pass.

Alex backed up, dragging her with him, and sat down on the cot in the back of the tent, which had the effect of landing her in his lap. She lurched as his hot breath touched her right ear. And then, oh, man, his lips moved against it.

"We're going to have to wait out the battle until it moves on, and then we'll bug out of here. We'll take whatever supplies we can carry in one trip down the mountain. But until then, no lights and no sound. Understood?"

She nodded and felt her hair moving against his cheek. His hand fell away from her mouth, and he lifted her off his lap.

He stood and moved into the corner. When he came back, he pressed something cold and heavy into her hand. She recognized the rough grip and heft of a pistol.

"Do you know how to use this?" he breathed.

She ran her fingers over the weapon in the dark.

"Luger .22 with an extended clip. Standard model. Check." She loaded the clip he passed her, clicked off the safety and rested her index finger beside the trigger guard as she laid the weapon in her lap.

"You can tell the make and model just by feel?" Alex blurted. He added grimly, "If we get out of here alive, you and I need to talk."

His right hand rested by his side, presumably with a weapon in it, as well. She shivered a little, belatedly registering that the night was growing cold around them quickly without their propane heater to ward off the chill. He held out his left arm, barely visible in the dark, and she accepted the invitation gratefully.

He tucked her close against his side. His body was solid and warm, and she had to admit she found it reassuring to cuddle up against him. A shell whistled overhead, and a tremendous explosion nearby sent dust raining down on them in the brief illumination.

How long they sat there listening to the artillery barrage blasting the valley to smithereens, she didn't know. An hour, maybe. The explosions ebbed and flowed, sometimes close and sometimes farther away. Small-arms fire announced that the rebels and local ground forces were engaging in direct combat close by.

She heard the high-pitched engine whine again. Another drone. But this time, the scream of its engine was followed immediately by the sound of ordnance exploding in airbursts nearby. An attack drone? Who in the hell had access to that kind of weaponry out here?

Yet another whistling scream pierced the night. A big explosion deafened Katie as a flash illuminated the darkness. She looked up and a little scream escaped her when she saw a black figure looming in the doorway of their tent. She yanked up her pistol to shoot the intruder, but Alex was faster. He slammed his hand over her pistol, shoving it down to the cot before she could pull the trigger.

What the—

He was on his feet, moving as quickly as a cat to the shadow in the door. He took the person by the arm and guided him or her inside.

It dawned on Katie that the shadow was much shorter than Alex. And clothed in voluminous robes. *Crap.* She'd almost shot a local woman.

"Talk to her," Alex ordered low. "But keep it quiet."

Katie nodded and waited out a momentary lull in the shooting. As a spray of small-arms fire started up again, she used the noise to murmur, "Can we help you?"

"My baby. It comes," a young voice moaned.

"Then you've come to the right place," Katie replied. "Lay down here, and Doctor Alex will take care of you."

"Keep her dressed," Alex ordered when Katie reached for the hem of the girl's burka.

"Why?"

"We may need to move her." He sat down at the foot of the cot to examine the patient with a flashlight he shielded with his hand.

"But she's having a baby," Katie replied blankly.

"Haven't you ever watched *Gone with the Wind?*" he retorted. "Babies don't care if the city is burning down around Mom. They come when they come."

"This isn't Atlanta, nor is it the nineteenth century," Katie whispered back. She'd watched enough women struggle with all their might to push out babies over the past two weeks to understand that during the middle of childbirth was no time to move a patient.

"Tell that to the soldiers out there," Alex retorted from between the girl's knees. "She's dilated eight centimeters. Time her contractions for me."

Ten centimeters was the magic number when Alex allowed women to start pushing. Some women went from eight to ten in a half hour. A few had taken hours to get there. Katie waited in tense silence for the girl's next contraction to start and end.

"Three minutes apart, one minute in duration," she reported in the rumbling aftermath of some sort of incoming missile.

"We've probably got a little time then," Alex remarked. "Stay with her. I'll be back."

Shocked, Katie watched him glide outside the tent and disappear into the night.

"Where—" the girl blurted in alarm.

Katie shushed her hastily. "He'll be back. He's just checking the battle. Stay as quiet as you can."

"Cursed, greedy Tatars," the girl muttered. "They think to destroy us. They are demons who rape our land. Steal the food from our mouths. Poison the wells, salt the fields. I curse them all unto the end of time—" She devolved into the local cough.

Katie frowned, not understanding the Tatar reference. Weren't they nomadic raiders from southern Russia from the time of, oh, Genghis Khan? The girl's language sounded old. Religious in nature. But clan rivalries and tribal feuding had been going on out here as long as humans had lived in these barren mountains. It was a revealing glimpse into mankind's violent and harsh past. Frankly, she found it miraculous that humans had survived their own homicidal tendencies to populate the planet.

In the flashes of artillery explosions, the girl looked to be in her late teens. And pretty. Really pretty. Her eyes were big and dark and doe-shaped, her black hair lush around a heart-shaped face that high-fashion models would envy. It seemed strange, though, that a girl this young would have made her way to Alex by herself.

"Does anyone know you're here?" Katie whispered to the girl.

Fear made the girl's eyes even bigger as she shook her head vigorously. "My family does not know I am pregnant."

Katie stared. "How is that possible?"

"I am not married. I wear big clothes. I pretend to eat a lot and tell them I am gaining weight. But I really don't eat much and try to stay thin."

In this culture, of all cultures, Katie supposed it might be possible to hide a pregnancy if a woman was really careful. Then the rest of this girl's dilemma hit her. An unmarried girl, pregnant. In a society where sex outside marriage was punishable by death. No wonder the girl had hidden the pregnancy.

"What will you do with your baby when it comes?"

Anger flared in the girl's eyes. "Kill it."

CHAPTER THREE

WHAT? KATIE'S JAW dropped at the hatred in the girl's voice. *What the hell?* She opened her mouth to ask what in the world was going on when a dark figure materialized in the doorway. She reached hastily for the pistol before she recognized Alex's familiar silhouette.

"We've got a problem," he murmured.

"No kidding," Katie replied, jerking her head toward the cot. "She wants to kill her baby."

Alex went still for a moment. Then he asked quietly, "Was she raped?"

Of course. Young. Beautiful. Unmarried. "I hadn't thought of that," Katie confessed. She turned to the girl and murmured a quick question.

The girl shook her head in the negative. Hmmm.

"Regardless," Alex interjected, "we may have to get out of here sooner rather than later. A line of rebel troops is advancing up the valley. If Karshan's local militia doesn't hold the road until daylight, we'll be overrun."

Katie frowned. "If the fight's on the road, how are we going to drive out of here?"

"As always, you grasp the crux of the situation unerringly," he muttered.

We're trapped? "Where will we go?"

He shrugged. "Up."

"Up the *mountain?*" she demanded in disbelief. "With her?" She jerked her head toward the laboring girl again.

"I scouted around a bit. Karshani tribesmen are entrenched in the village up the valley. Rebels have the road and the lower pass covered. Over the mountain will be the only safe retreat for us."

"But the girl—"

"She'll have to make do. I can't stop the war for her to have a baby. I'll do what I can for her." He moved toward the rear of the tent and his patient. "Keep an eye outside. Watch the road down where the river bends. If you see any movement, tell me immediately."

Katie nodded her understanding. The scene outside was surreal. Tracers streaked across the black sky like comets. Explosions peppered the hillsides, lighting up gun emplacements and clusters of shooters behind rocks and outcroppings.

The girl's bouts of heavy panting inside the tent came closer together and longer in duration. Katie heard Alex demonstrating breathing techniques, exhaling in short hard bursts. The girl mimicked him obediently. It wouldn't be long before the girl delivered. Thank God her labor was progressing quickly.

But not quickly enough. Headlights came into sight at the bend in the dirt road beside the river. "Vehicle's coming up the road," Katie announced.

"What kind?"

"Can't see yet. It's loud. Probably not civilian."

Alex swore quietly, and the girl let out a groan from behind the towel she was biting into.

The vehicle came into sight. *Crap.* "Armored personnel carrier," Katie reported urgently over her shoulder. It stopped halfway in view, and the front hatch opened.

"You're kidding," Alex muttered.

"I wouldn't joke about something like that. And I know my military vehicles. It's an APC. Late-model version with the wedge-shaped, anti-IED bottom."

Alex swore quietly again.

"Special Forces troops exiting it now," she mumbled. God knew, she recognized the gear and way of moving. Half her brothers were men just like that. She couldn't count how many times she'd stood by her father during training exercises watching soldiers egress APCs into simulated combat.

"Special Forces?" Alex echoed in dismay from the back of the tent.

"Yes," she answered with conviction. "They may be wearing civilian clothing and rebel colors, but *no way* are those regular soldiers."

A barrage of machine-gun fire exploded from over her right shoulder, and she jumped violently. Where had *that* come from? She craned her head to the right and spotted the muzzle flash up the valley a little ways. A very little ways. The weapon rat-a-tatted loudly, and the soldiers at the river hit the deck, diving for cover.

This was nuts. She was standing in the freaking middle of a no-kidding combat zone. The unreality of it struck her forcefully. She might have wanted adventure, but she didn't *do* combat. This was a bad dream. She was going to wake up any minute and it was all going to go away.

Alex joined her in the doorway, and she pointed out the action quickly. "Locals have the soldiers pinned down for the moment, but those troops will send out a patrol to flank the gunners and take out the position. The patrol will have to pass right by here to get to the gun," she whispered frantically.

He nodded in quick agreement with her assessment and breathed, "Time to go." He picked up a rucksack from the floor just inside the door and shouldered it. "Get the girl and follow me. I'll find us a route up the mountain."

Katie whirled and ran to the laboring girl. "We have to leave."

The girl stared up at her in disbelief.

"I know. But we're about to get overrun by soldiers who will shoot first and ask questions later. I'll help you."

Awkwardly, the patient sat up. Katie wedged a shoulder under her armpit and levered the unwieldy girl to her feet. A moan escaped her. Alex slipped outside and turned to the left, toward the advancing soldiers. Better them than the local gunners, Katie supposed, given that they had a laboring girl in tow. Although the soldiers would probably be inclined to shoot her and Alex for rendering medical aid to the locals anyway. *Because it was such a huge crime to help innocent girls give birth to tiny, future terrorists,* she thought bitterly.

Alex jumped up on the boulder beside their tent. The laboring girl reached up, and, with Katie hoisting from below and him pulling from above, they got her up onto the outcropping. What scrub there was up here was sparse and mostly dead. They had to rely on rocks and terrain for what little cover they could find.

Seeking cover and ways up the nearly impassable terrain, Alex doubled back to them often when one route dead-ended out and he had to find another. Katie put an arm around the girl's shoulders to steady her as they moved a few dozen yards up the steep slope. Without warning, the girl bent over, breath hissing between her teeth as she grasped her swollen belly. She devolved into a fit of coughing interspersed with low moans of pain.

Alex looked over his shoulder impatiently as Katie and the girl fell behind. He slid back down the gravel-strewn slope to them, pistol in hand, to wait out the contraction. Finally, the girl exhaled and nodded. They resumed picking their way up the hill.

During the girl's next contraction, Katie looked over her shoulder down the valley. She couldn't see the un-identified, definitely military, patrol headed their way, but she could feel it as surely as she felt the girl's fingers digging painfully into her forearm. A few more coughing breaths and the girl nodded once more.

They were able to go maybe thirty feet up the mountain between each contraction. It was agoniz-ingly slow, particularly when the gun emplacement lit up once more. Sure enough, soldiers down the hill fired back. At least a half-dozen weapons returned fire in a wide arc that would roll right over their tent any second.

They were maybe a hundred yards from their shel-ter when another contraction gripped the girl. This one drove her to her knees, and she doubled over, grasping her belly. "I have to push," the girl grunted.

"Not yet," Alex snapped under his breath when Katie translated the girl's words.

Katie relayed his order, but the girl shook her head. "You'll die if we have to leave you out here," Katie whispered frantically. "A few more minutes. We'll find a place to hide and then you can push."

"I can't go any farther," the girl moaned.

"Keep her quiet, or we'll all die," Alex bit out.

"I'm trying," Katie retorted, panic climbing into her throat.

The girl's contraction passed, and Katie heaved her to her feet. They made it only a dozen yards before the girl collapsed again, groaning into her hand pressed over her mouth.

Shouting erupted below them. Katie looked down as a burst of flame lit the night. The soldiers had just torched their tent. Cold terror washed over her. What if they hadn't left when they did? They'd be dead right now. The rebels probably had mistaken it for a local headquarters of some kind. The more immediate problem, though, was the wash of firelight illuminating the entire hillside.

"Get down," Alex ordered, yanking Katie and the girl down behind a waist-high boulder. A barrage of machine-gun fire raked the mountainside close enough to make Katie flatten herself to the ground.

Fear like she'd never known before roared through her. They were going to *die*. The three of them were not soldiers. They were barely armed, they had no gear and their only escape was up a forbidding mountain that only a seasoned climber—or a mountain goat—would attempt to scale.

Another drone flew past, barely higher than eye level, raking the ground with gunfire from a pair of machine guns mounted on its belly.

The girl's hands clamped around Katie's elbow just then and squeezed so tight the circulation in her hand felt entirely cut off. "Uh, Alex," she whispered. "This girl's going to deliver pretty soon."

Alex had picked up a few phrases in the local dialect, and he used one now, biting it out succinctly. "Don't push."

"Can't…stop…" the girl ground out from behind clenched teeth.

Katie translated grimly.

"We have to keep moving," Alex whispered in English. "We're not out of the line of fire, and the patrol will sweep the area looking for whoever was in that tent."

They would never outrun highly mobile soldiers. Katie shook her head in disbelief and denial, but it made no difference. He was right. She told the panting girl, "Crawl if you have to, but keep moving. Do you understand me?"

"I can't," the girl wailed under her breath.

It was becoming a familiar refrain, but Katie replied fiercely, "Find a way. I'll drag you if I have to."

Katie had to give the girl credit. She pushed up to her knees, moved her burka aside and staggered up the hill after Alex, using her hands for support on the steep hillside before her. She fell twice, and each time Katie bodily lifted the girl back to her feet. The next time they dived for cover, though, the girl's breathing changed. An element of really sharp pain entered her gasping breaths.

"She really can't go on," Katie told Alex. In a flash of mortar fire, Katie saw the frustration and futility that passed across his face. He nodded, though, and angled off to the right.

It was only a half-dozen yards to where he stopped

and waved for them to join him, but Katie didn't think she and the girl were ever going to make it to his side. Each step was a herculean effort for the girl, who was in so much pain she could not stand unaided. Only Katie's arm around her kept her upright. Thankfully, Alex rejoined them and lifted the girl in his arms. He moved quickly into the shadows.

Katie made the mistake of glancing down and saw that they stood at the top of a nearly vertical cliff face. Only the narrowest of ledges kept her from plunging hundreds of feet to the valley floor below. Sick to her stomach with terror and vertigo, she plastered herself to the rock wall at her back and edged forward. Alex ducked into a low opening, and she fell to her knees beside him in relief.

The three of them were crouched in a tiny crevasse that didn't rise to the exalted status of a cave. It was maybe eight feet deep at best and no more than three feet tall at the opening, narrowing to a few inches tall in the back. But it afforded them a little cover from the battle raging outside and a moment to catch their breaths.

The girl started swearing under her breath so colorfully that Katie felt an incongruous urge to laugh. Or maybe that was just hysteria threatening. Either way, the girl's voice broke on what would have been a scream had she not jammed her burka in her mouth and bitten down for all she was worth.

It was Alex's turn to swear. He unceremoniously shoved the girl onto her back to examine her. "Baby's trying to crown," he muttered. "Tell her to push with the next contraction."

Katie was so relieved she could cry as she relayed

the instruction to the girl. The contraction came, and the girl strained, bearing down in the age-old way as Katie supported her shoulders from behind.

"Again," Alex ordered.

"Again."

After several more contractions, Alex fumbled in the rucksack and pulled out a flashlight. Covering himself with the girl's burka, he took a quick look at affairs. When he emerged, he spoke so calmly in English, Katie's blood ran cold before she even comprehended his words.

"Tell her to rest for a while and just try to breathe through the contractions."

He'd *never* told a woman to take a break in the middle of a delivery before. Just the opposite in fact. He always had her give the women pep talks and tell them at all costs to keep pushing until it was over.

She relayed the instruction and then murmured, "What's up?"

"This kid's head is too big to pass through the pelvic opening. The baby can't be born."

"What do we do now?" she asked as calmly as her exploding alarm would let her.

"Two choices. Leave the girl and her baby here to die. Or do a C-section and save the kid."

"And the mother?"

"It's a major surgery. If blood loss doesn't get her, shock and hypothermia may. And then there's the problem of noise. If I cut her open without anesthesia, she's likely to scream her head off and get us all killed."

Katie stared at the shadows wreathing his face. How

in the hell were they supposed to choose between those options?

He stared back. At length, he muttered, "Welcome to playing God."

A barrage of gunfire below them made her jump. For a minute there she'd forgotten about the war raging outside. The girl lying on the ground beside her panted fast and hard as another contraction gripped her.

"What would you do?" Alex asked quietly.

Katie shook her head, horrified to the core of her being. "Ask the mother. It's her baby. Her life."

"How very pro-choice of you," Alex replied wryly. Then he said more sharply, "So do it. Ask her."

Katie was shocked that he had declined to make a unilateral decision. It was so very…human…of him. She turned to the mother and waited out the end of the contraction.

Holding the girl's hand, she said quietly, "Your baby is too big to be born this way. Doctor Alex can cut the baby from your belly, but he has no medicine for the pain. If you make any noise, we will all die." She took a deep breath and added reluctantly, "You may die from the surgery."

"If I have no surgery?" the girl asked.

Katie relayed the question, and Alex outlined the answer sentence by sentence as she translated.

"You will become exhausted eventually. The placenta will separate from your uterus. Your baby will suffocate and die, and you will begin to hemorrhage. That means you will bleed inside your body. You will die from blood loss."

The girl was silent, considering her options. "I hate this baby. I do not care if it lives. But I want to live."

Alex nodded briskly. "Then the baby must come out of you."

Katie watched as he pulled out a scalpel, clamps and what she recognized as suture materials. He spread a towel on the ground under the girl and another beside himself.

"How are we going to keep her quiet?" she asked.

"If we're lucky, she'll pass out fast."

"That's not encouraging."

"Since we're being so democratic about this, ask her," he suggested. "I'll try to time the incision for during an artillery barrage. She'll have to do the rest."

Katie spoke briefly to the girl. Determination entered the girl's eyes, and Katie thought that she was more scared than the girl at this point. The girl twisted a length of her burka and told Katie to hold it in her mouth for her when the time came.

"Ready?" Alex murmured from his crouched position between the girl's legs. The girl's grotesquely distended belly, now bared to the cold air, was pale in the darkness. How on earth was Alex going to do a C-section in these conditions?

The girl put the gag in her mouth, and Katie grasped the ends of it, her entire body shaking with terror. The girl wasn't shaking much less.

"Next explosion," Alex murmured, scalpel poised. *Kaboom!*

Alex slashed. The girl screamed. The night lit up and blood spouted black and wet from the girl's belly. A second slash, and the girl thrashed wildly.

"Hold her down," Alex ground out. "Placenta's separating. She's hemorrhaging."

Katie leaned on the cloth gag, pinning the girl's

head to the ground. A knee across the girl's shoulders helped hold her in place, while Alex knelt on the girl's thighs. He worked fast, and Katie did her level best not to look at the gore unfolding.

Instead, she stared into the girl's panicked, animalistic eyes. All humanity drained out of the girl as she screamed against the gag again and again. And then, just like that, the girl went limp. Her eyes glazed over.

Is she dead? Katie fumbled under the girl's jaw for a pulse.

"Thank God," Alex breathed. He worked even faster, hacking the baby free of its mother's body.

Katie was shocked at how fast Alex had the baby out. Thirty seconds, maybe, all told. A lifetime for that poor girl, though.

"I can't find a pulse," she told him frantically.

"First things first," he snapped. "Gotta get the kid breathing."

The baby let out a wail that he quickly muffled with a hand over its mouth. Alex shoved the baby at her fast. "Keep it quiet."

Like she had the first idea how to silence a newborn infant? The baby was slippery with blood and white, greasy gook. Quickly, she wrapped the child in the spare towel Alex had laid out and slipped the child down inside her coat for warmth, which was a trick while keeping a hand over the crying child's mouth. She hoped she wasn't suffocating the poor thing. What a hell of a way to be born.

"Hold the flashlight," Alex ordered.

She didn't have three hands, for crying out loud. But he was probably doing the work of three surgeons right now, so she didn't complain. Kneeling awkwardly, she kept the baby's mouth covered as it slid farther down in her coat and held the flashlight in her free hand where Alex pointed it.

He worked frantically on the mother, his hands flying.

"How's she doing?"

"Bleeding all over the place. I'm losing her," he gritted out.

Another round of gunfire from nearby made Katie jump and the baby cry even louder. She made hushing noises into her coat even though she doubted they would have any effect on the squalling infant.

Alex started to swear in a steady stream under his breath, and in the light of the next mortar, his face looked gray. She risked a glance down. There was blood everywhere. A huge pool of it lay under the girl. The formerly white towel was now black with it. And where Alex's hands worked inside the girl, his fingers disappeared in a flowing puddle of it. Streams of blood trickled down the girl's belly unchecked. Katie had never seen so much blood in all her life.

"Listen for a heartbeat," he ordered.

She laid her head on the girl's chest. The rib cage did not rise, and she heard only the swish of her own blood in her ear. God, she hated silence. But then a barrage of gunfire made it too loud for her to hear a thing, and that was worse. She hunted again, frantically, for a pulse under the girl's jaw. *Nothing*.

Tears welling in her eyes, she shook her head at Alex.

He continued to work in grim silence for several more minutes. But finally he went still. He stared down at the girl's body bleakly. And then all he said in a terrible, agonized whisper was, "Turn off the flashlight."

Her second hand freed, she turned to the business of quieting the crying infant. She maneuvered the hot little bundle inside her coat until it lay across her, the baby's head on her left breast. She remembered hearing somewhere that the sound of heartbeats calmed babies. It took a few moments, but it worked.

Alex shook himself out of wherever he'd gone mentally and crawled to the edge of the crevasse. "We've got to get out of here."

"What about her?" Katie glanced down at the corpse of the girl who'd been so brave and angry and determined to live.

"We have to leave her."

Every cell in Katie's being protested the notion of just abandoning the girl here like a discarded hunk of meat. Thankfully, Alex crawled back to the girl's side. Gently, he closed her eyelids before pulling the end of her burka across her face. He covered the bloody mess that had been the girl's belly with a towel and arranged the girl's robes over it all.

He placed his hand over the girl's heart and murmured barely loud enough for Katie to hear, "Rest in peace, and be with whatever God you worshipped in life."

The tears overflowed from Katie's eyes then, and she sucked back a sob. She was shocked when strong arms wrapped around her, dragging her up against a hard body. Between them was the hot bump of an infant torn from its mother's dying body. Katie didn't even know what sex it was. A hand pushed her face down onto his shoulder; his own face was buried in her hair. He shuddered against her while she cried into his neck.

But as the ominous *thwocking* of a helicopter became audible in the distance, he stilled and muttered into her hair, "If you want that baby to live, grieve later. Follow me now. Fast and silent."

CHAPTER FOUR

THE NEXT HOUR was a nightmare. The mountain was no less steep at the top than at the bottom, and the baby fussed occasionally, sending her into a cold panic as she tried frantically to shush the newborn. It didn't help matters that the battle raging below grew more intense as the night wore on. And who knew what lay over the mountain peak?

Alex was grim and silent, focused intently on finding a route up the mountain. He was quick to lend her a helping hand, though, or to haul her up over a particularly rough patch. As she'd correctly guessed, he was deceptively strong. And when her strength lagged and her will to go on faltered, he was indomitable.

And there was always that intense hug to think about. It had been more than simple comfort. He had let her inside his guard for just a minute. Made a human connection with her. Maybe even needed her for a second there.

Alex murmured from ahead, "Stay low. We're cresting the mountain. We don't want our silhouettes visible below."

She crawled across the open peak and huddled in the lee of a boulder just over the crest beside Alex.

"How's the baby?" he asked.

"Alive. It moves around now and then."

"Let me see it," Alex muttered.

She unzipped her coat and lifted the infant out. In a flash of mortar fire, she saw it was a baby girl. Said baby girl took immediate and loud umbrage at being exposed to the sharp chill, however, and started to squall.

Alex pulled a clean towel out of his pack and swaddled the infant in it after a fast examination. Thoughtfully, he passed the baby back to her, and Katie slipped the child back in her coat. It took a minute or so, but the baby quieted in the warm and dark next to Katie's heart.

"We have to get food for her," Katie whispered.

"She can go a day or two without eating, actually," Alex replied. "Most babies don't take in much nourishment in their first twenty-four hours."

Huh. Live and learn. "What about us?"

He shrugged. "We're another matter. We'll need water before long."

"Any bright ideas about what to do next?" she asked.

"Go downhill for a while."

She liked that idea a whole lot better than continuing to scale mountain peaks in the dark. With no climbing gear. And a baby stuffed down her coat.

Trying to stay oriented as to where they were, she pictured the map of this region they'd been showed in the D.U. offices. Another village lay at the head of this valley. Its name was something like Ghan or Ghun. She couldn't remember exactly. No telling if it was another Karshani clan village or belonged to some other clan entirely. As likely as not, the neighbors hated each other's guts.

This side of the mountain was more a slope than a

cliff, mostly made treacherous by loose, rolling gravel. She made much of the descent sliding on her butt; before long, they stood at the bottom of a narrow valley in deep darkness.

Alex shocked her by brushing off the seat of her jeans and finishing off by giving her ass the briefest of squeezes. So brief she wasn't sure if she'd imagined it or not. But not so brief that her breathing didn't accelerate sharply.

"Altitude getting to you?" he murmured.

Yeah, right. Altitude. "Gee, I don't know," she whispered back. "Maybe I should feel your butt and see if a sudden case of altitude sickness overcomes you."

"I dare you."

Oh, it was so on. She stepped right up behind him and slipped her hands down the waistband of his jeans. He lurched in shock as she slid her palms between his briefs and the denim and cupped strong, well-defined male cheeks that abruptly went rock hard.

"Not bad, Doctor. Not bad at all."

He whipped around, effectively yanking her hands out of his pants, and stared down at her. Enveloped in darkness and lust that rolled off him like sin, it crossed her mind that, perchance, she was playing with fire by messing with this man.

"Think before you go there with me," he rasped. "I'm not one of your milk-toast college boys."

The warning in his voice was clear. Although what, exactly, he was warning her about, she wasn't sure. That he wouldn't stand for mind games from her? Or that his tastes were darker than the average college co-ed's? Or maybe that getting involved with him would be an all-or-nothing proposition.

Was she prepared to go there with him? How far beyond her experience would he take her? Just how intense would sex with him be? Turned on and scared in equal measure, she let out a careful breath as he turned and stalked off into the night.

She'd wanted to be taken seriously. To be treated like an adult. For everyone to quit seeing a sweet, naive kid when they looked at her. But how much innocence was she willing to lose? If she didn't miss her guess, being with Alex Peters could cost her damn near all of hers.

They'd been hiking for maybe an hour when the baby commenced crying and nothing she could do would quiet the poor little thing.

Alex muttered, "She's hungry. Nursing after birth is an instinctive imperative. We probably won't shut her up shy of feeding her something."

"Any suggestions as to what to feed her?"

"Actually, yes." He slid his pack off his shoulders and rummaged in it, emerging with an IV bag. He poked a pinhole in one corner of it while she opened her coat and maneuvered the infant close to the opening while keeping the baby mostly inside the garment's warmth.

They tried unsuccessfully to squeeze some of the IV fluid into the child's mouth, but the baby wouldn't swallow it and only squalled louder.

"We've got to quiet her down," Alex bit out. "Once the artillery fire stops, people for miles around will hear her screaming."

"Any ideas?" Katie asked, frantically rocking the furious baby.

"She needs to suck to trigger her swallowing reflex."

"I already tried getting her to suck my finger as a makeshift pacifier and she wouldn't do it."

"She needs to suckle. As in a female breast." He threw her an expectant look.

Katie stared. "News flash, Doctor. My equipment is not currently in service for milk production."

"She doesn't need to get any milk. She just needs a breast to suck. Once she's sucking strongly, then we can squirt some IV fluid into her mouth and she'll swallow it."

An embarrassed impulse to refuse speared through her gut at the same time intellectual certainty that she would do it rolled through her brain. She tried unsuccessfully to juggle the baby and her coat and her shirt, until Alex's big, warm hands slipped inside her coat and took the baby. Awkwardly, she raised her shirt, baring her bra, which happened to be lacy and white and practically glowed in the dark.

"Not very practical lingerie for Zaghastan," he murmured in amusement.

The bastard sounded like he was enjoying the view a little too much. She glanced up, irritated, and muttered, "I wasn't expecting to show it to anyone while I was here."

"So you wear sexy lingerie entirely to please yourself? That's encouraging."

"How so?" she blurted. She wished the words back as soon as they left her mouth.

"You struck me as too...virginal...for that naughty bra. I'm glad to see I underestimated you."

Her gaze narrowed at the faint challenge simmering

in his voice. She reached for the edge of her bra cup and slowly, deliberately, pulled it down. Alex's gaze riveted on her flesh as the swell of her breast and its rosy nipple were revealed. His gaze flared like an arc welder, and her pulse spiked hard in response.

Without comment, he eased the infant to her breast. The baby was too mad or too inexperienced or both to know what to do, however.

"I apologize," he muttered.

"For what?"

"For this." He reached in front of the infant's mouth with his fingers and pinched her nipple. Hard. She jumped and would have squawked were they not in the middle of a war zone. Involuntarily, her back arched into his hand, trying unsuccessfully to ease the sharp pressure.

"Oww," she breathed.

He let go and made a small sound of satisfaction. "Better."

She ventured a look down and realized her nipple now jutted out, swollen and full.

"Rub it on the baby's face. Across her mouth," he instructed.

She did so, stunned at how erotic it was to be doing this in front of him. Without warning, the baby latched on and gave a tug that shot sensations all the way to her groin. "Oh!" she gasped.

One corner of Alex's mouth curved up knowingly. He reached between her breast and the baby with the IV bag and slipped the pinholed corner into the infant's mouth. She felt the baby swallow against her flesh.

"It's working," she breathed. "Do it again."

Working together, the two of them got a few ounces

of IV fluid down the baby, who fell asleep quickly after that. Alex hooked his finger under the lace and lifted it into place, running the back of his knuckle lightly across her nipple in the process. Damned if it didn't stand up proud and eager again, pushing impudently through the lace. And damned if he didn't stare down at it, his eyes ablaze, until her breath came short and fast.

"Zip up," he ordered sharply. "I don't need either of you catching a chill."

She scowled at his back until it occurred to her that it might have been sexual frustration putting that edge in his voice. Abruptly, she felt much better as she tucked the sleeping baby into her coat and zipped it up.

"We need to name her," she announced. "We can't just keep calling her 'the baby.'"

Alex threw her a startled look over his shoulder. "You do it. But, for God's sake, don't name her something native. Pick something American-sounding."

"Why?"

"We'll need to take her back to the States with us. Which means we'll need to pass her off as our baby. What would you name our daughter?"

Their baby? The notion was both thrilling and scary to contemplate. "How about Charlene?" It had been her grandmother's name.

"Slut I went to school with was named that. Try again."

"Alexandra?"

That earned her rolled eyes and a firm, "No."

"Catherine?"

"You want to name a baby after a violent, dead queen?"

"Fine. You come up with a name you like!"

"Katrina."

"Sounds a little grown-up for a tiny baby."

"She won't be a tiny baby for long. And you can call her a nickname like Kat or Trina in the meantime."

"Teeny Treeny?"

He groaned under his breath. "Call her Dawn. The sun will be coming up soon."

She actually liked the symbolism of a new day after the darkness of night. Goodness knew, this child had been born under the blackest of circumstances. And she couldn't think of any horrible nicknames other kids might come up with for it. "Dawn, it is."

"Speaking of dawn, we need to take cover soon," he commented.

"Why?"

"Given the size of last night's battle, I expect more drones will patrol the area today."

"Isn't the U.S. the only country with attack drones? Why would the good guys come after us?"

He whirled and demanded, low and angry, "Since when is the United States presumed to be the good guy?"

Her jaw dropped. She'd been raised among soldiers and cops dedicated to country and service…to the death. It was anathema in her home to suggest anything other than the United States was right and good and decent.

Alex huffed. "Don't get me wrong. Democracy is a hell of a lot better than the available alternatives. But spare me the religious fervor for mom, apple pie and the Stars and Stripes."

"What the hell did Uncle Sam do? Pee in your Wheaties?" she demanded.

Pain. Grief. Rage. Desolation. The emotions flitted through his eyes so quickly she could barely register them, let alone catalogue them. *What the—*

"Not on the list of approved topics for conversation between us," he bit out. He turned around and stomped off without waiting to see if she followed.

"If there's a list of approved topics, how come I didn't get a copy?" she called after him.

A mumbled retort floated back over his shoulder, "Above your pay grade."

Her eyes narrowed. She wasn't about to let him get away with blowing her off. But first she had to catch him, and he was practically jogging toward the head of the narrow valley now. She'd always hated it when her brothers used their superior size and strength to ditch her. In retrospect, she'd probably been an annoying pest more often than not, but she'd just wanted to be included. To this day, she hated being left behind.

Her brother's cryptic request to watch for signs of something weird with Alex resonated in her head. What was *up* with this guy?

"Slow down!" she finally had to call to Alex.

Nada.

"Please!"

That did it. He stopped without turning around and waited until she panted up behind him. The altitude was a killer when added to a strenuous hike. As soon as she drew within arm's length of him, he took off again, but thankfully at a more reasonable pace. In a few minutes, he murmured, "Keep an eye out for movement on that slope ahead. We're getting close to Ghun."

Mostly, she was occupied staring at the ground so she didn't twist an ankle or break her neck. She glanced where he indicated and saw a steep rock face looming. She groaned under her breath.

"I see caves up there," Alex commented. "It's too early in the year for shepherds to have brought their flocks up here, though, so they ought to be empty. No grass yet."

She snorted. *Nothing* grew up here. She was surprised to spot what looked like an organized network of caves all over the steep slope ahead. How could so many people support themselves off the dirt and dust of this valley? No stream of any kind flowed through the area. In the past two weeks, she'd learned just how critical water supplies were to native peoples.

As the first gray of predawn peeked over the mountains, Alex scrambled up the steep hill while she rested a bit. He came back soon and led her to a cave blessedly not far up the slope. Overlapping slabs of stone mostly obscured the entrance. They slipped past the rocks into the dark, and Alex audibly sighed in relief. Had he been that worried, then?

In the green light of a Cyalume stick, she looked around the high-ceilinged cave. The floor was flat, dry and reasonably clean. A few animal droppings and scattered bones proclaimed the presence of some small predator. Off to one side was a stone ledge about hip high covered with a framework of woven boughs and dried grass that looked like a crude bed. Near the entrance, the stone walls were blackened as if fires had been lit there.

A stack of firewood was piled in a corner, and Alex moved to it quickly. In a matter of minutes, he'd built a fire her Boy Scout brothers would have been proud of. Out of the steady wind, the silence in the cave was palpable. And it got on her nerves fast.

"Where'd a city slicker like you learn to lay a fire like that?" she asked to break the quiet.

Alex didn't deign to answer and merely shrugged as he pushed a series of smooth, melon-sized rocks close to the fire. The thin, dry wood crackled loudly and burned fast, but it heated up the small chamber surprisingly well. A thin layer of smoke accumulated near the ceiling, seeping sluggishly toward the rear of the cave. Must be a tunnel or vent back there. The back walls, which retreated into shadows—who knew how far back—were pocked with round holes at even intervals, big enough for her thumb to fit in. Maybe those were the vents.

Surprisingly little light seeped in as day broke outside, but that also meant very little cold seeped in, either. Before long, the cave was actually reasonably cozy, enough that she shed her coat and made a nest out of it for Dawn.

Alex unwrapped the infant and, at long last, trimmed the umbilical cord and wiped the last birth blood off her. He frowned down at her, and Katie moved to his side rapidly. "What's wrong?" she asked.

"Take a look at her. Notice anything odd?"

She stared down at the pink, chubby baby, who had adorable blond peach fuzz hair. Ten fingers. Ten toes. Two eyes. Two ears. Limbs of equal lengths. No visible deformities... *Whoa. What?*

"Blond hair?" she said questioningly. Every baby

they'd birthed so far had had black hair. *All* the locals she'd met were dark-haired.

"Exactly." He stared at her significantly.

"How did that happen?"

"The mom was an unmarried girl. Good-looking, right?" Alex asked tersely. "What color was her hair?"

"Yes, she was stunning. And she was dark-skinned and dark-haired like all the locals."

Alex murmured, "Too much pigment in Dawn's skin for her to be albino. Only way for her to have blond hair, then, is for her father to be Caucasian."

Katie's jaw dropped. "Where did a local girl meet a Caucasian?" To her knowledge, she and Alex were the only Caucasians for hundreds of miles around.

Alex snorted. "Soldiers. Spies. Civilian contractors. Drug dealers."

"And aid workers like us," she added, appalled.

"The way I heard it, we're the only aid workers foolish enough to venture into this area in years," he retorted.

She grimaced. "That's what the women have been saying to me, too. Okay, so strike aid workers from the list of possible fathers."

They stared down at the baby, who was settling down to sleep in her warm nest.

Alex announced without warning, "Strip off your clothes. All of them."

"I *beg* your pardon?"

He was already shrugging out of his coat and pulling the black turtleneck over his head. Lord, that man had acres of gorgeous muscle. He reached for his belt buckle and she squawked, "What are you doing?"

He looked up, and his gaze went from concentration on something worrisome to smoking hot in the blink of an eye. "Worried about delivering on the bet you lost?" he purred.

"No, I'm not worried," she lied belligerently. "I just don't think now is the time or place to collect."

He moved to stand a little too close to her for comfort, and she was abruptly aware of how much bigger than her he actually was. And stronger. And they were so very alone out in the middle of nowhere. Literally. He could force himself on her and there wouldn't be a soul around for miles to hear her scream.

"Angel, when I collect on our bet, it will not be in a squalid cave, and you will beg me for it."

Her eyes flashed as she instinctively rose to the challenge. "I don't beg."

The corner of his mouth turned up in that sardonic half smile of his. "Wanna bet?"

"No, thank you," she replied tartly. "I'm already indebted to you. I don't need to add to it."

"I still need you to strip. All the way down to your skin."

"Why?"

"I need to check for tracking devices in our clothes."

She blinked, shocked. "Excuse me?"

"Tracking devices. I need to make sure none were planted on the gear or clothing we bugged out with. I did a quick check before, but in light of last night's events, I need to do a more thorough search."

"Who on earth would want to track us?"

"I can think of any number of candidates, and some of them I'd rather not have knowing where we are."

"Like who?" It was starting to feel like all she did with him was ask questions.

"Not on the list of approved topics between us."

She scowled. "I'm not stripping unless you answer me."

His gaze snapped up to hers, and this time amusement flashed before he banked all emotion. "Fine. The CIA. Their Russian counterparts, the FSB. The U.S. Army. Various mob groups. That'll do for starters."

"Why would the mob track you? And which mob? What did you do to them?"

"I relieved both the Russian mob and the American Mafia of substantial funds some years ago and have yet to give them an opportunity to win any of them back. For that matter, the Ukrainians don't like me very much, either."

"What did you do?"

"I hung out in casinos they owned. In my rebellious youth, I went on a short-lived, but highly productive, gambling spree."

Math genius. Master's degree in probability. Cryptography postgrad… "How much did you take them for?" she blurted.

"A lot."

Huh. And he still had the money? *Well, well, well.* So the good doctor was rich, too? It hardly seemed fair given how smart, sexy and good-looking he was.

"Why would the CIA and FSB track you?"

He threw her a stubborn look and merely shimmied out of his black jeans. Dang, that man was built.

"Let me guess," she said wryly. "Not on the list."

"Bingo."

Oh, Lord. There went his underwear. *Yowza.* The good doctor was blessed in every single department of his life. She spun away quickly lest he catch her looking at his junk. The temperature in the cave shot up at least ten degrees as sexual heat abruptly filled the air.

"I'm not kidding about your clothes," he said grimly from behind her.

Which would be worse? Getting naked at the same time he was or waiting until he was fully dressed again and forcibly undressed her? Wow. That was about a toss-up. A tiny part of her loved the idea of him tearing her clothes off her.... Maybe it was the whole caveman vibe coming out of her deepest, darkest DNA. But she didn't have any spare clothing and needed what she had on to stay intact. Practical necessity won out, and she pulled her pink turtleneck over her head reluctantly.

Ohmigod. He was watching her. And he was stark naked. Gloriously, unconcernedly so. He'd already seen her in her bra—less than her bra. This was no big deal, right? Except her heart was jumping in her throat and her hands shook like leaves in a hurricane.

She reached for her jeans and unzipped them slowly. Pushed them off her hips reluctantly. Heat blossomed in her face as her lace thong was revealed. She could literally feel his blazing-hot stare taking in her pert little rear end. Men had been commenting on her derriere since she'd been old enough for it not to be creepy. She knew it was firm and high and lush enough to turn men on without Alex having to tell her so.

"Nice."

"Could you at least be a gentleman and turn your back?" she blurted.

"Kitten, I'm a lot of things, but a gentleman is not

one of them. You owe me sex anyway. I'm eventually going to see you naked, so why not now?"

Because she barely knew him. Because he was naked, too. Because part of her wanted him to take advantage of the situation, and she was a big, fat chicken about that part of herself. Fantasizing about a dark, dangerous man like Alex Peters was one thing. Being naked and alone with him for real was another thing altogether. She didn't want it to be that way, but it was. She was a fake, and she couldn't handle a man like him.

Damn.

The promise of sex hanging thick and heavy in the air pulsed between them, pulling her toward him. An urge to run her hands over that magnificent body, to pull him to her, to make love to him, surged within her, startling her. Sure, she felt attracted to guys at work and joked around with her girlfriends about jumping various guys' bones. But that was all in fun. This compulsion originated low in her belly, deep and primordial. Lust in its purest form. Mindless. Insistent.

"What's wrong?" he murmured.

She resorted to mumbling, "You're making me strip in front of you and you have to ask that?"

Something warm and soft dropped around her shoulders, making her lurch. It smelled of sandalwood and spice. His coat. "Sometimes I forget what an innocent you are. Wear this until I check out the rest of your clothes."

The driving need she'd experienced at the sight of his naked body subsided, and she all but cried in her relief as she tossed her thong and bra over her shoulder to him. *An innocent?* Was she really, in spite of her best efforts to get people to let her grow up—and then it hit her. Other people weren't preventing her from growing up. She was preventing herself from doing it. Chagrin roared through her. A real man was within arm's length, naked or close to it, and she owed him sex. All she had to do was reach out and take it. And yet...

And yet. Fear held her back.

Alex worked in silence, turning each piece of clothing inside out, running his fingers carefully over each seam, examining tags and pockets and anywhere else a burr might be attached.

"How big would a tracking device be?" she asked curiously without turning around to see if he was still starkers.

"Depends on how big a battery it has and how long the person who plants it wants it to work. A short-term device, say, for a single day, could be the size of a pinhead. Something a little longer term, like I'd expect to get used on us, might be the size of a grain of rice."

"Long grain or short grain?"

He chuckled briefly. "Okay. Your lingerie is clean." A big, tanned hand emerged over her right shoulder, the lacy bits dangling from his fingertips. She snatched them from his hand and maneuvered into them awkwardly underneath his coat. Who would have guessed two tiny scraps of fabric could make her feel so much better?

Her shirt took longer, and her jeans longer still, to check. But eventually he passed them over her shoulder, and she was safely clothed once more. But no sooner had she pulled the shirt back over her head than Dawn started to fuss.

"She's hungry again," Alex announced.

Katie had been around a lot of little kids in her day, but not many infants. She would take his word for it. She scooped up the baby and the IV bag that he held out to her and moved over by the fire with her back to him to coax the baby to drink a little more.

It took giving Dawn her breast again to get the infant to swallow, and Katie pinched her own nipple, mortified at how turned on doing it made her, before Dawn could find it and latch on. The sensation of the tiny mouth sucking vigorously at her breast was overwhelming and confusing. It felt good, but not in a sexual way.

It also felt very wrong. Like she was co-opting a moment that belonged to someone else. That poor dead girl should be doing this. Although, given how much she'd hated Dawn, Katie doubted the mother would have fed the child. More likely, she'd have drowned the baby or suffocated her. Katie clutched Dawn more tightly and fell in love a little.

"I need my coat back," Alex said apologetically. "I have to check it."

She passed him the garment, and he stepped close to drape her coat over her shoulders. As he did so, he paused to watch the baby suckling at her breast and swallowing the IV fluid Katie was sneaking into the baby's mouth.

"Beautiful sight," he said in a hushed voice.

She looked up at him in surprise. That was the last thing she'd expected to hear from the dark, sexy bachelor.

He reached down to cup the baby's tiny head in his

hand for a moment. "Such a rotten start in life, baby Dawn. I'm so sorry I couldn't save your mother."

"You did your best. And if that girl had lived, I expect she would have killed Dawn as soon as they left us. Maybe this is how it was supposed to work out—that the baby lived and the mother did not. Goodness knows, that girl would have had some tall explaining to do if and when she married. Not only would she not have been a virgin, but her body would have shown the signs of having borne a child. She would have been beaten to death if she was lucky. Perhaps a quick end on that mountain was the merciful way for her to go."

"God, the barbarism of it," Alex muttered.

"If we take Dawn to America, she'll grow up in a very different world."

"There's no 'if' about it. Not with that blond hair of hers. We have to take her with us. She'd be a pariah at best in this society and horribly abused at worst—assuming she were allowed to live at all."

Katie shuddered and cuddled the infant a little closer. She was starting to feel downright maternal toward the small bundle of squirming warmth.

Alex went back to the business of inspecting his coat and then all the gear in his emergency pack, which he spread out over the floor of the cave. She was surprised to recognize an array of survival gear in among the medical supplies—energy bars, matches, Cyalume sticks, compass, water purification tablets.

"How is it that you had a whole backpack of medical and survival supplies ready and waiting to go last night?" she asked.

He shrugged. "Call it a hunch. Those rebel forces

kept showing up at exactly our location and attacking, and it made me suspicious."

"Of?"

"Do you always ask so many questions?" he demanded.

"When people are being cryptic with me, absolutely," she declared.

He sighed. "I was suspicious of somebody not being happy we're out here."

"Are we in direct danger? And don't dodge the question. I grew up listening to cops and soldiers. I know exactly what kind of danger we're in if someone wants us dead."

He shrugged. "I won't ever bullshit you, Katie. That I promise. I may refuse to answer a question, but I won't lie. Deal?"

"Deal."

"I think someone not only knows we're out here, but wants us dead. Which makes me question Doctors Unlimited. They are supposedly the only people who know we're here. Someone within D.U. isn't who they claim to be."

"There's a mole? Why would anyone spy on a humanitarian aid group?"

"That is the question, is it not?"

She thought hard. Placing and maintaining a full-blown mole had to be a difficult and expensive proposition for a spy agency. Why go to all that trouble to watch a bunch of doctors and nurses.... Unless they were not just doctors and nurses? She looked up at Alex and asked soberly, "What do you think D.U. does besides render medical aid?"

"I don't know."

"If you had to guess?"

He shrugged. "That's obvious, isn't it? They insert people right in the middle of the hottest conflicts on the planet with covers that make them more or less immune to attack or arrest."

"Spies?" she breathed. "For whom?"

"You tell me."

She stared at him, shocked. "I don't know anything! I didn't even work for D.U. until they needed a Zaghastani translator for you."

Alex was studying her far too closely again. Like he was trying to look inside her soul and see what truth she was hiding from him.

"Maybe we're just being paranoid," she said a little desperately. "Maybe it's coincidence that the fighting has flared up in the places we've been."

He snorted. "I can calculate odds out to nine figures in my head in under a minute. And you don't want to know how many zeros line up after the probability of it being random chance."

She put her coat down on the rough bed and tucked Dawn back into her nest, now surrounded by hot rocks to keep her warm, and turned to Alex in the dancing firelight. "Do you trust D.U. enough to call and ask for transport out of here?"

A derisive snort was his only answer. Frankly, she shared the sentiment. If someone in the organization had set them up to be killed, she didn't want to talk to D.U., either. She asked, "What do we do now?" Interesting that she had complete faith in him to have an alternative plan. No doubt about it, he was one of the smartest people she'd ever met.

"We're going to get some rest and wait for dark."

A look of deep reluctance crossed his face. "There's a place I know…not too far from here… I was really hoping not to have to go there." Grim determination replaced the reluctance. "Can you hike twenty miles or so over rough terrain if we break it up into a couple of days of travel?"

"Depends on the terrain, but I guess so."

He sat down beside the fire, leaning back against a convenient rock. He held his arm out to the side. "Share the fire with me?"

She stared, shocked. He was inviting her to cuddle with him? He so wasn't a cuddly kind of guy! He was a torrid sex, love 'em and leave 'em kind of guy. Stunned, she sank down beside him and tentatively rested her head on his shoulder. His arm went lightly around her waist and she hesitantly did the same.

"What do you do to work out?" she murmured.

"Vigorous sex. You?"

She grinned and retorted, "Pole dancing, of course."

"Show me sometime?"

"Not on your life."

Silence fell between them, and she savored the slow, steady beat of his heart against her ear. The warmth of the fire and the flames' mesmerizing dance had lulled her mostly to sleep when he murmured under his breath, "I'm a devil you can't handle, angel. If you know what's good for you, you'll stay far, far away from me."

CHAPTER FIVE

ALEX SAVORED THE way Katie's body melted against his, fantasizing about how it would feel beneath his, thrashing in the throes of sex. Gradually, she slid down his torso in her sleep until her head ended up resting on his lap. That brought a whole new wave of forbidden fantasies springing to mind.

The sight of her mostly naked body danced in his mind's eye, burned on it indelibly. Lord, the things he wanted to do to her. And the sight of her breast with Dawn's head nuzzling it… He knew that wasn't supposed to be a sexy thing, but it had turned him on so bad he could hardly stand it. Someday, he would be the one sucking at her breast, bringing that flush of pleasure to her cheeks.

He snorted at himself. Must be some misplaced, infantile need to replace his absent mother. He always had been a breast man…

Although the sight of Katie's pert little behind cut in half by that strand of lace nestled between her cheeks was enough to make an ass man out of him in no time. Purely depraved fantasies came to mind about what he'd like to do to that part of her anatomy.

He tried to set aside the images, but for once, failed. Startled, he examined the problem. He always was able to compartmentalize the women in his life. They were something he stored in a drawer in his mind. When a need for sex became urgent, he opened up the drawer, hired a topflight prostitute, took care of the need and closed the female companionship drawer until next time.

But Katie was not so easy to stuff in a mental drawer. Undoubtedly, it was because they had to live together and interact 24/7. And now they shared responsibility for a newborn infant. He shuddered to recall the nightmare of Dawn's birth. As a trauma surgeon, he could accept that not every patient was savable. Even in a fully equipped operating room, he doubted Dawn's mother would have lived. Frankly, it was a minor miracle the baby had made it.

Katie shifted a little in his lap, and his thoughts lurched back to her. Dammit, he couldn't keep his mind off her. What was wrong with him?

Sleep. He needed sleep before tonight. But with his flesh rock hard and her face lying practically on top of his erection, there was no way he was getting any rest. What the hell. He closed his eyes and let his mind wander deep into the dark world of possibilities if Katie McCloud decided she ever wanted to climb down off her good-girl pedestal.

He spent the day dozing, helping feed and care for Dawn and speculating on who had planted both the primary burr in his coat and the smaller, secondary one in Katie's hiking boot. They'd been well hidden. Professionally hidden. It had taken an inch-by-inch, meticulous search and knowing what he was looking for to spot them.

He hadn't told Katie about either one. No need to panic her more than she already was. The quality of the bugs and how well they were hidden narrowed down the list of people who were following them a great deal. Even though the list of people who might wish him ill was long and distinguished, only an intelligence agency could be behind those tracking devices.

As dusk fell, he broke out bottles of water and mountain climbers' energy bars. He and Katie ate quickly, and she topped off baby Dawn with more of the IV fluid. The baby's birth weight had been excellent, he estimated somewhere around nine pounds, but the infant would need real food in the next day or so.

He sat in the cave entrance as darkness fell so his eyes could fully adjust to the dark. After about a half hour, he called inside quietly to Katie. "Ready to head out?"

She murmured an affirmative, and he heard her coat zip. They had fashioned a cloth sling for Dawn out of Katie's turtleneck that held the baby across Katie's torso and left her hands and arms free to balance herself. He hoped she wouldn't need them for the hike tonight. Too bad he didn't have a phone number for the people he was headed toward. He knew the GPS coordinates of where he was going, but he had no idea what the terrain between here and there would be like. He was not optimistic.

The sky was ominously dark and silent as they set out. Nearly as ominous as his mood. He was deeply irritated that it had come to using this emergency escape plan. It was a last resort, and he held no illusions about how high the cost of it would be. But what the hell else was he supposed to do with a woman and baby in tow?

He didn't like the quiet out here. In these rocky valleys, sound traveled forever. He'd been hoping for the sounds of battle to disguise the noise of their passage. Either the battle was finished in the Karshan Valley or had yet to begin tonight. He feared it was the former, which would mean whoever was tracking him was free to come after him. The first burr he'd thrown down a deep vertical shaft in the back of their little cave. The hole had been maybe eight feet across, and it had taken the empty water bottle he'd put it in many long seconds of falling before it clattered faintly below. The stone mountainside should block any outbound signal from it until its battery went dead.

He squatted beside the only tiny rivulet of running water they'd come across and turned the second burr loose in a second plastic water bottle to float downstream. He watched it bob out of sight in grim satisfaction.

"Can we drink this water?" Katie murmured.

"Not unless you want dysentery and trichinosis."

"Never mind." She laughed.

"We've got enough bottled water to get us where we're going," he commented. Assuming it only took them another day to get there. They topped the pass, and he paused to survey the terrain ahead. A vast, sloping plane angled away from them, and he mentally echoed Katie's sigh of relief when he murmured, "We're headed across that."

But the plain was deceptive, crisscrossed by gullies and littered with boulders and vicious dried bushes bearing thorns as long as his finger. How anyone survived here was beyond his comprehension.

They'd been hiking for maybe two hours and were

making decent time when he heard a noise that made his blood run cold. A motor.

"Get down," he bit out. They happened to be crossing a small ditch maybe five feet deep in total, and Katie crouched quickly, looking around nervously. She'd heard it, too.

He passed her the satellite radio and breathed, "If I'm not back in two hours, use the emergency frequency on that to call D.U. for a rescue."

"I'm not leaving you behind," she whispered back angrily.

"Thanks for the sentiment, but I'll be dead." On impulse, he leaned over and kissed her hard and fast on the mouth. He had *no* idea why he did it. And then he was up and out of the hole. He took a quick fix on three landmarks so he could find her again and then took off running low and quickly, zigzagging across the broken landscape.

The engine cut off abruptly. It sounded like a four-wheel ATV. Someone was *so* following them. He swore under his breath, slid his field knife out of its belt sheath and crept forward, hunting the hunter. The bastard behind them was in for a nasty surprise if he thought the do-gooder doctor was an easy mark. His father hadn't been a top Russian field operative for nothing. Alex had been groomed his entire youth to follow in his father's spy footsteps. And that included hand-to-hand combat training from the best—his old man.

It took him a matter of minutes to spot the stalker. The guy was good. Excellent, in fact. He was wearing civilian clothes and sporting a light brown beard, which made him a mercenary or a Special Forces operator most likely.

Alex picked his spot, perched high on a boulder and settled in to ambush the bastard as he crept past. It took almost ten minutes for the guy to draw even with his position.

Plenty of time for Alex to replay that insane kiss he'd planted on Katie before he'd left her. It had been for her comfort, right? Reassurance to her that he'd be back. That was all.

Plenty of time for Alex to consider the fact that, even if he took out this asshole, ten more just like him would swarm out after him and Katie and the baby.

Plenty of time for Alex to tell himself he wasn't in the business of killing people. Hell, he'd become a doctor in hopes of doing a little good in this world before he went to hell. But Katie and Dawn were depending on him. He might have been trained by a spy to be a spy, but that didn't mean he ran around assassinating people on a regular basis. A moment's doubt that he could pull this off passed through him.

But his father's training was too damned good. He shrugged off the doubt, locking it tightly in a little closet inside his mind. The moment called for calm. Focus. Fear and doubt were counterproductive, therefore, unnecessary.

He weighed all the options for after he took this first pursuer out, rank ordering them in decreasing desirability and probability of success. One plan emerged as the clear victor. A plan he hated with every fiber of his being. He'd spent his whole adult life trying to cut ties to his father, dammit. He'd even gone to jail to avoid the man's grasping fists.

First things first. He had to take care of this bastard on their tail. It was a risk to confront the tracker but more risky not to. An ambush out here would be the death of them all. And while he wasn't particularly concerned for his own survival, Katie was a young woman with most of her life ahead of her. And Dawn... She literally had her whole life in front of her. Weird how deep in his gut the urge to protect the infant ran. Must be some survival of the species instinct.

His target approached, and Alex focused all his senses on the man, his body coiled to spring. Thought ceased. Breath ceased. *Time* ceased to exist. *Now.* Alex leaped.

The guy was strong. Fast. As skilled as Alex had anticipated he would be. Although Alex had the element of surprise on his side, the stalker twisted violently in his arms and got in a hard elbow to his nose that had Alex seeing stars and hanging on for dear life. He didn't want to kill the guy. At least not before he forced him to tell him who he was working for.

But crap, this bastard was strong! Alex lost his grip and his opponent spun, a wicked blade in his right hand. There was no time for elegance. He lunged before the guy could get his bearings and slammed his own knife into his gut, ramming the tip of his blade up and under the ribs.

His follower went down, spouting blood everywhere. *Jesus. What a mess.*

"Who are you working for?" Alex demanded, already sliding his pack off his shoulders.

"Screw you," the guy snarled.

Alex pulled out an inflatable internal pressure bandage. It looked like a deflated condom. It was inserted into a puncture wound, inflated and the pressure stopped the bleeding from the inside out. It was designed for wounds exactly like the one he'd given his opponent.

"Know what this is?" he asked tersely.

"Yeah."

"You can have it if you tell me who you're working for. Otherwise, you're gonna bleed out in about two minutes. Your choice."

At least the guy didn't tell him to fuck off. In fact, the man actually stopped to consider the offer. Alex counted the seconds in his head. "Sixty seconds or so left, buddy. You should be starting to feel cold by now. Light-headed. Maybe even having trouble breathing while blood starts to back up into that lung I nicked."

The guy was still silent, his jaw muscles working convulsively.

"I've got nothing against you," Alex tried. "I'll even insert the pressure balloon for you. But I need to know who your bosses are."

"I don't know. I've only got an encrypted website URL. They send me a message and I turn on a burner phone they mail me."

"Got an active phone on you now?"

A pause. A rattling breath.

"If you die, I'm just gonna search you and take it, anyway. Then I'll leave the phone on until someone calls."

"Pouch. Left hip," the guy gasped. He was starting to make a death rattle when he inhaled.

Alex opened the canvas pouch quickly and pulled out a cell phone. Not fancy, not crappy. Anonymous.

"Gimme that balloon, Koronov!"

This guy knew his real name? That narrowed down the list of who might have sicced this man on him considerably. Alex knelt beside him and jammed the balloon into the wound. Unlike birthing babies, he had a ton of experience with knife wounds from his time working in the prison infirmary. With quick efficiency, he inflated the balloon bandage and blocked the bleeding. He applied butterfly bandages to hold the wound shut.

"Maybe you live, maybe you don't," Alex said briskly. "You waited a long time to play ball with me. Keep it clean and dry. Here's some tape and clean gauze for you. Rest and drink a bunch of fluids to replace the blood you lost. No strenuous activity for thirty days, and see a doctor ASAP for real stitches."

"You shitting me?" the guy muttered.

Alex shrugged as he rummaged in the guy's hip pocket and came up with a set of keys. "Like I said. It's nothing personal. If I wanted you dead, I'd have slit your throat when I first jumped you. Nice moves, by the way."

"Go to hell," the guy sighed as Alex tucked the phone and keys into his pocket.

"You're welcome," Alex replied drily.

He estimated the guy had hiked a quarter mile from wherever he'd stashed his vehicle in the time since the engine had gone silent. It took Alex a while to backtrack to about the right area and then hunt around until he spotted the brush-covered lump. But it was worth it as he started the four-wheeler's engine and roared into the night. Now they could reach their destination in one night, and maybe baby Dawn stood a real chance of surviving the fiasco of her birth, after all.

KATIE HUDDLED OVER the baby in panic as the engine came closer and closer and got louder and louder. *Please, God, let Alex not be dead.* Please let whoever was on that ATV go right on past her and Dawn. Should she use the radio now? Call for help while she still had a chance? The engine cut off, and she fumbled frantically at the radio. Dammit, she should have paid closer attention when Alex tried to teach her how to use it a few days ago.

"Katie," a familiar voice called out quietly.

She sagged, weak, nearly peeing her pants in her relief. "Over here," she replied.

She stood up and, when Alex reached her, threw her arms around him and squeezed the stuffing out of him. "I have never been so glad to see another human being in my entire life," she declared.

His arms closed around her tightly as she buried her face in his neck.

"How's the baby?"

"Fine. About ready to eat again. I think she won't need mother's little helpers to take the fluid and swallow it this time."

"Too bad. And your helpers are not little, by the way."

Her face heated up, and she was grateful for the darkness to hide her blush.

"I got us a ride. Unless, of course, you'd rather walk the last fifteen miles."

She laughed under her breath. "No, that's okay. Where'd you get the ATV?"

"Took it from its owner."

"Did you kill him?"

"I hope not. I stopped his bleeding. I give him fifty-fifty odds of making it."

She shrugged as she threw a leg on the seat behind Alex and settled Dawn in front of her. There was no time for compassion right now. There was a baby to get to food and warmth and her own life to protect. She wrapped her arms around his lean waist, savoring the strong, capable feel of him.

"Where are we going?" she shouted in Alex's ear over the engine noise.

"It's a secret," he called back.

They drove for a couple of hours, banging over the rough terrain uncomfortably. But it was a hell of a lot better than walking all the way. They wound up into the hills again. She was intensely grateful at not having to hike up the long climb to the pass. This time, the plain that opened beneath them as they topped the head of the valley was vast, stretching away in the starlight as far as she could see. It was to one side of this huge open plain that Alex guided the four-wheeler.

He paused to pull out his cell phone and use the GPS function to check his position yet again. He took a visual fix on something up in the hills and eased the ATV forward once more. In about ten minutes he stopped and turned off the ignition. "We're here," he announced.

She looked around and saw nothing but dirt and rocks and looming mountains nearby. "Where's here?"

"Follow me." Alex took off on foot up a steep, but short, hillside. With every step, the expression on his face waxed more thunderous. What about this hillside was making him so mad? Fury rolled off him in eddies and whorls that were practically visible to the naked eye.

He stopped at the base of a giant cliff, and she joined him, frowning. A cluster of crude carvings caught the moonlight and cast shadows that were definitely man-made. But they were just lines and dots. She'd never seen the Karshani people use any symbols like that when she'd been around them. Alex ran a hand across them and then his fingers fisted together.

He ground out, "I probably ought to give you a speech about having to kill you if you reveal what I'm about to show you. But, in fact, I doubt anyone would believe you if you told them, anyway."

Perplexed, she followed him into a high opening in the rocks that was more crevasse than actual cave. He stopped, and then passed her the Cyalume stick. "Hold this."

She took the glowing plastic tube and watched with interest as he pulled out his wallet and dug out a scrap of paper. He moved to one side of the narrow passage, and that was when she spotted the steel door. "WTF?" she breathed.

He threw her a grim look and proceeded to dial in a five-number combination on an old-fashioned rotary combination lock. He took a deep breath of resignation and huffed it out. Like this was some point of no return for him. He turned the massive handle and pulled.

The door moved a fraction of an inch but no more. "Help me," he grunted. "Thing's rusted shut."

She put her hands beside his and threw her weight into tugging. Together, they were able to slowly drag the rusted door open a foot or so. Alex took the Cyalume stick from her and slipped through the narrow opening first. Katie lifted Dawn to the side and squeezed through the gap after him. She coughed at the dust their feet had stirred up and looked around in the dim green glow.

It looked like a storeroom with wooden crates stacked high along the walls. Alex was moving away from her quickly, and she hurried after him murmuring, "I say again, what da heck?"

"Don't ask," he bit out.

The far wall of the space came into view. It wasn't a large supply depot or whatever it was, then—

She stared as she spotted an old-fashioned metal console with what looked like radios and circular dials mounted in it. Alex sat down in the metal chair in front of it and wiped off the glass dial faces with his sleeve. Her jaw dropped as she spied Cyrillic lettering.

"This is a Russian place? How on earth did you know about this? And the door's lock combination? And about this radio?"

"Later." He stood up and moved to one side of the console. A big round wheel was mounted there with a footlong handle protruding from it. He grabbed the handle and began turning the wheel slowly. It creaked and groaned.

"Get in my pack and pass me the petroleum jelly," he ordered.

She did as he asked and pulled out a small plastic container of the goop. Using his finger, he daubed the lubricant around the shaft of the wheel and commenced pushing at it again. The thing turned smoothly and silently this time. He picked up speed, cranking for a minute or so.

"Take over cranking the generator for me, will you?" he asked.

She shed her coat, laid Dawn down in it and then took over his position at the crank wheel. He sat back down at the console and flipped several switches. A small light came on, dim and flickering in rhythm with her cranking. But as she continued, the bulb glowed brighter and steadier.

Alex picked up a potato-sized microphone and held it to his mouth, speaking rapidly into it...*in fluent Russian.*

What. The. Hell?

CHAPTER SIX

ALEX SUPPOSED HE shouldn't have been surprised that he'd been forced into using the emergency supply dump that his father had told him about right before he'd come on this cursed mission. Hell, for all he knew, his father had engineered the rebels following him and Katie to force him to come here. To accept the massive favor and debt using this emergency Russian hidey-hole represented. How had his father found out about his job with Doctors Unlimited, anyway?

Peter Koronov was unapologetically a loyal Russian spy. The way he heard it, his father had never expressed or even pretended remorse to his CIA captors. Alex had no doubt that after his old man was repatriated to Mother Russia he'd received a fat promotion in the FSB. If only the bastard would give up already on recruiting him to follow in the Koronov family tradition of serving Russia.

That was why Alex had gone to jail, why he'd taken this obscure job that would put him well away from the United States on a regular basis. That and he owed society at large for the excesses of his youth. Not to mention, he *liked* being a doctor, dammit. Of course, his father would just say Alex liked playing God with other people's lives.

He'd been shocked by Peter's phone call just before

he'd left on his first D.U. assignment, and even more shocked when his old man made him copy down lat-long coordinates and a number combination. How had the guy known he would need the information unless his father had expected someone to come after his son in Zaghastan? Had this whole freaking assignment been a setup? If so, who'd done the setting up? The U.S. government or the Russian government?

Had Peter sicced the rebels on his own son with the intent to kill him? Was he that cold a bastard? Why would his father do a thing like that? Did it have to do with who Alex was working for? Lord knew, after the way he and Katie had been dogged, Alex didn't for a minute think Doctors Unlimited was entirely innocent. There was definitely a snake in its humanitarian grass.

Alex questioned his own arrogance in thinking that this mess might be all about him. His father might be that arrogant, but not him. Of course, his father would probably be right. Peter Koronov attracted trouble like a magnet. He'd tried so hard not to emulate his old man in that way, but he was beginning to think it was a lost cause. If the CIA and FSB wouldn't even let him deliver babies in the middle of nowhere in peace, his life was pretty much screwed.

Surely there was a reason beyond him that had larger forces at work. But what? And *why?* He was missing something critical. He felt it in his bones.

Static snapped and popped over the radio, and he fine-tuned the frequency slightly, holding his breath and praying it would work. If not, he could only hope there was enough gasoline stored somewhere in here for them to travel several hundred miles on the ATV, a prospect he did not relish.

He hated making this call with a purple passion. But as sure as the sun rose in the east, when that guy he'd stabbed reported in to whomever he worked for, more guys just like him would be coming. A lot more. All together this time. And with a woman and baby in tow, he didn't stand a snowball's chance in hell of avoiding them.

He made the distress call again.

Without warning, an answering voice crackled over the radio.

He had to yell into the microphone to be heard, but he relayed his position and the code words scribbled on the piece of paper from his wallet. There was a pause of nearly two interminable minutes, but then the voice at the other end of the radio returned and reported that transport would be dispatched to his position, ETA six hours.

It was done. He'd made a deal with the devil. Let hell's fury come. For surely it would, now.

He acknowledged the radio call and signed off. "You can stop cranking, Katie." He leaned back in the chair and pushed his hands through his hair in distress. He couldn't believe he'd just done that. But he had no choice. None at all.

She whipped around, staring at him in suspicion and shock. "Start talking," she demanded.

"Look. This was not my first preference for how to get out of here," he retorted. "But someone is trying to kill us, or at least me, and we've got a newborn in need of food and care. I had no choice."

"No choice to do what?"

"I called the Russians and asked for an emergency evacuation."

"Why?" She drew the syllable out in disbelief. He supposed he couldn't blame her. For all she knew, he was a vanilla American doctor who ran around doing humanitarian work. God knew, that was all he wanted to be.

"The guy following us, the one I took the ATV from, was American. Redneck, Bubba, *rah-rah-go-us* American. The kind of guy who wouldn't work for a foreign outfit. Which means whoever's out to get me— at least tonight—is not Russian. And neither will his friends be when they come looking for us. This was the only safe, fast egress route I could come up with on short notice." He fingered the cell phone he'd lifted off the guy. Who the hell would turn up at the other end of that thing?

Katie collapsed onto a crate, staring at him. "And how do you know how to contact Russians to ask for an evacuation? Why on earth would they actually come get you? Are you one of them?"

"Do you truly not know who I am?" It was clear she did not, but he was so used to the people around him treating him with automatic suspicion when they met him, he could hardly believe she didn't recognize him.

"You're Alex Peters, M.D."

He sighed. "Legally, that is true. I changed my name last year."

"Why?"

When he didn't answer right away, she just stared, waiting. She was really good at that. Did she learn it from her brothers? Or maybe from teaching five-year-olds? He sighed again. "My birth name is Alexei Petrovich Koronov."

It took a moment, but her face lit with recognition,

followed quickly by dismay. "Peter Koronov? The spy who was convicted of treason?" she blurted.

"My father."

"Oh my God."

So much for their flirtation and mutual attraction.... He jolted as her arms went around him.

"I'm so sorry, Alex."

He stood up, pushing her away, using his hands on her shoulders to keep her at arm's length. "What have you got to be sorry for?"

"I read about you. I remember wondering what would happen to the son when the father was sentenced to death."

He shrugged. "My old man was never in danger of being executed for treason. He was too valuable as a bargaining chip against the Russians. The CIA got back several high-level spies in trade for my father."

"So he's back in Russia?"

He nodded. "He's pretty well burned as a spy. His face is too well-known. I suppose he could get plastic surgery to change his appearance, but he's also sixty-four years old. That's getting up in years to be a field operative." He added drily, "I'm told it's a stressful and strenuous life."

Katie looked at him searchingly. "Is this why the CIA could be following you? Do they watch you?"

He shrugged. "Above my pay grade to know. I haven't been free for long enough to have figured it out."

"Free?" she echoed.

They hadn't told her about his prison time? He'd just assumed the people at Doctors Unlimited would have told her. After all, not many women would head out into the wilderness voluntarily and completely alone with a convicted felon. He swore violently under his breath. *Bastards.*

Katie pulled back a little in alarm. "What?"

"I'm sorry, Katie. I assumed they told you about me."

"They who? Told me what?"

"Doctors Unlimited. Told you about my past."

She frowned. "My brother told me you were really smart and went to college early. That you studied math. And, somewhere along the way, you apparently got a medical degree. D.U. didn't say anything at all about you."

His internal warning antennae wiggled wildly. "Who's your brother?"

"Mike. Mike McCloud. He knows I speak Zaghastani. He was chatting at a party with someone at D.U. who happened to mention they were looking for a Zaghastani translator. Mike hooked me up with this job."

"Didn't you already have a job?"

"I was just finishing up three years with Teachers Across America. Mike knew I was chafing against the idea of settling down to a permanent job as a kindergarten teacher someplace dull and boring."

She was seriously a kindergarten teacher? He'd half assumed that was just a cover story for her. Lord knew, practically everyone else who crossed his path worked for one spy agency or another. Good God, if she was who she said she was, she had no business running around in a virtual war zone with a man like him.

The one and only saving grace to her being out here was that she was apparently looking for adventure. She'd certainly found it. At least he hadn't completely misread her. The good girl might be looking to climb down off that pedestal of hers, after all.

And he was not the man to help her down. She was far too naive and pure for him. He might have already thrown his own soul away, but he had no right to destroy hers, too.

He sighed and asked, "Are you cold? There ought to be blankets in here somewhere. Maybe even a bed. After all, the radio operators had to have somewhere to sleep between shifts when this place was manned full-time."

At the mention of a bed, Katie's mobile features exploded in a variety of reactions. So transparent, she was. Definitely interested in sex with him and just as definitely afraid of it. Smart girl.

"You're very good at distracting me," she murmured. "Honestly, I could use more distraction, though. The past few days have freaked me out pretty bad."

"I bet." He had to give her credit. When the bullets had been flying overhead, she'd kept her wits about her, followed instructions and pushed herself well beyond exhaustion without a single word of complaint. She was allowed to fall apart a little now.

Reluctantly, he put his arms around her. "You've been very brave, Katie. Just a little while longer. We're almost out of this mess. Focus on the nice hot shower you can have as soon as we get back to civilization."

She muttered into his shirt, "You sure do know the way to a girl's heart."

"I highly doubt that," he murmured back. "I've never been any good at understanding women."

"I don't know." She sighed as she snuggled closer to him. "You're doing pretty good with me so far."

The strangest sensation coursed through him. Warmth. Affection, even. What the hell was that all about? He didn't do relationships, for God's sake. It was why he used hookers. They were all business. Pay the money; do the deed. No drama. No emotion. No connection. *Call me next time you're in town,* and they were out the door.

Katie's hands slipped around his neck, which had the effect of plastering her breasts against his chest. His abdominal muscles tightened in surprise while his brain sounded an alarm. "Katie," he mumbled, "we shouldn't—"

"Why not? Who's here to judge us?"

She had a point. Still...

"Kiss me, Alex. I need the distraction. And the sense of human connection."

"You don't want a connection with me, Katie. I'm no good at—"

"Kiss me. Now."

Who was he to say no to a demand like that? He'd be a cad to disappoint her and leave her hanging, right? Who was he kidding? He was a big enough asshole to take advantage of her vulnerability, and that was all there was to his motivation. Very slowly, he slipped his right hand around the back of her neck under the weight and warmth of her lush hair.

Her head tilted up and her lips parted slightly as she stared at him. Desire flared hard in his gut and that urge to plunder and debauch her roared through him, yet again. Yup, he was going to kiss her...and he was a complete asshole.

"Tell me what you're thinking," she whispered. "I can't read you."

Good lord, he hoped not! He *had* to step away from her. Save her from his brand of corruption. She was a decent kid. He should protect her innocence and purity and goodness. She was, in truth, all the things he wished he could be. All the things he'd been trying so flipping hard to be by going to medical school and taking this humanitarian aid job.

But damned if he could make his feet move an inch back from her or force his hands to slip off her satin flesh. Plan B—he had to get her to back away from him. Fast. Scare her. Find a way to warn her off his brand of corruption.

"I'm thinking about all the twisted ways I'd love to fuck you and use you," he replied baldly.

She did tense. For a moment. And then, dammit, she relaxed again. Looked up at him as trustingly as a lamb. Worse, she had the colossal foolishness to whisper, "I don't have much experience with...with that. But I'd like to learn. I'd like you to show me."

His eyes widened in genuine shock, and he flung himself backward. Away from her. He staggered a half-dozen more steps back before bursting out, "You have no idea what you're asking. I told you before—I'm not a good guy. I'm not Joe College, all-American boy."

"I know."

"Run from me, Katie. For the love of God, if you know what's good for you, don't get anywhere near me." He stabbed a hand into his short hair and whirled away from her, desperate to distance himself.

He heard her take a step forward, and he fled to the far end of the bunker, stopping only when his thighs bumped into a wooden crate. He looked left and right for an escape route, then spun to face his pursuer, as panicked as a cornered animal. She took another step toward him.

"Stop right there!" he barked.

Blessedly, she did.

"I spent the past five years in jail," he blurted. "I'm a convicted felon. I did hard time for DUI, reckless endangerment, resisting arrest and a bunch of other charges."

The other charges were mostly related to resisting arrest, taunting the court and baiting the judge, who steadfastly refused to throw the book at him until Alex finally broke down and asked the D.A. to convict him for his own safety. It had taken his lawyer some maneuvering to convince the judge to sentence Alex to four years in jail at her client's own request without ever revealing the real reason for it.

"Sit down," he ordered Katie. "Over there." He pointed at a crate far across the space from him.

She sank onto the edge of the crate, but damned if that determined look still wasn't gleaming in her baby blues.

"You are innocent. Inexperienced. Naive," he explained carefully. "I am the complete opposite. I am neither decent nor good nor respectable. Do you understand what I'm trying to say?"

"No. Explain it to me."

He huffed. "My father—" Dammit, would he always be defined by the shadow of his fricking father? "My father and I have always had a…difficult…relationship. We were not like a normal family. He used me as a cover while he spied against the United States. I was a tool to him. Not a son."

"He didn't love you? At all?" Katie asked in a small voice.

"How should I know? We never talked about feelings other than to teach me how not to have them. They're a weakness for spies. As long as I can remember, he spent our time together teaching me spycraft. I knew how to tail a subject like a pro by the time I was seven. How to slit a man's throat by age ten or so. He did his level best to turn me into Russia's ultimate weapon."

"Did he succeed?"

Alex snorted. "It doesn't matter if he did or not. Neither side trusts me farther than they can throw me. The CIA is terrified that Peter succeeded, and the FSB is terrified that he failed. I'm a liability either way. What I'm trying to say here is that he taught me how not to be a nice human being."

She absorbed that in silence for a minute. Then, "What happened to you when your dad was arrested?"

"I got sent off to boarding school and on to college while he was very publicly tried and convicted of treason. Everybody treated me like I was a criminal, too. After a while, I got so sick of trying to prove them wrong that I started doing my best to live down to everyone's rotten expectations of me. I was not immune to teenage angst, and I was a kid living in a world of adults. It probably didn't help matters that I never got to be a kid when I was one. I had some childhood rebellion to get out of my system."

"What did you do?"

She was going to make him spell it all out. Every last sordid bit of it. Unreasonable anger at her rattled in his gut. Maybe that was why he didn't pull any punches with her. "I didn't finish the PhD in cryptography that my father wanted me to get. I went to medical school against his wishes."

"Oooh. Medical school. You rebel, you," she teased.

He scowled. "I started to party. I drank and used drugs and gambled. Rebellion against my father carried to its logical extreme."

"And there were women?"

"Yes. There were a lot of women. Older than me. Experienced. I sought out women on whom I could work out my many issues and who would not expect any kind of a relationship with me." He stared into her eyes, willing her to hear what he was leaving unsaid.

But damned if her eyes didn't light with interest. Answering lust surged into his loins, but he suppressed it brutally. "Katie, as pleasurable as I might find showing that world to you, you do not want to explore my end of hell."

"You can't possibly know what I want or don't want," she retorted.

"I know you have no idea what you're asking for."

"So show me. Give me a taste of it."

He stared. If it were possible for his eyeballs to fall out of their sockets in shock, they would have rolled across the floor then and there. Could he do it? Could he give her a taste of the darkness and then back off when it got to be too much for her? Did he have that much self-control? "It wouldn't be the same without a fifth of whiskey and a half-dozen lines of coke," he mumbled.

"I have a good imagination. Try me."

He surged up off the crate and stormed down to the far end of the bunker, swearing luridly in Russian.

When he finally wound down and swung around to inform Katie in no uncertain terms that he couldn't do it, she was watching him blandly. Looking as satisfied as a recently fed cat. He eyed her suspiciously.

"How long until the cavalry comes to rescue us?" she asked mildly.

"Six hours, give or take."

Her mouth curved up in a smile that was pure sin. *Oh, God.* "No, Katie." She started walking toward him, her hips swinging provocatively. "I won't do it. I can't."

"Yes. You can," she purred. She reached for the hem of her turtleneck, which she'd converted back from sling duty to shirt duty. He darted forward and snatched her hands away from the fabric. He yanked her arms wide, and her body slammed into his. Resilient female curves pressed against him in every place it was wrong for them to press. He groaned in the back of his throat.

"Mmm. That's nice," she reported. "I think I like having my hands restrained."

"Stop that," he ground out.

Standing with her breasts crushed against his chest, she looked up at him. "I want it. You want it. We're both consenting adults. What's the problem?"

He closed his eyes. Willed himself to be strong. He would protect her if it cost him his sanity or even his soul.

"Kiss me, Alex. Show me something I've never done before."

Please, God, give him strength. Talk. If he could get her talking. Distract her. "What haven't you done?"

"It's probably faster to list what I have done. Let's

see. I've had sex, of course. But it was pretty boring. Basic missionary position involving some grunting and general messiness."

"Did you like it?" he asked unwillingly.

She looked up at him. "I thought we already established that I haven't had good sex, yet, given that I prefer ice cream to it."

He grinned reluctantly. "Duly noted."

"I tried to give a blow job once, but I had no idea what I was doing. The guy mentioned something about deep throating and then passed out."

"He passed out in the middle of getting a blow job?" Alex blurted incredulously.

It was Katie's turn to grin. "He was drunk."

Alex snorted. "Very drunk."

"I've kissed a fair bit. Gotten a hickey or two. Oh, and I gave a guy a hickey once," she announced in triumph.

"Has a man ever gone down on you?" he asked.

"Like oral sex?" she asked, a faint quaver in her voice. "No."

"Ever used any toys?"

She laughed. "I went online once to see if I could order a vibrator. My best friend said they're the best way to get an orgasm. But there were so many things to choose from I didn't know where to start."

He shook his head. "Babe in the woods," he muttered. *Cripes.* She was practically a virgin. She'd never had an orgasm? Not one?

She laid her hands on his chest, sliding her palms up to his shoulders and beyond, toying with the short hairs at the back of his neck. "Show me just one thing," she coaxed.

"When you're imagining sex, what do you think about?" he challenged.

"I don't understand."

"Do you imagine being told what to do? Tied up? Or do you fantasize about being in charge yourself? Telling the guy what to do and how to pleasure you. Do you envision a romantic encounter or wild sex?"

"Oh," she breathed.

He stared down at her, waiting. Two could play the patience game.

"Umm, I think I'd rather have the guy be in charge."

"And?" he murmured, his voice rougher than he would have liked. He didn't want her getting to him like this! But damned if he'd figured out how to block her out emotionally.

"I've had dreams a couple of times about being, umm, at a man's mercy. I woke up turned on."

"Good to know. Do you imagine it slow and sexy or hard and rough?"

The pulse at the base of her neck right where her collarbone ended jumped. He'd bet she was flushing, but it would take better light than this to tell if he was right. She caught her lower lip between her teeth, and he all but jumped her right then.

"I don't know," she answered slowly. "I'd have to try both, I suppose."

She was a natural-born temptress. Totally unaware of her own sensuality.

Still holding both of her wrists, he guided them behind her back. "Clasp your hands together," he instructed quietly. "And don't let go. Can you do that for me?"

"Uh-huh," she replied breathlessly.

How in the hell had she talked him into this? Why couldn't he seem to say no to her?

The position thrust her breasts up and out toward him and lifted her chin to expose the length of her neck. Very slowly, he reached for the hem of her ridiculously pink turtleneck and raised it up until her bra and the swelling cleft of her chest were exposed. He hooked his index fingers in both of the lace bra cups and drew them downward millimeter by slow millimeter, gradually circling the underside of her sweet, firm breasts, exposing them as he went.

He confessed, "I've been thinking about doing this ever since you suckled Dawn."

"So have I," she agreed shyly. "That and how you—" she finished in a rush "—made my nipple stand up for her to suck."

Without warning, he flicked both of his thumbnails across her rosy peaks. She gasped and—God save him—lifted her breasts a little more. "Again," she breathed.

In minor shock, he obliged. Her entire body strained toward him. "Tell me what it feels like," he ordered.

"Electricity is streaking through my whole body. It starts where you're…flicking me…and goes to my fingers and toes and…and…"

"And what?" he demanded with gentle force.

She whispered, "And between my legs."

Holy shit. His erection strained against his zipper until he thought the metal teeth might burst. Watching her face for the slightest sign of distress, he reached for her jeans and unzipped them inch by tantalizing inch.

"Spread your legs a little," he murmured. And then, "Wider, baby."

He splayed his fingers on her belly, and her muscles contracted sharply. He named all the muscles of the human abdomen in order from smallest to largest before he regained control of his raging lust enough to slide his fingers down over the flat, silky plane of her stomach slowly, then slip his fingertips under the elastic edge of her thong. The memory of that intensely sexy scrap of lace had him pausing yet again to force his breathing to slow. His dick throbbed insistently, and even his balls got into the act. Gritting his teeth, he continued his hand's downward descent.

"That feels amazing." She sighed.

His fingers slipped between swollen folds of flesh so plumped with desire they reminded him of a ripe peach, springy and juicy. Katie gasped, and he stopped immediately to let her accustom herself to what he was doing.

But she was having no part of that. Her hips undulated forward, rocking onto his hand hungrily. He separated her folds and found the slippery pearl nestled in between. He rubbed the pad of his middle finger around it once, twice.

"Ohmigosh," she cried more urgently.

He rubbed the length of his finger against her, probing her passage with the very tip of his finger. He collected some of the moisture there and smoothed it over her hotly throbbing flesh.

"Alex," she groaned. "Please."

"Please what?" he growled from behind his clenched teeth.

"More," she panted. "I want more."

"You want me inside you, here?" He slipped his finger a little way inside her tight, hot core. Her internal muscles tightened convulsively around his finger. He withdrew and then slid into her again, a little deeper. She groaned again. Apparently, words had failed her.

Hell. He was in hell. He couldn't have this woman. She was not for him. But he'd never wanted any woman worse in his entire life. *Satan's karmic joke.*

Angling his palm so it rubbed her with every stroke, he plunged his finger into her in a slow, maddening rhythm. His entire being ached to be inside her, to slam into her until he was lost in mindless lust, exploding in rage and release. But for once, this was not about him. He watched, eyes slitted, as she rode his finger, head thrown back, throat taut, breasts heaving. Her entire body undulated with more and more urgency.

In the past, had she been any other woman, he would have taken pleasure in driving her to the brink and then yanking his finger out of her, withholding the release she was so close to. He liked his women frustrated, begging, before he took them. But shockingly, he wanted to give Katie pleasure. He wanted to see her first orgasm, to watch it unfold across her face, to see what emotion flitted through her so expressive eyes.

Her body flowed with female juices around his finger, and her gasps turned into sharper moans. He matched the increased pace of her hip thrusts, reaching deeper inside her, seeking and finding the spot in the front of her passage where the most sensitive nerves passed close by.

"Ready?" he murmured, his voice low and charged.

"Yes, yes. Oh, God. Yes," she panted.

He increased the pressure of his palm against her swollen flesh and slammed three fingers into her without warning, stretching her and filling her fast and hard.

She cried out sharply as the orgasm ripped through her. While she shuddered from head to foot, he continued stroking her, drawing out the orgasm, savoring cry after cry torn from her throat. She crescendoed with a last keening cry that rippled out of her throat and sagged against him, spent. He eased out of her and pulled her shirt down gently.

And then a strange thing happened. An urge to hold her came over him. He never felt affectionate after sex. But here he was, drawing her close, savoring the aftershocks making her tremble against him so sweetly.

"Oh, my." She sighed against his chest.

He started as something soft and warm moved across his neck. She was kissing him! Women never kissed him. It was too intimate. Too personal. His sexual encounters were purely business; not to mention women didn't feel like kissing him after he was done using them.

"I had no idea," she breathed.

"Like I said before. You do not know what you're getting into. I can't let you go there."

She raised her head to stare up at him in the dying glow of the Cyalume stick. "If there's more of that to be had, I'm all for it," she declared.

"I've created a monster," he groaned.

She growled playfully in the back of her throat, "When can I learn how to do that to you?"

Her flirtatious question sobered him sharply. "I take my pleasures rather more intensely, Katie."

She shrugged. "If the end result is *that,* who cares how we get there?"

KATIE WATCHED, BEREFT, as Alex pushed away from her and strode to the far end of the bunker, or whatever it was. Her brothers and her father walked away the same way, never pausing, never looking back. They just left. It was like their entire life was divided into neat little compartments they switched on and off at their convenience. At home: turn on the family persona. Off to work: slam that person off and activate the soldier. In danger: switch on the killer. Out of danger: turn that switch off and don't think about the people they'd eliminated. At a bar after the mission with the guys: turn on the friends-and-buddies person. But in the meantime, the family back home was forced to sit patiently in their little corner, hearing nothing, waiting and worrying, never knowing if their loved ones were ever coming home. Or if they did return, whether or not it would be in a closed casket.

As a kid, she'd always vowed she would never love that kind of man. She'd had plenty of the stress of it already. And all she had to do was see the toll it took on her mother to know that loving a dangerous man was not for her.

Alex paced for long enough that she got tired of watching him. Eventually, in hopes of at least bringing him back to the present if not to her, she asked, "What's in these boxes?"

"Supplies," he answered absently.

"Any baby formula in here? And maybe some diapers?"

Alex looked up at her quickly. "Probably no diapers, but powdered milk is a possibility. And there are, no doubt, medical supplies. Rolls of gauze and cotton surgical pads..." He commenced moving around the perimeter of the space reading labels on the crates. "Bring me that crowbar, will you?"

The tool was leaning next to the radio, and she scooped it up, then joined Alex at a stack of smallish crates. He pried one open and pulled out several brown paper packages. "Voilà. Emergency diaper-making supplies."

Thank God. She was getting pretty low on clean corners of towels to wipe Dawn's bottom with. She moved to the baby and, using gauze pads and cloth tape, swaddled her in a reasonably decent makeshift diaper while Alex continued rummaging around. Woken by the diapering process, Dawn was over the whole business of not needing to eat and screamed lustily. No amount of rocking would calm her. She wanted real food, and she wanted it now.

"See what she thinks of this." He held out his hand to Katie.

Katie glanced up in distress and spied him holding a plastic water bottle full of a creamy white liquid. *Milk!* The lid had been replaced by what looked like the cutoff finger of a surgical glove. She smiled widely. "You're brilliant!"

"So I've been told," he replied drily.

Dawn had to be convinced of the appeal of both the makeshift bottle and its contents, but, eventually, she settled down to drinking her first real meal.

"We need to get her on proper formula," Alex commented. "She needs vitamin and mineral supplements designed for babies. But that powdered milk will give her some calories to hold her until our ride gets here."

Katie smiled warmly at him. "You take such good care of us. Thank you."

He stared, looking thunderstruck. "Me? Take care of anyone but myself? I can already hear people on several continents laughing their heads off at the concept."

"Then they don't know you very well," she declared.

He looked like she could knock him over with a feather. She shrugged. He might not be long-term relationship material, but he was a decent guy no matter who his father was, and she didn't care what anyone said. Not to mention he'd given her the first orgasm of her life.

She was getting to him. Bit by bit, he was letting down his guard with her. Eventually, he would let her all the way in. Of course, what she'd do when she got there, she had no idea. But he was a challenge she could not seem to resist. Exhausted by the strain of the past two days, she curled up on a stack of blankets with Katie and dozed off.

IT WAS IMPOSSIBLE to tell time in the cavernous dark of the bunker. When Alex shook her shoulder gently to wake her, she was disoriented and struggled to emerge from a delicious dream involving Alex's hand and her nether regions.

"Ride's here," he said.

"Oh!" She sat up quickly, disturbing Dawn, who squawked at the abrupt movement. All in all, she was a great baby and had been more than patient with all the traveling so far. Maybe she, too, understood at some level that their lives were on the line out here.

While she'd been asleep, Alex had rigged a better baby sling made out of a bedsheet. Katie passed it over her head and tucked Dawn into it with a grateful smile for him. After following him out of the bunker, it took both of them to haul the steel door shut, and she heard the tumblers of the lock fall into position.

"What was that place?"

"Leftover from the Russian occupation of this area a couple decades back. It's only for emergencies now. Served us well enough. That's what matters."

Of course, how in the hell he'd known of the bunker's existence was the big, unanswered question of the hour.

Alex jogged away from her, dropping red Cyalume sticks in a straight line. He even jumped on the ATV and drove off, continuing to drop red lights in a line that must have gone for a good half mile. *What on earth?*

She heard their ride before she saw it. As she stared in disbelief, a small cargo plane descended toward them and landed on the impromptu runway. It had twin propeller engines mounted on high wings and looked like a miniature, skinny C-130. It taxied up to the near end of the marked landing strip, and the rear cargo ramp started to open.

"Come on!" Alex yelled over the roar of the engines.

She ran after him, shielding Dawn from the dust storm the props kicked up as best she could. She raced up the metal ramp after Alex and into the dim interior of the cargo bay. A man in a gray flight suit gestured them into crude webbing seats along the sides of the aircraft and pushed buttons that raised the ramp while they strapped in.

Who on earth was Alex? How did he, an American citizen, have the power to make a single radio call and get an immediate evacuation by a Russian military aircraft? Granted, his father was a high-ranking FSB official. But high enough to rate this quick a rescue for his son?

Her impression had been that Alex and his father were not close. At all. Why then would the elder Koronov make a military aircraft available to Alex like this? What exactly was his relationship with his father... and more importantly with his father's government? Was Alex a more loyal son of Mother Russia than he let on? A frisson of cold, hard terror rippled down her spine. No wonder Mike had asked her to keep an eye on him.

She could play with this man, but she dared not genuinely care for him. Down that road lay disaster as surely as she was standing there.

The bird lifted off, bound for who knew where. What the hell had she gotten herself into now?

CHAPTER SEVEN

MICHAEL MCCLOUD SWORE as he watched the Antonov 26 lift off Zaghastani soil carrying his sister and the bastard who'd stabbed him. He—grudgingly—gave Koronov props for not killing him in cold blood. But the guy was a traitor like his father and seriously needed to die.

He couldn't believe Koronov had gotten the jump on him like that. But he probably should have expected it, given that the man had managed to slip out of the Karshan Valley alive. Thankfully, the bastard had gotten Katie out of there alive and unhurt, too. He supposed he owed him one for that.

He'd been pretty sure Katie was in over her head and might need emergency extraction at some point. What he hadn't counted on was a flipping Russian hit squad running with the local rebels and going full-out scorched earth on the Karshan pass and all its inhabitants. Even he, a hardened Spec Ops type, had been taken aback at the carnage.

Of course, now that he was half-gutted, he wasn't going to be able to reestablish contact with the damned Russian hit team to figure out why they were there and who was giving them orders. He wouldn't be at all surprised if Alex Koronov and his father were pulling the team's strings. It would explain how Alex kept managing to stay one step ahead of the "rebels" marauding through the region.

What the hell were the Koronovs up to?

Frustrated all to hell as the Antonov droned away into the ever-present haze of dust obscuring the rising sun, he cranked up his satellite phone and extended its long antenna. Reception out here sucked even on a sat phone, and he prayed to the electronic gods that the damned thing worked today.

Static crackled, and a tinny voice said, "Identify."

"It's Candyman. Current location and authentication to follow. Standby to copy."

When the guy at the other end indicated he was ready to copy, McCloud rattled off the lat-long coordinates from his GPS and the six-letter code from his onetime use pad. While he waited for verification, he tore the top sheet off the pad and lit it with a match. The flash paper burned brightly and was gone in a puff of ash almost as quickly as it ignited.

"You are authenticated. Go ahead, Candyman."

"I need a secure patch to a landline."

"Roger. Standby."

This pause took longer. It was a laborious process to use hopelessly out-of-date military command-post technology to turn a sat phone call into a secured telephone call. But eventually, the voice came back up. "You will hear three clicks, and the line will go live and secure."

The voice went away, and the familiar clicks followed. He dialed a memorized number he'd been given to report on Alex Koronov's activities. God knew who was on the other end.

An anonymous male voice answered the call. "Good evening."

Evening? That placed the guy in the Western Hemisphere. North or South America, because it was morning over here.

"Um, I was told to call this number to report on a…project."

"I'm familiar with your phone number. I was told to watch for it. I will relay your report."

Well, okay then. Sounded like somebody official. His report would move up through the layers of someone's bureaucracy. Some alphabet-named government agency if he had to guess.

"The target is not neutralized. Repeat, not neutralized. Departed this location approximately five minutes ago in an Antonov 26 aircraft painted in military gray. No tail numbers displayed. The aircraft was last seen turning northbound."

"Roger. Will relay."

"Do you have any further instructions for me?"

"Negative."

Now he could only pray that failure didn't lead to recriminations against him. He had no idea what the fallout would be from Koronov still being alive and free. He didn't know who'd given the order to watch Alex and to kill the guy if he did anything suspicious. If he knew that, maybe he could figure out what the motives of the person giving the kill order were. As it was, he was just a point-and-shoot assassin. He was supposed to do the job and not ask any questions.

But, hell, his clueless baby sister was out here! That gave him a right to ask a few damn questions.

No further instructions for him, huh? He had no

idea where that Antonov was headed, but it was a pretty good bet he wouldn't be able to follow it easily to its final destination. Screw killing Alex Peters. If the powers that be wanted the guy dead, they'd have to get themselves another operative to finish the job.

He disconnected that call and placed a new call to his military headquarters. "It's Candyman. You need me to go through the whole authentication process again?"

"Nah, McCloud. I recognize your voice. Go ahead. Whatchya need, buddy?"

"I need medevac from this location."

"What happened to your wheels?"

"Stolen by the bastard who stabbed me."

"Are you ambulatory?"

He looked down at the big gauze bandage plastered over his wound. It had a bright crimson stain in the middle of it about the diameter of a quarter. If he was gonna bleed out, he'd have done it by now. Koronov's internal pressure bandage was holding. "That's affirmative," he transmitted. "I can walk."

"Standby." Eventually the voice came back with, "Make your way to the following coordinates. Ready to copy?"

He pulled out a small pad of paper and a pen. "Go ahead."

THE RUSSIAN AIRCREW rigged up a miniature hammock for Dawn and took pleasure fussing over the baby until the vibrating drone of the propellers knocked both Dawn and Katie out.

Katie woke groggy enough that she thought she'd been out for a while. Alex was sleeping, and she didn't disturb him. As always, she lost herself in the beauty of his relaxed, unguarded features. If only she could bottle this Alex and keep him this way after he woke up. She sighed. If wishes were fishes, everyone would be eating tuna sandwiches.

Alex roused as the plane entered a bumpy descent and landed. Nervous to see where he had dragged her, she looked around curiously as she followed him out of the back of the aircraft.

Whoa. This is definitely not Kansas, Dorothy. The airport terminal was a tired, gray, three-story block of a building with a gently upcurving portico that tried to be modern and failed miserably. The structure looked at least fifty years old and was showing its age. "Time warp much?" she muttered.

Alex grimaced as though he was none too thrilled to be here—wherever here was—either.

"Where are we?" she asked.

"Osh."

"Sorry. Where?" The only Osh she knew of was Oshkosh. And this was emphatically not Wisconsin.

"Osh. In Kyrgyzstan. Second largest city in the country. Near the Uzbek border."

Right. And *that* helped her locate herself.

Alex grinned. "Not big on central Asian geography, huh?"

"Not much."

"Try this. Kyrgyzstan borders the northwestern-most corner of China. Or, if you fly due north out of Afghanistan or Pakistan, and cross over Tajikistan, you reach Kyrgyzstan. Osh is in the southwestern corner of the country. Located now?"

"More or less. The important question is, where

do I get that hot shower you promised me and proper baby supplies for Dawn?"

"Actually, we have one more hurdle to cross before you get your shower." She raised a questioning brow and he replied, "Kyrgyz Customs."

"I have my passport with me," she responded quickly.

"As do I. But we've got to get Dawn through, too."

Oh. Crap.

"I took the liberty of filling out a birth certificate for her and signing it," he muttered under his breath. "I listed you as the mother and me as the father. It'll save us a world of hassles. I hope you don't mind."

Her tummy fluttered at the idea of the three of them being a family, but she checked the notion, reminding herself she had no idea who this man was. He wasn't her type of guy, no matter how smoking hot he was. "I don't mind," she whispered back as an official-looking man in a uniform strode toward them.

"Interesting," Alex muttered. "The FSB didn't meet us. Must be waiting for us inside the terminal."

She stared at him in dismay as the customs agent got out of his pickup truck and strode over to them.

Alex spoke in rapid Russian with the fellow, who duly took their passports and examined them carefully. Katie felt helpless just standing there, but Alex seemed to be having no trouble charming the uniformed man. The discussion went back and forth for several minutes, and then, abruptly, the customs man went to the hood of his pickup truck, unfolded a small lap desk and stamped their passports. He handed over three slips of light green paper, as well.

"Temporary visas," Alex murmured.

She nodded and smiled at the Kyrgyz man, who smiled back and said something that made Alex laugh. The guy apparently offered them a ride to the terminal, because Alex opened the truck's passenger door for her, helped her inside and then climbed in the back of the crew cab. Dawn started to cry, for which Katie was grateful. It gave her an excuse not to have to smile and nod too much at the man beside her.

They piled out at the terminal, and Alex said under his breath, "And now for the next hurdle and our real challenge. Dodging the FSB, who will be lurking around here somewhere."

Her stomach dropped to her feet.

"Stick with me. I've done this before. Trained by a spy, remember?" Alex muttered.

Ha. He was trained *as* a spy. He might not admit it, but he might as well be one himself. Small problem with her, however: she was a kindergarten teacher, not Mata Hari!

He led her quickly through the bowels of the building, passing corroded luggage conveyor belts and laconic mechanics lounging about, smoking. He led her up a concrete stairwell so dark she could barely see the steps, and the door at the top of it opened on a flood of sunlight that completely blinded her. Squinting, she made out a taxi stand.

Alex helped her into a cab partway down the line of taxis and slid in beside her. He gave the driver directions, and the vehicle pulled away from the curb. Alex watched out the back carefully for several minutes, and she found herself following suit, even though she had no idea what to look for. Alex finally turned around to face front.

"That was easier than I thought it would be," she threw out as a test balloon.

"Agreed."

Hey! She got it right!

But then he added grimly, "Something's wrong." He slouched back against the vinyl upholstery, brooding.

As quickly as she'd relaxed, she was nervous again. In need of distraction from the spies out there somewhere looking for them, she asked, "What did the customs guy say that made you laugh?"

Alex arched one eyebrow at her. "He told me I have good taste in women."

Was she about to become one of his long string of conquests? Nowhere in their conversation so far about sex had there been any mention of an actual relationship. Clearly, Alex was not interested in commitments…even if he had legally declared himself Dawn's father. That was merely a ploy to deal with government red tape. She smiled emptily. "Yes, you do have excellent taste in women, if I do say so myself."

The city sliding past their windows was more modern than she expected, but more run-down than any modern city she'd ever seen. Occasional grand structures and a tall statue of Lenin in a big square spoke of the Soviet regime's time there, and bullet-pocked building facades spoke of more recent political upheavals. Every car that drew close behind them made her jumpy. Every time they stopped at a light, she panicked until they pulled forward again. *Sheesh.* How did Alex live with this paranoia as a kid?

The cab stopped in front of another gray, blocky building, and Alex announced, "Here's our hotel."

He opened her door for her and took Dawn as she

climbed out. Tense, she asked him, "Are we…you know…clear?"

"As far as I can tell. If not, they're better than me."

That actually reassured her slightly. He was really, really smart. They walked into the hotel lobby, and its shabby elegance dismayed her. "How are we going to pay for this?"

Alex shrugged. "I have rather significant resources at my disposal."

Oh, right. Compliments of his gambling habit. In short order, they were installed in a spacious, old-world room with tall windows and high ceilings. A crib was delivered for Dawn.

Katie had barely finished exploring the room and discovering the big, deep cast-iron bathtub when Alex said, "I'll leave you to a nice long soak while I go get supplies for Dawn."

She frowned. He was obviously planning to do other things while he was out, too, but she had no idea what. She just heard the subtle evasion in his voice. Phone-a-father maybe? Report in to his immediate FSB superior?

He left, and she stared at the telephone on the nightstand. She picked it up and managed to figure out how to make an overseas phone call. She dialed Mike's cell phone number, but, frustratingly, it passed through to voice mail. Worried about someone monitoring the hotel phone, she left a vague message about being safe and hoping to talk to him soon.

They probably ought to let Doctors Unlimited know what had happened and that they were alive, too. But Alex seemed in no rush to notify their employer, and after his suggestion that a mole within the organization might have given away their location to unfriendly forces, she was not eager to contact D.U., either. Not until she knew whether or not Alex's suspicions were legit.

For the moment, she got Dawn settled in her first real bed and headed eagerly for the bathroom and that lovely tub. Grabbing the little bottle of what she assumed was shampoo that sat on the counter, she ran a steaming hot bath for herself and slid into it blissfully.

Eventually, when the dirt had soaked out of her pores, she felt clean at last. She shampooed her hair within an inch of its life and eyed her filthy clothes piled on the floor. She climbed out of the tub and dried off, and then dropped the whole mess of clothes into the soapy bathwater. She did her best to scrub them clean, and the rinse water ran dark gray. Eventually, she gave up, wrung out her heavy, sodden garments and hung them to dry. *Note to self: hug the washer and dryer when I get back home and tell them how very much I love them both.*

She wrapped herself in one of the big bath towels, turbaned her hair in another towel and stepped into the main room to check on Dawn.

Alex looked up from the side of the crib, and took in her terry-cloth décolletage with a thoroughness that left her breathless. "I washed my clothes," she mumbled.

"I bought you new ones."

"Bless you."

He grinned. "They're in the bag on the bed."

A half-dozen bags lay on the bed. As she headed for the pile, she stared into the crib in surprise. Dawn wore a pink one-piece, a fuzzy, footie sleeper, and the distinctive bubble of a diaper was visible under it. Alex tucked a pink blanket around the sleeping baby as she stepped near.

"She's adorable," Katie cried under her breath. "Thank you so much for getting her something warm. I've been so worried about her getting chilled."

He shrugged and actually looked abashed. "She's been a trouper. It was high time to spoil our little princess a little."

Was he actually fond of Dawn? Who'd have guessed the big, bad bachelor spy would fall for a baby? Dawn's eyes were already huge and exotic like her mother's, a dark blue that Katie expected would turn a deep brown, also like her mother's. The baby's face was angelic, and there was something magical about the innocence clinging to her. She could see why it got to Alex. He seemed to have a bit of a weak spot for innocence. Who could blame him after the upbringing he'd had? Peter had done everything in his power to strip his son of his own innocence.

Katie rummaged through the bags and pulled out a pair of jeans, a gray T-shirt and a hoodie sweatshirt. They would fit well enough to get her home. But that was about all she could say about their fashion sensibilities. The outfit looked like something a construction worker would wear.

"There's more," Alex murmured from behind her.

She dug in the bottom of the bag and came up with a handful of sheer black nylon. It was a bra and matching bikini briefs trimmed with little red bows. Both were see-through and trashy, and her cheeks flamed. But the lingerie was clean, and that outweighed any objections she might have to its taste quotient.

"The only other option was granny panties and prison matron bras," he commented drily. "Given your predilection for skimpy lace, I figured you'd prefer those."

She retreated to the bathroom, slipped into the bra and panties and stared at herself in the mirror, shocked. She looked like a...a harlot. All she needed were fishnet stockings and garters to complete the look. But her bare legs topped by that black see-through nylon were pretty dirty all by themselves.

She jumped about a foot in the air when a voice said from the doorway, "I approve."

"Alex! You can't just barge in on a lady when she's dressing!"

"Why not? I've already seen you naked, and you've seen me naked. I've had my hands on your body, and as if that's not enough, I'm a doctor. I'm used to looking at naked bodies."

Yeah, and he had a long history with the kind of women who had no modesty and were at ease doing naughty things she hadn't even imagined. This kind of lingerie wouldn't faze them. But he was decent enough not to bring that up. "Doctors don't look at their patients in sexy underwear, do they?"

He shrugged. "Most of my patients to date have been male prison inmates. Not much black lace going on in that crowd." His lips twitched with humor. "And none of them could have pulled it off like you do, anyway."

She made a face at him. "Ha-ha. Very funny."

He pushed away from the door frame and advanced until he stood directly behind her, tall and dark in contrast to her light coloring. He'd changed into a black shirt and black dress slacks that made him look like a mobster. A drop-dead sexy mobster.

He stared over her shoulder at her body, his eyes blazing in the mirror, and she decided he actually looked more like a fallen angel looming behind her, waiting to claim her eternal soul.

Her pulse leaped at the raw lust in his expression. An urge to cover her girl parts nearly overcame her, but she suspected he would mock her for false modesty. After all, she'd had a screaming orgasm on his hand only hours ago. Truth be told, a tiny piece of her enjoyed having him look at her like that. Who knew she had an inner exhibitionist just waiting for trashy lingerie to draw her out? Or maybe it was the way Alex made her feel that made her bold. He treated her like a woman. A naive, fragile one, but it was a start. One way or another, she would figure out how to get him to show her all the gnarly things he knew about sex.

As if he was thinking about the exact same thing, he reached out slowly and placed his palm on the back of her neck. His hand was almost unnaturally hot. He ran his fingers up under her hair, lifting it off her neck and shoulders. Then, slowly, he dragged his fingertips downward, tracking her spine lower and lower. Past her shoulder blades, sliding inward at her waist and following the rising swell of her behind over the flimsy, slippery nylon. And then, oh my, lower still, down the cleft between her cheeks. She had to force herself not to leap away from his leisurely caress as it slid lower and pressed gently between her legs. Without his having to ask or urge, she moved her feet apart, opening herself to him.

Her head fell back, coming to rest on his shoulder as her eyes drifted closed. Through the crotch of the panties, his fingers played on her feminine flesh, which was all too eager to respond to the touch. His left hand touched her ribs. Slid around to her front. Cupped her left breast, lifting it and testing its weight. His thumb circled around her nipple, and it pebbled up beneath the thin nylon. Above and below, his fingers played with her, circling, stroking and teasing her body. Lust, hot and liquid, speared through her, and her knees went so weak she feared she might collapse.

Her body undulated against his, and she felt like one continuous puddle of molten desire. Something hot and firm touched her neck, his lips. His mouth opened and teeth closed on her skin there. He didn't bite her as much as he held her in place. It was primal and raw and sent bolts of electric pleasure zinging through her to gather at his magical fingertips in clusters of sensation that drove her crazy.

"Put your hands on the counter," he murmured.

She was standing several feet from the sink and had to lean forward to splay her fingers on the cold marble.

"Spread your legs wider."

He moved close behind her, his groin hot and hard against her behind. He reached up with both hands this time to fondle her breasts, which felt heavy and swollen in their nylon confines. His hands ran down her ribs to clasp her hips, and then they slid forward and down to grasp her inner thighs. He lifted her up slightly, tilting her hips forward until she was spread completely open to him from behind before he set her back on her feet. His magic fingers went to work on her flesh, casting their spell of pleasure on her body.

"Look at me," Alex ordered. "In the mirror."

She opened her eyes and stared at the tableau. Her half-dry hair was disheveled and her cheeks flushed, her eyes bright with lust. She looked nothing like herself. But then she spied Alex and was mesmerized. That intense fire burned in his eyes, which were black and so very alive as he looked at her body, devouring the sight of her undulating shamelessly on his fingers. The mere sight of him stroking her like that brought her to the brink of release, and the pressure built inside her rapidly toward an explosion.

"Don't come yet," Alex ordered sharply. "You will do it only when I say so."

She stared at him, stunned. The explosion retreated slightly as she asked, "How do I stop it?"

"You must discipline yourself. Hold it in. Restrain the impulse to lose control. If you fail, I will have to punish you." Something dark and dangerous passed through his eyes when he said that, and a frisson of alarm skittered through her. Wait a minute. This was Alex. He would never hurt her. And with that comforting realization, her lust expanded tenfold.

"Ah, ah, ah. No orgasm yet, pet," he warned.

She concentrated on the bolts of lightning zinging around wildly in her belly. More quickly than she could believe, they were aligning themselves like magnetic charges, and every last one of them centered on his fingers playing so cleverly between her legs. The energy built and built, and she fought like mad to stop it from reaching critical mass. But it was unbelievably hard as his fingers kept coaxing more and more voltage from her body.

"Alex, please," she pleaded. "I can't take it anymore."

"Yes, you can." His left hand gripped the back of her neck and pushed her head down until her elbows rested on the counter and her forehead rested on her forearms. Her back arched of its own volition, thrusting her rear end up into his hand. She felt wanton. The pose opened her entirely to his plunder, and her need to explode climbed a few more notches.

She groaned with pleasure and then moaned and then begged, "Please, Alex. I can't stand it."

"Almost, baby. Tell me how bad you want it."

"I'll do anything for you. Just let me come."

He leaned over her, covering her with his hot, hard body, pinning her to the cold, hard counter. He slipped his left index finger into her mouth and she sucked it mindlessly, desperate to do anything, everything, to gain his permission to explode.

His right index finger slipped inside the lace panty, poised at her convulsing entrance. "Ready?" he murmured in her ear.

She nodded, too overcome by lust to speak.

"Now," he ordered. "Come for me now."

He didn't even have to penetrate her with his finger. Just the thought of it plunging into her female heat made her detonate. She went up like a rocket, incinerating in a blazing glory that ripped a cry from her throat. On and on it went, tearing her apart from the inside out. She only belatedly realized it was Alex's name she was all but sobbing, so overwhelmed was she by wave after shuddering wave of unbearable pleasure.

Her knees did collapse then, but Alex lifted her with his strong hands and set her upright on her feet. He held her in his arms, pressed back tightly against his body. In the mirror, his hands were tanned and strong against her pale flesh. She smiled at him and was shocked at how sultry and well pleasured she looked.

"You really must teach me how to do that to you." She sighed, relaxing back against him.

"You're proving to be a more apt pupil than I anticipated," he replied in a detached tone.

"And the absent professor is back," she murmured drolly.

He frowned heavily at her, and she couldn't resist grinning back at him. "Never fear. I like both sides of you, Alex." Truth be told, she was beginning to suspect there were many more sides to this complex man than she'd yet seen. She probably ought to fear some of them, but mostly she was fascinated at the prospect of unraveling the mystery of him.

"You're such an open book," he commented.

"Is that bad?" She could envision a man like him wanting a complex and challenging woman.

"Lord, no. It's just unexpected. I'm so used to women with hidden agendas that I find myself not knowing exactly how to react to you." As she started to frown again, he added, "I like your honesty."

If only she was being as fully honest as he thought she was. How would he react if he found out her brother had sicced her on him to watch him? Or that she was intentionally trying to get him to let down his guard and cut loose physically and emotionally with her? Would he walk away? Or maybe, just maybe, would he let go of the dark streak he was currently keeping in check so tightly? The notion thrilled her like nothing she'd ever experienced before. And it made her nervous. No question, she was playing with fire.

She barely recognized the woman she was becoming all of a sudden. Since when was she such an adrenaline junkie? Since they'd nearly died on a mountainside and she'd learned how piercingly satisfying the thrill of cheating death could be?

She turned in Alex's arms and gave him a lopsided smile. "I think I hear the baby."

CHAPTER EIGHT

STILL WIPED OUT by their recent trek and by the emotional roller coaster that was life with Alex, she crawled into bed. While he took a shower, she promptly fell asleep.

Some time later she was jolted awake by Alex calling her name urgently. "Katie, wake up. *Now.*"

She sat up quickly but was deeply disoriented for a moment. *Hotel room. Dark outside. Crib— Oh, yeah. Dawn. Where— Oh, yeah. Osh. What—*

"Get up. We have to go right now. Hurry." Alex didn't look like he was kidding.

Alarm surged through her, and she was abruptly wide-awake and scared stiff. "What's going on?" she asked as she flew out of bed and yanked on her new clothing.

"I went out for food, and I wasn't able to shake my tail. I didn't think they'd find us so fast. I thought we'd have twenty-four hours to rest before we had to run. But I was wrong." He added under his breath, "Bastard. Wouldn't even let me catch my breath before he forced me back into the game."

Was he talking about his father? How could it be anyone else? Why was he running from Peter? Hadn't Koronov arranged their flight to safety? Why would the man turn around and chase his son then? Confused, she packed Dawn's gear in the diaper bag Alex had bought earlier, while he moved around the room wiping down surfaces with a handkerchief.

He didn't sound surprised that someone had figured out where they were. Only that it had happened so quickly. "Who followed you?" *Americans? Russians? Someone else?*

"Gather up our wet clothes. Put them in a bag. We'll toss them outside the hotel," he ordered tersely, overtly ignoring her question.

Fully into the spirit of "holy shit" now, she snatched up one of the plastic shopping bags and stuffed their wet clothes into it. She eased Dawn into her sling without waking the infant and nodded grimly to him that she was ready to run. From what, she had no idea.

She followed him quickly from the hotel room. No surprise, he headed for the back of the building and the service elevator. They entered it in tense silence. The doors whooshed closed, and Alex said quietly, "The good news is I don't think they know I spotted them."

"And the bad news?" she asked reluctantly.

"It's a professional surveillance team. I can't tell if it's Russian or American. My guess is Russians. But if the guy I stabbed was American and he saw our flight take off, it could as easily be a CIA team."

"What will they do if they catch us? Can't we just hand ourselves over to Americans and ask to go home?"

He snorted. "You forget who you're with. I'm the devil's spawn. The Americans would love any excuse to toss me in jail and throw away the key. And we're talking about spy agencies here, Katie. They don't play by the same rules as law enforcement agencies. It's

ops normal to torture and kill people, to make people
disappear never to be seen again. They're not nice
people."

Right. And he is one of them.

He murmured tersely, "Give me the baby. When we
leave the hotel, do exactly what I say, no questions,
no hesitation, no matter how weird it sounds. Okay?"

She nodded, terrified, as she passed him Dawn,
sleeping in her sling. Had Alex been this scared as
a little boy when he'd lived with Peter Koronov and
they'd had to do this sort of stuff? Who would teach
a young child how to be a spy? And *why?* What kinds
of scars did a life filled with this kind of fear leave
behind?

There was no more time to wonder, for the elevator
door opened. Alex headed for an exit, and she followed
him outside. It was cold, and her breath hung in the
air in a great white cloud around her head. Alex took
off down the alley behind the hotel at a quick walk,
sticking to the shadows.

She followed, doing her best to be quiet. Thankfully, she'd spent a lot of years skulking around in the
woods behind her parents' house playing hide-and-
seek with her brothers. They'd always won, of course,
but she considered herself reasonably stealthy. Alex
was dead silent in front of her.

He slipped around the corner into the street, and
she tried to mimic his fluid movement. "Try to look
normal," he whispered.

Normal. Right. She linked her arm in his and smiled
up at him. "Got it. Normal," she replied under her
breath.

They walked for maybe a block; then Alex swore quietly. "No good. They've spotted us."

Oh, crap. They walked another fifty feet or so, and, without warning, Alex yanked her to the side by her arm. She all but fell over as he dragged her into a convenience store. Once inside, he turned her loose and took off running for the rear of the store. She regained her balance and raced after him. A startled clerk stared at them. Alex called out something in Russian to the man, and the guy pointed. Alex swerved in that direction, and she veered after him.

They burst into a dim storeroom, tore through it and popped out the back door into another alley. A sprint down this one and Alex darted into the street. His long legs stretched out as he crossed the street and sprinted into a park of some kind. She pushed hard to keep up with him, and the baby bag banged against her back uncomfortably.

She spared a glance over her shoulder and was dismayed to see two dark figures running behind them. And the tails were closing in on them. Alex sped up even more, and she dug deep to keep up with him.

They came out of the other side of the park and Alex turned left, tearing down a side street and ducking into a restaurant. He said something to the manager and this time threw a handful of cash at the guy, who pointed to the back of the deserted dining room. This time they raced frantically through a kitchen. Alex yelled something to the cooks, who called something back to him.

Outside again, into the dark and cold.

"Not much farther," he grunted at her as they took off running yet again. Her lungs were starting to close up. Her respiratory tract didn't like the hot to cold to hot to cold routine. Not to mention the whole mad sprinting thing. She worked out regularly, but not with bad guys chasing her who intended to do who knew what if they caught her.

Alex turned one more corner, and they tore down a residential street. Row houses lined the block, maybe five stories tall and old-looking. He screeched to a stop without warning beside an ancient Volkswagen and bit out, "Keep watch."

She was more than glad to stand there, huffing hard. Meanwhile, Alex shocked her by pulling out his pistol and bashing the VW window with its butt. He let himself into the car quickly and gestured for her to get in. She raced around to the passenger side and climbed in. He thrust Dawn at her and bent down to hot-wire the car. In under a minute, the engine sputtered to life and he pulled away from the curb.

It was viciously cold with the wind whipping through the car, and she tucked Dawn inside her coat and held her close. The baby kept sleeping, though, so Katie guessed she must be warm enough for now.

"We've got to ditch this car. The broken window is too obvious," Alex said.

"Then why did you steal it?"

"You couldn't run forever, and neither could I with the baby."

"Where are we headed?"

"Airport. Lots of cars there. Long-term parking."

She frowned, not understanding.

"Watch behind us for any car that follows us for more than a few minutes."

It was hard to track individual cars at night using

only glimpses of vehicles as they passed under the sparse streetlights. But as best she could tell, no one followed them.

When they arrived at the airport, Alex guided the car into the long-term parking lot like a normal traveler and took a ticket from the automatic dispenser. He parked at the back of the lot and they got out.

"Start trying door handles until you find an unlocked one," he instructed under his breath. "If I tell you to get down, do it fast. I'll be watching the exit gate attendant."

They commenced creeping around the dark parking lot and she only had to dive for cover twice before Alex murmured, "Bingo."

He slipped into a small Ford via the unlocked driver's door and unlocked the passenger door for her. He tore apart the steering column and hot-wired the car, then did his best to more or less put the car back together. He handed her the parking ticket, which the owner had conveniently left on the dashboard for them. He started the car and docilely pulled up to the gate attendant.

Katie contained her shock as Alex casually pulled cash out of his wallet and paid the parking fee. He said something that sounded like a good-night to the attendant and drove out as pretty as he pleased.

"Now where?" she asked in minor shock. They'd just stolen *two* cars.

"Tashkent."

"Pardon me if my geography has failed me, but that isn't in Kyrgyzstan."

"Correct. It's the capital of Uzbekistan. But it's quite a bit closer than Bishkek, which is the capital of

Kyrgyzstan, and Tashkent does not lie across mountains on a dodgy highway with fractious weather. If we're lucky, our tails are Kyrgyz nationals and won't be able to follow us into Uzbekistan easily. The two countries don't like each other and our tails should get stopped at the border. Since we're traveling on U.S. passports, the Uzbeki border guys shouldn't hassle us."

She was sure she'd seen him give the Kyrgyz customs guy a Russian passport—dark red with an embossed gold double-headed eagle totally unlike her dark blue U.S. passport—but she elected not to bring that up just now. Not until she had a better idea of just how dangerous Alex would become if he thought she'd turned on him.

"Watch the rearview mirror. Check for any cars that follow us for a long time."

"What constitutes a long time?"

"More than, say, five minutes," he answered absently. He steered the car across Osh and headed west on a four-lane road that rapidly became a two-lane road. "Anyone back there?" he asked her for about the third time.

"Road's empty. What's the local time? The streets are deserted."

"It's about midnight. And it's a weeknight in a region with a large Muslim population. Not exactly a party crowd. I think we're clear for now."

She nodded and turned to face forward in her seat. "Okay, Alex. I'm on your side. But I think it's time for you to start talking. Who are you, and what the hell's going on?"

ALEX WINCED AT the questions but couldn't blame her for asking them. Problem was, very little of his life was on the list of things he was willing to talk about. Still, he owed her a few answers, at least.

"I haven't lied to you about anything. As the whole world knows, my father was a Russian spy who was caught when I was a kid."

"Are you really a doctor?"

"Yes."

"Why obstetrics?"

"I'm a trauma surgeon by training. All doctors get basic OB training, and I picked up a little extra practical experience so I could come over here on the Doctors Unlimited mission. Actually, delivering babies isn't that different from trauma medicine. It's explosive and high risk and you have to be prepared to react fast."

"Who were those men chasing us in Osh?"

"I don't know."

"Guess."

He sighed and considered the question. The Big Two were the obvious choices—the CIA and the FSB. It was a toss-up in his mind which bunch was trailing him.

What he couldn't figure out was why the tails had actually tried to catch him and Katie. Why hadn't the team just hung back and tracked where he went? Who wanted to actually apprehend him? That was a new and worrisome wrinkle in his ongoing dance with the intelligence services. Given that he'd stabbed an American and now this team was being so aggressive, he'd bet on the CIA. But based on her earlier question about turning themselves over to Americans, he wasn't inclined to tell her his guess.

Dammit, Katie was still waiting for an answer. That girl was preternaturally patient about getting answers to her questions. Must come from being a teacher. He said carefully, "My best guess is some intelligence agency. Which one, I couldn't say for sure. Why are they following us? We're Americans who came to town on a Russian military aircraft, and that would send up warning flags anywhere on earth."

She digested that evasive truth in silence, although he could practically hear the wheels turning in her head. If only she were a little less quick on the uptake. He'd promised her he would never lie to her, and he wouldn't. It had been a stupid promise, made on impulse, but he was stuck with it now. Still, that didn't mean he couldn't repackage the truth to his advantage.

"How is it you were able to call for that Russian plane to come get us? My brother was a Navy SEAL, and *maybe* on a mission he could have pulled off something like that. But that would have been the extent of it."

Her brother was a SEAL? Fuck. "Family connections," he said shortly.

"You called Daddy?" she blurted.

He made a disgusted sound. "Don't say it like that. It was a desperate last resort."

"Was your father paying back a favor owed or do you owe him one, now?"

Crap, that was an astute question. He hedged and answered, "Our relationship is…complicated."

"How so?"

He huffed. "It's hard to explain."

"Try."

"He's my father. My only family. He makes me crazy, but..." He didn't know how to finish the sentence. It wasn't something he ever tried to put into words.

"But he's your father and you want to make him proud. You want him to love you back. You want him to approve of you."

"I gather you've met my old man, then?" he responded wryly.

She laughed a little. "My dad's not the easiest man in the world to love, either. He's not as bad as your father, but he can be...demanding."

Alex snorted. "There's a word for my father. *Demanding.* Yeah, that about covers it." There was so much more to his relationship with Peter, but he wasn't prepared to discuss it with Katie. It wasn't that he was being dishonest with her. But, hell, his entire life was a series of half-truths and evasions. Why should his relationship with Katie be any different?

He and his father hadn't shared an honest moment between them in pretty much forever. But then, maybe that was how all spies did relationships. He might not work for an alphabet agency, but Alex knew himself to be a spy at heart, through and through. His father had been nothing if not thorough in training him.

Of course, Peter wanted him to become a field operative for the FSB in America in the worst way. But after Alex's stunt of putting himself in jail to avoid his old man, Peter knew not to ask him outright to become a Russian spy. No, it was Peter's intent to manipulate his son into doing his bidding and not to risk Alex turning him down outright. Which was why it had been such a big deal for Alex to break down and ask for that rescue, and why he'd known without a shadow of a doubt his old man would make the airlift happen. Peter would do anything to get his hooks into his prodigal son.

His old man couldn't seem to grasp that to Alex, "home" was America. Not Mother Russia. The last time they'd spoken about him working for the FSB when Alex was eighteen, they'd had a violent shouting match over it, in fact. His father had insisted that Alex was Russian in his heart and had wanted no part of hearing that his son preferred the corrupt, capitalist, imperialist regime in the United States.

He'd have thought the guy would have given up when Alex put himself in jail to avoid his aggressive recruiting tactics. But no. Even after four years in jail, his father was still coming after him. Peter had just learned to be more subtle and vicious about it. Tough. Alex still felt the same way. He was American—even if the U.S. government didn't trust him any farther than it could throw him. He couldn't blame the Americans.

"Who was following us back in Zaghastan?" Katie asked, startling him out of his bitter ruminations.

Alex sighed. Might as well burst her patriotic bubble a little. "I told you. The guy I jumped was American. I have no idea who he worked for." He didn't mention the burner phone resting in his pocket waiting to ring. He was deeply interested to see who eventually spoke on the other end of that phone. Fortunately, it was a cheap model without GPS tracking in it, so he could leave it on without fear of his position being tracked. He would need to obtain a charging cord for it soon. He'd hate to miss finding out who'd sent a killer after him because the damned phone went dead.

"Was it just me, or were those rebels who came up the valley the night Dawn was born trying to kill us?" she asked soberly.

"It was not just you. It looked to me like they deliberately torched our tent and then chased us."

"Were they American, too? Did the guy you attacked work with them?"

"I don't know." Personally, he doubted it. Given his father's insistence on telling him about that emergency bunker, he guessed Peter had knowledge of some Russian operation in the Karshan Valley that he'd thought would endanger his boy. Weird way of showing love for your kid. Knowingly send him into a death trap… but it was okay because he'd given Alex an escape route. His father was one twisted bastard.

"Why in the world would Americans attack us? Did they not know who we were?"

"Oh, I'm sure whoever came after us knew exactly who we were."

Katie's head whipped toward him. He swore mentally. He probably shouldn't have said that. He sighed. "Like I said before. I have enemies. I don't think that team was attacking you. I think they were attacking me."

"Who specifically would attack you and *why?*"

"I already told you. I don't know. But it could easily be one of several groups." And he wasn't about to list all of them off to her. The less she knew of him, the less danger she would be in.

Thankfully, a brightly lit border crossing loomed ahead of them, effectively distracting her. He passed

both of their passports and the birth certificate he'd
filled out on Dawn through his window to the border
guard. The fellow gave them a little grief over him
signing the baby's birth certificate until he explained
that he was a doctor and showed the guy his medical
pack. But soon enough, they were speeding onward
into the night. Hopefully, minus their Kyrgyz tails.

Tashkent was a larger city than Osh, somewhat
more modern, but it, too, suffered from a general sense
of post-Soviet decay. Independence might have been
emotionally satisfying to the southern states of the former USSR, but economically it had been disastrous.
None of the splinter states were strong enough to thrive
on their own in a competitive global economy.

Had they all hated their neighbors a little less, they
might have formed trade alliances and succeeded as
a trading bloc. But hundreds of years of tribal rivalries made that impossible. Once the former republics'
economies had tanked, social unrest followed and the
disaster was complete. In the chaos to follow, crime
and corruption had flourished, and the states were all
but failed.

It was nearing dawn as he chose a random hotel in
Tashkent because of its covered parking garage. No
sense flaunting their stolen car. He'd sell it tomorrow
on the black market, where no one would be inclined
to tell any authorities where it had come from.

He woke Katie, and she stumbled into the lobby
with him. She was alert enough to frown when he
pulled out five hundred American greenbacks to pay
for the room and for the clerk's discretion, but thankfully she didn't comment on it.

He took Dawn from her, mixed baby formula from

the can he'd bought back in Osh and gave the baby a bottle—in an actual baby bottle—while Katie collapsed in bed.

He had to admit, there was something deeply calming about holding a baby and feeding her. The sense of protectiveness that flowed through him was, frankly, shocking. He changed Dawn and laid her on several blankets on the floor that she wouldn't suffocate herself on. With a sigh of relief, he crawled into bed beside Katie. Almost immediately she rolled over and draped her sleeping self over him.

He tensed at first. He made a policy of never sleeping with his women. But she was not one of his usual prostitutes, and she seemed to genuinely like him. If only she knew what she was getting into, she would run screaming from him. Resolved to enjoy this novel, one-off, what-it-would-be-like-to-have-a-family experience, he closed his eyes and drifted off to sleep with a woman in his arms.

Katie took the next shift feeding Dawn and he took the following one. The three of them slept nearly twelve hours, and it was dark again outside when they finally roused for good.

"Feel better?" he asked Katie as she smiled sleepily at him from her pillow.

"Yes. Much. You?"

"Mmm-hmm." Come to think of it, he hadn't been this relaxed for as long as he could remember. "Interested in some supper?"

"I'm starving," she declared.

He laughed at her infectious good cheer. "Are you always so chipper when you wake up?"

"Pretty much. Are you always so serious and grim?"

"Pretty much."

She laughed at him and rolled out of bed. "I call dibs on the bathroom," she sang.

He lounged in bed and turned on the television. He found a Russian news channel and watched it lazily. Interesting how no news outlet had picked up on the use of attack drones in Zaghastan against civilians. Had it been done in one of several other countries in the region, there would have been an international outcry over it. *Hypocrites,* he mentally accused the newscasters.

Katie's voice drifted out of the bathroom as she sang a pop song at the top of her lungs. Something about halos. For an angel, Katie was pretty hot. He couldn't recall ever reminiscing about non-sex with a woman before, but he was definitely enjoying the memory of her swollen, hot flesh dancing on his fingers while she moaned her pleasure against his neck. He swore under his breath at the fact that he was going to need a cold shower when it was his turn for the bathroom.

Katie eventually emerged from the bathroom wrapped in one of the hotel's towels, her skin rosy and dewy, her face beautiful completely devoid of makeup. Her cosmetics had gotten torched back at the tent the night of their frantic flight from Zaghastan.

She went over to coo at Dawn, who was awake and learning how to wave her arms and legs around. A natural mother, Katie was.

He took a shower that relieved the worst of his frustration and shaved with the razor Katie had snagged when they fled Osh. He toweled dry and dressed, eager to spend the evening with her. She was a constant source of surprise to him.

The concierge recommended a good restaurant within walking distance and where Dawn would be welcome. They were most of the way to the place before Alex's internal warning system fired off. Loudly.

"Keep walking like everything's fine," he murmured to Katie from behind a pasted-on smile.

"Everything is fine, isn't it?"

"Nope. We've got company."

CHAPTER NINE

"Not again!" Katie exclaimed in dismay. "You're a freaking trouble magnet."

She's just now figuring that out? "Normal, dammit," he bit out.

She smiled back. "Exclamations of surprise are normal for me. Now what do we do?"

"We keep walking while I see how bad it is."

"What do you mean?"

"I need to get a head count and check out these guys' proficiency."

"Can I help?"

He glanced down at her, surprised. "What can you do?"

"If you stop to kiss me, we can look over each other's shoulders and check for bad guys or spies or whatever they are."

That was an excellent idea, actually. He pulled her into a shadow next to a building and wrapped her in his arms. Dawn was a warm and squirming mass between them, but she didn't seem to mind the group hug. Katie tilted her face up to him with what looked like a genuine smile and a spark of real desire in her eyes. It would be so easy to lose himself in her....

Their lips touched, and it dawned on him belatedly that this was the first time they'd ever *really* kissed.

She tasted like mint toothpaste and something sweet. Or maybe that was just the taste of surprise. Either way, he deepened the light kiss, slanting his mouth against hers and moving his lips more confidently. She reciprocated and, furthermore, touched the tip of his tongue with hers. *Well, then.*

His hand plunged into her hair, and he cupped her head, sucking at her with a hunger that shocked him. Only Dawn in the sling between them kept the kiss from becoming entirely carnal. Which was a good thing since he was supposed to be counting spies and not thinking about how he was going to steal the next piece of this angel's innocence. Out of the corner of his eye, he saw two men lounging on a street corner about two blocks back, lighting up cigarettes.

She murmured sexily against his mouth as she swayed into him, "I've got two guys across the street and down about a block and a half. And I think I see two more in the park across the street. But they're hiding in the shadows so I can't be sure."

Damn. They were never going to shake a six-man team. But at least he had a good ID on their tails now. Only the FSB had the resources in this part of the world to find them so fast and launch so many operatives in a matter of hours.

"The restaurant's just ahead," he muttered.

"We're going to eat with all these guys following us?"

"I doubt they'll try to snatch us in a public place with a lot of witnesses. Uzbekistan isn't publicly on friendly terms with the Russian FSB."

She fell silent beside him, absorbing the implications of who was following them. He held the door to the restaurant for her and sneaked a quick glance down the street and into the park. She was not wrong. Two more teams were out there. He swore mentally.

She let him order for her, which was a good call. The menu included such local delicacies as yak steak and eel. In deference to her American taste buds, he scanned the menu and ordered her roasted chicken. Absently, he chose the same for himself.

It had been suicide to come inside a building like this. Both the front and back exits would already be covered. But with Katie and Dawn in tow, he didn't dare confront the Russian agents directly. Were he alone, he'd risk a running shoot-out. But not with the girls depending on him.

Frustration at the limitations of playing spy with his little family in tow warred with a bizarre sense of protectiveness in his gut. He wasn't actually enjoying having a woman and child hanging around with him, was he? Surely not. He was a lone wolf. Always had been. Just like his father—

The realization broke over him in a rush of horror. He was just like his father.

In a mental non sequitur most likely borne of his mind shying away from *that* supremely unpleasant thought, it dawned on him that Katie was being un-characteristically silent across from him.

"How do you feel about separating from me?" he asked her.

Her eyes widened in sharp alarm. "I hate that idea!" she exclaimed under her breath. "I don't speak Russian or Uzbek, Dawn's documents are iffy, I have no money and I have no idea how to get home. I *need* you, Alex." She said it with such conviction he could almost believe she was referring to the emotional support he gave her. She was *depending* on him? That strange warmth passed through him again.

He turned over a half-dozen plans for getting out of this mess. None of them stood any statistical chance of working. He discarded them one by one in growing desperation until he was left with only one choice. The last choice. One he *hated*. This damned disaster was forcing him to call in favor after favor he dreaded paying back. Getting out of this latest pickle would put him in debt to people he'd really rather not owe anything to. Not that his opinion mattered for squat with six armed killers waiting for them outside.

Neither of them had any appetite, but he urged Katie to eat regardless. He had no idea when they would get a solid meal again. It was Spycraft 101 to sleep and eat whenever an opportunity arose to do either. As they finished choking down their meal, of which he'd tasted not a bite, he motioned over the maître d' and asked the fellow quietly to call them a cab and let him know the instant it arrived. He palmed a U.S. twenty and passed it to the guy, who smiled broadly.

"Have some dessert," Alex urged Katie. "The hotel's concierge told me the chocolate mousse here is excellent."

"Seriously?" she muttered.

"We have to kill a few minutes while our ride comes. It would look weird to just sit here doing nothing. And act happy."

She pasted on a bright smile. "Mmm. Chocolate. I can never say no to it." She added under her breath, "Even when I'm about to die."

"Might as well seize the moment and enjoy it," he replied grimly.

"Has your life always been like this?"

He frowned slightly. "I have never had any illusions that I would die of old age."

"What an awful way to live."

He'd never really stopped to think about it. It wasn't as if he had the choice to live some other way. His life was one long, ongoing tightrope walk without a net. He shrugged. "It is what it is."

She fell silent for a time and then said firmly, "I plan to live to a ripe old age and embarrass my great-grandchildren every chance I get."

His gut twisted. Then she'd better get far away from him as fast as she could. He said quietly, "I promise that, as soon as I can get you somewhere safe, I'll get out of your life and take my danger with me."

She looked like a puppy he'd just drop-kicked in the gut. *Dammit.* It took every ounce of his self-discipline not to take the words back, not to promise to stay with her as long as she would have him—

Whoa, there. Rewind. As long as she would have him? *Uh, no.* He didn't do long-term relationships. Hell, he didn't do *relationships.*

The chocolate dessert arrived, and he said quietly, "Be ready to go on a moment's notice. Speed will be vital. We'll go out front and jump in the cab waiting there. But we need to get out of here without drawing any attention to ourselves, so walk out of here at a normal but brisk pace. Got all that?"

She scooped up a spoonful of the creamy mousse and held it out to him. "Share it with me?"

Reluctantly, he accepted the offered bite of choco-

laty goodness. It was an apt metaphor for their relationship. He dashed her hopes, and she offered him
sweetness anyway. How in the hell did a woman get
to be her age and still be so damned naive?

The mousse slid off the cold metal spoon and melted
in his mouth, sinfully sweet with a hint of coffee bite
to offset the sugar. Just like her.

He watched as she took a bite.

"Oh my God, that's delicious," she groaned. His
male flesh stirred at the look of sheer hedonistic pleasure that filled her eyes. Screw the hit team outside.
He wanted to fall into her and put that look in her
eyes himself.

"You're falling behind on ooey-gooey goodness,"
she declared. "And come to think of it, you're behind
in the pleasure department, too. I owe you a couple of
major orgasms."

He nearly choked on the mouthful of mousse she'd
just given him. Not only was the bald observation unexpected, but it startled him. Prostitutes were paid
to pleasure him. He had no frame of reference for
a woman who wanted to give him pleasure for free.
Oh sure, tons of women had hit on him in the past.
But they'd had agendas. They were after his money
or his notoriety or the perceived sexiness of spies.
Curse James Bond, anyway. But none of them had
even known him, let alone *liked* him. And certainly
not enough to want to give him pleasure gratuitously.

He was saved from having to reply by the maître d'
raising a finger at him from by the front door.

"Time to go," he bit out.

Pasting on a brave, fake smile, Katie gathered Dawn
while he shouldered the baby bag. He placed his hand

in the small of her back and escorted her politely from the dining room. They hit the front door and, following his instructions, Katie raced down the steps and leaped into the cab with him right on her heels.

"Go. Now!" he yelled at the cabbie.

Startled, the guy peeled away from the curb hard.

"Two hundred dollars U.S. to get us to the American embassy as fast as you can," he told the driver. "Don't stop for anything or anyone."

The guy's eyes widened in alarm, but then greed kicked in as Alex peeled the bills out of his wallet where the cabbie could see them in the rearview mirror. The driver took him literally, running red lights and screeching through intersections to the sound of retreating car horns. The wild drive made it impossible for their tails to hide themselves, and a black Russian Chaika tore across Tashkent behind them.

"Another hundred bucks if I can borrow your cell phone," Alex said to the driver.

Without taking his eyes off the road, the guy flipped a cell phone into the backseat. Alex tossed the bills forward.

He contacted a local telephone operator and asked to be connected to the American embassy. *C'mon, c'mon,* he silently urged the slow phone system. That Chaika was getting damned close to them and might have orders to take them out.

"American embassy, Tashkent," a female voice said in his ear.

"My name is Alex Peters, and I'm American. I'm with an American woman named Katie McCloud. We're in a cab inbound to your embassy, and we're being chased by Russian FSB agents. Am requesting that you open the gates for us so we can drive directly into the compound."

"I'm sorry, sir. But that's not approved protocol—" the woman started.

He swore in desperation. "They're going to kidnap or kill us."

Katie plucked the phone out of his hands. "Let me handle this." Into the phone, she said, "My uncle Charlie—Charles McCloud, deputy director of plans, CIA—will verify my identity and authorize an emergency ingress to your location. Here's his cell phone number. Call him immediately. Tell him Baby Butt says hello. We'll call you back in five minutes." She disconnected the call and sat back.

Alex stared, dumbfounded. *Her uncle is a highranking CIA agent?* Blank shock rendered his brain nonfunctional.

"What?" she asked defensively as he continued to stare at her.

The implications were so staggering he couldn't even begin to think about them right now. He pushed them all aside to deal with the more immediate and pressing concern of the black car behind them. Regular operatives didn't get big fancy rides like that to tear around in. But he knew who *did* rate a Chaika. And it made his blood run cold.

He had to say something. Do something. Freezing up was not an option. "Baby Butt is your authenticator phrase?" he managed to mumble.

She rolled her eyes. "Uncle Charlie gave me the nickname when I was about eight. My brothers picked it up, and it took me most of high school to break them from calling me by it. Uncle Charlie will know without a doubt it's me when he hears it. It was the only thing I could think of on the fly that would let him know that I made the request."

"How much longer to the embassy?" he asked the driver.

"Five, six minutes at this speed," the guy answered.

"It's gonna be tight," Alex murmured.

It was more like four minutes when he rang up the American embassy. The receptionist picked up the line just as the driver said from the front seat, "It's up ahead. One minute. No more."

Alex looked back. The Chaika was maybe a hundred yards behind them, its big engine roaring like a lion on the hunt. Its bright lights shone, blocking any glimpse of the passengers inside. It would have blacked-out glass windows anyway.

"American embassy, Tashkent," the female voice said in his ear.

He passed the phone to Katie with a single terse instruction. "Hurry."

"It's me again, Katie McCloud. Are the gates open? We'll be there in about thirty seconds, and we're coming in hot."

He smiled reluctantly at the military terminology coming out of her entirely civilian mouth.

"Thanks so much," she chirped into the phone. "I'll be the blonde with the baby when we get out of the cab."

She'd done it. Mentally, he sagged in relief. He could *not* afford to get any deeper in debt to his father. The gut-melting gratitude of having dodged an actual, physical bullet poured through him. She had *no* idea how badly he didn't want the person in that black car behind them to catch him.

"Drive directly into the compound," he told the cabbie. "Don't slow down any more than you must to make the turn."

The cab didn't exactly stand up on two wheels as it careened around the corner into the embassy's driveway, but it wasn't far from doing so. The tires squealed in protest as the cab flew through the checkpoint out front. Two *very* armed marines leaped out to block the drive as the electric gate started to slide shut behind the cab.

Their driver slammed on the brakes and all but launched Alex and Katie into the front seat as the vehicle squealed into a half slide and screeched to a halt only feet from the back wall of the courtyard.

The driver turned off the ignition. The cab's interior was silent but for everyone's heavy breathing. If they got out of this mess alive, he would stop to ponder how an infant as young as Dawn seemed to sense life-threatening situations and go totally silent during them. Fascinating. But in the meantime…

"Keep your hands on the steering wheel in plain sight," Alex told the cabbie. To Katie he murmured, "Lace your hands behind your head and wait for the marines to come get us."

They sat quietly for a full minute before a half-dozen of the marines crowding the courtyard approached the car from every direction, assault rifles leveled at them.

To the driver, Alex said wryly, "Ever consider defecting to the United States? Now's your chance."

The guy smiled a little. "Can I take my wife but leave behind my teenaged kids?"

The marines gestured for them to roll down the windows and then proceeded to poke the muzzles of their weapons into the car. After that, it was pretty straightforward. They were ordered out of the car, thoroughly searched and their passports examined. The Americans were not particularly amused to find Alex's Russian passport—in his original name—along with his U.S. passport, even after he explained he was a dual citizen.

An assistant attaché eventually declared them non-hostile, although the woman threw a suspicious look in his direction when she said it. Clearly, she recognized the Koronov name on his Russian passport.

Katie was shown inside separately from him; the attaché was already making baby noises and cooing at Dawn before they hit the door. As for him, he was poked in the back none too gently by an assault rifle and escorted to an interrogation room in the bowels of the embassy.

A marine officer joined him eventually, a fat dossier under his arm. "You're a famous guy, Mr. Peters."

He shrugged. "My father is famous. Or infamous, as it were. I merely stand in the edge of his dubious spotlight from time to time."

"What are you doing in Tashkent?"

He told the story of working for Doctors Unlimited and their tent being overrun by rebels. He left out the bit about stabbing the American dressed as a civilian and the bit about the secret supply bunker or that the cargo plane that airlifted them out had been a Russian military aircraft. He picked up the tale in

Osh and finished it with their rather spectacular arrival at this embassy.

The marine was not a professional interrogator, but Alex was a professionally trained prisoner of war. His father had drilled him for hours on end as a kid in techniques of resisting interrogation. It was one of a spy's most powerful and necessary weapons—the ability to deceive, evade and lie with complete conviction.

The marine didn't ask about the American he'd stabbed in Zaghastan, which told Alex the American had not been CIA. Embassies were hotbeds of CIA activity, and news of an American operative stabbed in Zaghastan and badly wounded would have made the rounds of the embassies in this part of the world. He hoped the guy hadn't died. But the man had been stubborn and held out till the very last moment to trade information for that pressure balloon in his wound.

"What is your intent, Mr. Peters?"

"To travel back to the United States by the most expeditious means with Miss McCloud and her baby."

At the mention of Katie's name, all his shock and dismay from the cab slammed back into him. Uncle Charlie was a senior CIA official? Had she been sent on the D.U. mission to seduce him? To recruit him for the agency? Or, more likely, to *entrap* him into working for the American government? What were the odds that her assignment to help him was chance? His mind shied away from the math. The numbers did not look good for Katie.

Damn, she was talented. He'd bought her innocent-girl-looking-to-grow-up story hook, line and sinker. She must be laughing her ass off at him. Chagrin and a dose of wounded male pride surged through him.

Only his father had ever made him feel this way. Mentally, he congratulated her for correctly identifying an Achilles' heel he hadn't even known he possessed; he couldn't resist innocence. He was not used to being successfully hoodwinked. *Clever bitch.*

"About that baby," the marine interrupted his grim train of thought. "How is it your names are on the child's birth certificate?"

"I'm the physician of record at the birth. I am legally required to sign the birth certificate. As for naming us as the parents, Zaghastan has no system of adoption. Parentless children are informally passed around until they land with someone willing to raise them—or until they're drowned, suffocated or simply starved to death. In the absence of any custody laws and any family willing to raise a child, any responsible party who's willing to claim a child is pretty much allowed to do so. Particularly when the child would otherwise die. Rather than throw a helpless newborn on the uncertain mercy of strangers, we chose to declare ourselves her legal parents. Plus, it helped out with getting Dawn through customs in Osh."

"Being a parent is a big responsibility."

"Yes, it is," Alex replied evenly.

"Kids need a home. Parents who are around for them. A steady environment."

"I'm aware of that, Major. Do you have a point to make?"

Instead of answering, the marine changed subjects abruptly. "What are you planning to do when you reach the States?"

Jesus. Are they all going to try to recruit me? Did this guy want him to work for military intelligence or something? He snapped, "I expect I'll practice medicine. I am a physician, after all." No sense mentioning that he was wealthy enough not to have to work for several lifetimes. That would bring up all sorts of awkward questions about where his money came from.

So. Sweet, innocent Katie wasn't so sweet and innocent, after all, was she? And here he'd been, all worried about protecting her purity and naïveté. *Damn.* He should have taken her up on that pleading request of hers to debauch and corrupt her. At least he could have had a little fun before she started blackmailing him, or whatever she had in mind to force him into the CIA fold. *Damn her.*

"What do you want from us, Mr. Peters?"

"I would like you to help me purchase three plane tickets to Washington, D.C., which is my home, by the way. And then we'll need a ride and armed escort to the Tashkent International Airport at your earliest convenience. I expect you'd like to get me out of here nearly as much as I'd like to be gone."

The marine smiled a little unwillingly. "If you'll follow me, I'll show you to your room."

Interesting. The guy never asked why the FSB had been chasing them so aggressively. Did the marine know something he didn't? Or was it just so blindingly obvious who'd been in that Chaika, and why, that the guy didn't have to ask?

He was shocked that his father might actually be here in person. His old man must have pulled all kinds of strings to get permission to enter Uzbekistan on such short notice. One of the border guards must have been on the FSB payroll for Peter to have found him and Katie so fast.

It could *no*t be good that Peter was here. Calling in that favor pretty damned fast, wasn't he? Alex knew his father was hot and bothered to get him onto the FSB payroll, but, jeez.

He followed the marine to a hotel-like room for embassy guests. A wired and fully monitored room, no doubt. Would Katie join him here? Try to seduce him? Film the two of them having raunchy sex? God, she was just like all the rest—out to use him, treating him like a freak. Did any of them seriously think they could embarrass him into caving in to them? He snorted mentally. A person had to have a conscience, a soul, to be blackmailed. Last time he checked, he had neither.

KATIE WAS PERPLEXED as to why she and Alex had been separated, and, furthermore, why the nice lady attaché seemed prepared to keep them apart while they were in the embassy. Was this some sort of mental warfare? Against an American citizen? Alex had warned her that the CIA didn't play nice, even with its own people—maybe he wasn't wrong after all. Chilled, she tried to keep her expression calm and open as the woman showed her to a guest room and murmured something about seeing if there was a crib that could be sent up for Dawn.

Katie asked as casually as she could manage, "Are we in any trouble?"

The woman, middle-aged, bland and smoothly diplomatic, answered, "Of course not, Miss McCloud. Your uncle was clear in his instructions. We're to give you all the help you need and show you every courtesy."

"Where's Alex?"

"He's filling in a few details for us on how you came to be in a cab being chased onto safe soil."

Katie had lived around men with secrets and who avoided giving direct answers for too long to be fooled by the woman's soothing tone of voice. They were interrogating Alex. She suspected he could handle himself perfectly well if they were, however.

"Alex and I need to get back to the States. We need to report in to our employer, and I'm ready to sleep in my own bed."

The woman attaché laughed. "I hear you. If there's anything you need that's not in your room, just pick up the phone and let the operator know. Tashkent isn't exactly the hub of civilization, but we'll do our best to accommodate you."

She was being sweet-talked. Coddled. Her brothers did it all the time, and it pissed her off. In this situation, it made her suspicious, too. But it wasn't like she could rock the boat at this juncture. They had Alex, and she dared not say or do anything to jeopardize his fragile status with the American authorities.

If she called Uncle Charlie and demanded that he call off the embassy dogs, it would only make Alex look more suspicious. Like he actually had something to hide. He didn't, did he? God, she hoped not.

She settled Dawn in the playpen someone brought up and crawled into bed, not at all sleepy. They'd slept last night and all today. Cuddling with Alex had been really nice once he got over being awkward and uncomfortable with it. One more wall breached with him.

She missed him. Hopefully, he was okay. In desperate need of distraction, she turned on the TV and was startled to receive a raft of American networks. She channel surfed absently, unable to get her mind off Alex and where he was right now.

Who was in that black car that had chased them across Tashkent? Why had Alex seemed so much more concerned *after* a bunch of foot soldiers had morphed into that upscale car? She got that Alex would be a controversial figure in American intelligence circles. His father was a convicted spy for the enemy, for heaven's sake. But why would he be questioned so closely now? What was going on with him that he hadn't told her?

He'd been secretive from the start with her, but he'd been opening up in the past two days, giving her glimpses into his mind and into his past. The person she saw was lonely and in desperate need of love. She was a sucker for abandoned creatures, and Alex the child had been about as emotionally abandoned as they came.

Oh, he'd technically had a father… But she got the distinct impression that Peter Koronov had been more of a taskmaster than an actual parent. She highly doubted Alex even knew what it was to be loved.

Such a contrast to her big, rowdy, obnoxious family, where love and laughter were part of everything they said or did. She'd grown up petted and spoiled as the baby, the only girl after five boys. Her heart broke for the cold, isolated childhood Alex must have experienced. And then to be humiliated by his father's crimes…judged for the sins of the father…to bear Koronov's shame…no nonder Alex had changed his name.

Did she dare try to show Alex what love was? Or was she just opening herself up for disappointment and heartache? She refused to be just a convenient compartment in his life. If she let herself develop deeper feelings for him, it would kill her to have him walk away from her down the road.

He'd been clear in his intent to do so, promising to get out of her life as soon as she was safe. Her reckless desire to reach out to him warred with the caution of self-preservation. And there was Dawn to think about, too.

Her thoughts spun around and around until she was practically dizzy.

Dawn woke up, and she played with the baby to distract herself. Who was Dawn's father, anyway? When they got back to the States, should she go looking for the birth father or just take over raising the infant and not look back? Some intelligence outfit would have a rough idea who all had been in the Karshan Valley nine months ago, right? It was merely a matter of asking the right people the right questions. She couldn't imagine more than a handful of Caucasians had been in the Karshan region. All she would have to do was approach a few men, ask them a delicate question or two about a stunningly beautiful local girl and she'd locate Dawn's birth father. Easy peasy.

Her heart told her to walk away from looking for the man, but her head reluctantly told her she had to do the former. This was a child, not a stray cat. The birth father had a right to know he had a child. He had a right to choose whether or not to raise his daughter.

Did Peter Koronov have a choice about raising Alex? Had the birth mother foisted baby Alex off on Peter? Or had the Russian government ordered Peter to raise his son? To use his boy as a cover reason for emigrating to the United States? To hide behind Alex's mundane upbringing to spy on America?

She smoothed Dawn's hair, which was starting to grow a tiny bit and was coming in pale and blond and *so* not Zaghastani. Dawn opened her bright blue eyes and burped up at her. Katie laughed and scooped up the baby for a cuddle. She whispered into the baby's tummy, "Us girls, we'll show Alex what it's like to be loved and have a family, won't we?"

But as soon as the words left her mouth, doubt slammed into her. Easy to say. Hard to do. Was it worth the risk? Alex was an extraordinary man from what she'd seen of him so far.

Dawn gurgled back in what Katie swore sounded like agreement...or maybe she just had gas. Did she dare break through the walls Alex Peters hid behind and try to teach him how to love?

CHAPTER TEN

A DIFFERENT MARINE fetched Alex from his room the next morning and led him downstairs. He caught sight of Katie and Dawn at the foot of the stairs in the embassy foyer and relief jumped in his gut before he remembered.

She was not who she pretended to be.

He should have known. If life had taught him nothing else, it was that people were never who they said they were.

"There you are, Alex!" Katie cried. "We missed you, didn't we, Dawn?"

He stepped close to chuck the baby's cheek. "How'd she sleep last night?"

"As good as ever. She's a great baby."

He was vividly aware of the woman attaché from last night and the marine behind him paying close attention to his conversation with Katie. Looking for the two of them to send coded signals to each other? What did they know about Katie that he didn't?

"Shall we go?" the attaché chick said pleasantly.

The woman undoubtedly couldn't wait to get rid of him. The feeling was mutual. He was more than ready to get as far away from this part of the world as he could. Had Katie not pulled high-level strings with Uncle Charlie, he doubted they'd be leaving the embassy so easily this morning.

They stepped outside, and a limousine bearing diplomatic license plates waited for them. Katie, Dawn, attaché chick and he climbed inside. The marine officer from last night's interrogation was already waiting within, scowling. Alex mentally rolled his eyes. But, hey. He'd take the diplomatic protection no matter how grudgingly it was offered.

The ride to the airport was quiet. He was not willing to give the Americans any more ammunition to use against him than absolutely necessary. He was happy to sit back and let this be Uncle Charlie's gig. He was still staggered at the notion of Katie being a CIA operative. He'd *never* seen one as accomplished as she at giving no clues whatsoever to her training as a spy.

He ought to be furious with her. Looking to turn her or at least compromise her. But he couldn't seem to get past his towering disbelief. His gut just wouldn't wrap around the idea of her spying on him. Later. He had faith the rage would come later. And he would not hesitate to loose it upon her.

They arrived at the airport and were ushered onto the tarmac. An official in a suit led them up a staircase and into the passenger area of the terminal, bypassing the usual security checkpoints. Uncle Charlie must have some hard-core clout to have gotten the embassy to pull these kinds of strings for his niece. The marine from last night handed Alex a paper jacket containing plane tickets all the way through to Dulles Airport just outside Washington, D.C.

"Do you need us to stay until you board, Mr. Peters?" the attaché chick asked solicitously.

Gonna make him beg a little, was she? He answered with a calm he was far from feeling, "That would be helpful."

The woman added blandly, "We've spoken with the airport security staff and they're on high alert for any problems until you've left."

He'd bet. She'd probably told the Uzbekis that *he* was the primary threat. Alex sat down in a plastic chair in the waiting area and pretended to read yesterday's edition of *Pravda* that he'd picked up from the chair beside him. Katie paced back and forth with Dawn, who was uncharacteristically fussy this morning. Sensing disquiet in Katie, perhaps? Poor kid's sleep schedule must be wrecked by all the weird hours they'd been keeping.

Their flight to Moscow was just being called for preboarding—which they qualified for, not only because they had a baby, but because they needed not to die before they left Uzbekistan—when a commotion broke out at the security area across from their gate.

The marine escort leaped to his feet with Alex not far behind. A loud argument had broken out at the security checkpoint.

Katie rushed to Alex's side like a child running to a parent for safety. Man, she was a great actress. Hell, she'd fooled him, hadn't she?

"What is it?" she asked with credible fear quavering in her soprano voice.

He stared at the group of suited men trying to bully their way through the phalanx of security guards who'd appeared like magic in a thick cluster before the entry point. *Wow.* Those Uzbeki soldiers must have been lurking just out of sight the whole time. What had that

attaché told them about him, anyway? Hell, he supposed his Russian name alone probably would have
been enough to garner that sort of security presence.

"Ohmigod," Katie breathed.

He glanced at her and then followed the direction
of her incredulous stare through the heavy glass par-
tition. Behind the four suited men arguing stridently
with the security guards stood another man, apart and
aloof from the commotion. A face he hadn't seen in
years. His own face, but thirty years older.

"You look just like him," Katie said in wonder and
horror.

Peter Koronov. *What,* in the name of all that was
unholy, was *he* doing *here?* Cold, sick shock filled his
stomach until Alex felt like vomiting. It was one thing
to suspect his father was in that Chaika last night. It
was another thing altogether to know it. Was his old
man so certain Alex would cave in and come home
with him that Peter felt he could make an open approach like this?

"Does he want to talk with you?" she asked tightly.

Belatedly, the attaché chick spotted his old man
and stood abruptly, her hackles straight up and all but
growling aloud. As much for her benefit as Katie's,
Alex snarled, "I don't care if he wants to talk to me
or not. Wild horses couldn't drag me within speaking
distance of him."

He glared in hatred as his father slowly, deliberately lifted a cell phone to take a picture. Except he
didn't point the phone at Alex. The bastard pointed it
at Katie and Dawn. The phone moved slightly as the
man snapped another picture of the pair.

"Why is he taking pictures of me?" Katie asked nervously.

"Son of a bitch is trying to intimidate me. He's sending me a message."

"What message?"

Alex turned away violently. "Doesn't matter. I'll never play ball with him. I'm done with him." Big words. Empty threat. His old man had him by the short hairs, and they both knew it. *That* was the message Peter was here to send his wayward son.

"Talk is cheap, Mr. Peters," the marine muttered.

The marine had *no* idea how true that was. Alex snapped, "Put us on the plane. Now. At all costs, don't let him through that security checkpoint."

Attaché chick moved over to the loud argument at the checkpoint to add her two cents while the marine hustled him, Katie and Dawn aboard the jet.

First-class seats, huh? Wow. The embassy must really want to get rid of them bad to spring for the expensive tickets. He'd expected to be crammed in the worst seats on the plane by way of petty revenge for their spectacular arrival at the embassy last night. Most likely, these had been the only seats available on such short notice. Or, he thought sourly, maybe Uncle Charlie had even more clout than he'd given the guy credit for.

Katie fidgeted beside him. "Will your father try to shoot this plane down?"

It was entirely possible his father had the influence to call in an air strike on this plane. But last he heard, his father wanted him to work for the FSB, not kill him.

"Even he's not that vindictive," he murmured to

Katie, flashing her a false smile of reassurance. Not that he believed his own words for a minute. She seemed to buy his act and settled in her seat.

God, every way he looked, he saw nothing but betrayal. Katie was lying to him. His father was twisting his arm. His own government was hustling him out of town like a leper. Was there nowhere safe he could go? Nowhere to hide from all of them? He'd thought a remote corner of the planet in need of an obstetrician would have been far enough away from everyone that they would leave him alone. Apparently not.

He got the message loud and clear. Neither the CIA nor the FSB was going to leave him alone. Ever.

Half expecting the damned plane to get shot down, civilians and all, he held his breath through the take-off and climb out to altitude. He didn't relax until the dark blue of the Mediterranean Sea appeared outside his window as the plane finally descended into the massive sprawl of Istanbul.

He was not surprised when American embassy staff met them at the end of the jet bridge and escorted them to their connecting flight. The pair of men wore civilian suits but might as well have had signs around their necks saying, "United States Marine Corps badasses."

He wondered if they were there for security purposes or to make sure he and Katie didn't bolt from the airport. He suspected the embassy gang here didn't want him tarrying on Turkish soil any longer than absolutely necessary. Or maybe it was merely another demonstration of Uncle Charlie's power within the CIA. Either way, he was glad for the display of force. They boarded their plane for London without incident.

The same sort of welcoming committee met them

at Heathrow and politely booted them out of England, as well. Twenty-two miserable hours after they left Tashkent, they finally landed at Dulles International Airport outside Washington, D.C. Dawn was fed up with airplanes and on the verge of a major meltdown by the time they deplaned. Katie was frazzled with trying to keep the baby happy, and he was so tired he could hardly see straight. Lord, it was good to be back on his home turf, even if it was as hostile as everywhere else he'd run to.

They disembarked, and nobody ostensibly met them at the gate. He didn't doubt that security types were monitoring him and Katie closely on the airport's extensive camera network, but that was ops normal for his life. He was watched everywhere he went.

Yup, it was *really* good to be back on American soil. The long flights had been exhausting, but that was only the half of it. Here, he was on familiar ground. He knew the smells and sounds, the rhythms of American traffic; he could spot the people who didn't belong. People who were potential threats. Riddled with additional enemies though it might be, he knew the terrain. Plus, he had rights here. Resources. And the CIA could not legally operate on American soil. Not that such a pesky technicality slowed down the agency much.

Shockingly, the customs agent let him, Katie and Dawn pass without any hassles. They had no bags to collect, so they headed directly for a taxi stand.

Katie laughed a little and said, "It feels weird not to be looking over my shoulder for tails."

"Welcome home."

"Well, not technically. I live in Pennsylvania."

"Will you go there right away?" he asked innocently.

"I figure I'll have to stick around D.C. for a few days. The folks at Doctors Unlimited are going to want to hear the details of what happened to us."

Right. And she hadn't caught him in her snare yet, either.

She continued, "I was thinking about trying to find Dawn's birth father to let him know she exists."

Alex lurched. Okay, he hadn't seen that one coming. Good cover story. Believable. Credible excuse for sticking around town awhile longer. Smart cookies over at Langley. No flimsy cover stories for their operatives—no, sir.

A cabdriver opened his vehicle's doors for them. "No luggage?" the guy asked.

"No," Katie answered. And then she looked over at Alex. "Since you live here, can you recommend a hotel for me and Dawn? Something close to the D.U. offices, but not too expensive." She added ruefully, "I've been living on a starting teacher's salary and paying off student loans the past few years."

He leaned forward and gave the driver a street address on the border between Georgetown and northwest D.C. "You'll stay at my place," he announced grimly.

"No. I couldn't!"

"Why not? We've been living together for a while now."

"But…but…" she sputtered.

"You need help with the baby. I've got an extra room. This way I can keep an eye on you two." She smiled gratefully as if she'd taken his comment to mean that he wanted to keep her and Dawn safe. In point of fact, he'd meant it literally. He physically wanted to keep her close until he could figure out exactly what her marching orders from the CIA were.

Plus, his father had deliberately taken pictures of her and the baby. They were in more danger than Katie could imagine.... Even if she was a trained operative, she still didn't get it. Peter Koronov was devastatingly deadly when provoked.

KATIE LEANED FORWARD, interested, as the cab pulled to a stop in front of a turn-of-the-century building in a stupidly posh neighborhood. Just how much money had Alex ripped off the mob for in his gambling spree?

Alex paid off the cab from his stash of cash and led her inside. The interior lobby of the apartment building was sleek and modern in sharp contrast to the quaint exterior. They rode the elevator in silence to, no surprise, the top-floor penthouse. She *was* surprised, however, to discover that his condo took up the entire roof of the building. Besides being huge, it was open and airy, decorated with modern, clean-lined furnishings.

"Your decorator is superb," she commented. "To pull off a space this modern and yet keep it warm and inviting is no easy feat."

"Thanks. I'll tell her," he replied drily.

He'd been distant and remote with her ever since they'd left the embassy in Tashkent. Had something happened to him there to upset him? He was so hard to read most of the time. And she was usually pretty good at deciphering stoic men.

He showed her to a guest bedroom decorated in soft, pale shades of mossy green and cream. Its floor-

to-ceiling glass windows looked out on a rooftop ter-
race boasting a sleek, stainless steel swimming pool
and landscaping that managed to be as modern and
welcoming as the rest of the condo. A mix of old-world
perennials and stark cactus made for a stunning visual display.

"My God, this place is magnificent," she told him.

He shrugged. "It's relaxing."

"Do you have guests often?" she couldn't resist asking.

"Never."

He was back to one- and two-word sentences with
her, huh? Was it something she'd said or done? Her
resolve to reach past his emotional barriers wavered.
Had she set an impossible goal for herself?

"I'll see if I can have some baby stuff delivered,"
he said emotionlessly.

"You don't have to go to all that trouble," she replied quickly. "We'll only be here a day or two, I hope."

"Eager to get rid of me, are you?" He sounded genuinely surprised at that.

"Not at all. You've been a great companion and
saved my life more than once. I owe you huge." She
lifted her gaze to his, and for just an instant, memory
of what else she'd declared that she owed him blazed
in his eyes. How was it that light gray eyes could burn
so dark and hot?

He turned on his heel and walked out without a
word.

Dismayed, she played in the ultramodern bathroom
and gave Dawn her first real bath in the oversize cop-
per bowl that served as a sink. The baby splashed ex-
citedly and Katie laughed in delight when the baby

soaked her. She glanced up in the mirror as a movement caught her eye and saw Alex's silhouette just disappearing from the doorway. He'd been watching her and Dawn play together? Why? And why had he left?

She jumped in the shower while Dawn played on a towel on the heated floor. Maybe she could coax Alex into watching the baby for an hour or two this afternoon while she slipped out for a quick shopping trip. She was going to scream if she had to wear those clunky jeans and sweatshirt one more day. And she needed a curling wand and some makeup in the *worst* way.

Alex was noncommunicative when she made her request, and she took his grunt for assent. She grabbed her wallet, which was one of the few personal possessions of hers that had made it all the way back to America from Zaghastan. That and her passport. Oh, and her ugly hiking boots. That was about it.

She found a drugstore and stocked up on beauty supplies, and the clerk told her where the nearest shopping area was. She walked the half-dozen blocks to a retail area and sighed in delight at the sight of cute girl clothes in the storefronts. Lord, she'd missed civilization.

Before she left the first store, she took deep pleasure in ceremonially throwing out the construction worker jeans and hiking boots. She walked out wearing girl jeans that made her look like she actually had an ass and a cute pair of sandals. She bought several tops at the next store, and was just collecting her bags to check out when her cell phone vibrated.

She pulled it out of her pocket and saw she had a text from a phone number she didn't recognize. It read:

Buy a dress. D.U. invited us to a cocktail party tonight, and we need to go.

Alex knew how to text? Surprise, surprise. She texted back, How sexy?

How much more of your innocence do you want to lose?

She looked up at the clerk. "Turns out I'm not done shopping. Where to do you keep your LBDs?"

The salesgirl grinned. "Little black dresses are right over here. Are we doing the works?"

"Oh, yeah," Katie replied, grinning. She'd break through that man's walls whether he liked it or not. And she knew just the weapons to use on him....

BY THE TIME KATIE emerged from her bedroom, the babysitter had arrived. How Alex had managed to convince a full-blown nun to babysit Dawn for them, she had no idea. But she could rest easy knowing the baby was in great hands.

The wimpled woman in the living room introduced herself. "I'm Sister Mary Harris. I teach at the school Alex attended as a child."

"Really?" Katie responded, interested. "So you've known Alex for a long time then. I'd love to hear about him as a boy."

The gray-haired nun smiled secretively. "In my profession, we carry no tales."

"Can you at least give me a hint as to what kind of child he was?"

"Brilliant. Serious. Withdrawn."

"That sounds a lot like the adult now."

"Indeed."

Alex emerged from his bedroom, looking as magnificent in a tuxedo as she'd suspected he would. Her initial impression of James Bond over Rambo had been spot-on. He looked born to a tux. To Sister Mary Harris, he murmured, "You have my number if you need anything."

"Dawn and I will be fine. I've been taking care of babies for forty years."

Alex glanced in her direction. "The nuns run an orphanage along with the boarding school."

Katie nodded, pleased that he'd gotten Dawn such a highly qualified sitter. The elderly woman commented, "You two relax and have a nice evening. Dawn and I will have a lovely time together."

Alex glanced at Katie's raincoat, which was buttoned to her chin and belted at her waist. She caught the faint smirk that crossed his face. He knew full well she was hiding a hot little dress under there. At least she hoped he thought it was hot. It was hard to know how to impress a man who was such an accomplished womanizer.

She'd opted for simple and classy. The black minidress was halter-necked in front with a slit that plunged nearly to her waist. She was bare all the way to the waist in back. The fabric hugged her every curve, highlighting the sexy pout of her breasts. The cut of the garment allowed for no bra at all under it, and her breasts were boldly outlined by the clingy fabric.

She wore impossibly tall stilettos and prayed no one would chase her and Alex tonight. There was no way she could run in these shoes. She'd spent the afternoon getting her legs waxed and polished, and while she was at it, she'd gotten a Brazilian bikini wax. Her nether regions still stung a little from it, and she would have preferred to do it a day ago to let any irritation subside, but she'd had no choice on the timing.

"Shall we?" Alex murmured.

She nodded, jumping as his hand came to rest lightly on her waist. They said good-night to the sister and made their way to the elevator. He paused long enough to do something to a keypad outside his door; it looked like he had activated a security system.

They rode the elevator down in silence. He was apparently going to be his taciturn self tonight, and she was too nervous about going out in public in such skimpy clothing to make small talk. She supposed she shouldn't have been surprised by the limousine waiting in front of the building, but it was a shock after the past few weeks of primitive survival.

As the limo pulled away from the curb, she murmured, "It's hard to believe I was washing my hair in a bucket of cold river water only a few days ago. And now this."

He shrugged. "I've never set much stock in material things."

"Why the limo then?"

"It was convenient. And it makes a statement."

"To whom?"

He stared out the window as if he hadn't heard her question, but his lips were pressed together tightly. He'd heard her, all right. Why did he feel obliged to remind the staff at Doctors Unlimited that he was a wealthy guy? A statement of independence? A display of personal power? Or was Alex just thumbing his nose at them all, declaring that he didn't need them or their job?

Two weeks ago, she'd have seen the limo as him being an arrogant jerk. But now she knew the gesture for what it was—a flash of the insecure, unloved child demanding attention. He was a weird dichotomy of wounded child and confident man. But she supposed everybody carried around childhood baggage to some degree. Hers was not big secret, after all. Heck, the whole D.U. trip had been about declaring her independence from her childhood.

She was in no position to judge Alex for having his own baggage to haul around. Besides, under normal circumstances, when people weren't trying to kill him and he wasn't forced to interact with his father, she expected the child inside him was kept carefully locked away.

She might as well start her campaign to breach the Fortress of Alex Solitude. "Who all's going to be at this party?" she asked lightly.

He finally glanced over at her. "Worried you'll be underdressed?"

She raised one eyebrow at him. "I'm perfectly satisfied with my dress, thank you very much. I just wanted to get an idea of who to expect to meet."

The fire in his eyes flared momentarily and then settled once more. "Most of D.U.'s senior staff should be there. And a bunch of diplomatic types from countries that D.U. uses to insert its people into hot spots. Should be quite the United Nations."

It made sense. D.U. needed to stay on good terms with as many countries as possible so its doctors would be allowed to enter the countries to treat patients and to transit them to reach less friendly nations like Zaghastan, where doctors slipped in illegally to treat locals.

Interesting that Alex mentioned nothing about trying to spot the mole on the D.U. staff. Surely that was the main item on his personal agenda for tonight. Hell, after seducing Alex, it was the main item on hers!

The limo pulled up in front of the converted mansion that housed Doctors Unlimited. The driver opened the door for them, and Alex held a hand out to her. She laid her hand in his palm, and the contact was electric. No matter how antisocial Alex was being with her, the intensely sexual spark between them was still alive and well.

That dangerous darkness she found so irresistible came over him as he ushered her into the foyer. The spy had gone to work. He reached for her coat, and she held her breath nervously.

He lifted her coat off her shoulders and took a moment to look her over from neck to toes. "You do like to play with fire, don't you?" he said, low and rough.

"The hotter the better," she shot back.

"Careful, little girl. I can burn you bad enough you'll never recover."

"I dare you," she declared.

His eyelids dropped to half-mast and one corner of his mouth turned up. He said lightly, "You really shouldn't have done that."

"Chicken?" she challenged.

"I'm not one of your brothers, and I'm not ten years old. I don't indulge in childish dares."

"What do you indulge in? Why are you afraid to show me?"

He placed a hand on her waist and guided her toward the large reception area. He muttered under his breath, "All in good time, little lamb."

The threat simmering in his words sent shivers rippling down her spine. "About damn time," she breathed, mostly to herself.

Alex's eyes went a little blacker and his hand clenched her waist a little bit tighter. *Good.* She'd hate to think she was the only one having trouble breathing normally or concentrating on saying hello to the tuxedoed member of D.U.'s board of directors who stepped forward to meet them in concern. For the life of her, she couldn't dredge up the man's name.

"Are you two all right? We were appalled to hear about the massacre," he declared.

"Massacre?" Katie echoed, startled.

"Why, yes. Everybody in that village you were stationed beside—Karshan was it?—was killed in a rebel attack the same night you fled the area."

She stared, aghast.

"By the by, in the future, we'd appreciate it if you two contacted us sooner to let us know you're alive. There was quite a panic around the offices while we tried to find out your status."

Alex replied drily, "We were a little occupied avoiding being killed. I called as soon as I felt we were actually safe."

"But that wasn't until this morning," the man blustered.

"That's correct," Alex bit out. "Come, Katie," he ordered quietly.

She followed Alex obediently as he literally turned his back on the man and walked away. "And we're being intentionally rude to him why?" she asked under her breath.

"Because he's an ass, and I'll call in when I damn well please."

"Why's he an ass?"

"He sprang the news of the massacre on us to see what our reactions would be. The bastard was checking to make sure we had no part in perpetrating it."

"No way," she replied, appalled. "We were aid workers delivering babies."

"You forget—I'm the firstborn son of the devil."

She frowned up at him. "Why would they send you out if they thought you would turn on the people you're supposed to help?"

He lifted two flutes of champagne off the tray of pre-poured glasses and handed one to her with a tight smile. "To set me up."

"Is it possible you're being a wee bit paranoid?"

His smile stayed, but his eyes went grim. Angry. "It's not paranoia if the boogeyman is actually following you."

"Alex, I saw you work your tail off, delivering babies. I watched you fight like crazy to save that fourteen-year-old, and we both know how hard you tried to save Dawn's mother. You weren't out there to kill anyone."

"I nearly killed the guy who tracked us."

"But you didn't kill him, did you?"

"No."

"You tried to save him, in fact."

Alex shrugged in reluctant agreement.

"There you have it. You're not the monster you seem to think everyone sees when they look at you."

"It's not my imagination, Katie. Look at how people are avoiding us right now."

"Their loss," she replied stoutly. "I'm cute and fun, and you're endlessly fascinating to talk with."

"Just talk?" he murmured.

"You're fascinating in other ways, and you know it," she scolded lightly.

"Mmm. And don't forget it."

"Not bloody likely," she retorted.

He laughed dangerously, and heads swiveled in their direction. Too many heads and too fast. Everyone in the room seemed to be keeping an eye on Alex. Or maybe it was just that he and she made such a handsome couple. Or maybe Alex wasn't being excessively paranoid at all.

André Fortinay, director of Doctors Unlimited's operations, approached them, a jovial and obviously fake smile on his face. He pumped Alex's hand a little too enthusiastically. Katie knew Alex well enough to see the sarcasm in his expression as he greeted their boss.

"Glad to have you back safe and sound!" André boomed. He was a big, hearty man with an ample girth and down-home personality, completely unlike what Katie expected from a Frenchman.

"We're glad to be home," Alex replied evenly.

"What the hell happened over there?"

Alex shrugged. "We delivered babies as long as we could. When the rebels came, we fled. We made our way out by whatever means we could find, and here we are. Back in modern civilization."

André's pleasant gaze went less pleasant for just a moment, and then he was back to his cheerful, bluff self, declaring them brave and lucky as hell. Katie snorted mentally. Luck had nothing to do with their making it home alive. Alex's mad skills and his making a deal with the devil were the only reasons the three of them were safe and sound.

Speaking of Dawn, if the village her mother came from had been eradicated, that meant the infant likely had no surviving relatives from her mother's clan. It became more imperative than ever to find the child's birth father.

"Were there no survivors of the village at all?" Katie asked André.

"None. It was a horrific massacre."

"The rebels did it, you say?" Alex asked.

"That's what our sources tell us."

Alex asked casually, "Did your sources tell you about the high-tech attack drones, armored vehicles, laser-guided RPGs and air strikes?"

"Excuse me?" André asked urgently.

"Since when are the Zaghastani rebels armed like a first-world military force?" Alex bit out.

André looked distracted and moved away quickly.

"He's not our man," Alex muttered.

"We're looking for someone?" Katie asked low. She was right, after all. Alex's main reason in coming here tonight was to look for the mole.

"Someone from D.U. knew what they were sending us into."

"Why do you say that?"

"Why else would they send me?" he asked gently.

She frowned, not understanding.

"Think about it. I'm a pariah. I'm not even an obstetrician. Why would they send me in there unless I was expendable?"

"What about me?" Katie asked.

"You're collateral damage. Not to mention your obvious innocence and naive desire to do good works are the perfect cover for the fact that I was sent in as bait."

"To catch what?"

"Or who," he added. "Excellent question. My continued safety and yours may very well depend on answering it."

She smiled seductively and murmured, "When we get out of here, will you please tell me what the hell's going on?"

His gaze flashed for a moment and he blatantly looked down at her breasts. "Talk is not at the top of my agenda when we get out of here."

Her pulse went crazy and her thong got damp in a matter of seconds. But that other stuff, the who-was-trying-to-kill-them stuff, was important, dammit. She couldn't afford to let him distract her.

"What's the gambit tonight?" she asked. "Chat up everyone until someone reacts wrong?"

"Clever girl."

"Want me to flirt with them and throw them off balance?"

"No," he answered sharply. "You're mine."

Well, then. Didn't that just make her thong even a little more wet? They wandered around the reception for the next hour, making inconsequential small talk with any number of foreign dignitaries and staffers from D.U.

And then Katie turned around and lurched in shock against his arm. "What is it?" Alex asked quickly.

"Uncle Charlie just walked in."

Alex muttered something under his breath in Russian that she would assume was not an expression of joy.

Her uncle, a gray-haired man in his early sixties, who wore the decades elegantly, wasted no time coming over to her. "Katie, sweetie. Are you all right? You took ten years off my life with that phone call."

"Thanks so much for the help, Uncle Charlie. I couldn't think of who else to call on such short notice. I'm so sorry I bugged you."

"What's the point of having influence if I can't use it for good now and then?" he replied charmingly.

"Uncle Charlie, I'd like to introduce you to my working partner, Dr. Alex Peters."

"Mui vrestretilise prezhde," her uncle said to Alex.

Alex answered emotionlessly in English, "Yes, we have met before. When I was much younger."

Uncle Charlie switched to English. "Your father was a worthy adversary."

"I imagine he still is," Alex replied drily.

"Just so. What are you up to these days?"

"Delivering babies until I was rudely interrupted by a brush war."

Katie frowned. Uncle Charlie had a predatory glint in his eyes that she wasn't accustomed to. But she damned well recognized it from seeing it in Alex's eyes. Here was a master spy at work, not her mother's laid-back brother relaxing with family.

"How'd you two get out of Zaghastan? It sounded pretty dodgy over there."

"Several kind souls provided us with unexpected rides," Alex answered smoothly.

Rides, plural? Katie mentally frowned. *Oh.* Both

the plane and the four-wheeler Alex stole from the guy tracking them.

"Bit of luck for you," Charlie noted drily.

"Make no mistake, luck had nothing to do with it," Alex retorted.

Charlie's head dipped slightly as if acknowledging some coded message in Alex's words. "Maybe someday we will meet again in the wake of less stressful circumstances."

"Don't hold your breath," Alex snapped.

Somebody called a greeting to Uncle Charlie from across the room. "Don't be a stranger, Katie," he said smoothly. He gave her a peck on the cheek and drifted away.

Alex scowled into his champagne glass as if he was contemplating murdering someone sooner rather than later. She leaned on his forearm, bringing her barely clad breast into contact with his biceps, forcing him to acknowledge her. "What was that all about?"

"You tell me."

Danger rolled off him, wave after wave of it. He was seriously pissed off about something. As much as she wanted to break through his emotional walls, and as much as she wanted to try the brand of sex he preferred, she wasn't sure she wanted to go there with him this furious.

"I've seen enough," Alex announced.

Crud. She was hoping to get him to stick around a little longer, get a little more champagne down him, smooth the rough edges of his temper a little.

"You look disappointed," he muttered. "Scared to be alone with me?"

"A little. I was hoping to get some more booze down you."

"Why?"

"To mellow you out."

"For what I have in mind, nothing will mellow me out. Last chance to back out, lamb. You can go with Uncle Charlie or you can leave with me, now, and come to your slaughter."

She looked him square in eye. "I'm with you. How do they say it in poker? I'm all in."

"We'll see about that."

CHAPTER ELEVEN

KATIE'S HEART FLUTTERED as Alex handed her into the limousine. What fate had she just damned herself to? As the vehicle pulled out smoothly into the night, she felt like she was on a one-way ride to some dark place from which she would never return. It didn't help matters that Alex was sitting back in the shadows across from her looking positively demonic. But dammit, the guy needed someone in his life to be loyal to him for once. To have his back. To believe in him. And she was a sucker for hard-luck cases. Especially when they came packaged in such a gorgeous, hot man.

"What was all that stuff with Uncle Charlie about?" she tried again.

Nothing. No answer at all. Alex merely stared at her broodingly.

"Was he trying to recruit you or something?"

Again, nothing. Her trepidation climbed. The limo pulled up in front of his condo and Alex ordered her to wait in the car. He got out and looked up and down the street carefully before gesturing for her to join him. The limo pulled away quietly, and they were alone.

Alex gripped her arm tightly as he guided her inside. Was he afraid she'd bolt, or was he already asserting the dominance she expected from him tonight?

The elevator ride was silent. Tense. He entered a

lengthy number sequence on the keypad outside his front door and passed a magnetic card through the slot. A red light illuminated.

"Come into my lair, little lamb," he muttered darkly. "Uncle Charlie's a bastard to sacrifice you to me, by the way."

Sacrifice me? Huh?

They stepped into the open space, and there was no sign of Sister Mary Harris. Katie followed Alex to Dawn's bedroom and the nun was asleep in the bed beside Dawn's crib. The woman had a hand stretched out through the bars and resting on Dawn's mattress.

Alex explained, "Sister's as deaf as a post with her hearing aids out. She'll feel Dawn cry with her hand."

As he backed out of the bedroom, he scooped the twin hearing aids off the dresser top and pocketed them.

"Alex!" she exclaimed softly.

"You'll thank me later when you need to scream."

He pulled the door shut behind them.

Knees quivering more than a little, she followed him back into the dark living room. As he moved to the bar and poured himself a glass of whiskey, she asked, "Are you going to hurt me?"

"Do you want me to?"

"We already established that I don't have any idea what I'm getting myself into. I have no clue what's going to happen tonight. I only know I want to give you the same kind of pleasure you've given me."

He raised his glass to her in a silent toast and drained its contents. He untied his bow tie and let it hang around his neck as he stalked toward her, danger radiating from him.

"Do you, um, want me to take off my dress?" she asked nervously.

He paused directly in front of her. He flipped his right hand down sharply, and a small knife was abruptly in his fist. Where in the hell had that come from? She sucked in a sharp breath as he lifted the blade, running the flat of it along her shoulder to the neck of her dress.

No tenderness whatsoever was present in him. He was angry. Furious even. His expression was closed. *Crud.* What was it going to take to break through his walls to the man she knew—well, okay, that she *hoped*—was underneath it all?

With a quick flip of his wrist, he slashed the neck of her dress, never even nicking her skin. The dress sagged, revealing her left breast. Tension abruptly hung thickly in the air between them. This wasn't about love then. This was war.

Her nipple puckered hard in the cool air, and she gasped. But she held her ground and didn't run screaming. Frankly, she was pretty proud of herself.

He reached across her and sliced the other side of the neck, and the black flap that made up the halter front fell to her waist, leaving her entire chest naked to his gaze.

"Unzip the skirt," Alex ordered, his voice thick with desire.

It was nice to know he wasn't completely unaffected. In the past, he'd held himself so totally aloof from their sexual encounters she could scream. She had to get him to let go of whatever he was holding inside, no matter how over her head this got.

She reached around behind her waist and unzipped the dress's skirt slowly. If she was going to seduce him, then she might as well play the siren, right? She gave a single, sexy tug and the fabric slithered down over her hips to the floor, leaving her standing in a pool of black silk, wearing only a thong and high heels.

Alex walked all the way around her slowly, looking but not touching. Although the heat of his stare felt like it was going to incinerate her at any second. She reached for that naughty part of herself that had enjoyed wearing slinky lingerie for him in that hotel room before. After all, she was the one who'd insisted on this. She was sick of being a little girl. Sick of being discounted because of her naïveté. It was high time she acted out her secret fantasies. She'd known from the moment she'd met Alex that he was the kind of man who would go to as dark a place as she could imagine. Darker.

When he was standing in front of her once more, he reached around her head to remove the clip holding her hair in its French twist. Her hair tumbled down around her shoulders in thick waves and she couldn't resist giving her head a shake.

"Don't move," he ordered.

She stood there, a few wayward curls half across her face, and was surprised when he pulled out his cell phone and took a picture of her. He stepped back a few paces and took several more pictures of her in all her topless glory. He moved behind her and snapped her from behind. Given how skimpy her thong was, the shot wouldn't leave much to the imagination.

"Bend down," he ordered coldly, "and grab your ankles."

Embarrassment sprang to her cheeks in a hot rush. He was back there with his camera, and such a pose would be seriously lewd. *So. This is war to him, too, is it?*

"Do it," he bit out.

Eyes narrowed, she bent down brazenly and grabbed her ankles. She'd asked for him to bust through her sexual boundaries. She couldn't very well complain now that he was doing it. But then his finger hooked beneath the narrow thong and, crap, lifted it aside, revealing her most private parts. She hadn't the slightest doubt he was photographing those, as well. Serious doubt about her odds of winning this private war with him assailed her. She was a McCloud, dammit. And win or lose, McClouds never surrendered. She would see this thing through no matter what.

He moved back in front of her. "Unlike me, you still have a reputation to concern yourself with. If you ever want to teach again, you need these pictures to stay safely on my cell phone. Also, unlike me, you still have a soul."

"What does that have to do with anything?" she blurted.

"A person with no reputation and no soul is rather more difficult to blackmail."

She stared, shocked. "You plan to blackmail me? But I've got nothing you want. You're rich."

"I want your silence. These pictures are my insurance."

"Alex, what goes on in the bedroom stays in the bedroom. I would never kiss and tell."

He laughed shortly. "You'll do a lot more than kiss tonight, lamb."

She spotted a chink in his armor and pounced. "So far, you're all talk and no action."

That got a real laugh out of him. "Ahh, sweet Katie. You never fail to surprise me. You should be scared to death right about now, and yet you're goading me on. You're either incredibly brave or incredibly foolish."

She was undoubtedly both. Cocking her right hip and planting her fist on it, she demanded, "You gonna get busy, or am I taking charge around here?"

Abruptly serious, he snapped, "On your knees."

She did as he ordered and was not surprised when he reached for his zipper. He might consider it a win to get her in this position, but, frankly, she chalked it up as one point for her. She reached up and pushed aside his hands, a little surprised when he let her.

She slid his zipper down slowly, blatantly teasing him as she revealed his black silk boxers. Silk, huh? More of a hedonist than he let on, perchance? She reached through the flap to grasp his member, which was wide-awake. Hot. Hard. Satiny. She ran her fingernails down its length and was gratified by the growl her nails elicited.

She pushed the fabric aside and examined his male parts closely. She'd grown up with a bunch of boys and wasn't a stranger to their equipment. But this time, it was hers to play with. She explored every inch of him, learning his textures.

She knew how to proceed with a blow job in theory, but her experience with it was nil. But she wasn't about to give away her nervousness to the enemy at this juncture. Hesitantly, she leaned forward to taste him, and Alex sucked in a sharp breath. That was more like it. She was getting good and tired of all his damned self-control. She ran her tongue around the tip of him and then along his length. She swirled her tongue around the base of his penis and then back up the shaft.

His hand plunged into her hair at the back of her head and he pressed her down over him; her lips slid over his flesh. Her mouth filled with his heat, and she was gratified when Alex sucked in another, even sharper breath. She pulled back slightly and then slid forward again. She repeated the process until Alex was groaning aloud. She remembered what it had felt like when he'd driven her slowly out of her mind, and she did her best to return the favor.

Without warning, his hands clamped on the sides of her head and he pulled out of her. "Enough," he ground out.

Having to fight for control, was he? *Excellent!* Score another hit for her.

He pulled her to her feet and backed her up quickly. The cold quartz of the wet bar touched her hips. He hoisted her up onto the hard surface and pushed her down onto her back. He shoved her thighs apart. It seemed a little high for him to reach her with his—

Oh. He bent down toward her with his face. His mouth closed on her female flesh, and she cried out in shock and pleasure and embarrassment. But then his tongue swirled around the center of her throbbing lust and all sense of propriety evaporated.

He pushed her legs high and lifted his mouth away from her enough to mutter, "Grab your ankles."

It was a good thing she stretched as part of her regular fitness routine. But still, she felt wanton in the extreme clasping her ankles with her shoes still in those naughty stilettos. The position opened her entirely to his mouth and tongue. The wet, swirling, plunging heat of it brought her to the verge of climax almost immediately. She bit her lower lip hard, doing her best not to scream. A nun was sleeping in the next room, for crying out loud.

"You think you can hold out against me?" Alex growled against her inner thigh. "Think again." His mouth closed on her pulsing flesh, biting and sucking right to the edge of pain. She lurched up off the marble as the orgasm slammed into her, crying out into her forearm to muffle the noise.

"Again," he ordered.

She was surprised when his mouth closed on her, and in a matter of seconds another orgasm shot through her with the violence of a lightning bolt.

He grasped her thighs, pulling her forward on the slippery quartz, then grabbed her around the waist. He lifted her off the bar and turned her around, shoving her down over the back of the couch with her rear end high and vulnerable in the air.

The embarrassment started to return, but then something smooth and hot and throbbing pressed against her wet, wanting flesh. She braced herself for impact, but instead the invasion of her body by his happened by slow, maddening degrees.

Alex was prodigiously endowed, and he seemed to take pleasure in letting her take the full measure of him inch by torturously slow inch. The sensation was incredible. Her internal muscles stretched to accommodate him, pulsing around the invader, clasping at his flesh convulsively. He withdrew just as slowly, tantalizing her with a feeling of loss so acute she wanted to sob. *Dammit*. Score one for Alex.

He slammed into her all the way to the hilt, until

he touched her womb he was so deep inside her. She cried out in relief.

He withdrew again, and this time, she pleaded, "Again. Fill me again." *Crap.* She was losing control. Handing too much power over to him.

He slammed into her again, and she groaned. Over and over he filled her to bursting, his hips thrusting hard against her. She started to shudder, with her whole body this time, her muscles tightening and releasing in time with his invasions. The shudders built into a giant convulsion around him, and she shouted her release into the seat cushions.

He stood her upright and scooped her up in his arms, almost as if he knew she was too overwhelmed by the series of violent orgasms she'd just experienced to stand on her own. He carried her swiftly down the hallway to his bedroom and kicked the door shut behind him. He let her body slide down his, and she craved every masculine inch of him. He was still fully dressed—except for his open fly—and the starched tuxedo was rough against her highly sensitized skin.

"I can't get enough of you," she gasped.

He shoved her up against the wall, and she grabbed his shoulders and wrapped her right leg around his hips. He lifted her by the ass, and she wrapped her other leg around him as he entered her again. The hard wall gave her no recourse from his deep thrusts, and she shuddered in ecstasy with each one. He spun away from the wall and sat her on some sort of vanity. His arms swept everything on its surface to the floor with a crash, and this position gave him the right angle to press deep, then deeper still into her.

When that failed to satisfy him, however, he picked

her up again without pulling out of her. This time he backed her up against a heavy, soft drape. She grabbed the fabric high over her head and hung on for dear life as he drove up and into her with powerful, flexing thrusts of his buttocks beneath her calves. He used her weight against her, to drive her down onto him without recourse. This must be what plundering was. She was completely defenseless against him, and he took whatever he wanted from her body. And, God help her, she was glad to let him. Complete surrender roared through her, and she handed herself over to it. To him.

"Never stop," she groaned in an excess of pleasure.

"Sing for me, Katie. This room is soundproof."

Sing she did. She moaned and sobbed and even screamed as Alex drove her completely out of her mind. When her arms trembled with fatigue, he spun her away from the window and they bounced down onto his bed. Her body lifted wildly to his, matching his urgent rhythm, joining in the chase for whatever demons drove him.

He grabbed her hips and pulled her to him hard. She rose willingly in his hands, giving herself to him without reservation. She literally sobbed in gratitude as he filled her over and over, harder and harder, faster and faster. She lost herself in an alternate universe where nothing existed but Alex and the raging inferno between the two of them. If this was war, let it never end. Time ceased to have meaning as the conflagration roared around them, consuming everything she'd ever been before this moment.

And somewhere in the glorious madness, something shifted between them. Changed. It was as if he didn't know quite what to make of her unconditional surrender. Like it was unexpected. Reluctantly, at first, he absorbed it into himself. And as he did so, the violent edge left their sex. It was still hard and fast and he pounded deep inside her. But they both wanted it, strained together toward wherever it was heading. They drove each other higher in mutual wildness.

She urged him on, praising him and pleading with him. Finally, when all words failed her, and she was crying out in continuous, endless release, her body exploded and kept on exploding like the climax of a mighty fireworks display around him.

Alex's shout joined hers and he slammed into her one last time, staying buried deep within her for an eternity while his body pulsed within hers. For her part, she accepted everything he had to give her, pulling it deep into her soul.

She went limp beneath him, physically and emotionally drained, but she kept holding him tightly in her arms. Thankfully, he made no immediate effort to move away from her.

Gradually, her breathing slowed and his did the same. She registered that his bedroom was spacious and dark and cold. After a lovely eternity with his reassuring weight on top of her, pressing her deep into the mattress, he rolled away and got to his feet to stand beside the bed. He yanked the bed covers out from under her and then tossed them back up over her.

"Sleep," Alex ordered.

Ahh, chalk up another point for her. He was feeling his loss of control keenly enough to order her around now. Smiling into the darkness, she asked, "Aren't you going to join me?"

His shadow moved toward another doorway, not the one they'd come in earlier. "Maybe later."

Which, in Alex-speak, was a big, fat no. He slipped out of the room. She felt bereft all of a sudden. Abandoned. Why hadn't he stayed with her to cuddle? He had eventually let go of the terrible tension making him vibrate in explicable fury earlier. Or was this all part of his larger plan to convince her of what a twisted, unlovable bastard he was?

Thing was, he'd given her nothing but pleasure and more pleasure tonight. He talked a big game about not being a nice guy, but she had yet to see any real evidence of it.

She got that his life was complicated. That his father was an SOB. That both the CIA and the FSB made a hobby of harassing him, and that neither agency trusted him. But a little at a time, he seemed to be carving out a life for himself. He'd broken with his father when Peter went back to Russia. He'd gone to medical school. He'd landed a job with a humanitarian aid outfit. And now, he'd taken in a woman and a baby, for crying out loud. Where was the many-colored bastard he claimed to be?

He'd been tense and angry tonight, but she would eventually get him to talk about what had made him so uptight. Yeah, he'd been pretty aggressive with her at the start of their sex tonight, but it wasn't like she hadn't been goading him for days. And he'd changed his tune before they were done making love. For a minute there, they'd shared a real emotional connection. He could deny it all he liked, but she knew what she'd felt from him. And he knew it, too, or he wouldn't have bolted out of here the second he could walk. Yup, all in all, tonight had been a definite win for her.

But next time she wasn't letting him go when he tried to walk away from her.

CHAPTER TWELVE

ALEX POURED HIMSELF another glass of whiskey and
stared down into its amber depths in search of answers. How in the hell had she done that to him? She'd
stripped away every single urge from him to do anything but make her scream with pleasure. His M.O.
was to relish deprivation of pleasure. He didn't get off
on causing pain, but he always made sure the women
he had sex with didn't enjoy it particularly. He took
his pleasure alone. The shrinks all said it was a subconscious desire to punish his mother for leaving him.

But Katie, lamb-for-the-slaughter Katie, had
smashed the mold to smithereens. Katie, the CIA
plant trying to trap him into working for the agency.
Katie, the superb actress and damned liar. Except he'd
watched her body flush with pleasure, watched her
shudder with orgasm after orgasm, heard the cries torn
from her throat. Nobody—*nobody*—could fake all of
that. And he'd been completely, fucking totally unable to resist her.

He'd had sex with some seriously accomplished
high-dollar whores. Some had tried to fake enjoying themselves with him over the years because they
thought that was what he wanted. They hadn't understood it was the one thing he didn't want from them.
They'd been *professional* fakers, and they couldn't

have pulled off faking what had just happened between him and Katie half so well. No, Katie's reactions had been real.

What the hell does it mean?

Was it possible that she was actually who she said she was? A kindergarten teacher who'd been thrown in his path by sheer chance? And she just happened to have an uncle who was a high-ranking CIA official?

No way. Hell, he should be complimented that the CIA had sent its very best whore to seduce him.

He tossed down the whiskey in a single angry gulp. It burned its way to his gut like acid. He glared at the cell phone on its desk, now full of damning photographs of Katie in the most compromising possible positions. Why did she let him take the pictures in the first place? Shouldn't she have been the one trying to get damning photographs of him? She'd probably gone along with it to gain his trust. Yeah, that made sense.

There was *no chance* she was an innocent. Which left him with one logical course of action. He had to turn the woman who was trying to turn him. He had to addict her to him so completely that she served him over all others, that she abandoned any previous loyalties and clung only to him. And if that didn't work, he always had the pictures.

But something deep within him rebelled at the notion of brainwashing or blackmailing her. Tonight, her reaction to him had been entirely voluntary. Whore though she might be, she seemed genuinely attracted to him. No question she had truly enjoyed having sex with him. It was a first for him. *And it was addictive, dammit.*

He could not afford to indulge in any addictions

right now. The FSB and the CIA were breathing down his throat, both trying hard to rope him into working for them. Someone had hired that American in Zaghastan to kill him. At any minute, that person would send a more accomplished assassin after him, assuming it hadn't been done already.

God knew what game his father was playing now, but he dreaded what Peter would do to Katie and Dawn if Alex let either of them out of his sight.

He definitely could not afford to have feelings for sweet Katie McCloud. She might be by far the best sex he'd ever had, but he could *not* fall for her. Not now. Not ever. His head said to get rid of her immediately, but his lust shouted in no uncertain terms that he was not done with her yet. Did he dare continue sleeping with her? Was he strong enough to hold himself emotionally apart from her while he sated his bodily needs with her? *Hell.* It wasn't only his bodily needs she fulfilled, and he was a fool to pretend otherwise. He loved being loved a little.

He swore violently and tossed back another whiskey before stretching out on the couch in his office. He might have given her his bed tonight, but he wasn't about to give her his soul. Or at least what tiny piece of it he clung to precariously.

KATIE WOKE UP slowly. Soft cotton beneath her cheek and an insanely comfortable mattress lulled her back to sleep several times before she finally roused for good. The sheets were black. She frowned. Where was she—

Memory flooded back all at once of the D.U. party with Alex. Him cutting her dress off her. Everything that followed. She'd given herself over to him completely, and he'd made her scream like he'd said he would. Even now, a shudder of delight passed through her to remember the things he'd done to her and with her.

She sat up in the gigantic bed, stretching out the kinks, and looked around the big bedroom. The room was trashed. Their sex had apparently been as rambunctious as she remembered. But the far side of the comforter was still neatly tucked in.

He hadn't joined her last night, after she'd fallen asleep, then. No surprise. She seemed to freak him out more than a little. Which she chose to take as a good sign that she was getting through those emotional walls of his.

Naked, she climbed out of bed. There was no sign of her ruined dress anywhere. She peeked through a closed door and found a perfectly organized walk-in closet. Did Alex keep the thing that neat, or did he have a butler stashed around here somewhere?

She tried another door. This one led to the master bath. It retained a faint trace of humidity as if Alex had been in there since last night to shower. She did the same now. Funny how, ever since Zaghastan, she relished hot showers and the act of washing her hair so much more than before.

The hot water pounded away most of her soreness from last night. She dried off, wrapped the biggest towel she could find around herself and prayed for luck. All her clothes were in the guest bedroom, and there might still be a nun in the condo somewhere.

She sneaked into the hallway and crept down the hall to her room, freezing guiltily when she heard the nun's voice in the kitchen, talking to Dawn. Katie dived into the guest room and eased the door shut quickly. Breathing a sigh of relief, she blow-dried her hair, put on a little eye makeup and dressed.

Pasting on a bright smile, she stepped into the kitchen and called a cheery hello to Sister Mary Harris. Chicken that she was, Katie stuck her head in the refrigerator immediately and went hunting for orange juice rather than look the nun in the eye.

The nun looked up from a skillet of scrambled eggs loaded with chopped ham and minced vegetables. It looked insanely tasty. "I figured you'd be hungry after your big night last night," the nun announced.

Katie choked on the orange juice she was downing but managed not to spew it all over the counter. "Where's Alex?" she asked when she recovered her breath.

"He left a while ago. Said he'd be back later this morning."

Hmm. She didn't know whether to be worried by that or not. She supposed it was all part of his secretive personality not to share where he was going with her. "How's Dawn?"

"A perfect angel. Slept six hours last night between feedings. Eats well. Digestion regular."

Katie moved over to the baby, who was wriggling happily in a car seat strapped securely to a kitchen chair. Clever improvisation of a high chair. "Good morning, sweetie."

The baby gurgled almost as if answering her.

Sister Mary Harris commented, "She reacts to you like you're her mother. And yet Alex says she's not your biological child?"

"Alex delivered Dawn, but her mother died in child-birth. We were in the middle of a battle and had to flee, so we took Dawn with us."

"What does Alex think of her?" the nun asked care-fully.

"He's great with her. He feeds her and changes her and spoils her."

"Does he hold her?"

Katie turned her full attention on the nun, who sud-denly was very busy plating up the scrambled eggs and slices of bacon she pulled out of a warming drawer. "He does hold her. Quite often, in fact. Why do you ask?"

The nun sat down at the table, murmured a blessing and deliberately unfolded a napkin in her lap before answering. "Alex has never been one to show much af-fection. He never liked to touch others or be touched."

Katie frowned. "He held me a bunch during our escape from Zaghastan. I was scared a lot. And he cuddles with Dawn all the time."

"Indeed?" the nun blurted. She eyed Katie with re-newed interest, while Katie eyed her back in surprise.

She was first to look down, diving with gusto into her eggs. They ate in silence for several minutes be-fore Sister Mary Harris spoke up again. "I always be-lieved Alex was trying to punish himself by denying himself physical contact with others."

Katie looked up quickly. "Punish himself for what?"

The nun shrugged. "Maybe for driving his mother away. Later, he took the sins of the father upon him-self. No matter how often priests absolved him, he never seemed to believe them."

"How did he drive his mother away? He told me she left when he was a baby."

"She did. And he didn't. But he always had a tendency to take responsibility for everyone around him. He's a very protective person."

Interesting. "Tell me something, Sister. Has he always struggled to let people love him?"

The nun laughed merrily. "*Struggled* is not the word I would use. Flatly refusing to let people love him would be more accurate."

"Why's that?"

The nun leaned forward and said intently, "Where, in his past, did anyone give him the idea that he's lovable? His mother abandoned him. His father ignored him. He bounced from school to school as his father moved around the country. His only parent treated him like a spy recruit in need of constant correction and training. Where was the love?"

"Can you tell me more about his father?"

"Not really. We only saw him when he dropped off Alex at the beginning of each school year. And then, after his arrest, Alex was practically one of our orphans. To our knowledge, he has no other living family whatsoever. As I recall, a lawyer did an extensive search for someone to whom Alex could be given to raise."

"And there was no one?"

The nun shrugged. "No one came forward to claim him."

And didn't that comment just shed all kinds of light on Alex claiming Dawn the way he had? He knew what it was like to have no one at all. Katie stood and carried her plate and the nun's over to the sink. She rinsed them thoughtfully and put them into the dishwasher.

"I'll finish cleaning up here," the nun murmured.

Katie was drying her hands when her cell phone vibrated in her jeans pocket. She pulled it out quickly, hoping it was Alex.

It was not. Instead, the text read, I need to speak with you this morning. It's urgent. Has to do with your friend. My office, one hour. Say nothing to him about it.

She recognized the phone number and turned to ask the nun, "Do you need to be somewhere this morning, or could I duck out for a little while to take care of some business and leave you with Dawn?"

"I'm retired, dear. I don't have to be anywhere until I join my Maker. You go on. Dawn and I will have a stroll around Mr. Alex's lovely garden and then maybe take a little nap."

"Thank you," Katie said gratefully. On impulse she hugged the elderly nun. "For everything."

Sister Mary Harris patted Katie's cheek. "God bless you, child. And may you bless Alex. He needs you more than you know."

Stunned, Katie stared down at the small woman. "From your mouth to God's ear," she muttered.

The nun laughed gaily. "I'll see what I can do about that. Now go on. Dawn and I will be fine."

Katie hurried outside and walked down the block to the nearest Metro stop. She pulled out her Metro card, which had managed to survive a war zone and her wild escape from it. Her mind whirling from what the nun had revealed about Alex, she rode to the Langley stop.

After passing through the security checkpoint outside, she stopped at the visitor's desk at CIA headquarters. "I'm here to see Charles McCloud. He's expecting me."

CHAPTER THIRTEEN

ALEX STRODE UP to the receptionist's high counter at the expensive law firm in downtown Washington.

"Good morning, sir. May I help you?"

New girl. Didn't know him. And, furthermore, she was flirting with him. Today it irritated him, which irritated him even more. He ought to at least mentally size her up. But instead he had no desire at all to check her out. *Dammit.* He had it worse for Katie than he'd realized in his whiskey-induced fog last night.

Swearing to himself, he bit out, "Please tell Chester Morton that Alex Peters is here to see him. He's not expecting me."

"If y'all will take a seat, sir, I'll ring him right up. And if there's *any*thing I can do to make y'all comfortable, just lemme know," the girl drawled in a thick Southern accent.

He took the farthest chair away from the aggressively interested girl in the waiting area and opened the *Wall Street Journal* on his tablet computer. But he didn't read the news in front of him. Instead, his brain churned. Since when didn't he check out attractive young females? He wasn't a sexual predator by any means, but neither was he *dead.* He knew he was handsome. He knew the dark, dangerous aura that clung to him attracted a certain kind of woman. He was accustomed to women making overtures to him, and he generally returned the interest.

So, what the hell was wrong with him this morning?

He knew the answer to his mental questions. He just didn't want to accept it. Alex Peters was a player. A rolling stone. He wasn't the kind of man to settle down with one woman in domestic bliss. Ever. The past few weeks were an anomaly, and the sooner he got back to his regularly scheduled life, the better.

"Alex? This is a pleasant surprise, son. Come on back."

He looked up at his attorney and scowled. Why in the *hell* was he here today to do what he was about to do?

"What can I do for you?" Chester asked as he sat down behind his big desk.

Alex bit out, "What do you know about international adoption law?"

KATIE WAS SHOWN to her uncle's office by a highly intelligent-looking and friendly young man in a suit. The guy smiled winningly and threw out interested signals at her, which she pretended obliviousness to. He was the kind of guy she'd have been wildly attracted to a few weeks ago. Before she met a brilliant surgeon with a dark past and a darker soul.

"Hi, Uncle Charlie," she said wryly as the door closed behind her.

"Hi, kiddo. Have a seat."

"I gather this isn't a social visit?" she wasted no time asking.

Her uncle leaned back in his desk chair and shifted,

in the blink of an eye, into the master spy. "No. It isn't."

"What can I do for you?" she asked. She tried to keep her voice friendly. Open. But suspicion rattled around in her gut.

"I gather your trip to Zaghastan was rather eventful."

"That's a word for it."

"I'd like to hear about your experience."

She leaned back, studying the spy in front of her. Piercing intelligence shone in his eyes. She said pleasantly, "You're a busy man, and I've got places to go and things to do today. Why don't we just cut to the chase? What specifically do you want to know?"

Her uncle studied her in turn, and she had no doubt he was catching every microscopic hint she gave away of her thoughts and feelings. "I always did think your immediate family underestimated you."

He was trying to soften her up. Get her on his side before he sprang whatever he was going to spring on her. She didn't bother to respond to the compliment, even if it was gratifying to hear the words aloud.

"What did you see that last night in the Karshan Valley? Who attacked the village?"

She answered bluntly, "It was soldiers for sure. Trained Special Forces types, if I had to guess. They had extremely high-tech gear. Frankly, I thought it might be our guys."

"Not ours," Charles the spy answered promptly and definitively.

"Then whose?"

"That's what we'd like to know. What are the odds it was Russian military types looking for your friend?"

She frowned. "The Russian military helped us get out of Zaghastan. Why would they try to kill us and then turn around and help us?" She shook her head. "I don't see how it was Russians in the Karshan Valley."

"At least not Russian army," her uncle replied thoughtfully.

"What other Russians could it be?" she asked quickly.

Charles smiled broadly at her. "Exactly. They've all underestimated you."

"You're dodging the question."

He nodded. "I am, indeed."

"Well?"

He picked up a single sheet of paper from his desk. She saw typing on it. "This is classified. Highly classified, in fact. Came across my desk early this morning." He held it out to her.

Frowning, she took it and read it quickly.

Urgent traffic: Central Asia desk. Verification codes authenticated at 0613. EDT by Victor Echo Foxtrot Alpha. Eyes only. Top Secret. Begin message. Zaghastan station reports village of Ghun in Karshan Region attacked at 2300 hours local. All inhabitants killed. No survivors. Observer on ground verified in person at 0300 hours local. End message.

She looked up at her uncle, aghast. "What's going on over there?"

"You tell me. It's not the rebels' style to eradicate entire villages. They don't usually want to provoke the sort of reprisals that follow these sorts of actions.

Rival clans will band together to attack another clan that oversteps the rules of tribal warfare by too much."

"The enemy of my enemy is my friend?" she said wryly.

"Exactly."

"What is this, then?"

Charles took a deep breath. Released it. Seemed to consider whether or not to tell her the truth. And then he said, "Clans in that region have fought with each other since the dawn of time, more or less. In order to preserve their way of life, which includes a cottage industry of feuding and fighting, they tacitly agree not to destroy one another. They steal livestock and women, but they don't wipe each other out. Their enemies need to live on to fight another day, or else the warfare that is their way of life will disappear."

"In other words, they like the constant fighting but have to make sure nobody wins."

"In a nutshell, yes. I would like to think they don't actually like the fighting, rather they do not know any other way of life."

She leaned forward. "Okay. So wiping out Karshan and Ghun is not normal rebel behavior. Which brings us back to the question of who else is fighting with the rebels over there." She frowned as an idea occurred to her. "Or maybe it wasn't rebels at all. Maybe it was just someone impersonating rebels."

"Give the girl a gold star," Charles replied grimly. "Our analysts doubt the local rebels would have allowed foreigners embedded with them to wipe out either village."

"Sounds like your people have a good handle on what's going on over there. Why do you need me?"

"You got eyes on the fake rebels, directly. We're hoping you saw something that might give away the identity of the forces pretending to be rebels."

"I have no idea."

"That's why I'd like you to talk to a few of my people. They'll guide you through remembering details that might not seem important to you but which could be meaningful to them."

"Will they tell me what they figure out?"

"Why do you want to know?"

Suspicion exploded in her chest. *Crud.* Alex's paranoia was rubbing off on her! The first thing that came to her mind at her uncle's question was sharp alarm followed by a dozen possibilities for why he'd answered a question with a question and dodged giving her a straight answer.

Abruptly, she wasn't at all sure she was willing to talk to a U.S. government official about Dawn's parentage just yet. A sudden, sharp need to protect the infant overrode her curiosity about Dawn's father.

Her uncle was waiting with the patience of a Sphinx for an answer out of her. "Call me nosy," she replied lightly.

Charles smiled. "A true McCloud trait."

She smiled, relieved to have gotten past the awkward moment.

Charles took a sip from a coffee mug he hadn't touched until now. *Huh.* It was his turn to think over what he was going to say next. She mentally braced for his real gambit.

He started blandly enough. "There's another reason I wanted to talk with you this morning."

"I figured as much. If you only wanted to know

who the rebels were, you'd be talking with Alex, too. He's brilliant and freakishly observant. He's as likely to have noticed some detail that would give away the identity of the rebels as I am."

Charles threw her a hard look and muttered, "We really *did* underestimate you, didn't we?"

She didn't bother to reply. They both knew the answer to that one.

"Here's the thing, Katie. Alex Peters has steadfastly refused all of our overtures for the past decade. And all of a sudden, here you are, in a perfect position to observe him. Talk to him. Get to know him even. It's a gift from God."

"You want me to recruit him."

She didn't know whether to be outraged or merely saddened that her uncle would abuse their family connection like this. She supposed he thought he was doing the right thing. Everyone in her family was deeply patriotic.

"I wouldn't go so far as that," he replied quickly.

Smart man. He must have read her disgust in her body language. He'd backed off faster than she'd expected.

"What can you tell me about Alex?" she asked. Might as well take advantage of her uncle's position if he was planning to take advantage of hers.

"I expect you know more than I do."

"Indulge me," she replied lightly.

Charles pursed his lips, weighing her for a long moment. Then he leaned back in his desk chair, folded his hands across his stomach and assumed a storyteller's tone of voice. "To understand Alex, you first must understand his father...."

ALEX'S LAWYER STARED at him in open shock. "You're serious?" Chester blurted.

"As a heart attack," Alex replied firmly. "And Lord knows, I've got more money than I can ever spend."

"Your investments have done very well," the lawyer conceded. "I'll file the emergency guardianship request this morning."

"Text me when the judge approves it."

"Will do, Alex. As for the other stuff, it'll take us a few days to draw up the long-term guardianship paperwork and get the legal adoption started. The fact that there's no agent for the infant could be a bit of a hurdle, but our family law guys will come up with something. As for the trust fund, I can have it in place by the end of the week."

"Call me when the paperwork is ready to be signed."

"While you're here, how are things going? You're—" the lawyer paused delicately "—staying out of trouble?"

"If you mean, am I drinking and driving at the same time, I'm not. I'm not gambling, and I haven't hired a hooker since I went to jail. Haven't you heard?" he added sarcastically. "I'm doing humanitarian work now."

Chester rolled his eyes at him. "I worry about you, Alex. You've had a rough time of it."

He sighed. "I know you give a damn about me. I appreciate it, Chester." God knew, there weren't many people he could say that about.

"You've got so much potential to do great things. I'd like to see you achieve it."

He studied the lawyer, considering the man's words. Potential? That would involve having goals. Real passions in life.

"While I didn't expect you to start a family in quite this way, I think it'll be good for you," Chester announced.

A family? Alex's mind reared back in dismay. This wasn't a family. This was simply him looking out for a helpless infant with no family. A kid whose plight he could relate to and that he had the resources to mitigate. Nothing more. He wasn't emotionally attached to baby Dawn. He was just making sure the child had the financial wherewithal to be safe. He knew exactly what it felt like to be alone in the world at a young age and not know how he was going to pay for shelter or even a meal. It sucked.

Chester had stepped in and looked out for him many years ago when his life had imploded. The lawyer had quickly and quietly maneuvered Peter Koronov's financial holdings into a trust for Alex immediately after Peter was arrested. The lawyer had taken heat for doing it from the U.S. government, which had wanted to strip Peter of everything. But, thanks to Chester, Alex had been able to stay in school. Pay for a topflight education. And then, of course, he'd staked himself in the casinos and multiplied the contents of his checking accounts by a stupid amount.

Alex was just paying the favor forward. That was all. The million-dollar trust fund he was setting up for Dawn was a very small percentage of his overall worth.

"Now, all you have to do is find a wife to go with your daughter," Chester said jovially.

Alex jolted. A *wife?* Him? He snorted in derision, but an image of Katie in the throes of an orgasm flashed into his mind immediately, followed by the memory of what it felt like to hold her in his arms as she cuddled up to him.

Bah. He wasn't the marrying kind. Hell, he didn't even trust her. She was a *spy,* for God's sake. Or if she technically wasn't one, she damned well was working for one.

He supposed there was a certain twisted logic in his being so attracted to her. The only family he'd ever known was in the spy business, as well. He must equate love with spies—and lies and deception—at some deep, subconscious, *sick* level.

Screw that. He was done with the whole rotten, twisted head game.

He stood up abruptly, and Chester rose with him. "I'll be in touch, Alex."

"Thanks," he said shortly. An abrupt need to get the hell out of these claustrophobic offices rolled over him. He needed fresh air. Open space. Now.

KATIE KNEW MOST of what Uncle Charlie told her. Peter Koronov had lived and breathed espionage. He used his son as a cover to set up housekeeping in suburban Washington, D.C., and taught the boy the tools of the trade along the way. She hadn't heard that Peter had openly expected his son to spy for Russia, but it didn't surprise her. The rest of it, she'd pretty much pieced together.

She hadn't realized the extent of Alex's rebellion in his teens. He'd glossed over the wildness of his misspent youth, but she supposed she couldn't blame him for that. He was clearly trying to put it behind him now. She was shocked to hear that he'd begged a judge to throw him in jail. She was less shocked to hear the CIA's assessment that it had been an effort to hide from his father's aggressive recruiting tactics.

"Do you know how much money he won gambling?" she asked curiously.

"Our estimate is around ten million dollars."

Wow. No wonder the mob hated his guts.

Uncle Charlie added lightly, "I imagine that, if he has half-decent investment advisers, young Alex has parlayed that into quite a bit more by now. He wouldn't have spent any of it while he was in jail and could have just let the money multiply."

She ventured to ask the one question that had been nagging at her the most. "What do you know about his mother?"

Charlie started to open his mouth, and then he hesitated for just a nanosecond. Had she not known him so well, she wouldn't have spotted it. But it told her plenty. Whatever he told her next was not going to be the full truth. It could even be an outright lie. Still, she was interested to hear what the CIA would lie about to her.

He spoke slowly. "We have reason to believe she was a KGB employee. In what capacity, we have no idea. She could have been anything from a secretary to a full-blown field operative. She and Peter likely met while working. Our supposition is that the union was not sanctioned, and that a baby was entirely unsanctioned. She may or may not have been put to death for getting pregnant. Or it's simply possible she chose to pursue her career and left the child with Peter. Either way, the KGB exploited the child. A child explained why Peter emigrated to the U.S., and the boy made for a sympathetic cover when Peter set up shop as a single parent."

"Any guesses at all as to her identity?"

Charles shook his head in the negative.

Hmm. God, she'd love to know if he was telling the truth or not. She should have known she wouldn't get a straight answer, she supposed.

"Which leaves us with your Alex," her uncle said.

Her Alex? Is that how the CIA saw him? *Fascinating.*

Charlie continued, "We know he retains contacts within the FSB. We know they'd love to get their hooks into him. We suspect his father is actively working to recruit him. In fact, I'd be stunned to discover that Koronov isn't trying anything he can to pull his son into the FSB fold."

She studied her uncle thoughtfully. "So, you're hoping to turn Alex. Then what? To recruit him to work for you guys and send him into the FSB as a mole for you?"

He shrugged. "I can neither confirm nor deny that statement nor answer your question."

"Whatever," she muttered. She was right. "What makes you think the FSB will ever trust him?" she said louder. "The way I hear it, Alex has never made any secret of his preference for the United States over Russia. This is his home, and his loyalties lie here."

"It's not about loyalty. It's about leverage," Charles replied sharply. "Alex doesn't have to be the slightest bit loyal to Russia for his father to gain enough leverage to force Alex into working for him."

She turned that over in her mind and reluctantly saw the reasoning. If people could be bought or blackmailed or coerced, loyalty wouldn't really matter. The pressure that could be brought to bear to make someone serve a master—willingly or unwillingly—was ultimately more important than things like loyalty or patriotism. A dirty business, this espionage stuff. No wonder Alex was so cynical on the subject.

And no wonder he'd been so reluctant to call in favors from the Russian government. He'd understood full well that he was giving the FSB an opening to sink its hooks into him.

Sudden revelation crashed through her brain. *That* had been why that cargo plane came racing down to Zaghastan to pick them up! The Russian government—or at least his father—desperately wanted Alex to owe them his life.

The sacrifice he'd made to get the three of them out of Zaghastan had been larger, *much* larger, than she'd realized. Gratitude and renewed respect for him filled her.

Suddenly, today's meeting made perfect sense, too. Charlie did her a favor by pulling strings to get that embassy gate opened for her in Tashkent, and now he was collecting on it. These guys could either scratch your back and you scratched theirs in return, or they could twist your arm. *Take your pick.*

No wonder Alex was a head case if a man who operated from this perspective had raised him. Trying, but probably failing, to keep the cynicism out of her voice, she asked her uncle, "So, if I try to recruit Alex for you, what are you willing to do for me?"

"By God, you're a quick study," he muttered. "I suppose I'll owe you a favor."

Her eyes narrowed. "Bringing in the brilliant son

of a high-ranking FSB operative? You'll owe me more than a lousy favor. You'll owe me something huge."

"Agreed."

"What if I merely prevent Alex from working for the Russians? Would that be enough for you?"

"It would not be my ideal outcome, but it would admittedly be better than nothing."

She thought quickly. This might be her only chance ever to ask the question that had brought her there in the first place. If she could ask it in the context of having leverage over her uncle, he couldn't turn the answer against her…. She hoped. Before she chickened out and gave in to the warnings screaming in her gut, she spoke. "There is something you can do for me now, Uncle Charlie. Consider it a down payment on that future massive thing you'll owe me."

"You'll help with Alex then?" her uncle asked quickly.

"I need to know who the father of the infant we brought out with us is. And I need to find out quietly. Discreetly. Secretly, even."

Charles pursed his lips. He hadn't missed the fact that she hadn't agreed to work on Alex, yet. "Secretly is how we operate around here, Katie. I'm sure the baby's father is dead. Karshan was wiped out as completely as Ghun. What little satellite imagery we have of the area that night shows only two survivors successfully egressing the area into the Ghun Valley."

The CIA had been watching her and Alex's escape over that god-awful mountain that night? The idea made her feel exposed, even now, well after the fact. Was anything anyone did private anymore?

She wasn't at all sure she could trust her uncle, but

he clearly was desperate to get her to recruit Alex. And how else would she ever get the information she needed about Dawn? Reluctantly she admitted, "Dawn's father was not Zaghastani. He was Caucasian."

Her uncle stared at her, his jaw slightly open for several long seconds. Score one for her...she'd actually managed to shock him. He leaned forward and pushed a button on his phone. "I need a list of every male Caucasian observed entering the Karshan region from April to July of last year."

"Won't that weird request cause a lot of questions?" she blurted.

"Weird requests are normal around here. And our people know not to ask too many questions if they want to keep their jobs."

Good point. "How long will it take to get that list?"

"A day. Maybe two. Depends on how long it takes to make IDs of anyone we haven't already tagged. I'll let you know as soon as I have it."

She nodded her thanks.

"And you'll try to bring Alex around?"

That was a nice way of describing blatant coercion. "I'll test the waters," she said warily.

"And report back to me?"

"Sure." She got the message: obtaining that list of names would hinge on a positive progress report with Alex.

Charles stood up. "I'd see you out myself, but I have a meeting in a few minutes."

"Of course. Thanks for your help, Uncle Charlie," she said brightly.

His eyes narrowed. *Crud.* He'd caught that she was

poking at him a little. "If you ever want a job here at the agency, young lady, you let me know."

She laughed softly as she stepped out of his office. *Not a chance.* But it was nice to know that someone in her family finally got that she wasn't a totally brainless bimbo.

As another bright, handsome young man showed her out of the building, she let herself consider for a minute what it would be like to work here. Could she function in the cutthroat, survival-of-the-fittest environment of the CIA? Could she live with the secrets and half-truths and evasions? What would it be like to have an entire side of your life that nobody else knew about?

The mental exercise of imagining it was certainly enlightening when thinking about Alex. No wonder he didn't like to talk about himself or his feelings. It went a long way toward explaining his reluctance to engage in actual relationships, too. How could anyone let themselves feel something as vulnerable as love if their own identity, and everything and everyone around them, was a sham?

CHAPTER FOURTEEN

ALEX BURST OUT of the law firm into bright sunshine and took a half-dozen deep, calming breaths. *Christ.* What was that bout of claustrophobia all about? Even four years in prison had never made him feel that trapped.

No way was he getting married. The very idea flipped him out. *Home.* He needed to go home. Surround himself with safe and familiar things.

Right. And his eagerness to get back to his place had nothing to do with an emotional attachment to the baby or Katie. It was about lust. Pure and simple. He wanted to get Katie naked and blow her mind—

Dammit, this wasn't about making her happy! He merely wanted pleasure. Gratification. Yeah, that was all. He was just in lust with a girl. He'd screw her brains out and get this…infatuation…out of his system. He mentally spat on the word but allowed that he was, in fact, a little infatuated with Katie. Or at least with having sex with her.

Marginally calmer, he slid into his BMW and headed for home. But lurking in the back of his mind was the worrisome suspicion that he was lying to himself.

He barged into the condo and was irritated beyond all reason to discover that Katie was out. It didn't help that Sister Mary Harris smirked at his irritation. "I'll drive you back to the school," he snapped.

"Let me make you lunch first," she said firmly, moving into the kitchen.

He never had figured out how to successfully say no to a nun. They were *nuns,* after all. He huffed and followed her into the kitchen.

"Here. Feed the baby a bottle while I make us a bite to eat."

He took the bottle she thrust into his hands and scooped up Dawn from her baby seat. "Hey, cutie," he murmured. "How's my girl today?"

The nun glanced over at him and commented casually, "She likes you. Is really comfortable with you." He frowned at the nun, and she added, "The two of you look good together."

His frown deepened to an outright scowl. "You can get that idea right out of your head. Katie can raise her. I'm just putting the two of them up for a few days until Katie goes back to Pennsylvania." *And making legal arrangements to make Dawn independently wealthy and name Katie and myself Dawn's legal guardians.*

The nun's mouth twitched skeptically, but, thankfully, she let the subject drop. Which was good. He didn't feel like splitting semantic hairs with her. He was naming himself a guardian because of the resources he could offer Dawn throughout her life. And if she ever got in trouble, being her guardian would give him a legal right to dive in and fix everything.

Dawn lost the nipple of the bottle and squawked, and he turned his full attention to feeding the baby.

The condo's front door burst open, and he jerked in alarm before he remembered that Katie had a key to the place. This business of sharing his home, even temporarily, was unsettling.

"Oh!" she exclaimed. "You're back."

He frowned. She sounded evasive. Where had she been and what had she been doing? Reporting in to her superiors, perhaps? Eyes narrowed, he asked smoothly, "Where were you?" He couldn't wait to see how she answered that salvo.

"Langley. Uncle Charlie wanted to talk to me."

Holy shit. She freely admitted she'd gone to the mother ship for a debrief? Was she that confident she owned him after their epic sex last night? He mentally snorted. It would take a hell of a lot more than that to control him.

His mental antennae on full alert, he leaned back in the kitchen chair. "Do tell."

She set down her purse on the counter and turned around a little too fast to face him. Her face was hectic. "He tried to convince me to recruit you for the CIA."

Alex stared at her, dumbfounded. She admitted it? Just like that? What game was this she was playing with him? Although, on reflection, it was a brilliant ploy. The CIA had to know he would make her as one of theirs the moment he found out who her uncle was. They might as well have her make a direct approach to him. He would smell a lie a mile away, and lying to him would only piss him off.

"What are they offering?" he asked grimly.

Dawn started to fuss in his arms as if sensing his building temper. He tried to pass the baby off to Sister Mary Harris, but the nun was inexplicably too occupied making grilled cheese sandwiches all of a sudden to take her. He tamped down hard on his fury lest he disturb Dawn. The sister was forcing him to keep his cool on purpose.

Katie was speaking. "I personally have no idea what they could offer you that would entice you. It's not like you need money. And you've already declared yourself blackmail-proof. I have no reason not to believe you're being straightforward about that."

Unwilling humor tickled his gut. Completely unpredictable, she was. Truly refreshing. She had all the subtlety of a bull in a china shop when it came to espionage. Hell, that was part of her charm.

She continued speaking, a note of irritation entering her voice. "I suppose they'll have to find a way to twist your arm since they have no faith in your patriotism or loyalty to Uncle Sam. You should be careful."

She was *warning* him that her own agency was going to make a run at him? His mouth quirked with outright humor. "As recruiting speeches go, this is by far the worst one I've ever heard. You're not being the slightest bit convincing."

She snorted. "I'm not trying to convince you of anything. I'm just playing my uncle to get information on who Dawn's father is."

He leaned back hard in his chair. "Are you now? Any leads?" His mind raced with the implications of *that* little nugget. She was such a confident operative that she would play head games with one of the CIA's top spymasters? *Damn.* Kindergarten teacher, his ass. Just how long had she been training with the agency?

"Charlie's getting me a list of all the Caucasian males sighted in the Karshan Valley around nine months ago."

"What will dear Uncle Charlie do when he finds

out you're not actually going to try to hand me to him on a silver platter?"

She shrugged. "I don't care. I don't work for him."

She said that with such casual conviction he could almost believe she was telling the truth. *Almost.* God she was fantastic. Pure, unadulterated admiration for her skill rolled over him. If he'd had to fall for a spy, at least he'd fallen for the very best.

KATIE WAS TOO agitated to sit and let Alex stare at her like a bug under a microscope. She knew he'd be unhappy that Uncle Charlie had approached her. But just because her uncle was in the business of keeping secrets didn't mean that she had to be, too. Lies and evasions were foreign things to her. Distasteful things. Better to have been up front with Alex and make him mad than try to play games with him. Still, his amused reaction was unsettling. Didn't he believe her?

She set the table and puttered around, pretending to help Sister Mary Harris get lunch on the table. They ate mostly in silence, and as soon as they finished, she leaped up to clear the dishes.

Alex announced without warning, "Katie, I'd like you and Dawn to go with us when I take Sister Mary Harris back to the convent school."

She looked up quickly. "Why?"

He replied sardonically, "I have something to talk with you about, and it may make you unhappy. I thought I'd borrow a page out of the good sister's playbook and do it with Dawn present so you can't yell at me."

She glanced over at the elderly nun, who abruptly busied herself washing out a skillet with undue vigor.

What did Alex think would make her shouting mad? "I'm pretty hard to make yell," she said. "I've been a kindergarten teacher for a while, and you get good at keeping your cool around a bunch of little kids and their antics."

"Amen," the nun piped up fervently.

"Will you come?" Alex asked tersely.

It almost sounded like he was nervous at the idea of her turning him down. As if she could deny him anything. "Sure, if it's that important to you."

She went to Dawn's room to fetch the baby bag. When she returned, Alex was gone. "Where'd he go?" she asked Sister Mary Harris.

The nun smiled broadly. "He's outside installing Dawn's car seat in his BMW. And he's none too happy about having such a thing in his fancy sports car."

Katie smiled back, amused. She picked up the dozing baby and followed the nun to the parking lot behind the building. Alex was just emerging from the backseat of the powerful German sports coupe, looking more than a little hot and annoyed.

She commented drily, "This is the beginning of the end for you."

"How's that?" he retorted.

Katie tsked. "Baby seats. Bottles. Diapers. Before long, you'll be coaching Little League soccer and going to PTA meetings. Another bachelor playboy bites the dust."

The nun cackled, and Alex scowled. As he held the door for her, he muttered, "I'm not going down without a fight."

"We'll see about that, big guy," she replied breezily.

His gaze snapped to hers, and myriad emotions

played across his face for a moment. Alarm. Amusement. Challenge accepted. What was *that* about?

"Oh my, you're good for him, Katie, dear," Sister Mary Harris declared gleefully. As Alex helped her into the front passenger seat, the nun added, "I think you might just have met your match, young man."

Alex looked as though he might actually be sulking as he slid into the driver's seat and guided the car to the street. He drove them onto the curving, tree-lined Rock Creek Parkway, and traffic was light in the middle of the day like this. But it wasn't long before Katie noticed Alex watching the rearview mirror an inordinate amount.

"Problem?" she murmured.

"Yes, in fact."

She swiveled around in her seat to see if she could spot the tail. A forest-green SUV with blacked-out windows was maneuvering in and around cars behind them a little too aggressively. Dismayed, she demanded, "Are you followed *everywhere* you go, Alex?"

"This is worse than usual."

"Did I lead them to you?" she asked painfully.

"Nah. The CIA has known for years where I live. I bought the penthouse when I graduated from college."

"Were you old enough to own property?" she blurted.

He didn't answer and appeared to be focusing entirely on his driving at the moment. Sister Mary Harris answered for him, "You're correct, Katie. He was too young to enter into such a contract. His trust fund had to buy it for him, as I recall. I also recall it being quite frustrating to him at the time."

"Overachiever," she teased him.

Alex spared her an annoyed look in the rearview mirror as he sped up smoothly. Before long, the BMW was weaving in and out of traffic like a stunt vehicle. Sister Mary Harris started to pray under her breath in the front seat. Katie kept a close eye on Dawn, who, so far, was sleeping through the increasingly violent ride.

They accelerated onto the Beltway—a major highway circling Washington, D.C.—briefly. The green SUV flew onto the Beltway behind them. Alex dived off an exit at the last second and swerved onto surface streets once more. He ran red lights and screeched around corners, but no matter what he did, he couldn't seem to shake the big vehicle behind him.

"What do they want?" Katie demanded in exasperation.

Alex bit out, "Maybe just to harass us, maybe to catch us, maybe kill us. A high-speed auto crash would likely do the trick."

She didn't bother to tell him to be careful. He was an outstanding driver, much better than she was, and he knew full well he had a baby on board.

A screech of locked tires and a cacophony of blaring horns, followed by a car-on-car crunch behind them, ended the chase as quickly as it had begun. The big SUV had rammed into a pickup truck in an intersection, broadsiding the truck and spinning it around; its front end was mangled.

Alex decelerated, and Katie started to breathe again. Enough to ask, "Who was that?"

"Good question. I doubt Uncle Charlie sent his goons after us today. He thinks he's got me in the bag for now."

"What about the FSB?" she ventured to ask.

She caught his thoughtful frown in the rearview mirror. He replied slowly, "I don't think so. Peter just did me a big favor and expect to collect on it soon. Why would he kill me when he can use me instead?"

She said soberly, "I happen to think getting us that flight was worth it. I don't think Dawn would have stayed healthy too much longer without real food, and who knows what rebels or bandits we might have run into out there."

Alex just shrugged.

"That's me saying thank you," Katie added.

"You're welcome," he replied reluctantly.

Sister Mary Harris piped up, "I see I'll need to add you to my special prayer list, Alex."

"The one you keep for really bad sinners?" he asked wryly.

"No, young man. The one I keep for heroes in danger," she replied tartly.

Katie picked up the thread of the conversation once more. "So, if it wasn't the CIA and it wasn't the FSB, who *was* that?"

"Good question," Alex ground out. He threw her a warning look, as if he didn't want to talk about it anymore. Probably didn't want to air his dirty laundry in front of the nun and end up on her really bad sinners list.

She slumped in her seat, worried. How much danger were she and Dawn in as long as they stayed with him? No way was she dumping the infant on the foster care system if she could help it, although she didn't know squat about how to prevent that. Honestly, she didn't understand Dawn's legal status at all. She was afraid to ask questions about it for fear of the answers she'd get. But sooner or later, she would have to face all of it.

If Alex's enemies were this aggressive, she probably ought to get Dawn away from him. Problem was, he seemed so capable of protecting her and the baby. Was it better—safer—for them to stay or go? Her head said to go, but her heart shouted at her to stay.

The BMW pulled up in front of a pretty stone church with a big walled compound beside it. The roofs of buildings were visible inside. That must be the convent. A second three-story structure stood on the other side of the church. That must be the school Alex had gone to.

They escorted the nun inside, Alex carrying her overnight bag and Katie cradling Dawn, who blissfully slept through it all. They reached the cloistered portion of the convent, and Sister Mary Harris took her bag from Alex.

"Sister, could you wait for a moment while Katie and I have a private word?"

"Of course, Alex."

He took Dawn out of Katie's arms and passed her to the nun, then took Katie's arm and led her off a little ways down the stone hallway.

"This is the part where you piss me off, right?" When he didn't reply, she tried, "What's up?"

"I planned to have one conversation with you, but in light of that SUV, it now needs to be a different conversation."

"You're scaring me, Alex."

"Katie, what do you think of leaving Dawn with Sister Mary Harris, just for a day or two, while we figure out who was chasing us?"

"We need to hide Dawn?" she squeaked. *Crap! Just how dangerous are his enemies?* "Why don't I just take her home to Pennsylvania right now?"

He exhaled hard. "You and Dawn have been seen with me, which makes you two targets. You will be perceived as soft spots in my armor and exploited as such."

"Which is a roundabout way of you saying you don't think Dawn and I will be safe if we go home," she said reluctantly.

"Exactly."

"My dad's a retired cop. I can stay with him and my mom."

"He won't cut it against these guys. They'll come at you two with a team of hit men or even military operatives."

"*Who* will?"

"Not here. Not now. Besides, we're talking about Dawn."

"After you send her away, will you do the same to me?"

Chagrin passed across his face. He *was* planning to get rid of her!

"I wish I could. But the truth is you're probably safer with me than anywhere else. I know my enemy's tactics and have been thwarting them for a long time."

He wishes he could send me away? What the hell was last night, then? Oh, wait. He doesn't get emotionally involved with anyone, does he? Not even if he has mind-blowing sex with them. He might as well have sunk a dagger in her heart in that moment. She did her best to hide her devastation, but she probably failed miserably.

"Will this place be any safer for Dawn than your condo? It's a convent, for crying out loud. It's not like they have armed guards."

"It's also an orphanage. Where better to hide a baby than among a bunch of other babies? And the convent actually does have pretty decent security. When I was a student here, my father arranged to have a state-of-the-art security system installed. Another wealthy parent updated it a few years ago. She should be fine here."

Katie hesitated. The idea of being separated from Dawn felt like having her right arm cut off and her heart torn out of her chest.

"I'll miss her, too," Alex said quietly. "But it's for her safety. And I swear it'll only be for a little while."

His phone beeped with an incoming text just then, and he fished it out of his pocket, mumbling, "I'm expecting some important news. This may be it." He glanced at his phone and a look of relief crossed his face. "I had my lawyer file an emergency custody request for Dawn this morning. The judge has agreed to make you and me Dawn's temporary guardians."

Katie's jaw dropped in both relief and shock. But then she demanded, "You made us her guardians without asking me?"

"Why?" he asked sharply. "Don't you want to be her guardian?"

"I'd adopt her today if I knew how to do it!"

"Well, there you go. Dawn doesn't have to go into the foster care system, and we can continue to care for her."

"Until we have to hide her in a convent so she doesn't get kidnapped or killed."

Alex argued, "She'd be at much more risk of being kidnapped or killed in a foster home. She has already been linked to me, remember? My enemies will go after her whether she's near me or not. As her guardians, you and I can take direct action to keep her safe, up to and including hiding her somewhere safe."

"You don't have to talk me into the benefits of being her legal guardian," Katie snapped. "I'm delighted and relieved that you took this step. I'm just unhappy that you didn't talk to me about it and that our first act as her guardians is to leave her in a convent all by herself."

"She'll hardly be by herself. Sister Mary Harris will look after her day and night if I ask her to."

Katie sighed. She had no doubt the nun would take great care of Dawn. She was just freaked out at the idea of leaving the baby. They'd been together literally since the moment of her birth. "If Dawn has to stay in this place, I want her to be with someone she knows and who cares about her."

"The nuns care about all the babies they look after."

"You know what I mean," Katie snapped.

"I do." Alex strode down the hall to the nun, and Katie followed in his wake, supremely unhappy. The nun readily agreed to look after the infant while they sorted out whoever had been in that SUV behind them In fact, Sister Mary Harris seemed relieved to do so.

Katie kissed sleeping baby Dawn goodbye on the forehead and took one last, long breath of her sweet baby smell before passing off the baby bag to the nun. Despondently, she followed Alex back out to the car. She *hated* this. But what choice did she and Alex have?

Responsible parents didn't endanger their children. Period.

Not that it had stopped or even slowed down Alex's father from being a spy. She blurted, "Do you blame your father for engaging in something as dangerous as espionage at the same time he was your only caregiver?"

He was silent for a while before replying. "I never thought of it in those terms before. But I suppose I did. A little."

Past tense? "You don't blame him anymore? Have you forgiven him then?"

"Not at all," Alex answered coldly. "I simply choose not to think about him anymore."

"Never?" she asked, surprised.

"Not as a parent. He's simply the irritating bastard who harasses me from time to time."

Wow. The thought of cutting all ties with her family, physically and emotionally, was almost as painful as leaving Dawn behind had been. The mere thought of how lonely a child Alex must have been made her heart weep. Surprised at how upset the idea made her, she wiped a stray tear off her cheek.

"Don't cry for me," Alex said sharply. "Don't *ever* do that."

"Why not?"

"I prefer that no one care for me. Saves a world of hassles to avoid emotional ties of any kind."

She stared across the interior of the car at him. "Are you serious? You don't ever want any kind of emotional ties to another human being?"

"Correct."

"Then why on God's green earth did you make yourself one of Dawn's legal guardians?"

"Being a guardian has nothing to do with being a parent. It merely means I will provide support and resources to whoever raises her."

"Bullshit," she exploded. "You promised you'd never lie to me, Alex."

He all but drove off the road, he was scowling so heavily. And then it hit her. To be honest with her, he first had to be honest with himself. He was already emotionally invested in Dawn whether he wanted to admit it to himself or not.

"It's hard, isn't it?" she asked sympathetically.

"What is?"

"Giving up your grand isolation and stepping up to being an adult—"

Something big and fast-moving slammed into her side of the car and the BMW swerved violently. A black SUV had just sideswiped them, hard. Alex stomped on the accelerator. If she thought he'd driven fast before, that was nothing compared to the way he flung the BMW around now. She braced herself grimly in her seat and held on to the bent door for dear life as he tore across the suburbs like a madman.

It took five of the most nerve-racking minutes of her life for him to lose the big vehicle, but the superior speed and agility of the German sports car finally prevailed over the clumsier SUV. Five minutes didn't sound like long to her in the context of normal life, but when someone was trying to kill her, every second seemed to last an eternity. She was silent and didn't disturb Alex's intense concentration as he drove.

Eventually, the SUV disappeared behind them and Alex decelerated once more.

"We've got to ditch my car," he bit out.

"Because the damage is too obvious?"

"No. Because whoever's after us is tracking this vehicle somehow. I checked for bugs, but they're doing something else. Watching it on satellite or tracking the onboard computers somehow."

He pulled into a long-term parking lot next to a Metro stop. And then he did a strange thing. He took the key fob off its chain and left it prominently on the dashboard in the front windshield. "Leave your door unlocked," he muttered as she jumped out of the car. He did the same and put his window down for good measure.

"Are you trying to get it stolen?" she asked, confused.

"Yes. Then our thugs can follow around the thief for a while instead of us."

Ahh. A clever misdirection. "You're good at this spy stuff," she puffed as they ran for the Metro entrance.

They slowed down once they were underground. He answered belatedly, "I bloody well ought to be good at it after the way I was raised."

"I wish I could go back in time and hug that little boy. He must have been so lost and lonely."

"You don't miss what you never had," Alex retorted.

He was right. And he'd just described Alex, the man, in a nutshell. He'd never been loved; therefore, he didn't know what he was missing out on. Her resolve to show him strengthened once more.

"Now what?" she asked as they stepped onto a

Metro train. They fell into seats as it accelerated into a dark tunnel.

"We go to ground."

We, huh? Guess she wasn't going home to Pennsylvania anytime soon. Not until people quit trying to kill Alex or get to him through her. *Good.* It would give her time to teach him what love was. Whether he liked it or not....

CHAPTER FIFTEEN

ALEX KNEW THAT spies tended to think in terms of disappearing in the underbellies of cities. Therefore, he chose to hide right out in the open among crowds of tourists. His biggest problem was that he and Katie made a strikingly attractive couple. They would be memorable. *Oh, well.* They would just have to stay in their hotel room and find a way to occupy themselves for a few days. He could think of worse fates.

First, he took her to a crowded shopping mall only a few miles from where he lived—another ploy to throw off his pursuers.... Spies never returned to home base or anywhere near it if they got burned. The two of them needed to pick up yet another emergency wardrobe.

Katie acted startled as he led her into a posh Georgetown mall and handed her a credit card. "Preloaded debit card. Untraceable, of course," he bit out.

She looked appropriately surprised, like an amateur nonspy might. Golf claps for her performance. One thing he was growingly impressed with about her act was how consistently she held up the charade. She was flawless. Not even in the throes of sex could he spot a single hint of her true motives.

"Ill-gotten gambling profits?" she asked.

"Trust fund."

"You have a trust fund, too? Man! Some people have all the luck."

That made him snort in unwilling humor. "That's me. Daddy's little financial safe haven."

"Don't put yourself down like that," she said indignantly. "You're lovable no matter what you seem to think."

"Why would I want to be lovable? Love is for normal people."

"Love is for everyone," she retorted. "And, furthermore, I'm going to prove it to you, tonight."

His libido perked up at that. "Really?" he drawled. Still hadn't given up on the seduction angle, huh? No complaints from him if she wanted to give that her best shot. He was up for the challenge.

"I'm going to slip in here and pick up a little something to help me prove my point."

His mouth curved up sardonically as he realized they were standing in front of a high-end lingerie boutique. Her instructions from the CIA had apparently been to put a full-court press on him. *Interesting. Very interesting.*

Bags in hand three hours later—how in the hell did it take women three hours to pick out a few outfits and some new underwear?—he grabbed a cab and had it take them to a hotel near the Capitol that was known for its discretion and privacy. Not only would the staff carry no tales, but he suspected the rooms were heavily soundproofed. It was a favorite rendezvous spot for politicians and their extracurricular constituents.

They checked in and ordered room service while he eyed the glossy bag from that lingerie store. What *had* she picked up? She'd been entirely secretive about it and steadfastly refused to give him a sneak preview.

He was amused when Katie insisted on ordering supper for them and made a big production out of it. It was a strange sensation to have a women fussing over him like this. He'd certainly had women pamper him over the years. Some did it for money, and some did it in pursuit of their own ulterior motives. But none of them had ever done it in the name of demonstrating love.

What was her agenda, anyway? If she was out to blackmail him, she should have picked out the hotel. Arranged for a bugged and camera-infested room. But instead she'd let him pick the hotel.

He didn't see the CIA's angle, and Lord knew Katie was brilliant at giving nothing away. He had to ride this thing through until she made a slip...or, knowing her, just came out and blurted what she wanted from him.

Hard to believe that a man of his intellect and education could be so stymied by a supposed kindergarten teacher. But then, very little about her had turned out to be simple.

"You pick," Katie announced, handing him the TV remote.

"I beg your pardon?"

"Pick what you want to watch. You spoiled me last night, so tonight, I'm spoiling you."

If only. "I usually watch financial channels or news channels."

"Go for it," she declared. "This is your night."

He idly surfed through the usual news channels for a while until Katie piped up, "Do you ever watch sports? Or manly shows that involve heavy construction equipment or repossessing stuff? My brothers like to watch cop shows and crime-solving shows or anything involving men and balls."

He couldn't help grinning at the double entendre. "I did develop a fondness for basketball in prison. The inmates played a lot of it."

She plopped down on the end of the bed closest to the armchair he sprawled in. "What exactly did you do to end up in jail? You don't strike me as the felon type."

Ahh, here we go. Probing for details about his past. This was more like it. Settling in to the comfortable world of evasion and concealment, he told her exactly what was on the public record. "I drank and drove on the New Jersey Turnpike. In a Porsche. As fast as it would go. And, yes, I know how dumb that was, and, yes, I learned my lesson. I'll never, ever do it again."

"Were you in an accident? Somebody hurt or killed?"

"No and no."

"First offense?"

"Yup."

"Then how on earth did you end up in jail? My brother's a cop, and that seems pretty extreme for a first offense."

Crap. Her and her damned family connections again. He shrugged. "I'm no innocent victim, Katie. I've done a lot of bad things I didn't get caught for. Some of them were flatly illegal. I figure my karma's about even."

"Have you ever intentionally harmed another person or taken something from someone that they personally valued?" she demanded.

"I stole those two cars in Osh."

"Those don't count. You did it to save our lives and without any malicious intent."

"I keep telling you. I'm no saint."

"There's a world of difference between an angry, lonely kid venting and a hardened criminal hurting people and wrecking lives."

He shook his head, even though he did mentally concede the point to her. "What I don't understand, Katie, is why you're trying so hard to convince *me* of how noble and wonderful a person I am. Why do you care what I think of myself?"

"In the first place, I think it's healthy for people to have a positive self-image. In the second place, I'd like you to see yourself as lovable so you won't fight the idea so damned hard of someone else loving you."

Loving him? What the hell was she up to? The only reason she would say something like that was if she planned to be his long-term handler and use sex to control him. No way was he becoming a signed, sealed and delivered CIA asset. His father would kill him within the year.

He bolted from his seat and paced the spacious room, genuinely agitated. Finally he stopped. Enunciated clearly. "Katie. I do not want love."

She stared right back at him and said just as clearly and slowly, "Yes, you do."

He stared hard at her. Was she trying to tell him something? Maybe hinting that the CIA would take him out if he didn't become their asset? Horror rattled through him. If so, he was dead either way.

He threw up his hands and said, low and urgent, "No, Katie. I don't!"

"There's not a human being alive who doesn't want to be loved. Period. It's how we're wired."

"And, yet, here I stand," he snapped. "Doing just fine without it."

Her face fell. Her cheerful countenance slipped away, and her eyes went wide and hurt and moist. "It's me, isn't it?" she mumbled. "You just don't want me to love you."

He huffed, exasperated. Dammit, he really wished she wasn't such a sincere actress. "I have nothing against you. In fact, I find you attractive, fascinating even, and pleasant to be around when you're not getting ready to cry onto my shirt."

She whirled away from him, shoulders shaking suspiciously. Okay, act or not, he was an ass. Not to mention he really couldn't afford to drive her back into the arms of her handlers until he knew her play. He stepped close behind her and rested his hands lightly on her shoulders. "I'm sorry, Katie. I told you I can be a real jackass."

She sniffed. "You're only a jackass when you're trying to push me away. And that's not your fault. No one ever taught you how to love."

In a moment of brutal honesty, he responded, "I would have to know what you're talking about to be able to respond intelligently to that observation."

Katie laughed reluctantly. Not that he understood why she thought it was funny. But it was better than tears. A knock on the door made them both start, and he gestured her urgently out of the line of fire. Only after she was lurking in the shadowed doorway to the bathroom did he open the door an inch. Waiter. Table.

He powered down and threw the door open to let in their dinner.

He tipped the guy, and Katie shooed the waiter out when the fellow would have laid out their meal. The door closed and Alex turned to face her and the table. "What's all this?"

She uncovered the plates with a flourish, and he stared, surprised. Hot dogs. And piles of French fries. Ketchup. Mustard. Cups with chili, chopped onion and shredded cheese. "I didn't know how you like your dogs, so I ordered all the trimmings."

He shrugged. "No clue. I've never eaten a hot dog."

"I knew it!" she exclaimed. "Your father raised you like a European. A stuffy one. You need to chillax. Embrace your inner American. And Americans raise eating sloppy, fattening, unhealthy food to an art form."

He watched in amazement as she popped the lids off two bottles of beer and poured them into tall, frosty mugs. She handed him one and intoned solemnly, "Look out teeth, look out gums, look out belly, here it comes."

"Am I supposed to say something in return to that, um, poetic greatness?"

"Yes. You say 'bottoms up.' And then slug some beer down."

He lifted the glass to her. "Bottoms up." He couldn't help smirking. "I gather Americans like their beer and their women the same way?"

Katie laughed and lifted her beer glass to him saucily.

She was, without question, the strangest spy he'd ever encountered. He flipped the TV channel to a basketball game and, after a little experimentation, determined that he was a chili-dog-with-onions man. They kicked off their shoes and sat on the bed with their plates propped on their knees, swigging beer and watching the game.

Whether it was the combination of manly indulgences or the sheer brainlessness of it all, Alex found himself relaxing. "I don't ever recall intentionally doing nothing," he commented. "It's interesting."

"This is the part where you flop your arm over my shoulder and we veg out together."

He did as she suggested. "What's next?"

"Well, for most people, they get a little drunk and make a pass at whoever is closest of the appropriate gender for their tastes."

"Which helps explain the proliferation of STDs in this country," he added drily.

"Beer, Doctor. You definitely need more beer," Katie declared.

At her insistence, he downed several more beers, and he had to say he saw the appeal. Hard liquor slammed a man fast, but beer crept up on a guy slowly. Gave him a little more time to bid a fond farewell to his judgment as it slipped away.

Katie turned off the lights so only the flickering glow of the basketball game lit the room. She excused herself to the restroom for a minute. When she returned, she was wearing a white silk nightgown that barely skimmed the top of her thighs. It was simple and elegant, outlining her body's curves like a seductive whisper. He had to give her credit for great taste. She managed to look sexy and classy all at once. It was a sharp departure from most of the hookers he'd ever known.

"Like it?" she asked shyly from the doorway.

"I approve."

"Really? It's not too..."

She trailed off and he replied, his voice unaccountably rough, "No matter how you were going to finish that sentence, I assure you, it's not too anything. It's perfect. You're perfect."

"Great," she said brightly. "And as for you, Dr. Peters, shirt off and on your stomach."

"Only my shirt?" he asked wryly.

"It sounded weird to tell you to strip. But naked would be better for what I have in mind."

One eyebrow cocked questioningly, he chucked off his clothes and stretched out on his stomach. A silky leg went across his thighs, and Katie straddled his buttocks. Startled, he tensed.

Her hands landed in the middle of his back, soft and warm. "You're always so tense," she murmured. "We need to fix that."

"Why? Tense equates to prepared. Alert. I like tense."

"That's because you haven't tried relaxed," she retorted.

He generally didn't like back rubs, but he had to admit this one felt pretty damned good. Maybe it was the beer that had relaxed him in the first place, or maybe it was Katie's enthusiasm for the project that was contagious. Either way, he found himself sinking into a state of blissful contentment.

She kneaded her way across his shoulders and neck, then down either side of his spine, outward across his ribs and farther down his back. She pulled down hard on his hips, stretching his back before she went to work on his glutes and hamstrings. Down his calves to his feet, and then, holy crap, she sucked his big toe. Who the hell knew a toe was such an erogenous zone? His body went on full combat alert as her hot, wet tongue laved between his toes and then sucked them one by one.

He tried to roll over, to pull her up his body, but she used her position, seated on his thighs, to pin him down. He would have tensed or maybe even attacked if she'd ever shown the slightest bit of unarmed combat training. But as it was, he subsided cautiously.

Back up his legs she went, using her mouth to supplement her clever hands this time. She kissed and licked the backs of his knees until he actually squirmed, a novel sensation for him. He was usually in the business of making women squirm. He made the mistake of groaning, and, of course, Katie giggled and redoubled her tickle torture.

She nipped up the back of his right leg, and his breath caught as her mouth slid inward toward the juncture of his thighs. Her hands pushed and he let his legs fall apart for her.

She licked the underside of his shaft, and he about came off the mattress. It didn't help that her breasts were mashed against the backs of his legs and her hands were squeezing his glutes hungrily. Her mouth closed on his sac, and she took it gently into her mouth. Heat and moisture and a gentle pulling sensation roared through him, ripping through his belly and straight back down to his erection. He was abruptly so hard and heavy it hurt.

Her tongue delicately traced the length of him again, and then it swirled around the tip until he all but shouted his frustration aloud.

"Let me up," he growled.

"Nope. Not done with my massage," she answered blithely.

She kissed everything within reach of her mouth and tongue, invading his privacy until he didn't have any left and, furthermore, didn't give a damn about it. She reversed position and her hands started up his spine and her entire body followed until she was all but lying on top of him, a delicious silken blanket of woman and sex.

Her thigh nestled between his, rubbing his man parts where her mouth had left off, while she nipped across the back of his neck to his earlobe.

Her tongue swirled into his ear—crap, another erogenous zone he'd never discovered before now— and she whispered, "I love everything about you. Your body. Your mind. Your sense of humor. Your honor. The way you keep me safe. The way you make me feel—"

That was it. He couldn't take any more. He surged up beneath her, flipping over beneath her in a quick wrestling move. Once he was able to get his arm around her, it was an easy matter to use his superior weight and strength to reverse their positions.

He realized she was grinning up at him triumphantly. Her arms were wrapped around his neck, her legs around his hips, and she held him like she wasn't ever going to let go. Something cracked in his heart as the moment burned itself into his memory for all time.

He shifted position slightly and then pressed into

her, groaning as her internal muscles gripped him as tightly as her arms and legs. He stared down at her intensely, and she gazed back at him, her smile slowly fading into something deeper. Something raw and personal and unbearably intimate as their bodies fit together and found unison.

He made love to her in slow motion, one deliberate thrust at a time. He felt every inch of her, felt every little clasp and release, registered every nuance of expression across her face. It bordered on sensory overload.

How could he have raced through this act so many times before and never stopped to notice a thousand details that made it mind-blowing? The way her lower teeth caught at her lower lip now and again. The way her chin lifted every time he seated himself all the way inside her and rocked a little. The way the arch of her feet flexed and relaxed against his lower back.

It was exquisite. And he'd never experienced anything like it. Even the scrap of silk that was her slip thing sliding between them was delicious to his heightened senses.

Eventually, though, her breathing quickened; her heels became more urgent against his back. Her hands slid down to clutch his buttocks and pull him deeper. She surged up against him, and he let her suck him into the maelstrom. He plunged into her deeper and faster, harder and more urgent.

But all the while, he stared into her eyes and she into his. He saw her gaze fill with wonder and glaze with pleasure and finally black out in the moment of her release. She came back to him slowly, her gaze refocusing in awe. Then the awe transformed into a smile that lit her entire being from the inside out. It was beautiful. *She* was beautiful. In that instant, everything was right with the world.

He was loved. And it was good.

And it was...what?

CHAPTER SIXTEEN

KATIE WATCHED HAPPINESS fill Alex's gaze, and the conscious realization that he was happy followed soon after.

But then he rolled away from her abruptly, swearing luridly in Russian if his tone of voice was any indication. In English, he demanded, "What the hell are you trying to do to me?"

"Show you what it feels like to be loved and appreciated?"

"I'm not falling for it. You can't suck me in. I *won't* be suborned."

"Suborned?" she echoed, not understanding.

"It means bribed, blackmailed or corrupted," he spat. "Surely you learned it at the Farm." He jumped out of bed and strode to the far end of the room.

The Farm? As in the famous CIA training facility? *Huh?* She wasn't CIA. She sat up, yanking her silk nightgown down as far as it would go. Why couldn't the stupid thing be a gunnysack? "I know what the word means. You already made it crystal clear you're not blackmail-able, so why would I even try?"

"You tell me." He whirled and stalked back toward her.

Why was he lashing out like this? She hadn't done anything to—

Oh. She must have scared the hell out of him. Which meant she had gotten through his carefully constructed emotional armor, after all.

"There's nothing to be scared of," she said matter-of-factly. In her experience with five-year-olds, if she sounded like there was something to be scared of, no matter how hard she tried to convince a kid not to be afraid, she would fail.

"I will not be trapped!" he exclaimed. Away he went again, pacing the length of the spacious room.

"Okay," she said reasonably. "Who's trying to trap you?"

Her question stopped him cold. He stared at her like she was crazy. "Your CIA. My father and the FSB."

"Who else?"

"What do you mean?" he demanded.

"Well, there's obviously me. Who else?"

He frowned. "You admit to trying to trap me?"

"Not at all. I'm trying to understand who *you* think is trapping you." She threw her legs over the side of the bed and stood up. She wished she could go to him. Hold him. But she highly doubted he would let her touch him right now. She said carefully, "I think it's you trapping you."

He turned to stare at her. "How's that?"

God, she wished she could read him better. But he'd gone still and frozen, his face a mask. Did he realize he was clenching his fists at his sides like that? His voice gave away nothing. Was he angry? Surprised? Upset?

"You've built so many emotional walls to hide behind, so many rules to live your life by, that you've practically paralyzed yourself."

"Wouldn't you build walls in the same situations I've lived in?"

She sincerely hoped not. "I'm not you, so what I would do doesn't really matter. You did what you had to in order to survive. And you made it. Here you are."

"I don't need psychotherapy," he announced.

"Of course you don't. You need more sex."

That threw him. He looked over at her, startled. His need for control in bed made perfect sense now. He was desperately seeking control of his life. Look at how badly he'd flipped out when she took control of their lovemaking and took it to an emotional place not of his choosing. No matter how badly he subconsciously craved the affection and caring she'd shared with him, he could not allow himself to accept it if it wasn't of his taking.

"Go ahead, Alex. Take control. Make me beg. Do whatever you want to me. I dare you."

That dark fire flared in his eyes again, and the hurt little boy retreated, leaving behind the dangerous man who made her breathing speed up and her heartbeat go wonky. "You really do like to live dangerously, don't you?" he murmured.

"Show me how dangerously," she challenged him.

He stalked her slowly, pantherlike. An urge to bolt shivered through her, but she ignored it and stood her ground. He needed this.

Alex stopped in front of her. Reached out slowly and took the low neck of her silk gown in both hands and gave it a violent yank. She jumped as the fragile silk ripped apart in his powerful hands, tearing all the way down her front and falling away from her body in shreds.

He moved aggressively, then, backing her up hard against the wall and yanking her arms high over her head. His leg jammed between hers, forcing her to ride high on his leg. His head bent to her neck, and he bit her on the shoulder.

She cried out, not in pain but pleasure. Stunned, she arched into him, intensely attracted to his aggression. It turned him on, too, apparently.

He lifted her right knee, and she draped her leg around his hips as he rammed into her, filling her with his heat and hard length. He slammed her higher against the wall and she stood on tiptoe on her remaining foot. He yanked her left leg out from under her, forcing her to cling to his shoulders and wrap her legs tightly around his waist while he supported her bottom with both hands.

The position left her completely vulnerable to him. He slammed into her again, filling her and stretching her almost to the point of pain. She had no defense against his invasion, and he took full advantage of it, thrusting again and again into her.

If she was supposed to fight him, she refused. If she was supposed to be angry at him for this rough sex, she embraced it instead. He needed this, and she willingly gave it to him. In fact, she pulled his hips closer with her legs, pulled his head down to her neck again with her arms, offering herself to him freely to devour.

He growled and increased the force and intensity of the sex, and she urged him on, opening herself fully to him both physically and emotionally.

"More, Alex," she panted. "Give me all of you. Take all of me."

He growled as if frustrated by her reaction. He spun,

carrying her still impaled on him to the table. With a sweep of his left arm he sent the plates and glasses flying, laid her down on the edge of the table and drove into her. The hard surface at her back forced her to absorb the full ferocity of his sex, and he slammed all the way to her core.

"Yes," she groaned. "More. I want it all."

"You make me crazy," he ground out from behind clenched teeth.

"I want crazier," she panted back.

He grabbed her knees and shoved them wide. She helped by grabbing them and holding them. His eyes closed as he lost himself in her body, thrusting mindlessly, over and over.

She wondered if he realized he was slowing his angry thrusts. That they were becoming more strokes than attacks, long and slow and deep. In, then out. Over and over and over.

His hands came down on either side of her head as he braced himself, eyes still closed, making love to her. She let go of her knees. Gradually let her legs wrap around his waist. Found the rhythm with her own body, rising up to meet him as their bodies joined, stroking each other to a building climax. The now familiar tingling started at her extremities, racing from her fingers and toes toward her core, growing, growing, clawing at her insides until it all exploded and she cried out with the power and glory of it.

Alex's body tightened against hers. Took on a terrible urgency. She opened her eyes and stared up at him. His face was angelic, his eyes demonic, as he stared down at her, furious and desperate and lost.

Her internal muscles clutched at him. She surged

up against him one last time, and he detonated inside her. Pleasure ripped across his face, and he shuddered hard against her, once, twice. She held him close with her body and gaze and soul, absorbing his release into her, opening herself completely to him and taking him into her in every possible way.

And as abruptly as it had started, the storm was over. His body stilled, and he stared down at her, braced with his hands on either side of her head, his arms trembling a little.

He whispered, "What are you *doing* to me?"

Adding real emotion to an act he had managed to detach from his feelings in the past? Of course, she knew better than to say that aloud. He wasn't ready to hear the truth just yet. Better that he figure it out for himself.

He stepped back from her, and she sat up on the edge of the table, a little wobbly, the remnants of her silk camisole bedraggled at her sides.

"Sorry if the table was too hard," he said dismissively.

"The table's fine," she said lightly. "Next time we do it on the table, though, could you flip me over the other way?"

His startled gaze snapped to hers. "Like on your stomach?"

She turned and half leaned over the table, testing it with her palms. "Yes. I think I'd like that. Which would be better—for me to support myself with my hands or to lie flat?"

The expression in his eyes was floored. Was that supposed to have driven her away from him? Passionate sex? Mind-blowing pleasure? A moment of intimacy he could not deny, no matter how unwilling he was to admit it had happened? She snorted at the notion. She had his number now. And she wasn't going anywhere.

Across the room, his leather computer bag dinged. He'd had it in his car and carried it into the hotel with them earlier. Curious, she watched as he pulled his laptop out and opened it.

"Sonofabitch," he breathed.

"What is it?"

"A Skype call. From my father."

"What does he want?" she asked, curious.

"More to the point, how in the hell does he have my number?" Alex demanded sharply.

"He does work for the FSB. Last time I checked, they're a reasonably competent bunch with a fair number of resources for finding out something like that."

He just rolled his eyes at her.

"You gonna take the call?" she asked.

He stared at the screen for several long seconds before saying slowly, "Yes, I think I will."

She was relieved. She'd been raised on the theory that it was always better to know what your enemy was up to than to be in the dark about his actions.

Alex typed in a password and initiated the call while she dived for the bathroom and clothes.

Peter Koronov said something in Russian, and Alex replied in English, "I'm surprised, too. What do you want, Peter?"

He didn't call his father "Father"? *Ouch.*

Koronov answered, in accent-free, American English, "I was just checking to be sure that you and your little family made it home safely."

Alex answered drily, "You know by now that they are not my family, but rather a coworker and an orphaned infant. And as you can see, I am perfectly fine. If that's all you wanted, I'll sign off—"

"Alexei," his father said sharply.

Katie grinned as she zipped up her jeans. *So.* That was where Alex had learned that particular tone of voice. She slipped into the main room, being sure to stay out of the laptop camera's line of sight.

Koronov was speaking again. "I did you a favor and sent you that airplane. Now I need a favor from you in return. A small one that breaks no laws."

Alex leaned back from the screen. "How small?" he asked blandly.

She didn't have to see Alex's face to know the dark, angry predator would be flashing in his gaze. She could feel the danger rolling off him all the way over there.

"I need some information. A list of all the places your employer has medical teams deployed."

Her jaw sagged. Peter Koronov wanted Alex to spy on Doctors Unlimited? *Why?* What did it mean about D.U. that the FSB was poking around it?

Alex asked, "Tell me something first. What do you know about a pair of SUVs that engaged me earlier today?"

God, she wished she could see Koronov's face from there. But it was best that he not know Alex's "little family" was more than just a coworker and a random kid.

Koronov's voice was even, calm, when he replied, "Nothing. Do you need me to look into it?"

Alex frowned faintly. Thoughtfully. He believed

Peter? Then who *was* that in those SUVs? She'd privately assumed they were Russian intelligence. "A list of places D.U. has teams? That's all?"

Alex wasn't seriously considering getting Peter that list, was he?

"Names would be helpful, as well. Our government wouldn't want to accidentally interfere with their work for lack of recognizing them. Now, would it?"

"No. Of course not," Alex answered deadpan.

"How soon can you have it?"

"And then we're even?" Alex responded, ignoring the question.

"Is there any such thing?" Peter asked wryly.

Alex ignored that, too. "I'll contact you when I have it."

"Good boy." If she wasn't mistaken, Peter sounded faintly surprised. He bloody well should be. His son had just agreed to freaking spy on an American charity for him!

She waited impatiently for the call to disconnect. Alex had barely closed his laptop when she burst out, "What in the *hell* are you doing? Aren't you the one who's all hot and bothered not to get trapped? It sounds to me like you just ran headlong into your father's totally obvious trap!"

CHAPTER SEVENTEEN

HIS HEART BROKE a little. There it was. The slip from her that he'd been waiting for. She'd leaped too fast to D.U.'s defense when he'd pretended that he would help his father spy on the organization. Now he knew the play. The CIA had some sort of connection to the charity group and would run him as a spy from behind the cover of the aid organization.

Alex thought quickly. His best bet now was to turn her. Use her to his own ends. He stood up casually and moved over to his clothes strewn on the floor. Bent down and picked up his pants. Pulled them on. Zipped them. Reached for his shirt. Draped it across the back of a chair. Smoothed the fine cotton a little. He wasn't a professional actor, but a stellar performance was called for now.

"Well?" Katie demanded angrily.

He looked up at her grimly. "I grew up with that man. I know when not to cross him. He opened the call by referring to you and Dawn. Don't you see? He was threatening the two of you. I get him his list, or he comes after the two of you."

Katie's outrage deflated like a balloon with the air let out of it fast. "But, Alex, it's treason to spy."

"It's not treason to lift information from a private

company. Doctors Unlimited is not a government-sponsored organization."

"It's still theft."

"Hey, if the Russians merely want the information so they can stay out of our people's hair, where's the harm in that?"

"Seriously?" Katie's outrage was back, and she was magnificent in her fury. *Excellent.* He was counting on her blind patriotism to drive her response to him.

He shrugged. "It's no big deal. I just slip into André Fortinay's office, copy the master deployment list off his computer and forward it to my father. No harm, no foul. It doesn't hurt anybody at D.U. My father gets off my case for a while. And most importantly, you and Dawn are left alone."

The ends-justifies-the-means argument appeared to give Katie pause. But just for a moment. "It's *wrong,*" she said forcefully.

"Information like this has no cash value. I wouldn't even be charged with theft. Industrial espionage involves proprietary information that's vital to a moneymaking process or venture."

"You could still be charged with breaking and entering."

"I work there and have legal access to the offices. All I have to do is walk in. No breaking required to enter, babe."

"I cannot believe you're being so cavalier about this! I thought better of you."

Okay, that stung. But this was necessary. He had to goad her to action. Mentally, he cursed his father for pushing him into this corner. He'd thought there for a while that he was finally out from under his father's iron fist. Peter had mostly left him alone since he got out of prison, and he'd been praying Daddy dearest had gotten the memo when his son chose to go to jail rather than work for him. But no. The bastard was back, full-force, jerking him around and screwing up everything good in his life. Just like he always had.

A wave of despair washed over Alex, so deep and dark he couldn't breathe beneath its weight. This must be what drowning was like. It was a weak emotion he refused to give in to, but damn. Would the man never leave him alone? Would he never get a shot at happiness for himself?

The emotional connection Katie was offering him tempted him like no other vice he'd ever been exposed to. He could get addicted to her so easily. A little more time. A little more bonding—over Dawn, over their shared work—the two of them could have had it all. *And then along came Peter,* he thought bitterly. Now all that was left for him to do was finish destroying what Peter had just told him in no uncertain terms to wreck or else be forever vulnerable to his father's manipulations. He mentally cursed his father to hell and back.

Alex looked over at Katie coldly. "I already told you I'm no saint. This is the practical reality of my life. I walk a tightrope between men like your uncle and men like my father. It's not pretty, but it's how I stay alive. Deal with it or get out of my way."

Odd that it actually hurt to say those words. He examined the pain from any number of angles. Intriguing. Disturbing. Just how far gone was his heart to her? To the concept of a normal life that included family? And that love thing?

He tried to imagine never seeing Dawn again and thanked his lucky stars he'd already nailed down shared guardianship of the infant. Katie couldn't legally prevent him from seeing Dawn and being part of her life as she grew up. And if he remained part of Dawn's life, he would, perforce, remain part of Katie's. No matter how angry she was with him now, he could win her back. He always got his way in the end. Superior intellect, patience and cunning always prevailed, after all.

"If dealing and getting out of your way are my only choices," Katie declared, "I'm out."

"What?" he blurted in spite of his resolve to do this thing.

"I'm out. I thought I was getting through to you. Making a difference. That we had something special going. But I don't sleep with criminals."

"Getting the list is not criminal!"

"Maybe. But it's not *right*."

She was absolutely correct. But he wasn't about to tell her that. She was almost there. Almost ready to spite him. He would never, ever forgive his father for making him do this. Grimly, he pounded in the final nail into his own coffin. He steeled himself and managed a casual shrug. "Fine. If that's how you feel—get out."

She stared at him for a long minute. Long enough for her rage to melt. Long enough for her eyes to fill with tears. Long enough for him to call himself every foul name he could think of for doing this to her. But what choice did he have? He *had* to stay on the tightrope. And he had to get her to step off it. He had no net to catch either of them.

KATIE PICKED UP her purse and walked out of their hotel room. And he didn't stop her. She ignored the smirk a bellboy threw her as she crossed the lobby. The kid no doubt thought she was a hooker done with a job. Screw him. Her heart had just broken in a million sharp-edged pieces. Couldn't the kid see her bleeding out from the cuts?

She could *not* believe Alex would steal the list of names and places for his father. He hated Peter! She'd stormed out of the hotel and asked the doorman to hail her a cab before it occurred to her that family relationships weren't necessarily simple things. It was entirely possible that, as much as Alex claimed to hate his father, he also craved his father's approval. Maybe even his father's love.

She had, in fact, established tonight that Alex did appreciate and want love in spite of his big words to the contrary. Maybe he wanted his father to love him, too—

Dammit, she was not going to make excuses for Alex! It was wrong to steal that list, and that was all there was to it. But Lord, it hurt to realize that she hadn't gotten through to him.

Her mother had always said it was folly to try to change a man, but Katie had really thought she could save Alex from the darkness within himself. He'd seemed to want her to save him at some fundamental level of his being. How could she have read him so very wrong? It shook her confidence in her ability to understand people. Heck, it shook her confidence in people. She'd been so sure, deep down in her heart, that Alex was a good man. Until this abrupt and complete about-face from him proved her so terribly wrong.

It hurt now, but she suspected it would hurt more and for a very long time before she got over him. If she ever got over him. How could she ever look at Dawn and not see him? Her arms ached to hold the baby. Her baby.

She looked at her watch. It was after 10:00 p.m. Too late to visit the convent, darn it. But there was one other thing she could take care of tonight. Now, while she was still angry and the hurt hadn't taken over her soul. She had to do it before her resolve faltered.

She scrolled through her cell phone and found André Fortinay's emergency cell phone number. All D.U.'s field staff had the number.

He answered right away. "'Allo?" The faint French accent was noticeable in his voice tonight.

"André? I'm sorry to bother you this late. It's Katie McCloud. We have a problem…."

ALEX SANK INTO the armchair as the door shut behind Katie. He felt…empty. When would he ever learn? It was always this way when he was a kid. If he found something to love—a teddy bear or a stray cat or even a friend from school—his father tore it away from him. Told him to be tough. To have no feelings. Discipline his mind. How was the bastard still doing it to him?

No, wait. He was doing it to himself now. Alex swore violently as he grabbed a little bottle of whiskey out of the refrigerator and downed it in a single gulp. These minibottles weren't going to cut it. He called downstairs and had the bar send up a fifth of their best, with a fat tip if it could be there in five minutes or less.

The bottle was delivered and he took a healthy gulp. Better. He was getting plastered off his ass and praying oblivion lay in wait at the bottom of this bottle.

KATIE SAT IN a chair in the motel room she'd hastily found and checked into across town, as far from Alex as the Metro would take her. She stared at the gray carpet, her mind blank. She'd done it. She'd betrayed Alex. Gone behind his back and warned André Fortinay that Alex was planning to steal his master list of staff and their postings abroad.

The Frenchman's reaction had been odd. He'd seemed almost amused that Alex had told her what he planned to do. Of course, he'd been grateful for the heads-up, but he hadn't been nearly as alarmed at the moral breakdown in one of his doctors as she would have expected. He'd questioned her in some detail regarding Peter's phone call, what Alex had said afterward about the call and his decision to do what his father asked. Come to think of it, that had been about the time André started to chuckle.

There was nothing funny about this situation! It sucked. She'd just lost a man she'd been falling for hard. Lost him to his grasping father and to the dark urgings of his wounded soul. How in the hell was she supposed to compete with those? Apparently, the answer was that she couldn't win. Blood ran deep in families. Of all people, she knew that.

She sat there for a long time before finally crawling into bed and passing out.

Her cell phone's loud ring yanked her out of a dark dream sometime the next morning. She dove for the phone, heart racing. *Let it be Alex. Let it be Alex.*

Private caller.

She slammed the phone to her ear. "Alex?"

"Hi, honey. It's Mom. And who's this Alex fellow you're so breathlessly eager to talk to?"

Katie's heart dropped to her feet, and she sat down heavily on the edge of the bed. "Hi, Mom." She glanced at her bedside clock. Not even 8:00 a.m. yet." *Ugh.* "Why are you calling me so early?"

"Uncle Charlie called. Imagine my surprise when I found out you were back home and didn't give me a call to let me know you're safe."

"I'm sorry. It's been really crazy since I got back. I was going to call you, but I haven't had time."

"Not one single minute to let me know you're okay? I was worried about you, sweetie."

Katie scowled. "You don't make the boys call you every time they get back from a mission. And don't tell me they're boys and can take care of themselves, whereas I'm a weak, silly girl who can't do anything for herself."

Her mother chuckled. "That's what your father would say, honey. Not me. I raised you to be a strong, independent woman. And I do make your brothers call me whenever they get home. They're just embarrassed to admit it."

Katie smiled reluctantly. Her mother was barely five foot three and could kick butts and take names if her big, bad sons didn't do as she asked of them.

"Why are you calling me so early, Mom?"

"Mike's home. Apparently, he got hurt on his last trip and he's in a hospital in Washington, D.C. Charlie said you're in the Washington area, and I thought you might check in on your big brother for me. Your dad and I are driving down today, but in the meantime, Mike might like to see a familiar face."

"What hospital is he in?"

"Walter Reed facility in Bethesda. Do you know it?"

"Heard of it. I'll figure out where it is and go see what Mikey's got himself into now."

"Thanks, sweetie. How about Dad and I meet you at the hospital this afternoon? We can do dinner and you can tell us all about your trip to that something-stan place."

"That would be great."

She tried to go back to sleep, but she was wide-awake after the call. She gave up and got out of bed, showered and dressed. The motel front desk helped her find a car rental place, and an hour later, she was headed north to Chevy Chase and Dawn.

Sister Mary Harris was chipper when she came out to meet Katie in the waiting area. Even better, she was carrying a bundled pink blanket in her arms. Dawn was sleeping, but Katie didn't care and held the baby close, cooing over her and cuddling her.

"I've missed you so much, honey bunny," she whispered.

"She's a good baby," the nun reported. "Eats and sleeps like a champ and has a sunny personality."

"That's my girl," Katie murmured.

"How's Alex?" the nun asked without warning.

A shadow crossed Katie's heart, and she looked up at the nun sadly. "Not great. His father called him last night and wanted him to do something…unethical… for him. Alex agreed to do it."

Sister Mary Harris sat down on a stone bench and

gestured for Katie to sit beside her. "That man has always had his hooks deep into his son. You have to understand—Alex had no one else. His father isolated him from other children and other people. Made the boy totally dependent on him. You could even say he brainwashed young Alex."

"So you're saying Alex can't say no to his father?"

The nun sighed. "Alex said no plenty. Peter just made him pay every time he did. Alex used to come to school beaten black and blue."

Katie gulped.

"Any time we asked him about his bruises, Alex always claimed it was martial arts training or boxing lessons. And maybe it truly was." She added gently, "But maybe it wasn't."

Katie spoke with quiet desperation. "The thing Peter asked Alex to do last night isn't strictly illegal, yet it's morally wrong. But Alex said he would do it anyway. I lost him. I thought I was getting through to him, but I failed."

"The Lord doesn't give up on anyone the first time they fail, child. And that boy may do more illegal and immoral things before it's all said and done. But I believe in my heart that he wants to be a good person and is doing everything in his power to become a good person."

"You're saying I'm giving up on him too easily?"

The nun shrugged. "I learned long ago never to tell people what to do. You have to look inside your own heart and listen to the urgings of that small, quiet voice deep down inside you. You must do what you think is best for you. And for Dawn."

Katie exhaled hard. "I don't approve of what Alex is doing."

"That's what you think of him. What do you feel about him?"

A tear splashed onto Dawn's fuzzy blanket and trembled there delicately. "I think I'm falling in love with him a little." She added in a rush, "But that's not enough. I have to be able to trust him, to believe in him, to respect him, if we're going to build a life together."

"A family," the nun murmured.

"Exactly. I need a good man to raise Dawn with me. Not someone with no moral compass and living under the control of a monster."

The nun threw her a sympathetic look and closed her eyes, launching into silent prayer. Katie sat quietly beside the nun, absorbing the love and concern and compassion the elderly woman radiated.

Had she reacted rashly? Judged Alex too harshly? Given up on him too quickly? Remorse for that angry phone call last night to André Fortinay poured through her. What was done was done, though. She'd sabotaged Alex, and she couldn't take it back. She had no idea if he would even let her try to make amends to him. He'd been so angry last night. So cold and hard after the call from his father.

Sister Mary Harris commented reflectively, "I never thought I'd see Alex feed a baby a bottle comfortably, but he did that. And I never thought I'd see him let a woman spend the night with him, either."

Katie's gaze whipped to the nun, and her cheeks heated up. She blurted unwillingly, "You do know he's been with lots of women, right?"

The nun laughed gaily. "Of course I do."

Katie's jaw dropped. She could not believe she was having girl talk with an eighty-year-old nun.

"I'm not dead, you know. And just because I took a vow not to have sex doesn't mean I'm not aware that it exists."

"Umm. Wow. Okay," Katie mumbled.

The nun chuckled and patted her knee. "You're good for him. Better than any woman I've ever seen him with. Not that he actually has had any actual relationships with women. You're the only who's ever stuck around long enough to catch a glimpse of the real man."

"Yeah. And he does bad things and drove me away from him without batting an eyelash."

"Mark my words. He's batting an eyelash."

If he was, he bloody well wasn't letting her see it. Dawn woke and started to fuss as the telltale odor of a diaper in need of a change became evident.

"Let me take her, child. Just do me one favor, Katie, dear."

"What's that?"

"Think about it before you give up on Alex."

Katie climbed in her little rental car and sat in the parking lot of the convent for several long minutes. Was Sister Mary Harris right? Had she overreacted? Not given Alex a break he deserved? Hope fluttered in her breast like a bird trying to fly, and it was nearly impossible to think clearly around the emotion. One thing was for sure. She'd fallen hard for him and was way more invested in him emotionally than she'd realized before she'd walked out on him.

In a thoughtful frame of mind, she punched the address of Mike's hospital into the GPS and drove out of the parking lot. She was maybe halfway there when she finally started to be aware of her surroundings again. Had that red sedan been behind her when she'd pulled out of the convent's parking lot? She recalled seeing a car like that back in Chevy Chase. What were the odds it was going the exact same direction she was for so long?

Traffic thinned as she exited the Beltway onto surface streets. The red car exited behind her. She shot through a yellow light and was dismayed to see the car run the red light behind her, causing a flare of honking horns. She was being followed!

She was nowhere near the driver Alex was, and this subcompact car was no German sports car. She didn't stand a chance of losing the tail. What was the harm in someone knowing she'd gone to a hospital to visit a patient?

Goodness knew, Mike could take care of himself if anyone tried to mess with him. Last she'd heard, he worked for some superclassified military Special Ops group that operated way, way off the books. He was not a guy anyone should mess with in a dark alley.

Vividly aware of the tail behind her, Katie kept her driving as normal as possible until she pulled into the hospital's parking garage. The place was crammed, and she was forced to wind deeper and deeper into the underground structure in search of a parking spot. Finally, she found one at the very lowest level of the garage. She wedged into the space and got out, heading for the elevator in the claustrophobic gloom.

The man came out of nowhere. He wore a ski mask and made no secret of his intent to mug her. She held out her purse and started yelling for help. The guy batted her bag away as he charged her. His shoulder barreled into her, spinning her around. She slammed into a car and its alarm went off, blaring deafeningly. Not that anyone would come check it out way down here.

A fist connected hard with her jaw, snapping her head back and making her see stars. But she hadn't had five brothers for nothing. She lashed out with her foot, connected with the guy's shin so hard her toes shouted in pain.

She shouted, "Fire!" at the top of her lungs and prayed someone was within earshot and would come investigate.

Her attacker snarled wordlessly and slugged her in the stomach so hard it felt like something exploded inside her. She doubled over with a *whoof* of pain, right into the uppercut to the same spot on her jaw as before. He head snapped to the side. The concrete floor came up at her quickly, and that was the last thing she remembered.

CHAPTER EIGHTEEN

ALEX BLINKED, HALF-AWAKE, as his cell phone rang somewhere close by. His head was splitting in two. He pulled a pillow over his head to muffle the damned phone until it stopped ringing. Except even after the caller gave up, the ringing continued in his ears.

He rolled over to pass out again until his hangover abated.

The phone rang again.

Go away, whoever you are. As if he had to guess who it was. Katie.

The phone commenced ringing a third time.

Irritated all to hell, he rolled over on his back and slapped the nightstand with his outstretched hand. Groped around. Found the flat shape of his phone.

"Leave me the fuck alone," he snarled. "I told you, this is how I roll."

"I believe you've mistaken me for someone else, Mr. Peters."

Crap. Male voice. Formal. Unfamiliar. "Who is this?" he demanded.

"Charles McCloud. I thought you might like to know that Katie has been admitted to a hospital. She was attacked a little while ago."

Alex sat bolt upright and cursed as his head exploded and his gut revolted. *Holy shit. Katie.* Heading fast for the toilet, he bit out, "What hospital?"

"Walter Reed, Bethesda."

"Thanks." He disconnected the call so Katie's uncle wouldn't hear him puking up last night's whiskey. He ran cold water in the sink and stuck his head under it just long enough to drive the spikes out of his eyeballs. He toweled his hair as he raced around the room picking up and pulling on his discarded clothes. Keys. Where were his keys, dammit?

He snatched up his phone and wallet and ran down the hall for the elevator that a family was currently climbing into. He barely caught the thing and slipped inside. The parents eyed him warily as they rode down in silence. He must look like shit. *Tough.*

Katie was hurt. How bad was it? Who'd attacked her? Why in the hell had a high-ranking CIA official called to tell him? Had the CIA jumped her to get at him?

Head spinning, he climbed into his car and headed for the northwest D.C. suburb of Bethesda. What time was it, anyway? The car clock said nearly 10:00 a.m. When was Katie attacked? Last night? Had she lain somewhere alone for hours until someone found her? How bad was she hurt? Why hadn't she called him? The more questions he asked himself, the worse his head throbbed. The low-level hum of panic in his gut wasn't helping matters one bit, either.

Damn, he was out of practice at drinking. He'd forgotten how nasty he felt the day after. Time was when he hadn't cared if he felt like this. But today of all days, he wished his head was clearer, that he was in better shape to help Katie. He forced himself to pay attention to the cars behind him, to catalogue makes and models in a running list as vehicles came and went behind him. As far as he could tell in his debilitated state, he wasn't followed.

He rushed into the emergency room and went to the check-in desk. "Katie McCloud?" he bit out.

"You family?" the nurse asked briskly.

"Yes," he answered without hesitating. "How is she?"

"Come with me."

He followed the nurse through a set of swinging doors and down a hallway. "What happened?" he asked tersely.

"She was mugged in our parking garage. Lucky for her, someone found her pretty quickly."

"Have the police been called?"

"Don't know. I just work here."

"How bad is she hurt?"

"Contusions. Swelling. Was unconscious when they brought her in."

Unconscious? He'd kill whoever did this to her. He asked grimly, "Was she sexually assaulted?"

"Her clothing was intact when they brought her in."

Praise the Lord. "Purse missing?" he asked.

"No. It was on her shoulder. She must have fought the guy off until someone showed up to scare him off."

Either that or her mugging was no mugging at all. He *knew* the bastards from both intelligence services wouldn't hesitate to use her to get to him. This was *exactly* why his father had always preached never to get involved with anyone. Loved ones, even friends, were a liability a man like him could not afford.

He rounded the corner into a small room and

stopped in the doorway. Katie looked so pale and helpless tucked underneath a pile of blankets that his gut tightened in quick concern. A butterfly bandage on her left jaw covered a nasty lump. A scrape on her right forehead looked like sidewalk burn. She'd hit the ground, right there.

"Concussion?" he muttered over his shoulder to the nurse.

"Likely."

"Other injuries?"

"Internist will be in shortly."

He sat down on the edge of the bed and was alarmed at how slowly Katie's eyes fluttered open. "Hey, beautiful," he murmured. "I hear you tried to go a few rounds with a bad guy."

"What are you doing here?" she asked weakly.

"Your uncle called me."

A faint frown puckered her brow. "How'd he know?"

Alex shrugged. *Good damned question.* But he just smiled gently at Katie. "How do you feel?"

"About like you look."

His smile widened. There was the ol' McCloud spunk. "Can I get you anything?"

"An industrial-strength painkiller for my headache would be lovely. And a glass of water. I'm thirsty."

She would not be allowed to have anything to eat or drink until surgery was ruled out, but he didn't tell her that. A doctor stepped in just then and introduced himself briefly. "Well, young lady, your MRI shows no internal damage. Other than a mild concussion and that goose egg on your jaw, I'd say you're going to live.

Bet you'd like a painkiller long about now, though, wouldn't you? Are you allergic to any medications?"

"No."

"I'll have the nurse bring you something. Bland foods for twenty-four hours, and someone needs to stay with you around the clock for the next few days. Will that be you, sir?"

"Yes," Alex answered firmly. "And I'm familiar with concussion aftercare. I'm a physician."

"Perfect. We'll get her release paperwork going, then, and you'll be out of here, Miss McCloud."

"I don't need you to babysit me, Alex."

"Apparently, you do. Twelve hours by yourself and you end up in the emergency room."

She started to scowl, but it turned into a wince that seemed to derail her irritation.

Alex expedited her release—it helped that he was a doctor himself and could casually write a check for her medical expenses. Before long an orderly had pushed her out to the front exit.

The painkiller must be starting to take effect because Katie asked impatiently, "Can I please walk now?"

"Okay, now," the orderly finally said.

Alex jumped forward to help her to her feet, and she frowned hard at him. "I'm not helpless. My brothers have slugged me that hard by accident, and I just fell and hit my head. I'll be fine."

He refrained from listing the possible complications resulting from blows to the head and tucked her hand under his arm protectively. "You're coming back to my place."

"I need to see my brother first."

"Where's your brother?"

"Somewhere in this hospital. I was here to visit him."

Right. She'd been attacked in the hospital's parking garage. He was losing his touch, having failed to wonder why she'd been there in the first place. He wasn't *that* hungover. Or maybe he *was* that distracted by his worry for her.

They turned around and approached the hospital's information desk. He cut through the red tape briskly. "I'm Dr. Peters. I'm here to see a patient named McCloud."

"Michael McCloud," Katie supplied.

The receptionist answered promptly, "Third floor. Room 3017." It was good being a doctor sometimes.

Katie leaned against the elevator wall, and an urge to put an arm around her nearly overcame him. He frowned. Was he playing into the CIA's hands by feeling so protective of her?

They stepped out of the elevator and found her brother's room without too much trouble. "I'll wait outside," he said quietly.

"Come on in and meet one of the famous McCloud boys."

He followed her into the room and stopped in shock as he spied the man lying in the bed.

"You?" Michael McCloud demanded. "What the hell are *you* doing here?" He started to surge upright but subsided abruptly and lay back against his semi-inclined pillows, pressing a hand to his belly.

Damndamndamndamndamn. The guy he'd stabbed in Zaghastan had been her *brother?*

Katie was looking back and forth between the two of them in confusion. "You've met?" she asked.

Alex answered reluctantly, "You might say that."

"He's the fucker who stabbed me!" her brother exclaimed.

Katie whirled on him, wincing in pain as she did so. "You *stabbed* my brother?"

"Obviously, I didn't know who he was. He was the guy following us on that four-wheeler in Zaghastan. I jumped him and he pulled a knife on me. So, yeah, I stabbed him."

Her jaw dropped, and burgeoning outrage sparked in her bright blue eyes.

He added quickly, "In my own defense, I did treat his wound and save his life."

"But you stabbed him!"

"He attacked me. Of course I stabbed him. We were in the middle of a war zone and people were trying to kill us. He came at me with a knife, and I fought back. I'm not going to apologize for that."

"Get out," she snapped.

Okay, he probably deserved that. But she had a concussion of her own to deal with.

"Out. Now!" She was getting agitated, which wasn't great for her head. He threw up his hands and backed out of the room. But he went no farther than the nurse's station a few steps away. He begged a bottle of over-the-counter pain meds and downed a handful of the painkillers dry.

How in the hell was he going to make this right? He really hadn't borne any ill will toward her brother. It had been just business. War was violent and bloody. Kill or be killed. He'd actually shown extraordinary mercy in not killing the guy. By rights, she ought to be thanking him. But she wouldn't see it that way. He'd done the right thing—again—and again he wasn't going to get any credit for it.

Life really sucked sometimes.

In the meantime, he would head down to the parking garage to see if he could figure out who'd attacked her and if it had been a message to him.

KATIE MOVED TO her brother's side in concern. "What happened to you?"

"I was about to ask you the same thing. That bastard Koronov rough you up? I'll be happy to kill him for you."

"I was mugged. I'll be fine. Mild concussion and a few bumps. Nothing worse than you louts did to me as a kid."

"We never meant to hurt you. But you insisted on tagging along all the damned time and getting in the way."

She smiled crookedly at her big brother. "Yeah, I know. I was a pest."

"Cute pest."

"So, why are you in this joint, big guy?"

"Your boyfriend stabbed me. Damn near killed me, too, the bastard."

Katie frowned. Alex had nearly killed Mike? Her brother was literally a trained killer. She didn't know the details, but she'd heard bits and pieces of quiet conversation between her brothers now and then. And they all thought Mike was one serious badass.

"Did Alex catch you by surprise?" she asked, confused.

"Yeah. Ambushed me. And when I pulled a knife, he nailed me."

"Where'd you get poked?"

"Right here." He pointed to a spot just below his ribs on the left side of his stomach. So, he'd been facing Alex when he got stabbed. Which meant Mike had a chance to defend himself, and Alex had still gotten the drop on her brother? *Whoa.*

She knew Alex's father had trained the crap out of him, but she'd had no idea just how lethally he was trained until this very second. No wonder Alex was a head case. He'd never asked for any of that training. It had been forced on a little boy with no say in the matter. She really was starting to hate Peter Koronov. At least she'd thwarted the guy's attempt to get that list of D.U. staffers. Satisfaction coursed through her.

"Why didn't you tell me you were going to Zaghastan, too?" she demanded.

"Didn't know I was coming out to your neck of the woods to play until after you'd left and gone off the grid."

A few weeks ago, she'd have bought that line without question. But now, her lie detector antenna wiggled. He'd known roughly where she would be. It would have taken a single phone call to D.U. to find out where she was. They wouldn't have hesitated to tell him where to find his baby sister and look in on her, right?

She'd played a whole lot of poker for toothpicks with Mike over the years and knew his tells. It took her about two seconds to become convinced he was being evasive with her. Why wouldn't he be square with her? Did it have to do with protecting a cover for his job, or was it something else? Something he didn't want to admit? What had he been doing out there at the end of the world? For that matter, why had he pulled a knife on Alex?

"What took you to greater downtown Zaghastan, bro?"

"Work."

She rolled her eyes. "What kind of work?"

"Classified work."

"C'mon, Mike. I'm not a kid. I know what's going on in that region. Don't bullshit me. What were you doing?"

He shrugged a little under the bandages swathing his torso. "Observing."

"So you weren't one of the military types dressed up to look like rebels?"

His laser-sharp gaze snapped to hers, and his voice dropped to an urgent murmur. "What do you know about that?"

"Only what I saw with my own two eyes. Those 'rebels' were way too well armed to be locals. I know a trained soldier when I see one. I grew up with you guys, remember? Those supposed rebels were Spec Ops types."

He sighed. "Could you keep that to yourself? It's highly classified information."

She shrugged. "I'm just a civilian translator. A kindergarten teacher on a humanitarian trip abroad. Who's gonna ask me about something like that? Your secret's safe with me."

He snorted skeptically. "Not as long as you're hanging around with that guy. He's trouble."

It was her turn to snort. "Yeah, I noticed."

"Stay away from him, Katie. He's a big shark and you're a tiny little minnow."

God, she hated it when her brothers said things like that to her. It was just that kind of dismissal of her that had made her take the Zaghastan gig in the first place. "I'll let you get some rest. Mom and Dad are driving down to see you today. They'll be here this afternoon." On that note she let herself out of Mike's room.

She did not relish the interrogation her parents would subject her to when they saw her injuries and, moreover, when they heard she was hanging out with the guy who'd stabbed her brother. She didn't even need to hear that tirade to wince.

"You okay?" Alex asked in concern from nearby. She supposed she wasn't surprised he was still out there, waiting for her. Reluctant gratitude flowed through her.

"I was thinking about having to face my parents this evening."

"If it's what put that look of pain on your face, don't do it. Come to my place and rest."

"I thought you were avoiding your place."

He shrugged. "Everyone seems to know I'm involved with you, and they all know where I live, anyway. I'd rather be surrounded by known security measures and force the hostiles to come at me head-on if they're going to make a run at you."

"What about Dawn?"

"She's in a safe place."

"But I'm pretty sure the guy who jumped me followed me from the convent. I think they're using Dawn as bait to find us."

"All the more reason to let them find us when we're

nowhere near her," he ground out. "No one messes with me and mine without suffering the consequences." His expression was blacker and colder than she'd ever seen it. And yet it sent a frisson of warmth through her. If only that expression wasn't just for Dawn and he felt a little bit like that for her, too.

"I can't believe you stabbed my brother. Explain to me why you did it again?"

"He posed a threat to you and Dawn. He attacked me. I defended myself." He added grimly, "And not only spared his life, but saved it."

He sounded like he didn't expect her to believe him. Thing was, Mike didn't say anything to contradict that story. And Mike was incredibly tough. It wasn't like Alex picked on an innocent civilian. Something in the wall of anger she'd built up in her heart overnight cracked just a little.

He ushered her into his car in silence and pulled out into traffic. The tension in the rental vehicle was thick enough to cut with a knife. God, she hated this. Why wouldn't he let down his emotional guard with her anytime other than in bed?

She asked, "Do you know why special operators would be in the Karshan Valley posing as rebel soldiers?"

"Nope. If I did, then I could identify who they were and figure out who's screwing with us now."

They were almost to his place when her cell phone dinged an incoming email. She pulled it out of her purse and was startled to see the sender was Uncle Charlie. She opened the attached file and a short list of names scrolled down her phone.

"Who is it?" Alex asked tersely.

"It's the list from Uncle Charlie of outsiders in the Karshan Valley nine months ago," she announced.

Alex glanced over at her alertly. "Care to share?"

"Sure."

"Once we're inside and can't be overheard," he murmured as he parked the car.

"Paranoid much?" she quipped.

"I just got you out of the emergency room. Indulge me."

He did look pretty frazzled, now that he mentioned it. "Were you worried when you heard I was there?" she blurted.

He stopped in the act of closing her door and looked her square in the eye. "I've never been more terrified in my entire life."

Wow. At a loss for words, she followed him up to his condo in silence. In short order, he installed her on the living room sofa with a pile of pillows behind her and a blanket over her lap. Not until he handed her a bowl of chicken noodle soup, and made her down part of it, would he let her talk business again. His fussing over her made her alternately want to cry and scream. The guy was a doctor, for God's sake. Wasn't he supposed to feel compassion for his fellow man? Shouldn't that mean he was able to share his feelings with her? Surely his father hadn't burned all the feelings completely out of him. Nobody who felt nothing made love as passionately as Alex did. She wanted to grab him by the shoulders and shake him until he quit acting like a damned robot.

He startled her out of her thoughts by announcing, "Okay, let's see Uncle Charlie's list."

She'd read the list over and over in the car until she

had it memorized. Ten names were on it. She passed him her cell phone.

"Care to tell me why your brother's on this list?"

"He told me today he was in the area acting as a military observer."

"Hmm."

"What are you thinking?" she asked quickly. The combination of his intelligence training and raw brainpower could be leading him to all kinds of conclusions she wouldn't see in the list.

"The CIA informant—that's this guy here—and your brother are no surprise. But who's this guy, Archaki?"

"A Russian, I guess."

"Not Russian. Archaki is a Ukrainian name. So are these three. What do you want to bet they were traveling together?"

"Makes sense. But I'm only a kindergarten teacher, remember?"

"You can drop that act with me," he snapped. "We both know what you are."

She leaned back, stung. *What the heck does that mean?*

He stared at her hard, his mind obviously working in overdrive. Indecision crossed his face but gave way to irritation. He swore under his breath and pulled out his cell phone. He chose a number and she was startled at the lengthy series of numbers his phone dialed. *An overseas call?*

"It's me. Yes, I know what time it is in Moscow. No, I don't have the D.U. list yet. I'm working on it. Who's Yevgeny Archaki?"

Holy crap, he'd called his father. Was he so eager to

find Dawn's father and foist the baby off on the man that he would enlist his father's aid, even knowing all the strings that came attached to it?

Her heart fell at the mention of the list of Doctors Unlimited staff and that he was still planning to steal it. He listened for a surprisingly long time to his father's answer to who Archaki was, though, which distracted her. What was his father telling him?

"Thanks," Alex said reluctantly. "I'll tell you why another time. Yeah. I'll be in touch."

"Well?" she demanded as soon as he disconnected the call.

"Archaki's a Ukrainian mobster. Into trafficking and smuggling."

"What kind of trafficking? Drugs? Sex?"

"Yes," was Alex's chilling answer.

"What's a guy like that doing in the Karshan Valley?"

"Good question."

Alex left and returned with his laptop, settling in a chair across from her. "Sleep. I'm going to do a little research."

Even with all the tension between them, she still felt safe in his presence. Weird, that. Her head hurt, and she'd slept like crap last night. Even though it was barely past noon, she closed her eyes. But in a few seconds, they popped back open.

"Why did you call your father?"

"I beg your pardon?"

"Just now. Why did you call him? I thought you hated his guts."

Alex's gaze narrowed dangerously. "You never give up, do you?"

It was her turn to look confused.

"Okay. I'll play ball. I called Peter because he was the fastest means of obtaining information on Yevgeny Archaki."

"But doesn't he think you owe him a favor now?"

Alex shrugged, but she caught the brief shadow in his eyes.

"Why do you keep doing this to yourself?" she cried. "Why don't you cut ties with him and be done with the man once and for all?"

"You'd just love it if I did that, wouldn't you?" he bit out.

She answered softly, "No, Alex. It's sad for a child to cut off a parent. But I think he causes you more pain than a relationship with him is worth. I just don't want to see you get hurt by him anymore."

That earned her a frown tempered by confusion, skepticism and who knew what else. One thing she knew for sure. After their lovemaking last night, Alex was severely off balance. Which was a good thing, she supposed. If she could get him into bed a few more times, maybe she'd finally break down his emotional fortress and let the real man out.

But not right now. She ached from head to foot and her head throbbed. A nap first. Then more sex with Alex.

She dozed for the next few hours as Alex worked intently on the computer. It looked like he was conducting some sort of deep Web search. The third time he woke her up to have a look at her pupils and have her perform a few simple tasks like sticking her tongue out, smiling, spelling her name and touching her nose with each hand, the expression in his eyes was unusually grim.

"Am I dying, or have you found something?" she asked lightly.

"Samarium."

"Samar—huh?"

"Rare earth metal. Used in nuclear power plants, lasers and missile casings."

"Okay. That's meaningful because?"

"Because I found an obscure geological survey from a Ukrainian university reporting that samarium might be found near the surface and cheaply mined in the western end of the Hindu Kush, specifically in Zaghastan and more specifically in the Karshan district."

"There's no mining operation in that area," she responded. "Do you think people were in the Karshan Valley to scope it out?"

"Remember that cave we hid in the night we ran?"

She nodded, frowning.

"Remember those little bore holes all over the walls?"

"I do!" she exclaimed. "Was someone looking for this samarium stuff, you think?"

"Remember that really deep shaft at the back of the cave that we threw our trash down?"

"There *was* a mine in the area."

"I think locals were working it. Bringing up ore by hand and smelting it in local furnaces."

She recalled vividly the odd smell of the place. She'd put it down to the dried dung that was routinely burned for fuel. But maybe it had been something else entirely.

"Is samarium valuable?" she asked.

"They don't call it a *rare* earth metal for nothing. And its uses are primarily military. You do the math."

"Why do the Ukrainians need it? Are they building nukes and lasers?"

"Yevgeny Archaki's financials don't indicate he's doing deals with his government. Quite the opposite, in fact. He's said to despise the current regime in his country. Apparently, the feeling is mutual."

"Then why is he mining this stuff? There must be money in it or he wouldn't mess with it."

"Iran."

Whoa. And Zaghastan shared a border with Iran. It would be an easy matter to secretly mine samarium, pay locals to refine it, smuggle it across the border and sell it to the Iranians, who were undoubtedly eager to lay hands on the stuff.

"Until this very minute, we had no idea Yevgeny and company were possibly mining samarium. So why would he be trying to kill us here in the States, half a world away from his operation? It's not like we have any proof. Wouldn't men like my brother be a much more immediate threat to him? Why not kill Mike?"

Alex's mouth twitched wryly. "Who, exactly, does your brother work for?"

"Honestly, I don't know. He joined the army as soon as he got out of college."

"But that was…ten, twelve years ago?"

She nodded.

Alex replied, "He could be working for anyone now. For all we know, he could be a freelancer."

"Why does it matter?"

"It would help us figure out who else is poking around the Karshan Valley."

"And poking around us," she added.

He smiled darkly at her. "Ahh. She finally lets a hint of the brilliant spy within peek through."

She sighed. "I'm so not a spy. Seriously, I'm a kindergarten teacher. I just grew up in a houseful of cops and soldiers."

"Riiight," he drawled skeptically.

"I never claimed to be stupid," she retorted a shade defensively. "For what it's worth, it takes someone really on their toes to keep up with a bunch of five-year-olds."

"I believe you," he replied sincerely.

"If it makes you feel better, Uncle Charlie offered me a job when I saw him this week."

"That doesn't make me feel better at all," he answered a bit sharply.

"Want me to ask Uncle Charlie about this samarium angle and see what he says?" she offered.

"Actually, I'd rather see how your brother responds to a casual mention of samarium mining."

She frowned. "We're just going to drop that into a conversation about sports and the weather?"

A tiny smile flickered across his face for just an instant, and her heart beat a bit more hopefully. Was it possible for them to find their way back to each other, after all? It *was* decent of him to look out for her like this. And he'd looked ghastly when he'd come into her room. Worse than any hangover, no matter how epic, could account for.

His cell phone rang, and he glanced at it. "My lawyer," he murmured as he took the call.

Ooh. Maybe there was news about their application for long-term guardianship of Dawn. She glanced down at the list in her hand. One of these men was very likely Dawn's father. It had better not be Mike, or getting stabbed would be the least of his problems before she was done with him.

Alex exhaled hard, almost like he'd been punched in the gut and all the air driven out of him. He said only, "I'll be right there."

"What's wrong?" she asked quickly.

Alex glanced up at her, and she recoiled from the reptilian coldness in his eyes. They looked...dead. "My lawyer's been murdered. Some of his files were apparently broken into."

Foreboding roared through her. "Yours?"

Alex nodded grimly and disappeared into his office. She was deeply alarmed to see him chambering a round and holstering a pistol as he emerged. "I've engaged the crisis security system. You're effectively living in a fort. As long as you don't let anyone in, you're safe," he explained tersely. "No one. Understood?"

CHAPTER NINETEEN

WITHOUT ALEX THERE to hover over her and insist she stay on the couch, Katie paced the living room nervously. It felt like some sort of terrible net was closing in around her and Alex and Dawn. She couldn't see it, but the trap was about to spring.

Her head spun with the events of the past week. From the moment they'd left that tent in Zaghastan, somebody had been dogging their steps. What was so flipping special about the Karshan Valley?

Or was it Dawn? Did this have to do with her mysterious, unidentified father? She mentally crossed Mike off the list as a possible suspect in the mayhem. Not only was he the kind of man who would own up to a by-blow child and do right by the mother, he'd also been stabbed and hospitalized for most of the past week. He couldn't be the source of the car chases or the assault on her.

Reluctantly, she replayed the attack in the parking garage in her head. It had been so dark, and the guy had come at her so fast. She'd barely had time to defend herself, let alone register details. The man had been taller than she was. Heavier in build than Alex. Strong. She would never forget the feel of that rock-hard fist slamming into her face. It obviously hadn't been the first time he'd ever clocked someone. He'd been brutal and efficient. A professional thug, then. FSB? CIA? Or…what about the cluster of Slavic names Alex had determined were all associated with one another? Maybe her attacker this morning had been with the Ukrainian mob. The notion seemed silly to her, but she couldn't discount it.

Dawn's mother had denied being raped. Which meant she'd had an affair. The father had to have been in the valley for a while to pull that off. Urgently, Katie pulled out her cell phone and dialed Uncle Charlie.

"Hey, Katie-kins," he answered jovially. "Have you got good news for me?"

"Working on it. You know that list of names you sent me?"

"The guest list for the party? Of course."

What? Oh. Crap. This wasn't a secure line. "Exactly," she replied cheerfully. "Can you get me arrival and departure dates to go with it so I can make sure everyone's got rides?"

"Of course."

"Like…now?"

"No problem. I'll have my secretary send them over, kiddo."

She severely doubted Uncle Charlie was ever that perky for real at work. He must think her cell phone was not only unsecure, but was being monitored by someone unfriendly to him. And he *was* CIA. What enemy of the CIA had the power, the reach, to tap her phone—

The question had only to enter her mind for her to know the answer. The FSB. More specifically, Peter Koronov. Alex was convinced his father would come after her and Dawn to force Alex to work for him.

And, hey, it had worked. Alex was prepared to steal sensitive information from his own employer for Peter.

She commenced pacing again, but after about three laps of the spacious condo, her phone beeped an incoming email. The days and months in the list Charlie had forwarded her were all followed by this year's date. But she got the point. She ignored the year and focused on the days and months, instead.

Only the four Ukrainian names on her list and Mike had been in the Karshan Valley for more than a few days last year. In fact, the four Ukrainians had been there for the entire three-month window of time in question.

Alex thought Archaki was the leader of the bunch and the other three were probably his bodyguard flunkies. Doubtful a flunky would get enough time off to romance a local girl. More likely, Archaki had been the seducer.

Call her selfish, but she wasn't about to contact a mob boss to ask him if he'd like to take custody of his baby daughter. What the guy didn't know wouldn't hurt him. She would ask Alex to help her do whatever it took to adopt Dawn, and she'd take the baby home, get a job and settle down. And she'd raise the baby herself. God, it sounded good to leave behind all this fear and stress and mental pressure. Life with Alex was *exhausting.*

She called Alex's cell phone to tell him what she'd learned of Archaki's time in the Karshan Valley, but she was sent immediately to his voice mail. If Peter was tapping her phone, he was darned well tapping Alex's phone, too. She didn't leave a message.

Her cell phone rang moments after she disconnected her call, and she snatched it up eagerly.

"Alex?" she said quickly.

"Katie? Is that you?"

Sister Mary Harris. "Yes, Sister, it's me. Is everything okay with Dawn?"

"She's perfectly fine, dear. But there's been a break-in at the orphanage. It appears the thief got scared away when the alarms went off. I thought you and Alex ought to know."

Katie's blood literally ran cold. "Uh, thanks. I'll be right over."

"That's not necessary. The police are here and the thief didn't get anything. He just broke a window."

"Nonetheless. I'm on my way."

Katie ended the call, grabbed her car keys and screeched to a stop at Alex's front door. *Crap.* Would she get shot or electrocuted or something if she tried to leave the penthouse? She threw the door open, ducking as she did so. *Nada.* Cautiously, she stepped out into the hall. So far so good. Worried about just how far Alex's paranoia might extend, she bypassed the elevator and raced down the stairs instead.

Dusk was falling as she climbed into her car and headed out into the mess that was rush hour in D.C. She had no idea whether or not she was followed. There was no way to navigate the traffic chaos and watch her rearview mirror and actually spot anyone in the tangle of vehicles diving in and out of lanes, honking and turning on headlights in the failing light.

What was going on? If Dawn was being targeted now, surely Peter Koronov was behind it. But he was the person who'd had the security system at the orphanage installed in the first place. Wouldn't his guy know that it existed and, furthermore, know how to get around it? Or had the later upgrades to the system taken Peter's man by surprise?

Fury erupted in her gut that an innocent baby would be pulled into Peter's power struggle with his son. If that bastard did anything to hurt Dawn, he'd have *her* to deal with.

Two police cars were parked prominently in front of the convent, but she was appalled that she was able to walk inside the facility without a soul challenging her. Thankfully, a cop was stationed at the door to the cloistered section of the building. He spoke into the radio at his collar, relaying news of her arrival to Sister Mary Harris.

In a few minutes, the elderly nun appeared at the door and actually invited her in. Katie was under the impression that the public was not generally let into this area. This exception to the rules alarmed her almost more than anything else tonight. The nun looked exhausted and was showing every one of her eighty years this evening.

"How are you doing, Sister?" Katie asked gently. "Is there anything I can do to help?"

"I think we've got things under control. Thankfully, that security system Peter Koronov installed did its job. All the doors locked when someone without a security badge tried to gain entrance. Fellow had to break a beautiful stained-glass window to get out. Threw a chair through it. That window was nearly a hundred years old. Terrible loss…"

Katie was not particularly interested in the window. "How's Dawn?"

"A little fussy with all the activity."

"But she's safe?"

"Yes, of course, dear. A thief wouldn't bother the babies."

Ha. Any self-respecting thief wouldn't break into a freaking convent in the first place. "I'd like to see her, Sister."

"I understand. A little cuddle would calm both of you. Wait here."

Katie sank into a lovely bentwood rocking chair in a small alcove. The window overlooked a cheerful garden. In a few minutes, Sister Mary Harris returned with a blanket-wrapped bundle. "She's wide-awake, the little rascal. I think she's interested in all the noise and movement."

"That's my girl," Katie cooed softly. "Smart *and* beautiful." She inhaled the sweet baby smell of Dawn, and all was right with the world. Nobody was hurting her little girl while she drew breath. But she also couldn't leave the baby here. The intruder would be prepared next time. Dawn mustn't be here when that next time came.

"How about I rock her to sleep, Sister? I'd like a little time alone with her if that would be okay."

"Actually, that would be helpful. All the children are upset, and my sisters could use some help getting everyone to bed tonight."

"Go on, then. Dawn and I will be fine."

Katie waited until the nun's habit disappeared around the corner, and then she hurried to the exit. As she approached the door, she tucked Dawn inside her coat, laying the baby flat across her stomach. "Just like old times, eh, sweetie?" she murmured.

Thankfully, like old times, the sound of her heart-beat calmed and quieted the infant. She stepped out, nodding a greeting at the police officer. It was all she could do not to break into a mad dash for her car, but she forced herself to stroll casually across the park-ing lot.

She didn't breathe properly until the convent disap-peared behind her. *Now what?* She thought frantically as she navigated surface streets south toward down-town Washington. Her car was known, and she'd lay odds the convent was being watched. She had to as-sume she was being tailed. And then there was her cell phone. Uncle Charlie seemed convinced it was being monitored. And if the FSB could hear her calls, they could also use its GPS function to track her.

What would Alex do in this situation? He would do the unexpected. Okay, so what was "expected" of her? She'd just taken Dawn. The logical thing would be for her to head home. To Pennsylvania. She spied a home-less guy lounging in front of a closed store ahead and inspiration struck. She had a couple hundred bucks in her wallet. Hopefully, it would be enough.

She pulled into the alley about a half block beyond the guy and pulled out her cell phone. She turned it off and stuffed it deep into the seat cushions before scoop-ing up Dawn and hurrying back to the panhandler.

"Got a buck for a cup of coffee, lady?"

Right. Coffee. The guy stunk of drunk vomit. "I'll do better than that. I'll give you—" she opened her wallet to check the contents "—two hundred and sixty dollars if you'll take my car and drive it to Pittsburgh."

The guy's jaw dropped.

"You do know how to drive, don't you?"

"Yeah, lady. But Pittsburgh?"

"Just head out of D.C. toward Pennsylvania. You have to leave right now, though. Here are the keys."

"You crazy?"

"As a jaybird. You want the cash or not?"

"Hell, yeah."

"Take the Beltway to Highway 270 northwest out of town. It merges into Highway 70. Follow the signs to the Pennsylvania Turnpike. It'll take you straight into Pittsburgh."

"What am I supposed to do when I get there?"

"Ditch the car and get drunk off your ass. You might want to save enough money for a bus ticket back to D.C., though. I expect panhandlers do better here than in Pittsburgh."

The guy snatched the keys out of her hand. Whether he would actually head for Pennsylvania or merely drive to the nearest liquor store, she had no idea. But it was worth a try. The guy did get into the rental car and head for the Beltway, at least. She cringed back in the shadows of the store building as the traffic lights changed and a stream of cars rolled past. Good Lord willing, one of those was whoever'd tailed her from the convent.

She waited until the street was deserted to hurry down it toward the nearest Metro stop. She used spare change from her wallet to buy a one-way Metro ticket and fell gratefully into a plastic seat as the train crept out of the station. A few people jumped on the train at the last second, but none of them looked like FSB operatives to her. Not that she would be able to tell one from a harassed businessman, she supposed.

Dawn declared her opinion of the past few minutes'

worth of racing around and started to fuss. Katie rocked her quickly before she could get too wound up. Last thing she needed was to have everyone on the train notice and remember the tense woman with the screaming baby. Katie won the race against baby meltdown and got Dawn settled before screaming commenced. *Whew.*

The rhythmic noise and swaying of the train seemed to lull Dawn to sleep. The baby slept through several stops, and Katie sighed in relief.

Now what? Unpredictable. What would be unpredictable?

ALEX LOOKED INTO Chester Morton's office grimly. His lawyer's body had been removed already, but an obscene tape outline remained on the blood-coated desk, and a crime-scene team was hard at work collecting samples. He wasn't allowed into the room, of course, but he'd seen enough. Chester had been shot at his desk, and the man's computer was turned on; a dancing screen saver was still going strong. Which meant the killer had likely been able to access the lawyer's files.

"Time of death?" he asked Chester's secretary tersely.

"This morning sometime. The firm was closed for Good Friday."

Alex blinked. This was Easter weekend? He'd been so distracted by Katie he hadn't noticed. The woman continued tearfully, "Mr. Morton must have come in to catch up on some work. He must have surprised an intruder."

Or maybe the intruder had followed Morton and forced the man to reveal his passwords before killing him. Chester was far too security conscious not to have encrypted the hell out of his computer.

"Who knew Chester's passwords?" Alex asked grimly.

"Nobody—" The secretary broke off as the significance of the question dawned on her.

He was right then. The intruder had been after files. Alex turned to Chester's paralegal, who'd just walked up to them. "My files were copied, weren't they? All of them."

The young man frowned. "That's correct. How did you know?"

"Call it a hunch," Alex replied drily.

The paralegal continued, "Just the recent ones were copied. The custody paperwork and the trust-fund documents."

"Anything else?"

"All of Mr. Morton's recently opened documents were copied from the cache in his computer. We've notified the other clients affected, but…" The guy hesitated, and then added in an apologetic rush, "But he said that if anything bad ever happened to him, it would be because of you."

Alex's jaw tightened. Chester had been no dummy. He knew the ilk of Alex's enemies, perhaps better than anyone. Morton had been his father's attorney, too.

Why in the hell did someone go after the legal documents pertaining to *Dawn?* Only his father could be interested in the infant like this. But his father surely knew where the baby was already. What did the child's legal status or trust fund have to do with anything or anyone else?

Frowning, he pulled his vibrating cell phone out of

his pocket. He didn't recognize the number. "Yes?" he said brusquely.

"Thank God you answered, Alex. It's Sister Mary Harris. We have a problem."

His heart skipped a beat. "Is Dawn all right?" he demanded urgently.

"Well, that's the thing. Katie came to see her a little while ago, but now they're both gone. I'm sure Katie left with her."

"What?" He took off running down the hall, phone still plastered to his ear as he sprinted for his car. He listened in dismay to the details. A break-in. The nun had called Katie, who'd showed up shortly thereafter at the convent. *Dammit. Any idiot could figure out a threat to the baby would draw her out of my place.* Sister Mary Harris had brought Dawn to see her. Katie volunteered to rock her to sleep....

He leaped into his car and tore out of the law firm's parking lot. He dialed Katie's phone but got sent immediately to voice mail. Why in the *hell* would she turn off her phone? His alarm turned into panic as he headed for home. He tore into his condo, shouting her name. "Katie? Where are you?"

Only silence answered him. His panic became infused with helplessness. Where had she and Dawn gone? Had someone snatched them? Or had Katie fled on her own?

He got onto the internet and used an illegal site to find her father's cell phone number.

"Hello, Mr. McCloud. My name is Alex Peters, and I'm a friend of Katie's."

"You're the guy who stabbed my boy, aren't you?"

"Yes, sir, I am," he answered impatiently. "Have you heard from Katie tonight?"

"No, and she blew off a dinner date with us, too. What's wrong?" The cop in the man obviously smelled a problem.

"She's disappeared. If she contacts you, please have her call me immediately."

"Likewise, Peters. Have her call us."

"Will do."

"Can I help?" her father bit out.

"If you can, you'll be the first to know." Alex disconnected the call and stared at nothing. Katie knew her parents were in D.C. with Mike. Would she still head home to Pittsburgh with Dawn if they were all down here? His gut said she wouldn't. Who else would she turn to for help?

He called André Fortinay's emergency cell number.

"Good evening, Alex. What's up?"

"Have you heard from Katie McCloud tonight, sir?"

"No. Is something amiss?"

"She's disappeared with the infant we brought back from Zaghastan."

"What do you mean disappeared?"

"She's dropped off the grid. Completely. I'm worried that something might have happened to her."

"Did you two have some kind of falling-out?"

Alex rolled his eyes at the ceiling of his office. "No. We didn't. Look, this is totally unlike Katie. Something's wrong. Please have her call me if you hear from her."

"I will. Let me know if there's anything I can do," the Frenchman said.

"Will do."

Now what? He was out of ideas. He called Sister Mary Harris back. "I need more information," he said without preamble. "Is Katie's car still in your parking lot?"

"I don't know. Let me check."

He waited in an agony of impatience while the elderly nun made her way to a window in the front of the convent. "What does it look like?" she finally asked.

Crap. What did she rent? He thought back fast to the hospital parking garage. "Cobalt-blue mini-sedan."

"No blue cars here. She must be taking the baby someplace safe. I'm sure she's bringing Dawn to see you. I wish she'd told me she was going to take Dawn out, though. I've been worried—"

He hung up on the nun's nattering. He had no time for that. If Katie was in her car, she should have been here well before now. Unless she was trying to shake a tail. His mind threatened to vapor lock. *Think, dammit.* If she was in a car, she was traceable. He considered his options and headed for his car once more.

A half hour later found him barging past the receptionist at Walter Reed Hospital with a terse explanation that he was a doctor and there was a crisis with a patient. The woman subsided as he leaped into an elevator.

He slowed only when he hit the doorway of Michael McCloud's room. If he didn't miss his guess, Katie's brother had the contacts and resources to track his little sister now and not wait the twenty-four hours the police required before they would take action.

"What the hell are you doing here?" McCloud growled.

Her brother was alone in his room. *Good.* This

needed to be a private conversation, and he doubted McCloud's family would voluntarily leave Mike alone with the man who'd stabbed him. "Katie's in trouble."

McCloud's truculent expression evaporated in an instant. "What's wrong?"

"My lawyer was murdered today and the files pertaining to Dawn—she's the baby we brought back from Zaghastan with us—were stolen. Katie and Dawn disappeared a little over an hour ago. Her phone's turned off. I think she's in a car. No idea if she's alone or with a captor. I need to find the vehicle ASAP. It's a rental, so it should have a tracking chip in it."

Alex held out his cell phone to Mike. Without hesitating, Katie's brother snatched it and punched in a number. *Thank God.* He hadn't judged the guy wrong.

"It's Candyman. Emergency authentication Charlie Whiskey Three One Tango Tango."

Alex scribbled down the make and model of the car and the rental company on the napkin beside Mike's dinner tray while they waited for the authentication to be verified.

Abruptly, Mike started talking. He relayed the information on Katie's car with a request to use government security overrides to get a license plate number and initiate immediate tracking on the vehicle due to a possible hostage situation.

That ought to get folks on the other end of the line hopping.

The person at the other end of the phone said something that made Mike swear violently, though. Then he said, "Fine. I'll pull my own damned strings."

He disconnected the call and started dialing another number.

"Problem?" Alex asked.

"My people have no authority to request the trace." He added grimly, "But there's more than one way to skin a cat."

Alex grinned darkly. He liked the way this guy rolled.

"Uncle Charlie? It's me, Mikey. Katie's in trouble." A pause. "No, he's here with me right now. He's the one looking for her. She's disappeared with her kid."

Realizing belatedly that Mike was trying to talk around the issue on the assumption that the phone might be bugged, Alex said quickly, "My cell phone has 256-bit encryption. It's secure."

"Bless you," Mikey muttered. "Charlie, this line's secure at my end. How's your end?" A short pause and then Mike said quickly, "We think she's in a chipped rental car and have reason to suspect hostile action against her and the baby. Can you have your people pull a license plate number and track the chip?" He relayed the car's data to his uncle quickly.

Mike ended the call and passed the phone back to Alex. "That's more like it," he growled. "Now we'll get some action. And in the meantime, what the hell's going on? Tell me everything."

Alex was glad to have a trained operative to dump everything on. Maybe Mike could see some connection he'd missed. "After I stabbed you, Katie and I caught a plane hop to Osh. From there we headed for Tashkent. We were followed in both cities. Had a little trouble with my old man. He's—"

Mike interrupted. "I know who your father is."

Alex nodded tersely. "I took Katie to my place in D.C. It's a fortress. But we got picked up on the street and tailed. We hid the baby in an orphanage with an old friend of mine for safety. Katie was attacked on her way to visit you this afternoon, and my lawyer was killed soon after that."

"Christ, dude. Who'd you piss off?"

Alex shrugged. "Wish I knew. I was at my lawyer's office when I got the call that Katie and the baby had disappeared from the orphanage."

"Any guesses as to who's tailing you?" Mike demanded.

"Pros for sure. Maybe FSB. Maybe CIA."

"What do they want?"

Alex snorted. "They want me to work for them."

"You think they're making a run at Katie and the kid to twist your arm?"

"Possibly." He corrected himself angrily, "Hell, probably."

"Any other possible players?"

He frowned thoughtfully. "It's a long shot, but Katie's been poking around trying to find out who Dawn's birth father is."

"Wouldn't that be a local from Karshan?" Mike asked in surprise.

"Dawn's blonde and blue-eyed. Birth father's Caucasian."

"Son of a bitch," Mike breathed. "So Katie's been kicking rocks. Who'd she expose?"

"I was hoping you could help me with that. What were you doing in Zaghastan?"

"You know the drill. That's classified."

"Just listen then. Someone's been chasing Katie and me pretty much continuously since the Karshan Valley, starting with you. I thought for a while that it was all about me. God knows, I've got plenty of enemies with the manpower to follow me around and hassle me."

"But?"

"But Katie got this idea that we should find Dawn's birth father and let him know he had a kid. She asked for a list of names from your uncle of all the Caucasian men in the Karshan Valley nine months ago. A guy named Yevgeny Archaki was on it."

Mike shook his head. He obviously hadn't heard of the guy.

"Ukrainian mafia. Arms dealer, drug lord. Smuggler."

"And?"

"Tell me something. Did you ever find any poppy fields in that area? Any evidence to indicate that opium production or smuggling was going on?"

"No. Nothing like that," Mike said firmly. Alex saw no tells of deception at all. The guy was telling him the truth.

"How about weapons dealing? Any arms runners passing through there?"

"Negative."

"Then why would a guy like Archaki spend months in a godforsaken place like the Karshan Valley?"

"I got nothin'. You got a theory?"

"Yes, in fact. I do." He exhaled hard. "This is a little crazy, McCloud, but go with me for a minute." He described the caves with the bore holes in their walls and the deep shaft in the cave he and Katie had hidden in. He then described the chronic cough the locals all seemed to have, and the weird smell in the valley.

"Yeah, I noticed that stench," Mike piped up. "I tracked it to those big communal ovens they used."

"I don't think those were ovens. I think they were smelters." That sent Mike's eyebrows up, but he listened in silence as Alex continued. "I took a close look at this Archaki character. No political ties. Purely a businessman. Wouldn't go to the Karshan Valley unless there was money in it for him. With me so far?"

Mike nodded, watching him intently. Alex saw where Katie got her smarts from. It was a family trait.

He continued, "So, I did a little research on what he could be doing there to turn a profit. Like you, I saw no evidence of drug production or arms trade through the valley. Population wasn't high enough to support human trafficking. Plus, I'd have heard of girls disappearing from my patients."

Mike nodded, following his logic closely.

"Ever heard of samarium?" Alex asked.

Katie's brother frowned. "Sounds like something from my chemistry class."

"Good guess. It's a rare earth element. It's used a lot in control rods for nuclear reactors. It's also used in lasers and as a hardening agent in missile casings. It's highly heat resistant. It's always found in nature in conjunction with other minerals. It has to be melted down and separated from the nuisance minerals it's found with. That smelting process stinks to high heaven."

"Let me guess," Mike supplied drily. "There's samarium in the Karshan Valley."

"Give the man a gold star."

"Was Archaki getting this stuff for the Ukraine?"

Alex shook his head. "The guy hates the current regime in Kiev. And besides, both Russia and Ukraine have sources of it within their own borders. Unless you saw heavy transport trucks or cargo planes coming into the Karshan Valley routinely, we're looking at a local buyer."

"Christ!" Mike burst out. "Iran's a stone's throw from the Karshan Valley, and they'd have all kinds of military uses for the stuff. Do you think this Archaki guy was getting samarium from the locals and selling it to the Iranians?"

"Did you see locals hauling baskets down out of the hills? They'd be heavy. Full of rocks. Maybe an occasional truck coming and going like it picked up a heavy cargo and hauled it out?"

Mike nodded just once, very slowly. Alex understood. The guy couldn't say anything to him, but if Alex were to guess correctly, he could nod.

"If the locals were smelting it in those ovens in the middle of their villages, they'd ingest a crap-ton of the stuff," Alex pointed out. He didn't like having to reveal the next bit to an employee of the U.S. government, but he needed this man's help. Mike had been on the ground in Zaghastan for *months* more than him and Katie. He was the single most likely person to know who they'd pissed off in Zaghastan and who might have kidnapped Katie.

"And?" Mike prompted warily.

"Katie and I saw the rebels coming that last night. We both thought they moved like soldiers. Spec Ops types. Those weren't local rebels at all. Surely you saw them, too."

Mike nodded firmly.

Jesus H. Christ. It was one thing to suspect sinister layers to an event. It was another to have it confirmed for him. Alex's pulse sped up. He only hoped he wasn't on the right track all the way to the horrible, logical conclusion.

"Go on," Mike urged.

"For argument's sake, let's assume Charlie gave Katie the complete list and didn't omit any of his own people. Your name was the only obviously American one on the list, by which I'm going to assume you were working solo out there."

Mike nodded infinitesimally.

Alex finished heavily, "Which means that Spec Ops squad wasn't American."

Mike nodded more obviously.

"Those were undoubtedly the guys who slaughtered everyone in the Karshan village that night. They're probably the same team that took out the village in the next valley over, too."

"Logical," Mike commented cautiously. Which Alex interpreted to mean that Mike didn't know that for sure but agreed with Alex's conjecture.

"The team we saw had attack drones. RPGs. *Helicopters.* That was no Ukrainian mob job. That was a full-blown, state-sponsored military attack."

Mike's eyes opened wide as he saw where Alex was going.

"Yeah," Alex muttered. "The Russians."

"Why?" Mike breathed. "This samarium stuff?"

"There's plenty of it in the Caucasus Mountains. They don't need it."

"Then what are we looking at—" Mike started. He broke off as the hallway door opened. Alex spun, his hands going up defensively.

KATIE WAITED UNTIL the last minute before the Metro train pulled out of a random station to jump off it. She raced for the exit and didn't see anyone hurrying after her. As far as her limited spycraft could tell, she hadn't been followed as she emerged into the night.

"Cab, lady?"

Katie started. "Umm. Yes." *Impulse. Operate on impulse.* She slid into the cab's backseat and took a look around at where she was. She recognized the neighborhood with a start.

"Where to?"

She gave the guy the address of the Doctors Unlimited offices only a few blocks away. She couldn't go tearing around out in the open where Alex's enemies would spot her and Dawn, for goodness' sake. And besides, she needed a phone to make a call.

"GOOD EVENING, MR. MCCLOUD," a male voice said from the doorway.

"Hey, Doc Kowalski," Mike said.

Alex relaxed fractionally. If McCloud knew the guy, he wouldn't kill the man. Except something wasn't right about the set of the doctor's shoulders. They were hunched too high. The guy was wicked tense. Alex slid quietly to the side, slightly behind the doctor. Mike noted the movement and arched a questioning brow.

"We got some interesting lab results back on you just now, Mr. McCloud," the doctor said. He glanced over his shoulder at Alex. "If your guest would step out into the hallway for a minute, I'd like to go over them with you."

"He stays," McCloud said tersely.

Interesting. Katie's brother must sense the doctor's

abnormal tension, too. Or maybe he just trusted Alex's instincts. Operators tended to listen to their guts more than the average bear.

"Uh, okay. It turns out you test positive for exposure to radioactive isotopes. Have you been inside a nuclear power plant recently, or had a large ionic dose X-ray in the past few weeks?"

"No. And no."

Alex piped up. "What specific isotopes did the chromatograph spike on?"

The doctor frowned. "The spike was consistent with unrefined uranium."

Alex's jaw dropped, but not nearly as far as Mike's. "Uranium?" McCloud demanded. "There must be some mistake."

"No mistake. The techs ran the tests twice. They were startled by the first results and verified them for me."

"Health ramifications?" Alex bit out. He'd studied radiation poisoning superficially in his medical training but was no expert in the subject.

"The levels aren't life threatening but do bear watching. You'll have a slightly increased cancer risk. And you should probably avoid any more X-rays for the remainder of your life. We can discuss chelation to remove some of the isotopes you've ingested from your liver and kidneys."

"That I've *ingested?*" McCloud asked incredulously.

"Most likely way for radioactive cells to show up in your liver and kidneys is to swallow them. A recheck of your CT scan revealed trace amounts of uranium in your lungs, as well. We initially thought the specks were an anomaly in the scan itself." He added, "You must have inhaled dust containing trace amounts of the isotope for it to end up in your lungs."

Alex's mind raced, and he really, really hated the direction it was going in. He asked reluctantly, "Excuse me, Doctor. Did Mr. McCloud test positive for any rare earth metals, or just the uranium?"

"We picked up trace amounts of thorium, samarite and iron dust in his lung tissue."

Ho. Lee. Crap. The implications of that all but paralyzed his brain. He caught Mike's eye behind the doctor's back and jerked his head toward the door.

Mike caught his meaning and said, "Thanks for the heads-up, Doc. I'll try to remember where I might have gotten exposed to something like that and let you know. Right now, I'm tired. I'd like to rest a little if you don't mind."

The doctor nodded and left. Alex tucked a chair under the doorknob behind the guy and then turned to Mike. The two men traded grim looks. Uranium in the Karshan Valley was a game changer. Big-time.

"Russia and Ukraine have their own internal sources of uranium. I can't imagine they'd send a mobster after a small, crude source of it for them, anyway."

"So Archaki was out there for himself. A business deal."

"With who?" Alex muttered aloud.

"I didn't see any long-distance trucks or cargo planes come through there. Like you said before, the buyer had to be local—" McCloud broke off and looked faintly ill.

Alex closed his eyes in dismay. Zaghastan's western border with Iran again. He looked up at Katie's brother, and the same realization was clear in his appalled stare.

KATIE WALKED UP to the front door of the Doctors Unlimited building and prayed her entry code would work at night when the building was not open for business. She punched in the sequence, and a green light went on over the pad. She tugged at the door, and, blessedly, it opened.

She slipped inside, grateful to be off the street. She'd felt like a rat out in the open just waiting to get picked off by some flying predator that would swoop down, smash into her and whisk her away to eat at its leisure.

A phone. She needed a phone. Creeping through the darkened lobby, she felt like a criminal, and fear pounded through her. Heck, if she got caught, she'd just tell whoever caught her that she worked here. It was like Alex had said the night he'd agreed to steal the personnel list. It wasn't a crime to enter a building she rightfully belonged in.

Nope. The pep talk didn't work. She still felt like a criminal and in terror of getting caught.

She eased around the receptionist's desk and stared down at the oversize phone and the raft of buttons on its face. She picked up the receiver and reached for the dial buttons.

No dial tone. What was up with that? She wiggled the phone line coming into the top of the table set. Nothing. Squatting down, she reached under the desk to jiggle the line down there. Still no dial tone. *Crap.*

She headed through the lobby toward the stairs and

the offices on the second floor. She slipped into the first one at the top of the stairs and hurried to the desk. Dammit, this phone didn't have a dial tone, either! She thought she detected a faint electrical hum as if the line was live, just not giving her an outbound dial tone. The whole building's phone system wasn't out then. Did Doctors Unlimited turn its phones *off* at night?

She went back out to the hall, frustrated. And spied André Fortinay's door across the landing. If anyone's phone would work all the time, it would be his. She headed for the director's office. On his desk, she spied two telephones: a regular one like the other office had and an old-fashioned dial phone. She picked up that one. A dial tone hummed in her ear. *Bingo*.

She reached for the phone to dial Alex's cell when she was arrested by the sight of a big, round Rolodex file sitting beside the phone. The card she could see in the dim streetlight coming in the window read *Nigeria*.

It made sense that D.U.'s director would have contacts to pretty much every country on earth. Curious, she gave the thing a spin. Country names flew past in alphabetical order, along with contact names and information on intelligence agencies, military commanders and a host of other VIP contacts the leader of a global aid organization might need to call.

Frowning, she rolled to the *R*s. There were several cards for Russia. Russia: Kremlin. Russia: Prime Minister. Russia: FSB.

She stared. André Fortinay had a contact at the FSB? It was probably someone high ranking. High enough to know Peter Koronov probably. She should give the man a call. Tell him to back off his son…

The idea broke across her brain without warning,

like a rogue wave swelling up out of the depths of her mind to capsize all her other thoughts. What was the one thing she could offer Peter Koronov that would get him to leave his son alone?

With a clarity so sharp it hurt, she knew.

She reached for the phone's dial and, one by one, rolled the numbers around its face.

"So. THOSE FAKE REBELS were Spetsnaz, after all," Mike breathed.

Alex nodded. He'd suspected the Spec Ops team he and Katie had seen was the elite Russian Special Forces unit, but he'd never dared put it into words.

Mike continued, "Were the Russians there to stop the Iranians from getting uranium? Hell, if our side had known what was up, we'd have wiped out that village."

"I don't think it's that simple."

"Explain," Mike bit out.

Alex forged on grimly, "My father is intimately familiar with the interior workings of the Russian government."

Mike snorted at that little piece of understatement.

"It's far from a homogenous beast. There are factions within it and factions within factions."

"Sounds like the U.S. government," Mike commented wryly.

Alex snorted in turn. "I don't necessarily think the intent of that Spetsnaz team was to stop uranium from being smuggled to Iran. I think the intent could have been to protect the smuggling operation."

"How does wiping out two villages do that?"

"The arrival of an American doctor in the area had

to freak out whoever was sponsoring the uranium smuggling. I might spot the signs of uranium toxicity in the locals. I was a liability that had to be eliminated. Except Katie and I were moving fast, going from village to village and laying low. Local women were hiding our tracks, too, which would have made us hard to locate and take out."

"I can vouch for that. I was trying to keep an eye out for Katie, and my people had a hell of a time keeping tabs on you two."

Alex smiled briefly. A high compliment from a man in Mike's line of work. "For all the Russians knew, I already was onto them. I might already have reported back to Doctors Unlimited that I was seeing uranium poisoning among the locals. They had no choice but to wipe out the physical evidence."

"By killing all the locals?"

Alex nodded grimly. "If D.U. filed a formal report, the International Atomic Energy Agency and/or the United Nations would have immediately sent a team out to test the locals for evidence of illegal uranium mining and trafficking."

Both of them knew that, in the game of global nuclear brinksmanship, the lives of a few hundred natives in a place no one had ever heard of were meaningless. Governments wouldn't hesitate to slaughter a local tribe to protect a secret this big.

"Why haven't they killed you?" Mike demanded.

"Oh, they've been trying. But I'm a slippery bastard."

"Yeah, I noticed," Mike noted drily.

Alex shrugged. He wouldn't apologize for stabbing

the guy. McCloud been following them and pulled a knife on him. His expression went dark once more.

"The Russians need to kill my sister, too. Don't they?"

"Probably. She may be a know-nothing civilian, but she may have seen and heard too much while she was hanging around out there with me." He sucked in a sharp breath as his mind made the next leap.

"What?" McCloud demanded sharply.

"Not only do the Russians have to kill the two of us, but they particularly *have* to kill Dawn. And furthermore, they have to dispose of her body."

"Why the kid?" Mike asked sharply.

"She's the only survivor from the Karshan Valley massacre. If her mother was exposed to uranium, she'd have absorbed some of it across her mother's placenta."

"Son of a bitch," Mike breathed.

"She's the only remaining evidence of illegal uranium mining and smuggling."

"So you're telling me the whole fucking Russian government is out to kill one baby?"

"At least a powerful faction within it. A faction that would like to see Iran become a nuclear power. If Tehran nuked Israel, the U.S. would have a gigantic mess on its hands for decades to come. This would be a deep source of satisfaction in the Kremlin. Not to mention give it plenty of room to maneuver in other parts of the world while the U.S. was distracted."

Mike added, "And the price of oil would go sky-high. Russia would make a freaking fortune."

"This faction would no doubt love to see the U.S. quaking in its boots over the possibility of Iran lobbing a nuke at Washington."

"Jesus."

"It's possible I'm wrong," Alex said.

"You're not."

The two men traded grim looks. Where in the hell was Katie? She had no idea the danger she and Dawn were in.

CHAPTER TWENTY

THE MAN WHO answered Katie's call was stunned at her request. She lied and said that André had sanctioned this call and would appreciate whatever cooperation the anonymous Russian could give her. It was an emergency. The man rattled off a phone number, which she copied down on a sticky pad on André's desk. She thanked the man for his help and disconnected the call. She dialed the second number.

It rang with a funny electronic buzz. Once. Twice. On the third ring, it picked up.

"André! It is the middle of the night in Washington. To what do I owe this call?"

André Fortinay knew Peter Koronov? *Holy crap.* She had no time to stop and think about that just now. "Umm, Mr. Koronov?"

"Who is this?" he demanded sharply.

"My name is Katie McCloud. I'm—"

"The young woman who has seduced my son. Yes. I know who you are. How did you get this phone number?"

"I stole a number from André's desk and lied to the FSB man who answered it."

"Resourceful," he commented. She thought maybe she detected a hint of humor in that single word. She sure hoped so.

"I'm sorry to bother you, but I have a proposition for you."

"Do you now? This should be interesting."

"You want Alex to work for you, yes?"

"I'm not going to walk into such a blatant trap—"

She cut him off. "Fine. You and I both know the answer anyway. And you and I also know what the odds are of Alex doing it voluntarily. But I think I can help you."

Silence. She had his attention now.

"Alex will never work for you as long as I am in his life. He would never jeopardize my safety that way. You taught him very well that friends and family are a liability a spy cannot afford. He knows he dare not love anyone or else you'll come after them."

More silence. More importantly, no denial from Koronov.

"I cannot deliver Alex to you, and I'm not willing to commit treason against my country. But I can leave Alex. If I do, I can guarantee you he will not become involved with another woman for a very long time."

Of course, she could only guarantee it if her leaving him broke Alex's heart. And she was far from sure that she had such power over Alex. But Peter didn't know that.

"You are lovers, you and Alex?"

"Yes, sir."

"Is the child his?"

"No, sir. Alex delivered the baby, but the mother died. We brought her out with us when we left Zaghastan."

"Ahh. That is a shame."

Why? Alarm exploded in her gut at the regretful tone in Koronov's voice.

"Tell me something. Why do you make this offer to me, Miss McCloud?"

She avoided the whole issue of loving Alex enough to sacrifice her feelings for him so he could be safe. Be at peace. Breathe. She answered obliquely, "It's a trade I'm offering, Mr. Koronov. I leave Alex, and you agree to leave him alone."

"Define leaving him alone."

"Don't split semantic hairs with me," she snapped. "I'm making you a generous offer. You back off of Alex. Let him live his own life. Be his own man. Quit trying to get your hooks in him and suck him into working for you."

"Why would I agree to such a thing?"

"Because currently, he'll die before he works for you. But if he loses me, if I tear his heart out in the process, he may just come back to you someday. Trust me. Right now you've got nothing. This is the only chance you've got at ever winning him over. I'm offering you a shot at getting your son back."

ALEX JUMPED AS his cell phone rang. He yanked it out of his pocket. When he heard her voice, he nearly passed out in relief. "Thank God, Katie. Are you and Dawn okay?"

"Yes. We're fine."

His antenna stood straight up and wiggled violently. She didn't sound okay. She sounded damned strange, in fact. Distant. Like she might be in shock.

"I'm sorry, Alex. I didn't know where to go or what to do when—"

He cut her off sharply. "Not over the phone. Can you tell me where you are without being too specific?"

"Umm, I suppose." A pause, then, "Do you remember where I wore that sexy little black dress on our first date?"

"Got it. I'll be there as soon as I can."

CHAPTER TWENTY-ONE

"Dude, you gotta slow down."

Alex glanced over at Mike in the passenger seat of the rented Porsche coupe and took his foot off the accelerator. Again.

"You okay?" he asked Katie's brother. The guy was still recovering from a serious stab wound but had flatly refused to stay in the hospital doing nothing to protect his little sister when she was in trouble. Alex couldn't blame him.

"I'll live," Mike bit out. "How much longer till we're there?"

The guy must be in severe pain. But Alex wasn't going to coddle him. He'd demanded that Alex help him slip out of the hospital. He would have done the same if he were laid up and Katie was in trouble.

Realization slammed into him like a runaway train. He'd move heaven and earth to protect Katie if she were in trouble. No. *No.* He couldn't feel that way....

Alex's world was collapsing in on him faster than he could prop it up. And it was all because of Katie and Dawn. Never before had he had anyone else to worry about beside himself. But the two of them changed the whole damned equation. Something—someone—mattered now. And it made him vulnerable to everyone who'd ever coveted a piece of his hide. Cold terror poured over him. Life as he knew it was over.

They drove a few more minutes, and the underbellies of thick rain clouds glowed pink.

"We gonna make a direct approach?" Mike gritted out.

The question jolted him. He hadn't given any thought to doing anything other than parking out front and using his access code to walk in the front door. Mike's question was a sharp reminder to get his head in the game and not assume everything was hunkydory.

Alex shook his head. "Let's play it cautiously. I have no reason to believe she's been followed, but there's no harm in being careful."

"The Russians will make a run at her as soon as they know where she is."

Mike was right. What were the odds someone had monitored Katie's call to him? Would that person know where she'd hinted at being? Or maybe just trace her phone? Or—

He swore violently and hit the call back button on his phone. It rang. And rang. Dammit, she wasn't picking up! He threw his phone down and stood on the accelerator.

"What's wrong?" Mike asked sharply.

"She's got Dawn with her."

"And?"

"The intruder to the convent passed through the nursery briefly as he fled the scene."

Mike swore low and hard. "Bastard had time to plant a tracker on the baby." He added tightly, "As soon as we've got her and the kid locked down safe, I'm telling her to dump your ass like a hot potato."

Alex mentally winced. If she were his sister and she was involved with a high-risk asset like him, he'd do the exact same thing.

"I'm telling ya, Al. You gotta slow down. If we get hauled in for going supersonic on the Beltway, we won't be able to help Katie at all."

He eased off the accelerator yet again, even though every nerve in his body was screaming at him to stand on the pedal. His phone rang again, and he pounced on it.

"Katie?"

"Sorry, no. André Fortinay here. I just got—"

He cut his boss off sharply. "This conversation needs to happen on a secure line."

"I'm secure at my end," Fortinay replied, surprised.

"Me, too. Continue."

"Right. I just got a notification that Katie McCloud's employee code was used to access the Doctors Unlimited building a little while ago. Shortly thereafter, the emergency phone on my desk was used to make two calls to Moscow. Know anything about that?"

Moscow? WTF?

"No, sir. I'm on my way over there now, though."

"Wait…I'm getting…standby…"

Alex exited the highway and turned toward the D.U. building. *Five minutes, Katie. Don't do anything insane for the next five minutes.* Like call freaking Moscow. Three guesses who she'd called, and the first two didn't count.

Fortinay bit out, low and fast, "Security cameras are showing movement outside the D.U. building. Assume hostiles. Do not make a direct approach. Repeat—no direct approach."

Damn. The guy sounded like an FSB operations controller—

Not FSB. CIA. *Son. Of. A. Bitch.*

Fortinay was speaking again. "Alternate approach. I've got visual on hostiles. Armed and dangerous. Go to this address. Wait for me there. My ETA five minutes. Say yours."

"Three minutes."

"Do not go in by yourself, Alex. Do you hear me?"

"Yes, sir." What on God's green earth was going on?

He flipped his phone at Mike. "See if you can raise the number Katie called me from. We've got to warn her to stay put. The building she's in is surrounded by armed hostiles."

Mike swore in a continuous stream that echoed Alex's thoughts as he punched the redial button over and over.

Alex parked the car down the street from the address Fortinay had given him. They were a block over from the D.U. building, and this apartment building's property line backed up on the Doctors Unlimited backyard. "How mobile are you?" he asked Mike.

"I can walk. Run a little."

"How sneaky can you be?"

"As sneaky as you need." Mike bared his teeth in what passed for a grin from a predator about to strike. "Where are we headed?"

"Ten o'clock. Thirty yards," he murmured.

Mike's eyelids barely flickered in acknowledgment

as they moved out, easing silently down the street, sticking to the shadows and shapes of cars and shrubs.

The apartment building was quiet. Dark with only a single light fixture burning inside the front vestibule. As they neared the building, the dim glow from inside the building abruptly went black.

Alex, on point, froze. He crouched for long seconds in the lee of a Volvo until he caught a slight movement just inside the target building. *Ahh.* He knew that silhouette. "C'mon," he whispered over his shoulder to Mike. "A friendly unscrewed the lightbulb for us."

Mike grunted under his breath in acknowledgment, and they moved out.

KATIE DIDN'T WANT to talk to Peter Koronov again. The red phone was ringing insistently enough in Fortinay's office that it was starting to piss her off. Every minute or so, it set up a new caterwauling. *Give it up already.*

She'd retreated to the main floor as far away from the noise of the phone as she could. The last thing she needed was for Dawn to wake up and start hollering.

Katie thought there might be a small doctor's office somewhere in the building. It was a source of joking that an entire building full of doctors had no facilities for treating any patients, and she recalled something about Fortinay mentioning the examining room in the back of the house. She could stand to find a kitchen, too. Surely this old mansion had one somewhere. It had started life as a private home, after all.

Dawn would need a bottle of some kind eventually, not to mention a diaper. If Katie got out of this mess alive with the baby, she was never leaving her house again without a diaper and a tub of baby formula. She found the tiny medical office and poked around for supplies to construct yet another makeshift diaper for Dawn. Note to self: never try to be a superspy with a newborn infant in tow. Or more accurately, never try *again*.

She'd rigged up another tape-and-gauze affair for later when Dawn needed a change and was heading for what she hoped would be a kitchen when she heard a sound. Like someone moving. Close.

Her pulse leaped in alarm. She froze, listening intently. Nothing. Closing her eyes, she replayed the sound in her head in an attempt to identify and locate it. Someone moving. Outside. It hadn't been anything as dramatic as a twig snapping, but there had been a rustle of bare branches, as if someone had brushed up against a bush under the window.

At any other time in her life, she'd have blown it off as some kids walking past. But not tonight. Not now, with Russians trying to kill her and Alex. Not on a chilly spring night when no sane person was creeping around after midnight in the dark and cold.

She jumped as the phone started to ring again upstairs, jangling through the ominous stillness inside the cavernous building. The police. She should call the police. Creeping stealthily herself, she eased toward the grand staircase and up toward the only working phone, step by painfully terrified step.

ALEX SLIPPED INTO the unlocked vestibule quickly, ducking low, and Mike followed suit. The hulking form of André Fortinay took up most of the deep shadows by the door. The man wasted no time on pleasantries and asked tersely, under his breath, "Any idea who could be following Katie McCloud with guys who move like commandos?"

"Russian military," Alex answered equally tersely. "Long story, but the upshot is I think uranium is being smuggled out of the Karshan Valley. Someone's worried that Katie and I found evidence of uranium poisoning in the locals during our medical mission there."

"Hence the two of you have to be silenced," André concluded.

"Correct."

"Status report?" Alex bit out.

"The D.U. alarms don't show an incursion. Yet. The team is either not in the building or has totally disabled the alarms. The hidden cameras outside appear to be working normally but have not picked up movement in a few minutes. Perhaps our commandos have hunkered down to do a little surveillance or wait for instructions before they move on Miss McCloud."

"In other words, Katie's alone and unharmed inside the building or already dead." It was Alex's turn to conclude.

"I've got reinforcements coming, but it takes time to discreetly assemble a wet squad on U.S. soil."

"And in the meantime?"

"I thought we might join Miss McCloud inside the Doctors Unlimited building."

Alex stared at the craters where the man's eyes would normally be. "How?"

"Certain precautions have been taken for an eventuality such as this. Follow me."

Fortinay turned and walked swiftly down the long hall to the back of the apartment building. He opened an interior door and disappeared quickly down a narrow flight of steps. Alex and Mike exchanged questioning looks and followed.

The basement of the building was dank, cold, low-ceilinged and pitch-black. Fortinay pulled out his cell phone and turned it on, then used its glowing face as a makeshift flashlight. All three men had to duck to avoid hitting their heads on the bountiful pipes and conduits running along the ceiling. They passed a set of hurricane fence storage units and stepped into a boiler room. A large furnace blew loudly.

Fortinay slipped behind the commercial heating unit, and Alex nodded in comprehension. A tunnel connected this building to the D.U. building. He stepped through the even lower doorway into a tunnel no more than five feet tall. Ancient parallel steel tracks announced this was an old coal tunnel.

For a big man, Fortinay moved quietly in front of him. Alex half ran, crouching behind D.U.'s leader as his curiosity mounted. Secret escape tunnels? Hidden security cameras? His father's request for the names and locations of the deployed staff members had been the beginning of his suspicions, but tonight's revelations sealed the deal. Doctors Unlimited was not just some innocent foreign aid bunch. He would bet a year's salary the organization was a CIA front.

It made sense. They sent "medical personnel" to the front lines of every hot spot on the planet, often before more well-known aid groups like the Red Cross or Red Crescent arrived. Their personnel had front-row seats for the breaking crises in the world. It was the perfect cover for intelligence observers. All under the innocent guise of helping victims of war and violence.

Fortinay paused at the end of the tunnel and squatted down. The glow from his phone showed a black canvas duffel bag lying on the floor. André unzipped it and pulled out two pistols and several spare clips, which he passed over his shoulder to Alex and Mike without even glancing up at them. The two men accepted the weapons in grim silence.

Alex was more surprised when André lifted out an Israeli Tavor—the weapon was a compact urban assault weapon, light, maneuverable, quick to fire and easy to handle. How in the hell had André gotten his hands on one of those? The Israeli army wasn't sharing them with anyone.

Armed to the teeth, André eased open the door. Alex slipped past him and moved quickly and quietly up the stairs on the other side. *Be alive, Katie. Please, God. Be alive.*

YET AGAIN, DAWN seemed to sense Katie's fear and had gone silent and tense against her breast. When this was all over, Katie vowed never to put Dawn in a scary situation again as long as she lived. Surely she was scarring the baby for life. But it wasn't like she had any choice in the matter. Staying alive was the first priority. Mental health concerns had to come second for now.

She'd retreated to Fortinay's office with the intent of answering the phone the next time it rang and telling Peter Koronov he had his deal and to leave her alone.

But strangely, alarmingly, it had quit ringing right after she'd heard the movement outside. Were the two somehow connected? Who was out there creeping around the D.U. building? She didn't like this one bit. Her fear and tension were almost more than she could stand. Were it not for Dawn huddled tightly against her, she'd have run screaming from there and confronted the lurker before now.

She tucked herself under André's big desk, feeling silly hiding under it like a naughty child and wishing she could make herself invisible and walk out of there unseen. Incongruously, it popped into her head to wonder if Alex had ever felt this way as a child.

She hoped he wasn't being followed and harassed, too. Of course, he knew how to lose a tail like a pro—

What was that?

It sounded like a door squeaking faintly. *Crap.* Was someone else inside the building? How did they get in? Who were they? She picked up the red phone and dialed 9-1-1 as quietly as she could. Not that a phone was great at keeping the noise down when it dialed.

"9-1-1. State your emergency and give me your location, please."

"I'm alone in the Doctors Unlimited building in northwest D.C., and I think someone just broke in."

"I've got response on the way, ma'am," the efficient voice said emotionlessly. "Where exactly are you in the building?"

"Umm, under a desk on the second—"

The line went dead.

Oh. My. God.

ALEX FROZE AT the sound of a murmuring voice. It cut off even as he listened for it. Upstairs. Muffled, like it was in an office. Mike gestured urgently; he'd heard it, too.

André mouthed soundlessly, "My office." He held

his hand to his ear like he was mimicking talking into a telephone.

That would be Katie. Alex took off running across the big lobby that had once been a grand entry hall. The ceiling was four stories overhead, a glass rotunda in it letting in far too much starlight for his taste.

An explosion of gunfire sent him diving for cover behind the big marble table in the middle of the foyer. The huge vase of cut flowers on it exploded, showering him with cold droplets of water.

The front door imploded as a barrage of automatic weapons fire slammed into it, shattering wood and glass. He rolled and came to his feet, sprinting for the stairs and taking them two and three at a time in a dodging, zigzagging series of random leaps.

So much for stealth.

"Katie!" he shouted.

A pair of weapons from inside the building returned fire in short, controlled bursts. André and Mike laying down suppression fire. Bless them. They were badly outgunned, but at least they might be able to buy him a little time to find Katie and get her the hell out of there before they all died.

He dived into Fortinay's office and left the door open behind him. Closed doors were one of the most dangerous obstacles to surmount in an emergency egress. Better to be able to peek around door frames or leap through a doorway unannounced and surprise your foe.

"Katie?" he whispered in a lull in the gunfire. "It's Alex."

"Thank God." A fast-moving object flew out from under André's desk and launched itself at him. He caught an armful of woman and baby with a grunt of surprise.

"Let's go," he said.

She nodded and fell in behind him as he crept toward the door.

He jolted, though, as a dark form raced around the corner, announcing, low and hard, "It's Mike."

Alex jerked his pistol up and away from Katie's brother, whom he'd almost killed…again. He had to stop doing that.

"They're breaching the front door. Should be through in sixty seconds. André's laying charges on the staircase. Told me to get you guys to the back of the house."

Alex nodded tersely and herded Katie out into the hall, tucked under his arm. They ran together down the central hall toward the conference room and chief financial officer's office at the back of the second story.

"Fire escape?" Mike bit out.

"No," Alex replied.

"What about ladders?" Katie piped up. "Wouldn't an office have to have some way for workers getting out of the upper floors to meet city safety codes?"

They spun into the CFO's office and Alex cleared it quickly. "Feel free to look for a ladder while Mike and I figure out how to slow these bastards down."

Katie nodded and headed for a closet while Mike tossed him a grenade and a spool of thin wire. Working frantically, Alex rigged a knee-high trip wire and wrapped it around the belly of the grenade and its handle. Very carefully, he pulled the pin and snugged it into a nest of wadded paper he'd pulled from a wastebasket to hold the explosive upright. He and Mike high-stepped over the wire and backed into the office just as a tremendous explosion rocked the building.

Alex checked the grenade in a panic. It hadn't been shaken free of its nest. *Good to go.*

"Trip wire," he announced to Fortinay as the big man barreled down the hall.

They stepped over the wire and dodged into the office as the first bullets zinged down the hall. Damn, these guys were fast! How had they gotten up the stairs and past André's explosive charges like that? The only answer was they were Special Forces and well trained. Alex swore under his breath.

Fortinay locked the office door and gestured for them to retreat into the conference room. Alex asked urgently, "Is there a way out of here?"

He grinned and nodded. "Help me out, guys."

Alex and Mike moved over to the window and the big wooden chest André was unlatching.

"Open the window and help me toss this out."

"What is it?" Katie asked.

"Emergency escape slide."

"Like on an airplane?" she squeaked.

"The very same."

Alex, Mike and André gave a mighty heave as running footsteps pounded down the hall. They threw the big container outside. An orange strip of vinyl unrolled and commenced inflating all at once.

"Cool," Katie breathed.

Alex winced. He could think of a dozen things that could go horribly wrong in the next few seconds that would get her killed.

"I'll go first," Mike announced. "When I wave, you join me, Kat—"

Kaboom.

The door exploded inward as the goons outside hit his trip wire. The concussion felt to Alex like someone had hit him in both ears with sledgehammers. A dark shape loomed in the ruined doorway, and Mike dived out the window. Alex dropped and squeezed off a half-dozen shots.

Body armor. Dammit.

Katie was climbing over the sill awkwardly with the baby in her arms. He was pretty sure Dawn was screaming her head off, but all he could hear at the moment was a massive roaring noise.

He rolled behind the long conference table, popped up and took careful aim. Only way to defeat body armor was to take a head shot. He popped off two rounds and something black and liquid exploded out of the intruder's face. The guy crumpled and another black shape stepped into the void. *Crap!*

"C'mon, Alex!" he heard dimly.

He pulled his trigger. Out of ammo. And this was his last clip. He measured the distance from the table to the window. He was dead.

He waved for André to go on without him. He would make a death charge and draw the hostiles' fire long enough for the others to get down the slide and safely away from the structure.

Time slowed around him. The roaring became silence as the tableau unfolded. Chips of wood and lead slugs flew every which way. Fortinay's bulk disappeared over the windowsill. Alex rose to his feet. He shouted but could not hear his voice as he began his charge. His final grand gesture.

He ran toward the intruder's weapons and recognized the stubby, efficient shapes of AK-47s. The irony of dying from a Russian weapon was rich. He thought briefly, sadly, of his father. He no longer had any hate left for Peter. Not even contempt. Just pity.

He was sorry he wasn't going to get to see Dawn grow up. Would she be as beautiful as her birth mother had been? Katie would do a great job raising her.

Katie.

All else cleared from his mind but images of her. Washing her hair in a bucket. Laughing. Teasing him. Fleeing danger. And the sex. God, the sex. It had been so much more with her. They'd…connected. Hell, they'd all but become one. Sex had been freaking transcendental with her. Above all else, he was sorry he wasn't going to get to make love with her again.

He charged forward across the open space and opened his arms, embracing the bullets to come. Embracing death. A burst of relief at finally stepping off the nerve-racking tightrope of his life washed over him. So this was it. The end. Something hot grazed across his cheek, spinning him around. And then something hard and heavy slammed into his back between the shoulder blades. The last thing he registered was an explosion of pain as his legs dropped out from under him and he went down like a rock.

CHAPTER TWENTY-TWO

FORTINAY WHOOSHED DOWN the slide, his momentum carrying him to her side as Katie waited frantically for Alex to follow André. A barrage of gunfire made her flinch violently, and she all but jumped up and down in her panic. *Where is Alex?*

Her boss grabbed her upper arm and commenced dragging her away from the window. Or at least trying to. She cried out, "We have to wait for him!"

"He went down, Katie. He's not coming. Crazy bastard threw himself at the gunmen so we could get away."

Stunned, she stared at Fortinay. "Wait. What?"

"Alex is dead. Right now we must run or die."

Shock rolled over her like fog filling a valley. Dawn's howl finally registered, though, and the piercing wail spurred Katie into clumsy motion. *Must save the baby. But Alex...*

André's long legs took monster strides that were nearly impossible to keep up with, and Katie had no more time for thought as they tore away from the Doctors Unlimited building with Mike leading the way.

The screams of sirens—a lot of them—shredded the night, and Mike finally slowed. Stopped. Pressed a hand over his stab wound. "Dammit. I'm bleeding again," he muttered.

"Lemme see," Fortinay snapped. Mike lifted his hand away. "You tore your stitches all to hell, man. You got any internal sutures in there?"

Mike nodded with a grimace.

"C'mon. Fire trucks and SWAT will bring an ambulance with them. You've got to get to a hospital pronto and get that wound opened up and repaired, again. What were you thinking running around out here with an injury like that?"

"I was thinking about saving my sister's life," her brother bit out.

"Noble idiot," she panted. She looked behind them, and fire glowed in the upper windows of the D.U. offices. "What happened to him? We have to go back in there and find him. If he's still alive he'll need medical care—"

"Katie," André said gently. "He ran straight at a cluster of three Spetsnaz guys pumping lead from AK-47s as fast as they could fire. He was at point-blank range. A child couldn't miss from that distance. He drew their fire so the rest of us could get away. There's no way he survived."

A scream started deep inside Katie's head, so piercing it couldn't escape her skull. Her knees buckled, and Fortinay jumped forward and managed to get an arm around her waist at the last second before she went down. "Come, Katie. You have to keep moving. We're not quite there yet."

Wherever there was. Not that she cared. If Alex was dead, nothing else mattered. She could not believe he'd sacrificed himself like that. He'd never struck her as having a death wish. He'd seemed desperate for redemption, though. To prove his honor and his worth to his father, at least. While she wasn't the least bit surprised he'd been a hero in the end, she was shocked that he'd given his life for her and Dawn and Mike and André. He must have felt a great deal more for all of them than he'd let on to have sacrificed his life for them.

That bastard! Fury, hot and irrational, burst forth in her bosom, searing her and shocking her. She swung back to grief in the blink of an eye. *This must be shock.*

André led her and Mike around the burning D.U. building and into a throng of fire trucks, police cars and assorted emergency vehicles clogging the street. An ambulance pulled up, and André dragged them toward it.

He turned her brother over to a pair of stone-faced EMTs, who pushed Mike down onto a gurney. One of them pulled out a condomlike thing and stuffed it in her brother's wound, which made him cuss hard enough to get in trouble from their mother.

Meanwhile, she looked around frantically for who was in charge of this circus. She had to tell someone where Alex was inside so they could bring him out. She just couldn't wrap her brain around the idea of him being gone. She couldn't bring herself to even think the D-word.

The EMTs tried to push Mike into their ambulance, but he squawked, "I'm not going anywhere until I talk with you, André. I have critical information for you."

His urgency penetrated the fog in her brain as Fortinay leaned over her brother and listened grimly. Did Mike know something about Alex? Hope leaped in her breast. A little voice in a far corner of her brain told her hope was irrational, but she didn't care. Until they showed her Alex's lifeless, charred body, she refused to believe he was…that D-thing.

Whatever Mike muttered to André put a thunderstruck look on Fortinay's face. Her hope grew a little more.

A commotion erupted in the entrance to the Doctors Unlimited building as a firefighter was hustled out of the smoking hulk. André's spine stiffened as he looked over the crowd that closed in around the man.

She couldn't see a thing and literally tugged on her boss's sleeve. "What's happening?" Was it Alex? Had they rescued him?

"Katie, you and Dawn need to come with me. Quickly. Quietly."

"Where are we going?"

André didn't answer, but instead plowed into the crowd of uniformed law enforcement types. He led her to a big white van, unmarked and innocuous. It looked like a local delivery vehicle that had mistakenly been swept up in the maelstrom that had overtaken this quiet street. André looked around surreptitiously, opened its back door and helped her inside quickly.

It looked like one of those TV-show vans with a mobile surveillance command center hidden inside it. Computers and monitors lined one side of the interior. A bench backed up against the other. A man slumped on the bench, a bulky blanket wrapped around his shoulders.

He glanced up, and Katie's knees did collapse out from under her then.

But Alex surged up off the bench and caught her around the waist in a crushing embrace that made Dawn fuss. She threw her arms around Alex's neck and hung on for dear life.

"You're not a hallucination?" she whispered.

"Nope. I'm alive."

"How?" André demanded. "I watched you charge those guys, and they opened up on you!"

"Bastards fired all around me. I think they were trying to get you."

"Not me," Fortinay bit out. The two men's stares met and then both turned to Katie.

"What? Me? Those commandos only wanted to kill me?"

Alex ignored her question and instead said, "I took what felt like a bunch of beanbag rounds in the back."

Katie was stunned. Beanbag rounds hurt like hell and left big bruises—she'd seen them on her brothers when they were in training. And while beanbags knocked people down when fired out of weapons, they rarely injured a person seriously and never killed them.

André scowled. "You think they had specific orders not to kill you then?"

Her jaw dropped. "Your father must have given that order." She continued the line of logic. "Why on earth are your father's men trying to kill *me?* Heck, I just made a deal with him—"

She broke off but not soon enough.

Alex lifted Dawn out of her arms and passed the baby to André. She felt the van lurch into motion, but none of that mattered. Only the gathering fury in Alex's eyes was important. She didn't wait for the storm to break and blurted, "I called your father on André's crisis phone. I offered him a deal. I'm supposed to leave you—and break your heart in the process—and in return he agreed to leave you completely alone if and until you decide to approach him someday."

"Why?" Alex rasped the syllable with a horrible gasp of dismay and betrayal.

"Because I love you, Alex!"

"You told my old man you'd break my heart because you *love* me?"

She reached up and planted her palms on his cheeks, willing understanding through her fingertips and into his brain. "You're caught between two worlds. Neither of them will let go, and they're tearing you apart, Alex. Your father and people like my uncle are destroying you inch by inch. *And you're letting them.* I care for you too much to stand by and do nothing while you self-destruct."

He frowned down at her like she was speaking in tongues, her words meaningless gibberish he could not comprehend no matter how hard he tried.

"I love you, Alex," she whispered. "But I can't have you. They'll use me the same way they're using you to get you to do what they want. And I'm not willing to let them rip me apart limb from limb. I like being alive. I like being emotionally whole. And I have a baby to raise."

"What makes you think they'll let you raise that baby in peace?"

She shrugged. "Because I won't play their game.

I'm stepping off their fast train to disaster. You—you seem addicted to the ride. But I'm done with all of this." She added tiredly, "I quit."

THE VAN ROCKED to a stop and André Fortinay threw open the back door. Alex watched Katie jump out numbly. He felt as though he'd fallen into some sort of weird mental catatonia where nothing made sense anymore. He could watch events happening around him, see colors and hear sounds, but none of it computed.

"If you'll come with us," André murmured to him. "I need to take tissue samples from Dawn and run them through our lab."

Dawn. Innocent, abandoned Dawn with whom he shared so very much in common. That tiny stripe of bright hope peeking over a grim and gray horizon. His brain latched on to the imagery of that ray of light as a warm and happy thing. Proof that he'd lived through the perils of night—of memories that came calling in the wee hours, of fears crowding forward, of the brutal honesty that crept over him from time to time and informed him he was a failure at every aspect of being human.

Must. Protect. Dawn.

It was enough. It got him up off the bench. Moving forward. Going through the motions of being alive, for now, at least. He focused on the baby. Fixed an image of her in his mind. She was enough to keep him breathing.

But she was not enough to fill his soul.

For that, he needed…Katie.

Her name burst across his existence, his mind, his

heart, his *essence.* She was that which brought him fully to life. She made him feel. She gave him love. And in so doing, showed him that love existed within him, still. He'd been so sure Peter had burned it all out of him. But the bastard had missed a tiny piece of it hidden somewhere way, way deep down where cold, loveless Peter had not known to look for it to kill it.

But Katie had found it. Nurtured it.

And now he'd lost her. Because, if he understood her correctly, she loved him too much to watch him destroy himself.

In a fog, he sat in a plastic chair in a hallway. White walls. Fluorescent lights. Underground, if he had to guess. Antiseptic. CIA lab, probably.

Dawn shouted for rescue in a room nearby, and Katie came out carrying her in a few minutes, looking haggard.

"Poked her with a needle?" he asked woodenly.

"Poor baby. And they removed her umbilical stump and plucked out a few of her head hairs. Those big meanies," Katie cooed to the infant.

Dawn settled quickly. Of course it helped that someone had come up with a bottle of formula for the baby and a clean diaper. Simple needs, Dawn had. Sustenance, maintenance and love.

Were his needs that simple, too?

"Katie, we need to talk—"

A door opened nearby, and André poked his head out. "You two want to step in here for a moment?"

Katie glanced up at Alex in distress.

Tentatively, he put a steadying hand on the small of her back. He exhaled the breath he was holding when she leaned into his arm just a little. *Thank God.* She didn't flinch away from him like most women did by the time he was done with them.

He followed Katie into a small examining room. He recognized the equipment around the space and identified it all by rote.

Fortinay spoke briskly. "Preliminary results are back on Dawn's blood. Radioactive isotopes in it indicate exposure to unrefined uranium. These results in combination with Mike McCloud's are conclusive. She's the smoking gun."

Katie stared. "She's the...what?"

Alex spoke gently. "All along we thought everyone was trying to kill us. But it was Dawn they were after. She's the only local survivor of the Karshan Valley massacre. The only remaining proof that Yevgeny Archaki and his crew were paying the natives to mine and crudely smelt small amounts of uranium that he was smuggling into Iran."

"Uranium? I thought it was samarium."

Alex nodded. "Samarium always comes linked with other minerals, and one of its base minerals is uranium."

"Oh, my God. So who were all those guys at the D.U. building?"

"Russian Spetsnaz. Someone within the Russian government was eager to see the uranium smuggling continue and couldn't let a doctor treat the locals and possibly identify their uranium dust poisoning."

"Or Heaven forbid," Katie added, "bring out blood and tissue samples that would prove what Archaki was doing with their secret blessing."

No surprise, Katie's arms tightened convulsively around Dawn.

"Alex, we have to keep her safe."

"And we will."

Fortinay piped up. "Once we have the final data from Dawn's samples, we will present it to the powers that be in the U.S. government, and they will no doubt…discuss the issue with their Russian counterparts. There will be no need to eliminate Dawn and dispose of her body once the cat is out of the bag. She should be perfectly safe from here on out."

"Did your father send that team in to kill her?" Katie asked him in sudden horror.

"He certainly had something to do with the team or else they wouldn't have fired beanbags at me instead of live rounds."

Katie frowned. "Not to put too fine a point on it, but why didn't he let them kill you?"

"For the same reason he accepted your offer. Hope. He holds out hope that one day I will come back to the fold."

"Is he right to hang on to that hope?" André interjected.

Alex looked the CIA man in the eye. "You know I can't answer that question if I want to live to see tomorrow."

"You'll always be walking on a tightrope, won't you?" Katie asked sadly.

He glanced over at André in silent request. The big man nodded and slipped out of the room, lifting Dawn out of Katie's arms as he went.

Alex was surprised when Katie rounded on him immediately, demanding, "Why in the hell did you run at those guns? Are you crazy?"

"No. Well, maybe yes. You see, I love you."

She stared blankly at him. "You what?"

"I love you." The words came out a little more strongly this time. With more conviction.

"Are you *serious?*"

He frowned at her patent disbelief. "Yes. I am. I promised you I would never lie to you, remember?"

"But…"

He waited for her objections to spill out. Her denial. Her *rejection.* He braced himself for the blow.

"Oh, Alex." She launched herself at him like a missile slamming into his chest, leaping into his arms and literally wrapping herself around him.

Gratitude for her forgiving nature wove through his shock as he clutched her tightly against him. Her legs went around his waist, and he backed her up against the wall, kissing her with all the ferocity of his need.

"Screw my father," he muttered against her mouth.

"I'd rather screw you." She laughed.

"That can be arranged."

"What are we going to do about your father? I promised him I would break your heart."

"Trust me. You did. You just happened to put it back together, too."

She kissed him again, sweetly this time, exploring this new and fragile thing between them. He closed his eyes, savoring the taste of love on his tongue in delight.

"I don't think your dad's going to like it if we stay together."

"I'm certain he won't like it."

"Will he try to kill me?"

"How do you feel about tightrope walking as a hobby?"

She drew back from him a little. "Will you teach me how?"

"Stick with me, kid. I'm the best. I'll teach you everything I know."

She snuggled a little closer. "Mmm. Sounds interesting."

He laughed in spite of himself. "You're incorrigible."

"And you love it."

He kissed the tip of her nose. "I can't promise that this will be easy. But I can promise that it will always be interesting."

"Deal."

She looped her arm around his waist as they headed for the hall and to Dawn to make their little family complete. He watched with pride as Katie stepped forward to scoop the infant out of André's arms.

"We all good?" Fortinay murmured over the girls' heads.

Alex nodded and couldn't keep a broad grin from creeping across his face. "We're good."

"Great!" the Frenchman said brightly. "I hear they're in desperate need of doctors on the Syrian border. The civil unrest in the region is still throwing refugees on the international aid network like crazy."

"Syria?" Katie exclaimed. "Who wants to go someplace you can't take your blow-dryer?"

Alex grinned down at her. "You mean and have it work?"

She stuck her tongue out at him.

He said more seriously, "Zaghastan didn't turn out so bad, did it?"

She smiled softly. "No, indeed. Best trip of my life."

"Ha. You ain't seen nuthin' yet."

Her smile widened. "I can't wait."

Truth be told, neither could he. For the first time in his life, he had the rest of his life to look forward to. "We'll do this together, yes?"

He thought her eyes actually filled a little with tears. "Yes, Alex. Together. You and me against the world."

And they kissed to seal the deal.

* * * * *

Don't miss Cindy Dees's next HQN available in August 2014!

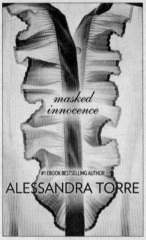

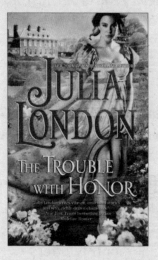

ReaderService.com

Manage your account online!

- Review your order history
- Manage your payments
- Update your address

*We've designed
the Harlequin® Reader Service
website just for you.*

Enjoy all the features!

- Reader excerpts from any series
- Respond to mailings and
  special monthly offers
- Discover new series available to you
- Browse the Bonus Bucks catalog
- Share your feedback

Visit us at:
ReaderService.com